"Go ahead," Trinity whispered, "kill me."

She had tried to escape, but Breck had pinned her against the door, the knife gripped in his left hand near her temple, where she could peripherally see its silver flash, his right hand around the exposed column of her neck. Everything about him spelled man; everything about him spelled power; everything about him spelled fury—a cold fury directed solely at her.

Rage coursed through her, as well as some other emotion. His belly brushed hers, his thighs rubbed against hers, his manhood nestled in the apex of her legs . . . and anger was metamorphosing into passion.

And that made her defiant. She tilted her head up in challenge.

Breck was sorely tempted to do *something* physical. Like take the knife and try to cut her out of his . . .

The word *heart* came to mind, but he instantly rejected it. Of course, there was one other physical option, which the lower part of his body seemed to think of before the rest of him did. . . .

China Star

Karen Keast

Harlequin Books

TORONTO • NEW YORK • LONDON
AMSTERDAM • PARIS • SYDNEY • HAMBURG
STOCKHOLM • ATHENS • TOKYO • MILAN

*To Diane Wicker Davis, who so faithfully
held my hand as I traveled the past,
and who, when asked how I could get a
Chinese woman to America before the great
1850s emigration, sagely advised:
"Have the* Enterprise *beam her down."*

*Also for M,
for always and forever.*

Harlequin Historical first edition January 1989

Second edition September 1990

ISBN 0-373-15139-X

KAREN KEAST

is the critically acclaimed author of more than a dozen contemporary romantic novels; *China Star* marks her stunning debut in the historical arena. A resident of Shreveport, Louisiana, she shares her home with her husband and two cats.

Prologue

Sacramento, California
Summer, 1854

Aunt Lilly had gotten the wrong doll.

Eight-year-old Trinity stared down at the porcelain-faced doll in her hands, her small, exasperated sigh accusing adults of being endlessly tiresome creatures. Didn't Aunt Lilly know this doll was not to play with? Certainly not to sleep with, because Mamma said it would break if squashed beneath a sleeping little girl. Which was the last thing Trinity wanted to do, because she thought it was the prettiest doll in the world. Aunt Cherry said it was Chinese. All Trinity knew was that the doll, with its dark, almond-shaped eyes, its raven hair intricately knotted on its head and pierced with ornamental ivory pins, and its silken flowered robe, looked just like her mother.

Daring the scolding she would inevitably get from Aunt Lilly, who'd gone downstairs to warm her a glass of milk, Trinity decided to exchange this doll for the gingham-dressed rag doll she slept with. She knew, too, that her mamma would be mad—it was a rule that Trinity was never to bother her mother when her mother had a gentleman friend with her—but surely Mamma would understand that she couldn't sleep with her porcelain-faced doll.

Opening the door of Aunt Lilly's bedroom, Trinity bunched her white lawn gown in her petite fist, raised the lace-trimmed hem above her ankles, and rushed barefoot along the worn

scarlet carpet of the hallway. Her long black hair, wavy from
its daytime braiding, floated about her delicate shoulders.

The thick, intoxicating smell of numerous perfumes blended
with the heavy, hazy heat of the summer night. The lacy curtain of the hall window billowed lazily, provocatively, while
shadows crept inside to mingle with the faint glow of oil lan-
terns deliberately, discreetly, kept few and low-burning. Trinity told herself she wasn't afraid of the near-darkness, yet she
hastened her footsteps and concentrated on the music coming
from the parlor downstairs. Aunt Prissy was playing the piano.
A man was laughing. Another man joined in. Then there was
the sound of Aunt Flo's muffled, husky voice. Which caused
everyone to laugh loudly.

Trinity cringed. Sometimes the noise woke her up and she
had to cup her hands over her ears in order to go back to sleep.
The time of night she liked best was after the house had quieted, after the men had left, and after Mamma had carried her
from whichever of her aunts' beds she was sleeping in back to
her own. Sometimes, but not often, she slept all night with her
mother. If it was still noisy, her mother would sing to her in a
soft, lulling voice; while it wasn't as loud as Aunt Prissy's
playing or the laughter, it seemed to blot out everything else
with its gentleness.

Racing past her aunts' closed doors—she was never allowed
to visit if their doors were shut—she heard a giggle coming
from Aunt Belle's room. Trinity wondered exactly what went
on behind those closed doors. She had asked once, but her
mother had said simply, "Nothing." It didn't sound like nothing to Trinity. Once she'd been frightened by a strange growling and panting. Another time she'd heard some very bad
words, which her mother had said she must never repeat, because ladies didn't say such things.

And Trinity did so want to be a lady. Just like her mamma.

Hearing the racket downstairs grow louder, Trinity halted at
the top of the steps and faded back into the shadows, peeping
out only enough to see the thickset man who was talking to
Aunt Ruby.

"I swear, Ruby, you got the best-looking girls in town," the
man said. His boots, scruffy and caked with the mud of Sacramento's dirt streets, provided a sharp contrast to the brightly
polished brass spittoon nearby. The man had made an effort to
spruce himself up. He had on a clean shirt and trousers, though

both had as many wrinkles as his weather-burned face. "A man could fair go crazy trying to choose," he added, his eyes taking in the women in the parlor with the enthusiasm of a child taking in a Christmas morn.

Ruby smiled, her carmine-red lips sliding back from white teeth, while her purple satin dress, cut low to reveal the ivory of her plump breasts, tightly cupped her voluptuous, if slightly worn, curves. In her brown hair she wore a single black ostrich plume that hugged her rouge-dusted cheek. She carried a black lace fan, which she sometimes let Trinity hold in her small, eager hands. When Ruby spoke, her voice was soft and naturally sultry. It was the same tone she'd use tomorrow, the same tone she used every Sunday, to teach Sunday school to her girls, whom she'd force to gather, amid yawns and grumbling, on the stairway. "Then why don't you let me choose for you?"

The man grinned, then ventured, "I hear you got a slanty-eyed Chinese—"

"Sorry, Su-Ling's entertaining someone else." Catching the eye of a blond-haired, blue-eyed woman who looked more girl than woman, Ruby said, "Why don't you try Anna Louise? Anna Louise, come here, darlin'. I want you to take good care of Lester here. He's been up there mining himself some of that shiny gold of Sutter's." Ruby lowered her thick-lashed eyes to the front of the man's pants. "I do declare, I think he's brought a hard nugget with him."

The man laughed and preened. He would have paid any price Ruby Landry set on her girls. Every hard man in need of a soft woman knew that Ruby ran the best brothel in town. Her girls were clean and pretty and . . . ladies. Damned if they weren't whorin' ladies!

Anna Louise smiled, shyly, becomingly, and beckoned to the man to join her in the downstairs bedroom whose door she'd just opened. Trinity wondered if they were going to have a tea party like the one she and Aunt Anna Louise had had that afternoon, sipping pretend tea from tiny cups that sat in tiny saucers.

In the last second before the door shut, the man reached out and slid his hand into the slit of Anna Louise's pink silk wrapper. Trinity glanced away, as if she knew instinctively it was something she shouldn't have seen.

"You got a shot of whiskey and a wicked woman to aid a man in gettin' through a hell-hot Saturday night?"

Ruby turned toward the boisterous man who'd just opened the front door. From his wink and Ruby's smile, it was obvious he was a frequent customer. As Ruby escorted the man into the parlor, her breast nudging his arm, Trinity seized the moment to scamper unnoticed down the stairs.

She ran across the cool wooden floor of the entryway, past the kitchen, where she heard Aunt Lilly humming, and past the side door, which led to the back alley, where she wasn't allowed to play because Mamma said that lawless riffraff prowled there. Trinity wasn't really certain what lawless riffraff was, but she thought it must be a beast like the wild animals in the books her mother read to her.

In seconds Trinity stood before the door of the room she shared with her mother. For the first time since charging from Aunt Lilly's bedroom, she had qualms about what she was doing. What if her mother looked at her with disappointment in her eyes because she'd disobeyed her? Would her mother still be in the strange mood she'd been in ever since they'd gone out that afternoon for a walk? The childish reservations vanished almost as soon as they appeared, and Trinity reached for the doorknob, turned it, and stepped into the room.

Suddenly she stopped.

The room was the same, yet not at all the same. It had the same dark walnut furniture crowded together, the same canary-yellow curtains lapping at the open windows, the same faint, sweet smell of the perfume her mother wore and would sometimes playfully dab behind Trinity's ears as Trinity stood worshipfully at her side, the same globed oil lamp spewing filtered light, the same gingham doll carelessly lying on the floor.

Doll.

Floor.

Mother.

Why was her mother lying on the floor? Her hair tossed about her like black midnight? Her face unnaturally white? Her eyes closed? With something red oozing from the folds of her pretty silk robe?

And why was there a man kneeling beside her? A knife in his hand? The same red something smeared on his shirt?

Trinity openly studied the stranger, who watched her with the same startled intensity. Blond hair, as pale as new moonlight, curled about his head as if threaded there by eternally restless fingers, while his face was lean, angular, and browned by long hours in the hot sun. He had a broad, furrowed forehead and thick, tawny eyebrows above wide-set eyes. Cold, misty blue eyes that would have been almost transparent had it not been for some dark emotion hidden deep within, an emotion that said they'd seen everything and cared little for any of it. They evinced a guardedness, an aloofness, an implacable hardness Trinity could not verbally define but felt nonetheless within her child's heart. She grew afraid.

"Mamma?" she whispered.

At the desperate word, the man stood ... slowly, cautiously. Trinity's eyes lowered to the knife. The red-stained knife. The knife he gripped tightly, presenting the back of his hand to her. Curious, Trinity stared at the scar marking the hand's tanned flesh. It was white and crudely resembled a five-pronged star. The sight was indelibly etched on her impressionable young mind. Somehow the scar frightened her more.

Her heart suddenly pounded in her chest; her ears roared like thunder.

"Come here, little girl," the man rasped, his voice as black as the night. Reaching out, he took a step toward her.

Trinity stepped back. Then stepped back again. In her clumsy haste, she dropped the doll. It shattered at her feet, splintering both the silence and the innocence of her childhood.

And then she screamed.

Chapter One

San Francisco, California
August, 1872

The night crawled with darkness.

Overhead, a frustrated moon slid in defeat behind a gauzy screen of whipped gray clouds, while out over the still bay, where ships reposed in bobbing slumber, lightning chased across the hot summer sky. Behind it came a whimper of thunder.

At the threatening sound, Trinity Lee scooped up a handful of her skirt and quickened her leather-booted steps into a pace totally out of character for the elderly woman she appeared to be. She had gotten the message as she'd walked off stage from the last curtain call and had been so eager to comply with the summons that she hadn't taken time to change clothes or shed her heavy theatrical makeup. Now, as she entered the fringes of the Chinese section of San Francisco, she thanked her over-zealousness. The Chinese quarter at night was no place for an attractive young woman. Despite the plaudits she received, she never actually thought of herself as pretty, simply as different.

Given her Eurasian ancestry, she deemed the label fitting. One newspaper reporter had written that her face was "the best possible blend of two worlds" and had then gone on to wax eloquent about "raven hair, almond-shaped, whiskey-tinted eyes, a flare of cheeks, a dash of a chin, skin the color of dusky honey, and two lips made only to whisper the sweetest of words."

Trinity had thought the remark a tedious display of meaningless syllables. She had thought the newspaperman equally tedious. At the beginning of her stage career, he, working for a prestigious San Francisco newspaper, had hounded her mercilessly about the identity of her parents. With the coy smile she was now famous for, she had insisted, despite the obvious implausibility, that her parents were the elderly Chinese couple who'd raised her, the couple whose name she'd taken for the stage. Other reporters had probed, as well, but none had gleaned any information beyond that, which only made her more mysteriously alluring. Some even suggested the silence was calculated to win attention. She didn't care what anyone thought. She had never talked about her real parents, nor would she ever. How could she? Her father she didn't know at all, not even a name, while her mother she had known painfully well. How did you tell a stranger that your mother was a prostitute? A prostitute who'd been murdered in cold blood?

The grave questions effectively linked the past with the present. Was it possible that Ch'en Yung at last had the information she'd so long sought? Was it possible that an eighteen-year search would come to an end this night? Those possibilities sent Trinity's heart tumbling in wild anticipation, and she raced onward across dirt streets now dusty from lack of rain.

Two-story frame buildings rose around her, some painted, some bare wood—a livery, a laundry, a grocery declaring the medicinal value of herbal tea—all closed this Saturday evening. The pungent smell of spice and the stench of sewage permeated the rain-heavy air, while the singsong sound of Chinese, impenetrable and irritating to the foreign ear, struck like the plucked notes of an ill-tuned lute. A small, mangy dog yipped at the heels of passersby, while two Chinese men—"celestials," as they had come to be called—rocked on their haunches in a riveting game of dice. Against the outside wall of a noisy saloon leaned a man with a glassy-eyed stare. Trinity wondered if he'd just staggered out of one of the opium dens, where for a generous share of his weekly pay a man could buy a pipe guaranteed to diminish all his earthly cares.

Lightning forked, thunder rumbled, and in that second Trinity saw Ch'en Yung. Standing in the entrance to an alley, he was wearing black pants, a floppy shirt, and the traditional wide-brimmed straw hat that rose to a conical point. From beneath the hat snaked a single black braid of hair. Despite his small stature—perhaps in defiance of it—he stood at an imposing angle, with his shoulders thrown back proudly, his eyes piercing rather than scanning the night. He looked exactly like the powerful tong leader he was, capable of mediating differences between Oriental factions, capable of violence if one faction insisted on encroaching on another's territory or rights.

Trinity couldn't help remembering him, however, as the little boy she'd so often played with. After the death of her mother, through an arrangement she'd never clearly understood, she'd been placed in the home of a generous, caring Chinese couple. Ch'en Yung, a distant young cousin to the Lees, immediately befriended the frightened child. Still, even now, years after the kind and loving Lees' natural deaths, those months of transition were painful memories. Memories she never consciously allowed herself to dwell on.

Because of the dark pull of the past, because of the promise of what lay ahead, she hastened her steps. Before she reached Ch'en, she saw his wary walnut-brown eyes scan her quickly— from her netted hair to her wrinkled face to her matronly dress—before dismissing her as no one he knew. Trinity was smiling slightly when she stopped in front of him.

"Do you forget so soon, Ch'en, the girl who could outclimb you?" Though they saw each other only infrequently as adults, the warm bond of friendship emerged each time they did.

Ch'en Yung's eyes narrowed, probed, before he cautiously asked, "Trinity?"

Her answer was a widening of her smile.

His own lips eased upward. "There was no shame in being beaten by you," he said, his English slow but precise. "You could outrun the wind and outclimb the stars."

The last word reminded Trinity of why she was there. She sobered instantly. "You've found him?" she asked softly, her heart drumming faster.

Ch'en's smile faded. Though he was but a few years Trinity's senior—twenty-nine to her twenty-six—he suddenly looked much older. "I have found a man with a scar."

"On the back of his right hand?"

Ch'en nodded, his braid flicking like the tongue of a serpent.

"A star?"

In answer, Ch'en picked up a stick and scrawled a primitive design in the dust. At the sight of it, Trinity's breath shallowed. Long-ago fear washed hotly over her. Chasing it, however, was the sweet, sweet taste of revenge.

"Where?" she asked, unable to get more than the one word out, unable to make it rise above a whisper.

"Virginia City."

"Nevada?" Trinity asked. Virginia City was the mining town her friend Ellie had moved to the year before. When petite Ellie Grayson had left the acting troupe to marry burly miner Neil Oates, Trinity had given her her sincerest blessing. It seemed that fate was now blessing Trinity.

"Yes," Ch'en said. "A Chinese man working in the town said such a man is there. He owns a railroad. The Sierra Virginia."

"And does—" Trinity swallowed back the heartbeat lodged in her throat "—does this man have a name?"

For as long as Trinity could remember, she had sought this nameless man, asking subtle but persistent questions as she'd toured the length and breadth of the country while performing. Ch'en had known of her search ever since they'd shared their youthful secrets. Through the years they had spoken little of her quest. That very silence had indicated its seriousness.

"Madison Brecker," her friend said quietly.

Madison Brecker.

Trinity hugged the name tightly to her, not in love, but in purest hate. Before her eyes swirled the bitter vision of blond hair and pale, winter-chilled blue eyes. As she savored, worshiped these profane images, she was oblivious to the marble-size drops of rain that began to splatter about her. Finally a growl of thunder recalled her attention, and she reached for the reticule dangling at her side, knowing as she did so that no amount of money could adequately pay for the information she'd just received.

Sensing her intent, Ch'en Yung stilled her hand with his. "We are blood," he said, referring to the fact that they were raised together.

"But what you have given me—"

"Is nothing you would not have given me."

Moved, she whispered, "Thank you."

The hand on hers momentarily tightened. "Go," Ch'en said, angling his head in a quick command. "Outrun the rain."

Their eyes merged and spoke of the binding things of friendship. Abruptly hiking her skirt up, she started off in the direction from which she'd come. She'd taken only a few steps, however, when Ch'en called out.

"Trinity?"

She stopped, turned and noted idly that the rain, drop by drop, was obliterating the star drawn in the dirt.

"Now that you have found him, what will you do to this . . . Madison Brecker?"

A thousand memories, as soft as satin, as delicate as lace, came tripping so vividly that Trinity feared she might smother in their sweet poignancy. She remembered the melodious sound of her mother's voice, the majestic beauty of her simple smile, the feel of her hand protectively closing about her own—large to small, mother to daughter, lady to lady. She remembered tea parties, bedtime stories, and a porcelain doll. A shattered porcelain doll.

Her eyes never wavering, her voice never faltering, Trinity answered, "Kill him."

During the first week of September, the Virginia City newspaper, the *Territorial Enterprise*, ran a banner headline stating that the Sierra Virginia Railroad had been brazenly robbed of the incoming mining payrolls, a sum conservatively estimated at twenty thousand dollars. The thief had gotten away, the newspaper lamented in the satirical fashion it was widely known for, "with nary a scratch to his bodacious rascality and with even less a scratch to his identity." The same edition of the newspaper reported that famed actress Trinity Lee had arrived in town via the same train to visit her longtime friend Mrs. Ellie Grayson Oates.

Two weeks later the newspaper carried another headline, this one fairly shouting that the Sierra Virginia had been robbed yet again, by a man not matching the description of the first. The reporter went on to voice the question on everyone's lips: Was there a gang involved? The paper also ran an article about disgruntled mine owners threatening to once again turn to Wells Fargo for payroll deliveries if the thefts didn't cease. Madison Brecker, owner of the Sierra Virginia Railroad, was quoted as saying that he was so certain of thwarting the thieves that he'd personally make good the past losses and any unlikely future losses. He also stated that Pinkerton's, the celebrated detective agency, had been called in. Again, almost as an afterthought to the robbery mayhem, the newspaper reported that Trinity Lee had returned to Virginia City to visit her friend, and that rumor had it that the renowned actress was planning to bring her current play to town.

On the first of October, rumor became fact.

To a passenger, those aboard that Reno-Virginia City run were spiked upon the horns of a dilemma. Did they spend their time hoping for a glimpse of Trinity Lee, who was ensconced in the plush private car at the rear of the train, or did they spend their time praying that they didn't get a glimpse of the now-notorious Vanishing Gang? If pressed for the truth, however, many would have had to admit to a secret longing to see both.

"Well, I think it's plum scary the way they disappear right in the middle of a robbery," Maude Terrill announced to her husband as she cradled a jar of persimmon jelly in the folds of her brown worsted dress. Once a month she donned her Sunday-best brown velvet bonnet trimmed with brown grosgrain ribbon, brown feathers, and black lace to travel to Reno to visit her sister. Once a month, as a reward for having done so, she returned with a jar of persimmon jelly.

Dub Terrill considered the gift more punishment than reward. To his way of thinking, the jelly was tart enough to pucker anything at twenty paces, most of which he was certain the Almighty had never intended to be puckered. To her statement, he now replied with a disinterested "Mmm."

It was all the encouragement his wife needed. "Marybeth said the first robber had dark brown eyes that looked like the gateways to hell."

"Marybeth didn't see his eyes," Dub Terrill pointed out logically as he slumped into as restful a posture as the seat would allow. "Nobody seen hide nor hair nor eye of him 'cept the railroad employee riding watch over the safe in the baggage car."

"I know," Maude said impatiently, "but Marybeth was on board, and that's what she heard Dick Kingsman—that's the man who was riding watch—say. 'Gateways to hell,' he said." Maude made an appropriate sighing sound. "Poor Marybeth. If I'd been her, I would have fainted dead away."

In actuality, Maude Terrill would never truly forgive her neighbor Marybeth for having been aboard when she herself hadn't. Maude had missed the first robbery by only one vexing day. The second robbery had been in the middle of the month—payrolls were delivered the first and the fifteenth—so she hadn't even come close to witnessing that one, but it had so whetted her appetite that she had made it her business to return home with the next payroll shipment.

"You'd give two days of your life to come face-to-face with a real train robber," her husband said, accurately judging his wife. "You'd probably even ask for his John Hancock, though I doubt the cuss could do more than give you his *X*."

Maude gave an offended *harrumph*. "That just goes to show your ignorance, Dub Terrill. I would, too, faint dead away."

"Yeah, well," her husband replied, his eyes at sleepy half-mast, his thoughts already drifting toward the Eurasian beauty on board, "if the train's robbed, and if the rascal comes into the passenger car demanding our valuables, right before you faint see if you can unload that persimmon jelly. It'd serve the durned scoundrel right."

"Dub Terrill, you're a mean-spirited man," Maude replied absently, her mind recreating the delicious adventure of which her husband had spoken. She could see a tall, dark train robber standing before her, gun in hand, demanding her valuables or, better yet, her virtue. Suddenly a taller, darker man, his Pinkerton badge—did Pinkerton agents carry badges? No matter!—his Pinkerton badge gleaming in the sunlight, his gun smoking, came to her rescue. Maude's heart pounded at the fantasy, and she wondered if the Pinkerton agent who'd been called in was on board right now. Her eyes roamed—selectively, however, to only the handsome men. Was it the man with the incredibly broad shoulders? Or the one with the sandy-colored cap of hair? Or perhaps the one...

Oliver Truxtun, his Pinkerton badge—a facsimile of an open eye, below which was inscribed the promise WE NEVER SLEEP—tucked into the inside breast pocket of his jacket, his gun heavy against his lean hip, sat in the very back of the monotonously swaying passenger car. Tall, thin, with a face that was totally unprepossessing, he could claim not one impressive feature, unless one was inclined to single out his hooked, hawklike nose or the thick, prematurely gray mustache beneath it. Though his nondescript features were not necessarily those he would have chosen, he didn't complain. His plain looks enabled him to blend into his surroundings; in his line of work that was most beneficial. And people, because he was so unthreatening, were inclined to talk to him, with the result that he'd never failed in any job he'd been assigned to. Oliver Truxtun always, one way or another, got his man.

With deceptive laziness, his wood-brown eyes scanned the car, absorbing the subtlest of movements, drinking in every nuance of the passengers' expressions. He saw a ruddy-cheeked little boy's excitement as he pressed his nose against the autumn-chilled window to watch the scenery speed by—bush-dotted foothills that periodically flattened into seas of sagebrush whose golden pods burst into puffs at the first touch of the wind. He saw, too, how the fastidiously dressed woman up front brushed disgustedly at the cinders that rushed into the car when the conductor, the "jack-in-office," as he was known, opened the front door. And he'd have bet money that Mr. Conductor wasn't nearly as relaxed as he pretended to be. In fact, the car was well-nigh filled with a brittle expectancy that encompassed everyone, from the old maid who jumped when the locomotive screeched its shrill whistle, to the men whose hands stayed unusually near their guns, to the woman in brown who kept fiddling with the jar of jelly.

Unhurriedly, as if he had all the time in the world, Oliver Truxtun eased his hand into the slit of his jacket and dragged his watch out of the pocket of his waistcoat. Its gold fob dangled onto his flat stomach before his blunt thumb popped open the lid to reveal the watch face. Ten minutes till four. Every fifteen minutes he took a quiet walk through the train, paying special attention to the one other passenger car, which was filled with way passengers—short-haul travelers who'd gotten on at Carson City for the last leg of the run into Virginia City. From there, he went to check out the baggage car, where the safe was kept.

The first thing he'd done after getting on board at Reno was to determine the car's arrangement: engine, tender, two flatcars carrying lumber, one boxcar stacked with mining supplies (no train robber hid within; he'd personally checked), two passenger cars, the baggage car, and the private car of Miss Trinity Lee. The gut instinct that rarely failed him said that if someone was going to rob the train, that someone was presently on board.

And this time the sonofabitch was gonna have a helluva time disappearing!

Pocketing his watch, Oliver Truxtun settled down to a ten-minute wait before repeating his rounds. Because he was a man first and a Pinkerton agent second, he allowed himself a fleeting thought of Trinity Lee. He wondered if she was as pretty as everyone said.

"Do you think she is, Mamma?"

"Do I think who is what?" Harriet Dawson replied, her nimble fingers knitting a woolen sock. "Sit up straight, dear. You're slumping."

Sixteen-year-old Victoria complied by pulling up her shoulders. "Trinity Lee. Do you think she's as pretty as everyone says?"

"Perhaps so, perhaps not."

A wistful look skipped through Victoria's wildflower-blue eyes. "Just imagine wearing all those beautiful clothes..."

"There's more important things than wearing beautiful clothes."

"...and having your hair done up in all those beautiful styles..."

"There's more important things than beautiful hair."

"...and having men look at you as if—"

"That's enough, Victoria," Mrs. Dawson said sternly.

Victoria sighed and wished that her mother wouldn't treat her as if she were a child. She knew what went on between men and women. Well, sort of. She and her girlfriends had talked about it and had come to some general, and rather exciting, conclusions.

"Can I go to the play?"

"*May* I. And no. It wouldn't be seemly for a young girl to go to a play."

Undaunted, Victoria added, "I'm going to be an actress."

"Of course you're not, dear."

Ah, but she was, Victoria thought. She knew that, as an actress, Trinity Lee had what her mother called a "reputation." Victoria also knew that men openly admired her, and that women secretly envied her.

"Why is a reputation a bad thing?"

Sensing the direction of the conversation, Mrs. Dawson nipped it in its nascent bud. "That's enough, Victoria."

Victoria sighed, slumped, then guiltily straightened her shoulders once more. "Do you think he will?"

"Do I think who will what?"

"Do you think the train robber will rob the train?"

"I daresay he'd be foolish to try."

"Breck would be furious."

"Mr. Brecker to you. And well he should be furious."

There was a pause. Then: "Why don't people like Br—Mr. Brecker?"

Harriet Dawson turned her eyes from her knitting to her daughter. "It isn't that they don't like him. It's just that they don't . . . they don't know him. And he lives differently from most God-fearing folks."

Drifter, Victoria mused. That was the word she'd heard her papa use. And he'd made it sound like something bad. Sort of like a "reputation." The funny thing was—and maybe this was what having a "reputation" meant—she saw the women eyeing Madison Brecker with more than casual interest. In fact, one of her girlfriends had heard a friend of her mother's say she wouldn't mind engaging Mr. Brecker in— "What's a quick tumble in the hay?"

Shock sped across Harriet Dawson's face. "That's quite enough, young lady! And square up those shoulders!"

Victoria sighed, squared, and wondered what on earth she'd said to set her mamma off so. She then let her mind wander to tumbles and train robbers and Trinity Lee. Of the last, she thought dreamily, *I wonder what she's doing at this very moment.*

At the moment in question, Trinity was remaking her face into that of a man. With the experienced application of theatrical makeup and the strategic placement of bits of hair, she had bushed her eyebrows, hollowed her cheeks, widened her chin, and fringed a mustache above her scaled-down upper lip. She was now putting the finishing touches on a scar that ran from her hairline to her temple. This was her giveaway recognition feature. Everyone robbed wanted to think himself clever enough to notice some telltale clue to the masked man's identity. For the first robbery, Trinity had worn a hairpiece so auburn it had been certain to attract attention. For the second, she had limped. The only thing she'd done with consistency was wear glasses, hoping to shield the distinctive shape of her eyes.

Grasping a brush dusted with dark powder, she dabbed at the epicanthus in an attempt to minimize it, refusing to acknowledge that her hand was trembling. Now was not the time to indulge in second thoughts. Resolutely slipping on wire-framed glasses, she fitted the curved wire behind her ears, then grabbed a felt hat from the elegantly made bed. She had braided her waist-length hair and crossed the braids at the back of her head. She now pulled the worn hat securely down over them, tucking any renegade strands upward.

The hardest part done, she allowed herself to take a deep, calming breath...and to admire the fabricated man who stared back from the ornate silver-plated mirror above the marble-topped mahogany washstand.

When had the idea of robbery first occurred to her?

She couldn't honestly pinpoint the moment. Certainly it had been after she'd written her friend in Virginia City and skillfully, subtly, to attract as little attention as possible, inquired about one Madison Brecker. Trinity had needed to completely satisfy herself that this truly was the man she sought. Perhaps the seed of the idea had been sown by her friend's reply.

Madison Brecker was a newcomer, a loner, a man who volunteered nothing about his past, though rumors ran rampant. He had surprised everyone months before by buying the Sierra Virginia Railroad from Wilson Booth, who had overextended himself financially when he'd laid down track between Reno and Carson City. Madison Brecker had taken money he'd earned in the silver mines and, with some astute card-playing, parlayed his funds into a sum substantial enough to buy the railroad and finish laying the track. Gossip further whispered that everything he had was sunk into the endeavor and that operating that railroad had become almost a religion for him.

Trinity had taken the letter to mean that she had found Madison Brecker's Achilles' heel. But what was she to do with this discovery? It was then that things, like pieces of a puzzle, had started falling into place. The sown seed had begun to sprout. A new but increasingly dear friend of hers, Jedediah McCook, had offered her the use of his private railway car for any traveling she chose to do. How easy it would be, using Ellie as her destination, to travel on the Sierra Virginia, rob it of its payroll money, then disappear into the sanctuary of her private car. Add to that the fact that she was an expert with makeup. Even her longtime friend Ch'en hadn't recognized her when last they'd met.

The flower had blossomed, fully, completely, with all its menacing implications. Yet Trinity had forced herself not to rush into any hasty decisions. More and more, however, she had found the idea of financially destroying Madison Brecker before killing him—she was always astounded at how calmly she considered the latter—appealing. Being rich in patience—a patience honed to perfection by the long search, a patience perhaps even rooted in her Oriental heritage—she had had no qualms about a little delay.

The deciding factor, however, had been the first robbery. It had been so easy. Too easy. Robbery shouldn't be that easy. But, Lord, it had been satisfying! Particularly when she'd learned that Madison Brecker himself was standing behind the losses. That had freed her conscience to continue, for she had searched her brain endlessly for a way to return the money, no questions asked, to the mining companies, for her quarrel was with Brecker, not them. No, she preferred to view his standing behind the losses as an open invitation for her to continue. Which was exactly what she was going to do. At least until she had discredited the Sierra Virginia. Or grown tired of the sport.

Untying the sash at her waist, Trinity allowed the jonquil-yellow silk wrapper, which looked ludicrous with her masculine face, to glide from her shoulders. She tossed it onto the bed, where it lay like a conspicuous splash of sunshine against the emerald-and-crimson velvet spread. Snatching a roll of cotton batting, she positioned it under her arms and bound it across her breasts, wishing for the first time that she had a smaller bosom.

Despite the tension gushing through her veins, a smile briefly touched Trinity's lips. Ellie, in her own laughter-laced words, stuffed "half of the continental United States" into the front of her dress to produce the desired décolletage. Ellie. Bawdy, yet intrinsically naive. And always so pure of heart, so kind, so charitable in thought and deed. Trinity's smile faded. What would her friend say if she knew what she was preparing to do?

Deliberately refusing to answer her own question, Trinity pinned the batting in place, grabbed the man's plaid shirt from the bed, and rolled her shoulders into it. With quick, tense movements, she slipped on the man's pants, tucked the tails of the shirt inside, and cinched the waist—why did it have to be so infuriatingly small?—with a slim leather belt. Next, she slid her feet into scruffy boots. She then donned a jacket and, reaching into the pocket, produced a red-and-white bandanna, which she tied across her nose and mouth. Instantly, she became aware of her warm, trapped breath—and the quickened pace of her breathing.

Easy, Trinity. You can't afford a case of nerves.

Affordable or not, however, her nervous agitation accelerated when her fingers curled around the handle of the Colt revolver. Its cool blue-gray steel and sinister weight fleetingly curdled the courage in her stomach. Detesting herself for the weakness, she cocked the gun, checked for at least the dozenth time to see that it was unloaded—she wouldn't have anyone accidentally hurt—and rammed it into her waistband. Jerking on her leather gloves, she hurriedly worked her soft woman's hands into their concealing depths and started for the door.

In one last bid, the plush railroad car begged her to stay within its safe confines. The carved, gilded mahogany paneling, the stained-glass windows, the frescoed roof, all beckoned with their luxurious reasoning, telling her she didn't have to go through with this. The rich, pleated drapes vowed to wrap her in their damask safekeeping, while the floor, carpeted with a costly Brussels, promised to discreetly absorb her footsteps should she choose to turn back.

But she didn't turn back. The past wouldn't let her. Madison Brecker had acted decisively when he'd killed her mother. She would be no less decisive now.

That thought burning in her soul, that thought leading the way with its malignant light, Trinity twisted the knob and pulled open the door.

Chapter Two

A cool October wind slid across the unmasked portion of Trinity's cheeks. It fluttered the triangular tip of the bandanna, spitting the tail back into her mouth; it snatched at the brim of her hat. Bowing her head to its gentle but insistent assault, Trinity wasted no more time on nerves or indecision.

As she had twice before, she stepped to the railing of the private car, hiked up a boot, and, anchoring her hands on the overhang of the adjacent baggage car, dexterously pulled herself up and forward. For a fraction of a second, she struggled for balance. Then she found it, distributing her weight evenly on both feet. As she stood on the tiny platform of the car, the wind whipped at her pant legs, making of them flapping black flags.

Because the back door of the baggage car was blocked by mailbags, which she'd noted both times she'd been in the car, she didn't fear detection from that quarter. The door obviously wasn't used. Still, she wasted no time in hoisting herself onto the car roof. To do so, she had to struggle, her fingers digging and curling for any advantage, chief among them the steel grab irons conveniently provided for just that purpose. She was reminded of the dozens of unclimbable trees she'd scaled all the way to their harrowing tops.

One last heave and she was on the roof, flat on her belly. She allowed herself a long, steadying breath. The wind rushed over her, filled with bits of charred cinders. Overhead, smoke bellowed, as if belched from the stomach of the brass-bound beast. The whistle, curt and shrill, startled the midafternoon silence of the countryside.

Bucking the wind, Trinity pushed to her hands and knees and began crawling the length of the jostling car. Bracing herself on one knee, stretching for a new handhold, she inched forward as noiselessly as possible. Occasionally the car creaked, but whether it was because of her or just the normal sounds imposed by constant motion, she couldn't say. She prayed fervently that, whichever it was, it drew no one's attention.

A third of the way down the car, her knee struck something. A sharp pain shot through her kneecap. In swift reaction, she uttered a cry.

Inside the baggage car, seated on the wooden floor, Dick Kingsman halted in the act of shuffling the deck of cards—the "railroad bible," as both employees and passengers called it.

"D'you hear somethin'?" the baggageman asked, cocking his head and straining to search through the sounds around him. He was as skittish as a mare that had never been bred. Twice he'd been robbed, and twice he'd had to look into the cold, hard eyes of Madison Brecker and explain what had happened. To his way of thinking, facing Madison Brecker twice was two times too many for any man, however brave. There were two things a smart man learned up front: You didn't mess with Madison Brecker, and you didn't mess with Madison Brecker. Not that his boss had blamed him for the holdups, but then again, he hadn't patted him on the back and said, "Nice job, Dick ol' boy."

All Hollis Reed, the off-duty brakeman who was hitching a ride back to Virginia City, heard was the *ker-chung, ker-chung, ker-chung* of iron wheel meeting iron rail. The sound was intensified because they had slid open the side door about two feet in order to pull some fresh air into the stuffy baggage car. Of course, they'd been careful to keep the door closed when the train had pulled into the Carson City depot. There'd been no need to issue a brazen invitation to any itchy trigger finger in town.

"I don't hear nothing 'cept what we're supposed to hear," Hollis answered. "What do you hear?"

Dick paused before saying, "Nothin'. I guess."

"Then let me hear those cards leaving your hands for mine. And while you're at it, let me hear my luck changing."

Still Dick hesitated, but when one normal sound piled up on top of another, he ran out of excuses and started to shuffle the cards. Hell, he thought, he'd just let that Pinkerton gent do all the worrying.

In seconds both men had their hands full of cards, and their heads full of the moment.

Trinity rubbed her hand across her aching knee. Come morning, there would be a bruise. She shifted her attention from her knee to the object it had struck—a smokestack some six to eight inches in diameter and about an inch high. In her haste, she'd overlooked it. She forced her mind from the pain and back to the task at hand.

Hurrying as quietly as she could, she reached the edge of the car. With the adroitness she'd employed in getting to the car's top, she now climbed, dangled, and swung herself downward. The floor seemed inordinately solid under her feet. Trinity ignored the possibility that it might only be her legs feeling inordinately rubbery.

She glanced quickly about. This was the trickiest part, the least controllable aspect of the robbery. Standing at the door of the baggage car awaiting admittance, she was vulnerable to the unexpected appearance of a restless passenger out for a breath of air.

Without wasting a moment, Trinity pulled the gun from her waistband and rapped sharply on the door. She wondered if her plan would work . . . if the Pinkerton agent was on board . . . if the deafening roar in her ears was the chugging of the train or the thudding of her heart.

At the knock, Dick Kingsman stopped dead in the act of picking a card from the fan splayed across his palm. He quickly looked over at Hollis Reed, who had just as quickly looked over at him. Both men waited.

"Hey, it's Dancey. Everything all right in there?"

The two men visibly relaxed.

"It's Dancey," Dick said unnecessarily, laying his cards facedown and pulling himself to his feet.

Dancey Harlan was the conductor of the Sierra Virginia, a rough-hewn man with a quixotic nature that blended whiskey-drinking and ear-curling swearing with a penchant for preaching religion.

Trinity listened to the clicking of the door's lock. Her plan had succeeded. The first time she'd robbed the train, the door had been trustingly unlocked. The second time she'd called the baggage clerk by name, and he'd naively opened the locked door for her. Knowing that ploy would no longer work—no one could be that stupid!—she had deepened her voice, called upon her acting skills, and prayed she could mimic the conductor. At least enough to confuse a man who was probably already nervous with anticipation.

The door opened. Dick Kingsman was smiling when he said, "What the heck you want, Dan—"

The smile faded as the question was swallowed up by the unfriendly barrel of a Colt revolver. The baggage clerk's eyes, a rainy gray, grew so big Trinity feared they would burst. The man was on the young side of twenty, an age when proof of masculinity meant all. The repeated robberies were bound to be taking their emasculating toll. She had a ridiculous impulse to apologize.

Instead, she listened to Dick Kingsman's muttered "*She-it*" and watched as he disgustedly plopped his hands onto his hips. Immediately, he remembered that he was in the throes of a robbery and rushed his hands heavenward.

Behind him, Hollis Reed, older, but with eyes as wide as Dick's, jumped to his feet, scattering the only winning hand he'd had all afternoon. He, too, reached for the sky as if there were some precious something to be plucked from there and he was determined to get his share of it.

Trinity stepped into the car, closed the door behind her, and tripped the lock. Letting the gun do the talking, she motioned toward the safe. Dick Kingsman knew the ritual all too well. With shaking fingers, he dialed the safe combination, a combination he was certain he wouldn't know for much longer. Mr. Brecker would probably fire him on the spot this time. Hell, he hadn't even been wearing his gun! But Sweet Jesus, he'd thought it was Dancey!

Locking in the last number, Kingsman lifted the lever. Nothing happened. The safe was locked as tightly as it had been moments before. Perspiration popping out on his face, he whirled and stammered, "I—I must've dialed a wrong number."

Trinity calmly motioned for him to try again. In truth, however, she wanted to scream, "Hurry! Hurry!" Her heart was pounding a hurting rhythm, and had been ever since she'd discovered that she was confronting two men instead of the expected one. Although the other one hadn't so much as blinked an eye. In fact, she decided, if she were to blow in his direction, he'd probably topple over.

The thought flitted through her mind that escaping from two men wasn't going to be as easy as escaping from one. Another thought flitted behind the first: That she should tie the second man up. But with what? An idea occurred to her, and she jerked the gun toward the passenger valises stacked along the right side of the baggage car.

"What?" Hollis asked, practically jumping out of his skin now that the robber's attention was focused on him.

"Open," Trinity growled.

"The bags?" he asked, certain he'd misunderstood.

She kicked a carpetbag with the toe of her boot, indicating that he was right and that he was to lose no time. He didn't. Nervously, allowing his hands to creep downward, he eased past the figure with the gun, fell to his knees, and threw open the carpetbag. Trinity motioned for him to back away. Her gun still trained on the two men, she squatted down and began to rummage through the contents. A dress. A chemise. A corset. A pair of drawers. The last she laid aside before searching out another pair.

The click of the safe was loud in the tense, rattling baggage car. Trinity glanced up.

"Got it!" Dick Kingsman announced proudly. "You'll want these bills in a sack, won't you?" he added, now downright accommodating. He assumed what everyone was assuming—namely, that the robberies were part and parcel the work of the same gang.

Trinity nodded. "Hurry!"

In seconds, he handed her a cloth sack filled with paper money. In return, she handed him two pairs of women's drawers. His look of surprise was everything it should have been.

"Tie him," she ordered, nodding toward his friend, who looked equally surprised and highly offended by what she was proposing.

"But—" both men said at once.

"Tie him!"

His trembling hand outstretched, Kingsman stepped forward.

* * *

At the precise moment an embarrassed Hollis Reed, his hands and feet bound by a woman's lacy unmentionables, was squirming on the floor of the baggage car, Oliver Truxtun rose from his seat to begin his appointed rounds. His eyes met those of Dancey Harlan. A quiet understanding passed between the two men.

A similar, though not silent, understanding had just been reached by Trinity and Dick Kingsman: The latter was to count to one hundred before opening the door or risk not making it to his next birthday.

She had just placed her hand upon the knob of that door when Oliver Truxtun's knock sounded. It sent reverberations echoing through the door and Trinity's heart.

She jerked her hand away.

The knock came again, hard and insistent.

Instinctively, Trinity stepped back. Damn! she thought. Holy damn!

"Kingsman?" the Pinkerton agent called out.

Trinity glanced quickly in the direction of the wide-eyed Dick Kingsman. "Answer him!" she whispered through gritted teeth.

"Uh...yeah?" the young man said in compliance, his voice shallow, his eyes pinned to those concealed by the wire-framed glasses.

"Everything all right?"

A pause followed. A slowly unfolding pause. Trinity, her eyes narrowed, angled the gun at the baggage clerk's chest.

"Yeah...yeah...sure!" he gushed, one word tripping over the next.

"Let me in," Oliver Truxtun ordered.

At the command, three separate thoughts were drawn forth.

We're gonna get the little weasel now, a prone Hollis Reed thought, fighting back the sneeze that was threatening as a result of inhaling the dust on the floor.

Maybe I can hang on to my job yet, Dick Kingsman thought.

Followed by Trinity's exquisitely heartfelt *Holy, holy hell!*

Stepping around Hollis Reed, Trinity edged her way past a slew of crates, trunks and bags, one of which still lay gutted and exposed, as she headed toward the rear of the car, away from the front door and certain detection. Several sacks of mail were stacked haphazardly—and incommodiously—against the back door.

"Kingsman?" Truxtun called out. He was jiggling the doorknob now.

Trinity could feel the man's suspicion, a thick, hot force crouched beyond the barrier of the closed door. She could also feel her heart scampering in a wild, uneven rhythm.

"Stall him," she ordered. "And move these bags."

"Uh—uh—" Dick stammered, "just a minute." As he spoke, he dragged one sack, then another and another, out of the way.

Trinity stepped forward, tried the door and found it locked. Her heart rose into her throat.

"Kingsman!" Oliver Truxton shouted, his fist pounding against the other door.

Trinity fumbled with the lock.

"Kingsman, open up!"

She could hear the voices joining that of the man who was insisting on gaining admission. Vaguely she wondered if he was the Pinkerton agent hired by Madison Brecker. Frantic now, she grappled with the lock, but the leather gloves only guaranteed her clumsiness. Sliding her hand beneath the mask, she pulled the glove from her left hand with her teeth, tried the lock again, and was rewarded by a clicking sound. Pulling the glove from her mouth and slinging the bag of money over her shoulder, she yanked open the door.

"Don't try anything stupid," she ordered, her voice naturally octaves lower because of her increased breathiness.

"No...no..." Kingsman assured her, unknowingly backing away as if to prove that he could be trusted.

Trinity slammed the door behind her and scurried over the baggage car platform and into her private coach. Two things crossed her mind in tandem: Why had she never insisted on going out the back door before? It was certainly easier than retracing her over-the-top route. And if she didn't get a decent breath soon, she was going to pass out.

Inside the baggage car, Dick Kingsman hurried toward the door Oliver Truxtun was threatening to shoot the lock off of. "I'm coming!" he shouted.

Hollis Reed, still prostrate on the floor, was trying to worm his way to the door, as well. He had also breathed as much dust as he could without giving in to the inevitable. Sucking in air, he sneezed violently. Dick Kingsman, who at that moment was stepping over the wriggling form of his friend, lost his balance and fell, his lower lip slamming hostilely against the floor. Both Hollis Reed and Dick Kingsman yelped as a shot rang out and the door was thrown wide.

Thus it was that Oliver Truxtun, Dancey Harlan, and a bevy of curious passengers found the brakeman of the Sierra Virginia Railroad bound up in two pairs of lace-trimmed ladies' drawers with the baggageman sprawled unceremoniously atop him, the latter's lip bleeding profusely, and both men's pride irreparably bruised.

Ten minutes later, when the knock sounded on the elegantly carved wooden door of the private coach, an outwardly composed and very feminine-looking Trinity answered the summons.

"Yes?" she said around a brilliant smile that made her recently—and furiously—scrubbed cheeks ache. "Why, it's Mr. Harlan, isn't it?"

She knew unequivocally that it was Dancey Harlan who stood before her, wearing his black conductor's suit and cap and his pendulous gold railroad watch. Even without the trappings of his position, she would have known him. He had a massive, mountainous build, a smothered, gravelly voice, and a totally hairless head with a jagged scar running out from under the cap all the way down to the nape of his neck. She'd heard that he took his cap off for few people and that he never discussed the scalping that had rendered him bald. She knew all this because, like the good actress she was, she'd studied the role she was playing, and for a few seconds this afternoon she'd been Dancey Harlan.

"Yes, ma'am," Dancey now answered. "I'm checking to see if you're all right."

"All right?" Trinity allowed her eyes to widen just that little bit that artfully suggested realization. "Oh, my, I did hear something, didn't I? I thought I heard a shot, but then I convinced myself I hadn't."

"Yes, ma'am, I'm 'fraid you did." Dancey Harlan's square jaw tightened until Trinity could almost see his back teeth grinding together. "The train was robbed. Slicker than Satan slithering into your soul."

Trinity spoke not a word. Instead, in the consummate gesture of distress, she brought her hand to her breast.

"There, there, it's nothing for you to worry about," the big man said in a gruff, comforting voice, making Trinity experience a momentary pang of guilt. "It's over."

"Did—did you get—"

"No, ma'am, the sonofabitch got clean away." So accustomed to swearing was Dancey that he rarely noticed when he did. This time, however, he stumbled over an apology. "I mean . . . what I meant to say . . ."

"I quite understand," Trinity interjected. "The man does sound of questionable ancestry. All the men do." Making it sound like just the appropriate afterthought, she added, "You do suspect a gang, don't you?"

"That's the idea making the rounds."

"And I hear Mr. Brecker is personally making good the mining companies' losses."

"Yes, ma'am, he is."

"How very . . . noble." The word she'd really wanted to use was *prudent*. With the irate miners growing more irate by the minute, Mr. Brecker was simply acting with placating prudence. He was also acting in a way that few people could financially afford for any great length of time.

Trinity felt a rush of satisfaction. It was dark and sweet, like a poisoned confection melting on a hungry tongue.

"I just wanted to check with you, ma'am. To see if you were all right. And to see if maybe you'd seen something, which I reckon you didn't."

"No. No, I'm sorry to say."

"We'll be pulling into Virginia City—" he slid the watch from its fob "—within the quarter hour."

Trinity heard not a syllable of Dancey Harlan's last words. She was too busy scraping her heart up from where it had sunk into the deepest corner of her stomach. For held within the hand that was so routinely replacing the watch was a glove.

A man's leather glove.

A familiar man's leather glove.

The leather glove she'd worn to rob the train.

"Th-thank you," she somehow managed to say.

*   *   *

News of the robbery spread through town before the train rolled to a complete stop. It skipped through the crowd waiting to meet friends and family, falling with special interest on the ears of Ellie Grayson Oates, before jumping like quick summer lightning to C Street, the town's main thoroughfare. It buzzed around the assay office of Firman Gill, where he and Neil Oates, manager of the Chollar mine, were engaged in conversation. Both men agreed that the miners' already raw dispositions were going to be further chafed and that, all in all, it was another bad blow to Madison Brecker.

From there the news hummed through the gold-and-navy-blue lobby of the Chastain Hotel, which Wilson Booth, former owner of the Sierra Virginia Railroad, was at that moment exiting after a most satisfying carnal assignation with a married woman. Upon receipt of the report, he simply smiled, nodded a greeting to the woman's husband, who'd just entered the hotel, and began whistling "Her Bright Smile Haunts Me Still."

Over at the Last Drink Saloon, the news was greeted with surprise, anger, and *I-told-you-so*s, depending on the sobriety of the listener. Standing at the brass-railed counter, her auburn hair scattered fetchingly about her shoulders, Millie Rhea felt a deep heartache for Breck. She also felt a keen disappointment. This probably meant he wouldn't be coming to her tonight, though why he came to her at all still mystified her. The truth was, the same women who looked askance at his shadowed background would gladly writhe beneath him, given half a chance. He, however, preferred to pay for his pleasure, insisting that that way both parties knew where they stood. Or, in this case, lay.

The news, now whipped to a fury, screeched to a halt, a wary halt, just outside a cubbyhole office wedged between a cobbler's shop and a drugstore. Inside, Madison Brecker—Breck—was doing what he spent eighteen out of every twenty-four hours doing: Poring over the consuming business of the Sierra Virginia Railroad. The office, like the man, was austere. Both dealt only in necessities. In the case of the office, there was an oak desk, a worn sofa, a safe, a filing cabinet, a coat tree that listed lamely, a bare wooden floor, a cast-iron stove, and an uncurtained window through which peeped the weak autumn sun. The man, dressed with equal simplicity, wrote in a ledger with an economy of motion. Even the cadence of his breathing, a rhythm that made the muscles of his chest swell against his black cotton shirt, seemed controlled and stripped to its crisp essence.

The news was finally forced inside by the young boy who kept the station floor swept and the spittoons emptied. He was all arms and legs and the gangly promise of manhood. He was also out of breath, having run all the way upon being dispatched by Dancey Harlan to fetch the railroad's owner.

"Mr. Brecker—" he panted, at the same time slinging wide the door until its glass rattled. His shoes almost threw off sparks as he skidded to a halt.

Breck glanced up.

"Mr. Brecker, sir—" the boy took a deep breath "—you better come quick. The train...it's been robbed again. And the sonofabi—" he amended Dancey's word, lest news that he'd used it travel back to his choir-singing mamma "—the man got away."

The announcement was met by silence. Dead silence. Already a pale blue, Breck's eyes faded to a colorless chill that not only threatened to crack the brittle irises, but also to freeze anyone unlucky enough to be caught in the path of their gaze.

The young boy took a timorous step backward.

Suddenly, seemingly all in one motion, Breck jabbed the ink-moist pen into its holder, jumped from the chair, leaving it to rock boisterously back and forth on its springs, and jerked his jacket from the coat tree. He was out the door like a shot, and, though he wasn't running, the lengthy stride of his longer legs forced the boy to rush to keep at his side.

The heels of Breck's boots crashed against the wooden sidewalk, the deafening sound sending all but a few scurrying. Hugging the sides of the buildings, the townspeople watched him. What they saw was a tall, lean, narrow-hipped man, whose broad shoulders rolled fluidly as he walked. His blond hair, golden as wheat and as rich in texture as the finest brocade, slashed across a sun-burnished forehead—a forehead deeply creased from his thirty-six years and from the harsh life he'd lived—and fell bluntly against the nape of his neck. The length of his hair always left men thinking he was about a week in need of a trim, while women thought it looked appealingly wild. Even wickedly so.

No one who watched was surprised that he didn't wear a gun. He seldom did. He seldom needed to. The knife he always carried in his boot, combined with his extraordinary skill and speed, demanded respect aplenty.

"Sorry, Breck," someone ventured.

"Did they get the fellow?" another dared.

"Give us the word and we'll form up a 601," a third voice said, referring to a vigilante group in California.

Stony-faced, Breck silently moved onward toward the depot. If hard work and brutal devotion weren't enough, what in hell did a man have to do to carve a something out of the chunk of nothing that was his life? he wondered bitterly. And why, after years of it not mattering, had it suddenly become so important to him that he do so? All he allowed himself in answer was the admission that he'd invested far more than money in the railroad venture. He'd invested his heart and his spirit and what was left of his battered soul.

The crowd, whose size had increased fourfold with townspeople eager to absorb all they could of the excitement, was alive with murmurs and mumblings and a keen agitation.

"I'm sure I don't know what the world is coming to," Harriet Dawson harped as she waded through the crowd, dragging her reluctant daughter behind her. "Come along, Victoria. And straighten those shoulders."

"Yes, Mamma," the dutiful young lady replied absently, for she was remembering the tousled look of Dick Kingsman, his hair wild, his clothes dirty, his lip swollen and bleeding, and imagining the bravery with which he must have faced down the train robber.

"Why, I almost fainted dead away at the sound of that shot," bright-eyed Maude Terrill proclaimed, gesturing erratically with her jar of persimmon jelly.

"Careful where you aim that jelly," Dub Terrill answered. "You don't want to pucker the whole of Virginia City."

At Breck's sullen approach, the murmurs, in the rippling rhythm of a tide washing ashore, faded to whispers and speculation. Heads turned, people stepped aside, until the crowd, as if it had been cleaved in half by a sharp knife, parted— slowly...slowly....

Slowly, her eyes searching the crowd for her friend Ellie, Trinity negotiated the last step of the private car. She looked the very picture of composure, the most elegant example of fashion. Her walking suit of sky-blue foulard fell over a short, flounced underskirt edged with a ruche of champagne-colored ribbon, its shade very near that of her eyes. The overskirt, equally flounced, was rounded up at the sides, where it was drawn into two large bows. Perched atop her braided black hair was a frothy hat of champagne-colored velvet, accented with thin ribbon and Mechlin lace. In her hand she carried a fawn-colored, beribboned silk parasol.

Her elegance was beyond question. Her seeming composure, however, was a sophisticated lie that could be laid at the feet of her acting ability, for the gloved hand resting within the folds of her skirt, and the hand clinging just a little too tightly to the parasol, were trembling like leaves in the face of a brisk wind.

The sight of the glove in the conductor's hand had sent her senses reeling, even though she knew there was nothing to link her to it. She had thrown the matching glove out the window of the moving train, watching with unqualified relief as it disappeared into the dry, deserted landscape. But the money, which could unquestionably tie her to the crime, was still in her possession, tucked within one of the many trunks that would soon be unloaded behind her. She knew that abandoning one while keeping the other was irrational, but free-flowing adrenaline did not lend itself to rationality.

Assuring herself that she would have to be more careful in the future, she caught sight of Ellie Oates, smiled, waved, and started toward her friend. She failed to notice that the crowd's chatter had fallen to a hush and that, one by one, the people were parting to let a dark power pass among them. Trinity had just quickened her pace when the couple directly in front of her, half of which was a woman carrying a jar of something, veered to the side, leaving Trinity with only one possible course of action: to plow straight into the figure of the man bearing resolutely down on her.

It all happened in the span of a second, yet for Trinity time stood frighteningly still. She first became aware of a rock-hard chest flung hard against her in haste, followed by the hurtful manacle of the two hands that rushed to grasp her upper arms. In reflex, her eyes sailed up the front of the man's jet-black shirt, which she could see beneath the equally black jacket. She absently noted that the shirt was buttoned high with pearl-white buttons that ran toward the shoulder, then downward, in an asymmetrical line. Above the chaste opening, the hollow of his throat, visibly ticking with his excited pulse, appeared pointedly vulnerable, even seductively alluring, by contrast with the rest of the man. His neck, corded with thick muscles and deeply tanned, rose strongly before jutting into a sharp, arrogant chin. From there she saw two lips, the top imposingly thin, even rigid, the bottom interestingly full, before noticing the rakish way his hair fanned the collar of his jacket. She angled her head and met his . . .

Blue eyes.

Cold. Hard. Dangerous. Eyes blistering with a wintry-bright, starless-night chill. Eyes that were empty and vacant and a stranger to warm emotions. Eyes that for eighteen years had haunted her while asleep and awake.

As if the sight of him had summoned up a specter from some mysterious, mist-filled world, she heard the shattering of a porcelain doll, heard an eight-year-old's fear gurgling through her veins, heard a child's scream. And felt the endless loneliness of losing someone she'd loved.

The second passed. Convinced that the woman was steadied, Breck removed his hands from her arms, stepped back, and, without a word, hastened on.

Trinity whirled, watched him leap onto the train and heard him thunder in the direction of a hawk-nosed man, "What in the bloody goddamned hell am I paying you for?"

Chapter Three

Oliver Truxtun blinked not one dark eye at Breck's scathing question. Instead, he walked back inside the passenger car, which was now filled only with railroad employees. Calmly, collectedly, he sat in the far back seat he'd occupied earlier and glanced up at the scowling man waiting for an answer.

"I believe what the bloody goddamned hell you're paying the agency for is to apprehend the men robbing your train," he said. "Which I assure you we will."

The icy condemnation in Breck's eyes in no way lessened. "Was anything said about it being before the sonsofbitches drain me dry?"

"These things take time," Oliver Truxtun noted.

"And my money," Breck countered, his deep, throaty voice frosted with rage.

The Pinkerton agent paused, appraising the man who'd stormed into the agency's San Francisco office weeks before, demanding the best operative they had. "I want these men," Truxtun said, simply but with feeling.

Breck noted how the plurality of the agency had suddenly been reduced to the singularity of this one man. Yes, he thought, Oliver Truxtum was like a dog with a bone. Or, more in keeping with his looks, like a hawk who relentlessly searched out his prey, then, with great satisfaction, moved in for the kill. In fact, he could easily imagine that Oliver Truxtun looked upon today's defeat as a personal affront. Which was fine with him. He was in favor of whatever it took to keep a fire lit under the man. He just hoped to hell he could afford the flame long enough to get some results.

Slowly Breck released the agent from his gaze and started to walk—stalk—down the narrow aisle. Man by man, his eyes met those of his employees, who were in a scattered pattern that suggested they'd been fired from an unsteady shotgun. There was Dancey Harlan, the only man he could truly claim as a friend, though even in this relationship, Breck, who'd been nursed on loneliness, could not give the whole of himself; Hollis Reed, who squirmed and flushed pink; young Dick Kingsman, who wouldn't even look him in the eye; Charlie Knott, the best engineer on any railroad, long or short line; and, finally, Abe Dustin, his mighty-muscled fireman, who looked perpetually sweaty and permanently costive, as if he'd spent too much time with wood to have much to say to people.

Breck turned, hiked a black boot onto the edge of the front seat in a movement that pulled his tight Levi's jeans even tighter, and, leaning forward, draped his arms across his raised knee. No one was fooled into thinking the moment was as casual as the man now appeared.

"Well," Breck drawled, "does somebody want to tell me what the hell happened?" When no one spoke, he tacked on sarcastically, "Please, not everyone at once."

Dick Kingsman, the logical narrator of the events, shifted, glanced up, glanced down, then forced himself to confront the closed face of his employer. His former employer, in all probability. He swallowed. "It, uh . . . it was a little before four, I guess. Hollis and I were pl—" He'd started to say that he and Hollis were playing cards but figured it was unnatural to ask a man to add a few more inches to the rope that was going to hang him. "Hollis was keeping me company in the baggage car. I thought I heard somethin', asked Hollis if he did, then decided it was my imagination. Three, four minutes later, there was this knock on the door. We waited, and then the voice said somethin' like 'It's me, Dancey. Is everything all right in there?'"

Dancey Harlan interrupted him. "The sow-sucking bastard sounded just like me. But then, the good book says that Satan can speak in tongues. But I'll be hanged in hell if I like him mimicking me!" During his impassioned discourse, Dancey dragged his conductor's cap from his head, passed his hand across his scarred, naked scalp, and replaced the cap.

Breck refrained from saying that he seriously doubted they were dealing firsthand with Satan. More likely, they had encountered one of his greedier human disciples. The robber's vocal capabilities did intrigue him, however. "He sounded like Dancey?"

"I swear to God," Dick Kingsman said, restating what was really his only defense before tiptoeing into "I didn't even put on my gun, I was so sure."

Hollis Reed joined in. "He did sound just like him. I'd have staked my life on it being Dancey."

Breck let Kingsman's not wearing his gun slide by and filed the information about the robber's voice under the heading of Interesting. "Go on," he urged.

Dick Kingsman did. Fact piled upon fact, and, with the cumulative layering of each, the robber grew viler, meaner, a man no one in his right mind would have refused. The baggage clerk prudently overlooked the part where he'd been forced to tie Hollis up with women's drawers. And the part where he'd fallen over Hollis and busted his lip. Which he now unknowingly raised his fingers to.

"Did you get a lick in at him?" Breck asked, noticing the man's injury, which was beginning to swell in earnest. Breck was prepared to enjoy even as small a victory as that.

Dick drew his hand quickly, guiltily, from his mouth. "No. No, sir, I—I fell... I mean, I stumbled over—over Hollis." This last was said so softly that it was almost a whisper.

Breck's tawny eyebrows rose. "You fell over Hollis?"

"Yeah. He, uh . . . He, uh . . . The robber made me tie him up."

Something in the way Hollis Reed turned from rose to crimson alerted Breck that there was more here to pursue. Which he did by simply staring. Silently staring.

Until Dick was forced to add, "With women's drawers."

"With what?"

"Women's drawers. He forced me to tie Hollis up with drawers he took from a passenger's valise."

A sudden twinkle sparked in Dancey Harlan's eyes, while Charlie Knott's lips twitched. Even Abe Dustin seemed to be toying with a snicker.

"Let me get this straight," Breck said, not even remotely sharing in the humor. "At a few minutes to four o'clock, a robber, disguising his voice as Dancey's, gained entrance to the baggage car, where the clerk wasn't even wearing his gun, robbed me blind—'' He stopped and asked a pertinent question: "I guess he did get the full twenty-two thousand?"

Dick nodded miserably.

"Robbed me blind," Breck continued, "then forced the clerk to tie up Hollis with women's underwear and made his getaway while the Pinkerton agent I'm paying a royal fortune pounds at the door and the clerk falls like a bumbling idiot over Hollis."

Reluctantly, Dick nodded again.

"Damnation!" Breck said, straightening and hauling his hands to his hips.

For a minute, no one said anything. Suddenly, as if this information might make some amends, Dick blurted out, "Dancey found his glove."

Breck looked up sharply.

Oliver Truxtun quietly passed the glove to Dancey, who tossed it the short distance to his employer and friend. Effortlessly, Breck caught it. He studied it. A man's brown glove. New. Still smelling very much of leather. Nothing, however, to categorize it as unique. Turning it over, Breck slipped his fingers inside. The glove barely came to his knuckles.

"Was the guy short like the other two?" Breck asked.

"Uh . . . yeah, I guess," Dick replied, reluctant to add insult to injury by admitting he'd been overpowered by a man smaller than himself.

"And did he wear glasses?"

"Yeah, he did," Dick answered. "Just like the other two."

Breck nodded, though he wasn't certain of just where his thoughts were headed. "Anything else you remember about him?"

The others could almost see the young man's mind searching for a visual image. It was Hollis Reed, however, who remembered.

"A scar!" the brakeman cried out. "I remember he had a scar about here." He brought his hand to his temple and marked off an inch or so that disappeared into his hairline.

"That's right!" Dick said excitedly. "He did."

Breck said nothing, disappointing both Dick Kingsman and Hollis Reed, who each thought the scar a fat, juicy plum to hand out under the lean circumstances. Instead, Breck was reflecting on the subjects of red hair, a limp and a scar. Something didn't seem quite right, he mused. Everything seemed just a little too obvious. He glanced down at the glove. Three men of small stature. Three men wearing glasses. Three men, each with a distinctive eye-catching characteristic. Was it possible that everyone had jumped to the wrong conclusion? Was it possible that there wasn't a gang involved, but simply a single man? Breck glanced up—and into the eyes of Oliver Truxtun. In that moment, without a word spoken, Breck was certain the same idea had just crossed the Pinkerton agent's mind.

"Unless someone can remember anything else," Breck said, glancing away from Truxtun, "let's get back to work." His jaw tightened in renewed anger. "If anyone wants me, I'll be out shaking the trees for twenty-two grand."

As Breck passed back down the aisle, Dancey caught his attention and spoke so no one else could hear. "I've got a little money saved—"

"You keep it," Breck told him. "Spend it on cheap whiskey and expensive women." He smiled. It was a rare occurrence, and it momentarily thawed the chill in his eyes. "Or is that expensive whiskey and cheap women?"

"On a Saturday night, I'll take either," his friend replied, "and thank the Almighty for the combination."

Breck's smile widened briefly, then disappeared entirely as he squeezed his friend's shoulder in silent thanks before stepping on toward the rear of the car. As he neared Dick Kingsman, the young man lowred his eyes.

"Kingsman?"

Dick snapped his head up.

"Get on over to Doc Dawson's and let him look at that lip."

"Yes, sir."

"And next time, wear your gun. And don't open the door to anyone. Even if you think it's me."

Next time. Those were the prettiest words Dick Kingsman had ever heard. "Yes, sir. I mean, no, sir," he said, his voice suddenly as light as a butterfly's flight.

Breck walked on toward Oliver Truxtun and held out the glove. "I believe this is your department."

The detective took it, and Breck headed outside, his long legs clearing the steps in seconds. The hungry crowd had fed on the crumbs of gossip and dispersed. In the silence, the sun was getting low. Breck wondered if a symbolic sun was also setting on the Sierra Virginia, or at least on his ownership of it. At the same instant the defeatist thought was born, Breck killed it.

Hell, no! he thought. He wouldn't give up that easily. He was going to prove to this miserable town, and to the whole stinking world, that Madison Brecker was somebody. He was going to prove, once and for all, that he was something more than "Brecker's brat."

On second glance, Ellie Grayson Oates was almost pretty.

On first, she was merely a short mass of freckles, blond, unruly curls, and too-large eyes, all of which seemed to bob and dance with her perpetual motion. In seconds, however, short was perceived as petite, the freckles were seen as appealing imperfections on her fair skin, and her blond curls seemed pertly spirited. As for her eyes, their lime-green color became far more important than size, while her ceaseless motion... Well, her ceaseless motion remained a jarring element to those of quieter sensibilities, yet one tolerantly overlooked it because Ellie was Ellie, which was to say that she was never still, almost pretty, and infinitely worth knowing.

It was this exuberant Ellie who threw herself into Trinity's arms the moment the door of the most elaborately appointed room in the Chastain Hotel closed. "I'm so glad to see you!" she squealed.

"It's only been two weeks," Trinity pointed out, though her hug was no less fierce. In fact, so fierce was it that two hats were tilted askew.

"But a long two weeks. Here, let me look at you," Ellie said, holding Trinity at arm's length, but keeping her hands firmly enfolded in her own. "Good. You've stopped shaking."

A note of fear hummed in Trinity's ears. "What?"

"You were shaking at the station, though I daresay you had every reason to. Being present at three robberies in two months is quite enough to make anyone shake. Tell me," she said, her green eyes bubbling with uncontainable excitement, "did you see anything? Hear anything?"

Trinity eased her hands from those of her friend and, one by one, began to pluck the fine kid gloves from her fingers. "No. No, I didn't." She wished her friend hadn't caught her trembling, but since she had, Trinity was pleased Ellie had attributed it to the robbery. Obviously, Ellie, possibly because she couldn't see over the heads of the crowd, possibly because it had all happened so quickly, hadn't seen her collide with Madison Brecker. The truth was, she'd been on the verge of bringing the initial case of trembling under control when she'd run—literally—into the one man who had the power to start it up anew. Despite their proximity following each robbery, they had not, until today, come face-to-face. After the first robbery, she'd deliberately avoided him, and after the second, he'd hurried off to San Francisco to hire the Pinkerton agency's services. She had known the moment of confrontation would come, had even longed for it, but she had found herself unprepared for it when it had. Even now, she felt the blizzardlike cold of his eyes. Shivering at the icy fingers suddenly walking up her spine, she repeated, "No. I neither saw nor heard anything."

"Well, I think it's all very exciting," Ellie said, untying her hat, sailing it into a chair, and swishing the copious skirt of her Dolly Varden walking suit while en route to the velvet-draped window, where she peered down into the street below.

"You would," Trinity said, smiling despite the subject.

"And a little sad."

Trinity glanced up as she, too, divested herself of her hat. She laid it on the rose velvet bedspread bordered with rippling yards of chenille balls. "Sad? Why?"

Ellie shrugged. "I don't know. I guess these people must need the money very badly. You must need something very badly to hurt someone else to get it, don't you think?"

The words, unintentionally sharper than daggers, gouged into Trinity's conscience. Not because she regretted what she was doing, but because she didn't regret it at all. One night, eighteen years ago, Madison Brecker had robbed her of her innocence, stolen a chunk of her humanity, and filled her heart with bitter hatred.

"What I think," she answered, "is that not everyone is as nice as you." She turned away, lest her friend see something in her face that bespoke the harshness in her soul. Without warning, she heard the snap of the fastener on one of the trunks stacked just inside the door. She whirled. "What are you doing?"

Ellie, ball of boundless energy that she was, slipped her hand to the other fastener. "Helping you unpack, of course. It'll only take us a minute—"

"No!" Trinity cried as she rushed forward and splayed her hands wide across the top of the trunk containing the money. At the realization that her reaction must seem strange to her friend, she softened her voice. "No. I won't hear of it. I want to spend this time visiting with you."

"But we can visit tonight at the dinner party," Ellie said, frowning slightly, although she let herself be led toward the bed.

"But not without interruption," Trinity persisted, easing onto the bed and encouraging her friend to do so, as well. "Tell me about this Mr. and Mrs. Anthony who have so graciously volunteered to give me a welcoming dinner."

In typical fashion, Ellie let the curious moment pass and jumped immediately to the next subject offered. She giggled.

Trinity frowned. "Oh, no. What does that mean?"

"They used to own the laundry."

"The laundry?" Trinity asked, unable to square this information with what she'd heard of the couple. Namely, that they were incredibly wealthy. Two of the wealthiest people in the state of Nevada.

Ellie nodded. "Mr. Anthony struck a rich vein of silver in the Comstock Lode. One of the richest in the area." She sighed dramatically. "They just don't seem to be able to stop the money from coming in."

Trinity smiled.

"They've built this enormous mansion, so gaudy you have to close one eye to look at it, and they dress even worse." Suddenly, her kind heart insisted that maybe she'd taken the teasing too far. "But they're really nice people. And they've certainly spared no expense for tonight. They've even brought French champagne and caviar all the way from San Francisco. As a matter of fact, it was probably on the train with you."

Trinity had an image of all the crates in the baggage car and wondered if perhaps the champagne and caviar had been stored within one of them.

Ellie giggled again, a fey little laugh. "If the robber had known about them, he'd probably have stolen them, too."

Trinity's heart skipped a tiny beat. She wondered irritably if it was destined to do so with every mention of the robberies. "Oh, I suspect," she said, with as much casualness as she could muster, "that he had other priorities."

"I don't know. Gossip says that four masked men robbed Wells Fargo a few weeks ago, and when they discovered ladies aboard and a magnum of champagne in the stagecoach's boot, they spread a blanket on the ground and robber and passenger alike had a party."

"Do you believe that?" Trinity asked with a grin.

Ellie considered. "No, I guess I don't." Her face brightened. "Yes, I think I do. And I hope they all had a roll on the ground later."

The comment was so singularly Ellie, naive yet bawdy, that Trinity laughed. "Ellie Oates, will you never change?"

They both agreed she probably wouldn't.

Minutes and several topics later, Ellie asked, "When does the troupe arrive?"

"Tomorrow. With a dress rehearsal planned for tomorrow night. I understand the presentation is the next night."

Ellie nodded. "I'm dying to get back on the stage." When the acting troupe had found out they would be playing Virginia City, they had all insisted that their former associate take a part. Ellie had needed little encouragement. "All of Virginia City will be there Wednesday night when the curtain goes up."

Trinity couldn't help but wonder if all of Virginia City included Madison Brecker. The thought that it might brought another frigid feeling. Slowly, she rose from the bed and walked toward the washstand. There, she tipped the pale pink floral-painted pitcher, saying as water splashed gently into the matching bowl, "I saw Madison Brecker at the station."

Ellie, unaware of the thumping of Trinity's heart, responded as if the comment were quite an ordinary one. "I certainly wouldn't have wanted to be the one to break the news of another robbery to him."

"He did seem ... upset," Trinity said, trailing her fingers through the cool water.

Ellie, too, slipped from the bed and stepped to the window. "Believe me, Breck doesn't get upset. He simply makes certain someone else does."

The remark had the effect of increasing the rhythm of Trinity's already thudding heart.

"Not that I can say I blame him in this case," Ellie said. "The miners are about ready to skin him alive—or, worse, pull their business. Not that they'd pull it all. They're desperately dependent on the railroad to bring in lumber and supplies and carry the ore out for processing, but Neil says the robberies are a terrible discredit to Breck's reputation as a businessman. And that the only reason they're continuing to ship their payrolls by rail is because Breck's absorbing the loss. Though I don't know how much longer that can last. Anyway, Neil says it's a shame, because Breck has always treated him and the other miners fairly."

Trinity reached for the embroidered linen hand towel and thought, How interesting. An honest murderer. What she said, however, was, "You said that he's a drifter." She hoped her query sounded sufficiently disinterested.

"Mmm," Ellie answered, plopping down in the nearest chair. "He's secretive about his past, but rumor says he's originally from St. Louis. He arrived here about six, seven months ago."

"What else does rumor say?" Trinity asked carefully.

"That he's killed," Ellie replied matter-of-factly, adding, "more than once. And that he wouldn't hesitate to do it again."

At the mention of the word *killed*, Trinity's hands paused. She resumed drying them, then laid the towel aside. "How barbaric."

"Mind you, it's only rumor, but then, if only a tenth of what people say is true, it's still reason to regard Breck with respect. Ben Buford—he owns the Buford Mine—said he knew Breck's father. Said he was killed in a gunfight. Seems that Breck's father called a man out for cheating at poker, and the man shot him. Before the week was over, the man, who everyone said really was cheating, was found dead...his throat cut. Ben says it was common belief that 'Brecker's brat'—that's what they called Breck—had killed him, even though he was only fourteen. After that, Ben says, Breck disappeared completely."

Not completely, Trinity thought. At some point he'd gone to Sacramento, where he'd killed her mother.

"Do you think he's wanted?" Trinity asked, trying to dispel the smothering feelings that recalling her mother's death always prompted.

Ellie, too long in one place, began to prowl the room once more. Trinity moved to stand before the trunk containing the ill-gotten money.

"I don't know," Ellie answered. "There's killing, and then there's killing."

"Yes," Trinity replied, musing that there were, indeed, two kinds of killing. The kind he'd perpetrated against her mother, and the justifiable kind she would perpetrate against him.

"All I know for certain," Ellie said, a wanton smile curving her lips, "is that, wanted by the law or not, he wears the tightest pants I've ever seen. Why, his Levi's are enough to make a woman's heart stop."

The conversation had taken an unexpected turn, and Trinity forced herself to respond in the way she knew was expected of her. She smiled. Just a little wantonly herself. "Ellie Oates, you're shameless. And married."

"Neil says I can look all I want as long as I don't touch."

Both women's smiles widened, Trinity thinking that she couldn't, if forced to take an oath, have said how tight Madison Brecker's pants had been, or even if he'd been wearing any. She'd been stopped cold—and that was the word—by his eyes.

Ellie's smile faded, replaced by a look of curiosity. "Why have you been asking about him so often?"

The question snuffed out Trinity's smile. "No special reason," she heard herself saying. "I wasn't even aware I was."

"You have been. For weeks now."

Trinity shrugged, searching for something that would get her off the hook. She grabbed for the first thing that came to mind. "A friend mentioned his name, that's all." She refrained from saying that the friend was Ch'en Yung. "It's not important," she added, quickly returning to the subject of that evening's party.

After a discussion of clothes, time, and conveyance, Ellie announced that she must take her leave. As the two were parting, a bright light jumped into Ellie's eyes.

"Can you keep a secret?"

Instantly intrigued, Trinity replied, "What?"

"I think I'm pregnant," she announced, hastening to add, "but don't say anything to Neil. I haven't told him yet. I want to be certain first."

"Have you been to the doctor?"

"Heavens, no. Doc Dawson would have it all over town before I could even get to Neil with the news." She smiled. "But I know I am. A woman knows these things."

Trinity raised her hand to cup the cheek of the woman who was dearer to her than any sister she might have had. "I'm so happy for you. You'll be a wonderful mother."

Ellie laid her hand atop Trinity's. Suddenly, both women's eyes were awash with tears.

"I'm so happy, too," Ellie said. "Not just about the baby, but about Neil, my life—everything. I only wish you could find someone to love as much as I love Neil."

Later, once she was alone, Trinity sat thinking about Ellie's parting wish. How could Trinity tell her that there was no room in her heart for love when it was so full of hate?

Ellie was right. The Anthony mansion was gaudy, a baroque-revival monstrosity whose heavy ornateness threatened to smother all who moved amid its curved, ornamental furniture and its deep-purple draperies. The Anthonys themselves had likewise been accurately depicted. Both Mrs. Anthony, bigbosomed and bigger-hipped, and Mr. Anthony, a short, bandy-legged man with a huge chest and thick neck, were elaborately overdressed in colors that warred blatantly with each other's attire. They were also delightfully nice people and cordial hosts.

Trinity, however, wished she were anywhere other than where she was. Every conversation, wherever it began, always ended with talk about the robbery. Which she understood as normal, just as she tried to accept as normal the little prickles of unease she experienced each time the subject came up. Now, satiated with talk and little prickles, she reached for a glass of champagne that a formally dressed servant offered her on a gleaming silver tray and weaved her way among the groupings of people, smiling and nodding and smiling again. Bits of conversation wafted to her.

"...third time in two months..."

"...totally lawless..."

"They oughta hang 'em high when they catch 'em."

Trinity's hand tightened around the glass as she moved on toward another assemblage of guests.

"...women's drawers..."

"Women's drawers?"

"I swear it."

"Who said?"

"Doc Dawson. He treated Dick Kingsman. Doc Dawson said that Dick said... How are you, Miss Lee? We're looking forward to Wednesday night."

Trinity smiled, replied graciously, and stepped on by, only to hear the same subject repeated.

"...women's drawers..."

"Someone said they belonged to Maude Terrill."

Someone sniggered behind his champagne.

"I'll just bet she almost fainted dead away."

There was another round of badly stifled laughter.

Trinity walked past the group, headed now for the fan-leafed palm at the rear of the room. To get there, she had to skirt one last covey of conversationalists.

"I can tell you I just about fainted dead away when I heard what that scoundrel had done with my unmentionables," the woman, whom Trinity had met earlier, said. "Why, I just can't suffer them next to me, knowing what wickedness they've been a party to."

Trinity's lips nipped into a smile, which broadened when she caught the muffled words of Maude Terrill's husband—Dub, she thought his name was—which were spoken to the gentleman by his side. "I'll bet you a shot of bourbon and branch water over at the Last Drink that she's wearing them right now."

Having reached her destination, Trinity brought her glass to her lips and sipped the cool champagne. For these precious few moments, she would bask in her solitude. Around her, the chatter ebbed and flowed, and she noted idly that more guests were arriving by the minute. In the last group, she saw Ellie, whom she had thought would be there earlier. She watched as Ellie scanned the sea of faces, settled on hers, and started directly for her, stopping only for an occasional greeting.

"I thought we'd never get here," Ellie complained, taking Trinity's hand. The yards of silk skirt, in a yellow-green shade high fashion called tilleul, rustled as the petite young woman leaned over to peck her friend's cheek.

On her heels arrived her husband. Neil Oates was a big, brawny man, tall enough to make two of his wife. He was also a hardworking man, a man of simple thoughts and simple tastes, a man who'd had the wisdom to marry a woman who adored him. That he adored her in exchange was more than obvious.

"Trinity," he said, giving her a huge hug, "nice to see you."

"Good to see you, Neil."

"Sorry we're late," he replied, out of habit placing his hand at his wife's back.

Trinity, noting the tender gesture, wondered what it would be like to be loved that devotedly.

"Some of the miners went into a panic when they heard the train had been robbed again," Neil explained, "but Breck called a meeting to allay everyone's fears. And to pay every-

one off with his own money, which I guess he got a loan from
the bank for. Anyway... Hey, that's just what I could use," he
threw in when a tray of drinks came his way. "You want one,
darlin'?"

Ellie shook her head. As Trinity set her empty glass back on
the tray, she noted that papers—posters of some kind—were
being passed among the guests. She idly wondered what they
were.

"Anyway, that's why we're late." Neil took a hearty gulp of
the imported champagne. "So you two are gonna perform together again, huh?"

From there, talk slipped to the performance Wednesday
night. It was still the topic of conversation when a tall, thin,
white-haired man and a tall, thin, dark-haired woman joined
the trio.

"Miss Lee, I'm Doc Dawson. And this is my wife, Harriet."

Trinity's eyes met those of Harriet Dawson, and immediately she sensed the woman's coolness, her censure. She didn't
have to search for the reason behind them. Trinity was an—if
asked to say the word, the woman would barely be able to get
it beyond her sanctimonious lips—*actress*. It followed, therefore, that she must be a loose woman. On the surface, women
like Harriet Dawson amused Trinity. Below the surface, on
those rare occasions when Trinity admitted it, they hurt her.

Cool though Mrs. Dawson was, Trinity observed that the
woman scanned her dress, sherry-colored off-the-shoulder satin
trimmed in chocolate-brown lace, with something just short of
envy. The doctor's wife went the entire distance toward the
mean sin, however, regarding Trinity's hair. Puffed above the
ears and crown in an Oriental style, it was skewered with two
ornamental pins—*kanzashis*. The heads of the golden pins were
delicate butterflies in flight.

"Mrs. Dawson," Trinity said.

The woman's eyes lowered from Trinity's fashionable coiffure. "Miss Lee," she returned with affected politeness.

Beyond her, Trinity saw the posters still making the rounds.

"We have seats for Wednesday night," Doc Dawson said.

"Wonderful," Trinity responded with a smile. "I hope we're
at our best."

"We're even bringing our daughter, Victoria."

"Wonder—"

Mrs. Dawson interrupted Trinity. "She has other plans."

"Are you sure?" her husband asked. "I thought she wanted to go—"

"Quite," Mrs. Dawson said.

Trinity understood completely. "Perhaps I can send her a signed program." The two women stood locked in silent battle, for there was no way Harriet Dawson could refuse the generous offer.

"Thank you," she was finally, grudgingly, forced to say.

"Bitch," Ellie said around such a sweet smile when the couple walked away that both Trinity and Neil dissolved into laughter.

Tears of laughter were still shining in Trinity's honey-colored eyes moments later, when the papers that had been circulating throughout the room finally reached the little trio.

"Ah," Neil commented, "Breck said he was going to do this." After studying the two posters, he handed them to Trinity.

She took them, glanced down and felt her breath flee from her lungs. WANTED: $1,500 REWARD was printed in bold black letters across each poster. Below the lettering was a drawing, each devoted to one of the first two train robbers. What Trinity saw, however, was simply two different versions of herself. Ignoring the stay-calm messages her brain was sending out, her gloved hand trembled, sending one of the flyers fluttering to the gaudy purple carpet.

Before she could bend to retrieve it, a hand snaked out of nowhere and beat her to it. It was a large, work-roughened hand. A sun-darkened hand. A hand that bore a scar in the shape of a crude star.

Chapter Four

The child in Trinity reacted with fear, her heart erupting into a wildly pounding rhythm, while the adult in her reacted with anger, her wildly pounding heart pumping thick, black hate. It was the consummate actress in her, however, who seized control and shackled the dual emotions. With self-preserving detachment, she watched Madison Brecker straighten up in a movement so slow it was mesmerizing; she watched his cool, remote eyes fix on hers; she watched his scarred hand thrust the poster forward. She took it without looking down, unable to drag her eyes away from his.

"Breck, I thought you said you weren't coming," Neil said, his voice comfortingly normal in what had become a lengthy silence. He pushed his hand forward in greeting.

Breck, again with a notable lack of haste, drew his eyes from Trinity's and extended his hand. "I needed to talk to the sheriff," he explained, adding in acknowledgment as he looked past Neil to his wife, "Ellie."

Ellie's lips bobbed into a brisk smile. "Breck, I'd like you to meet my dearest and best friend, Trinity Lee. Trinity, this is Madison—"

"We've met," Breck interrupted, his eyes—eyes the pale, washed-out blue of a winter sky—once more shifting to Trinity.

She was telling herself that, if she could just hold body and soul together for a few minutes, she could play out her charade undetected when the words fell about her with their razor sharpness. For the briefest of moments, her mind conjured up the image of her mother sprawled dead on the floor, a man— this man—kneeling before her, a little girl—herself—stepping back, back, back, out of fear. Instinctively, Trinity took a small step backward. Surely, however, Madison Brecker wasn't referring to that night eighteen years before. Surely he couldn't know she was that child. Surely...

"This afternoon," he clarified. "At the train station."

"Oh," Trinity answered, the incident having completely slipped her mind in favor of the more dramatic meeting in the past. "Why, I think you're right," she said, knowing full well he was. A sudden smile, half artistry, half sincerity, crossed her lips. "I'm afraid I must plead guilty to not always watching where I'm going."

"And I confess I was more than a little distracted myself." A grim tightness claimed his lips even as he spoke.

"But rightly so, I hear." Trinity told herself that avoiding the topic of the robbery would appear odd, and odd was something she couldn't afford to appear. "I heard the thief got away. Have you no leads at all?"

"Few," he answered. A servant arrived at his side to offer a glass of champagne. "Could I get a bourbon and water, instead?"

"Certainly, sir," the servant responded.

Trinity watched the man walk away, wishing that she, too, could absent herself from Madison Brecker's presence—and that he had responded to her question about leads with a definite *no*. She assured herself that she could live with his answer. Just as she could live with being forced to stand there and hold the incriminating posters. She wouldn't look at them. Or maybe she should look at them. Would it seem peculiar if she didn't? But would she give something away if she did?

"I understand this one left a glove behind," Neil commented after a few minutes of predictable talk about the robbery.

The statement snagged Trinity's attention, along with that of her friend.

"A glove?" Ellie asked.

"Yeah," Breck replied, "a leather glove. Unfortunately, quite ordinary. Thanks," he added, taking the bourbon and water the servant had returned with, the squat glass nestled among the taller glasses of champagne.

On impulse, Trinity reached for a tulip-shaped glass and, in its place, stuffed the wanted posters. She smiled engagingly, victoriously, at the waiter.

Smart, Trinity, smart, she thought as she watched the posters being carried away.

"The only distinguishing thing about the glove is that it's small," Breck was saying. Trinity watched as he downed half his drink, as if he were trying to scald away the bitter fact that the glove offered nothing more in the way of a clue.

Stupid, Trinity, stupid. Why did you have to drop that glove? she thought, slipping her free hand into the folds of her skirt, as if the man before her were perceptive enough to tell from looking that the glove would just fit her hand. She noted out of the corner of her eye that the posters had been removed from the tray and were circulating among the guests once more. She gave a silent moan of protest and took a courteous step to one side as Doc Dawson joined the group.

"Glove, eh?" the good doctor said.

"Small?" Dub Terrill chimed in. "Well, I can tell you there ain't nothing smellier than a pint-size polecat."

The subject of conversation seemed as set as a three-day-old bread pudding, and there wasn't a thing Trinity could do about it except let the words flow around her. In a town that was notoriously lawless—Ellie had once told her it averaged a funeral a day, although a funeral never coincided with the train's arrival, since pallbearers were wont to abandon a coffin in the middle of the street in order to greet the incoming train—everyone appeared preoccupied with the robberies. Apparently, they appealed to everyone's sense of adventure and need for self-righteous indignation, which out-and-out murder could not inspire, since one was too busy grappling with the cloying sadness that the human race had sunk lower than the underground tunnels being mined nearby.

Murder. Had Madison Brecker murdered her mother out of anger? Had they been quarreling about God only knew what? Or was the murder merely the product of theft? Had he merely intended to take what little money she had, any way he had to? And what did it feel like to kill, to snuff out a human life? Like nothing, Trinity thought in answer to this last question as she studied Breck from behind an uptilted champagne glass. For this man, it would feel like nothing. She sensed that he had been stripped of all human emotion, though for what reason she could not fathom. The nothingness shone dully from the blue blankness of his eyes. Somehow, somewhere along the way, he had become different from other men. It was a difference expressed in a thousand ways.

The most obvious lay in his appearance. The other men were dressed in their finery, starched shirtfronts and cutaway coats, while Breck wore denim pants, the durable invention of Levi Strauss. That they were every bit as tight as Ellie had suggested, and every bit as breathtaking, Trinity ignored. Or tried to. By concentrating on the black shirt, the one he'd been wearing at the station. Instead of the jet-black jacket, however, he now wore one of buckskin only a shade darker than his wheat-pale hair.

His hair, too, was different—too long on his head, too sparse on his face to make him blend in with a roomful of trimmed cuts, profuse beards, and manicured mustaches. Blend. That was what he couldn't do, either physically or emotionally, for even as he stood among the other guests, he stood singularly apart.

Slowly, his eyes found hers, trapping them with a cool stare. A frisson scampered along her spine, and she thought, *No, I was wrong. He does feel. But only the darker, baser emotions.* Before he could read her thoughts, which she wasn't at all sure he couldn't do, she lowered her eyes.

Her eyes. There was something intriguing about her almond-shaped, whiskey-brown eyes, Breck thought as he watched her lower those eyes from his. He'd thought them intriguing from the moment he arrived at the party; they had seemed familiar, and he'd suddenly realized, from yards away, that she was the one he'd collided with at the depot. But, standing only two feet away, as he was now, he sensed a familiarity that went farther back than that afternoon. Had he met this woman before? Hardly likely, he thought. Their lives, hers glamorous, his one of unadorned survival, were worlds apart. Possibly her eyes, like her raven-black hair, which she wore in a distinctly Oriental style, reminded him of someone else, a gentle someone else. Yes, he thought, it was the Oriental background that made him link her with Su-Ling.

Su-Ling. Even after all this time, the memory of her brought the sting of pain. To rid himself of it, he tipped the glass to his lips, swallowed, and let the fiery liquor burn away the brutal past.

Would this conversation never end? Breck thought minutes later as chatter about the robberies continued full steam.

Would this evening never end? Trinity thought, wanting to
scream at the relentless talk of theft. To add to her discomfort, she'd discreetly watched the wanted posters move from
hand to hand, tormenting herself with the thought that some
clever person in the group—probably Madison Brecker himself; his cold eyes evinced a keen intelligence—would suddenly
announce, "Why, Miss Lee, these sketches look very much like
you."

Trinity glanced up sharply, aware that Madison Brecker had,
indeed, spoken to her. She could not, however, if her life had
been staked upon it, have repeated what he had said, nor could
she have said exactly when he had broken from the others and
edged to her side.

"I beg your pardon?"

"I said, I seem to be robbed every time you come to town."

Trinity's heart stopped in midbeat, and she quickly searched
his face. Something in the relaxed set of his lean jaw convinced her that his remark had been idle rather than accusing.
Her heart began to beat again, and the coy smile she was famous for, a smile somewhere between she-devil and angel,
somewhere between saint and sinner, spread across her lips.

"Why, Mr. Brecker, no woman wants to be thought of as bad
luck."

Before Breck could respond, dinner was announced. If relief could be calculated in dollars, at the precise moment when
Mrs. Anthony, her heavy bosom wobbling, her bustled derriere jiggling, beckoned her guests toward the massive, ornate
dining room, Trinity became a wealthy woman. That wealth
grew as dinner progressed, for, as accommodating Fate would
have it, she was seated at the opposite end of the table from
Breck, and not once when she glanced up did she find him
looking in her direction. Her only discomfort came in the form
of Breck's protracted discussion with the sheriff, who sat across
from him. With Trinity's active imagination, it wasn't too hard
to believe they'd soon piece two and two together and immediately arrest her. As soon as dinner was concluded, however,
she saw Neil approach Breck, ending the latter's conversation
with the officer of the law. Relief once more flooded Trinity.

As she rose from her dining chair—she'd been seated next to
a gregarious representative of the *Enterprise*, who, like all reporters, was more interested in her past than her present—she
sought out Ellie. The instant she saw her, she knew something

was wrong. Even at a distance, the woman looked pale. Excusing herself, she hastened toward her friend, who had risen from the table and reseated herself in a chair flanking an elaborate claw-footed side table.

"Ellie?"

The woman glanced up and smiled sheepishly. "I've gone and done a silly thing. I got sick at my stomach . . . in front of Neil. He hovers over me like an overprotective mother hen when I'm not feeling well."

"Is it the—" Trinity lowered her voice "—baby?"

Ellie nodded, then groaned. "Plus a nip of champagne and some man's odious cheroot. I have this theory that a man buys the same quality in cigars as he buys in prostitutes, and let me assure you, this man must bed the cheapest on the Line."

Trinity recognized the name of the section of town where the ladies of the evening, or the ladies of whatever-the-hour-of-the-day-if-the-money-was-right, stayed. She smiled. "Have you told Neil?"

"About my theory?" Ellie teased.

Trinity gave her friend a look of mock sternness. "You're going to have to, you know."

"I know. It's just that I shan't be able to lift as much as a little finger after that, and—"

"I've found you a ride," Neil said, interrupting his wife.

"I'm fine now, Neil. I can walk."

"Thunderation you can!" Neil Oates returned. "A while ago you were about to puke in your dessert."

"So delicately put, dear," Ellie said. "Besides, that was a while ago. I feel fi—"

"Talk some sense into her, Trinity."

"You really do look a little peaked yet," Trinity offered. She chased back the protest she saw coming with, "It's only a buggy ride."

Since much of Virginia City was traversable on foot, buggies were used only sporadically, usually by residents of outlying areas or by someone trying to put on airs or show off a new bonnet.

"But who'll see Trinity back to the hotel?" Ellie asked. It had been prearranged that the owner of Piper's Opera House, the theatre where the play was to be performed, would escort Trinity to the dinner party, and that her friends would see to her return.

"I think I can manage to find my way back to the hotel," Trinity said.

"I've already arranged—" Neil began, but he was cut off.

"The buggy's out front."

At the sound of the deep, masculine, and disturbingly familiar voice, Trinity whirled. Her eyes raced to those of Madison Brecker. His had sought out hers, as well, but lingered only a moment before sliding to Ellie. "How are you feeling?"

"I'm fine. Truly I am. It was just a passing thing."

"Thanks for the buggy," Neil said, ignoring his wife.

"My pleasure. I rented it from Schooner." Schooner O'Hurley, a red-haired, red-mustachioed Irishman, owned one of the finest liveries on B Street. He also rented out his merchandise at a price that didn't rob a man blind.

Neil nodded. "I'll return it. Oh, and thanks for escorting Trinity back to the Chastain."

Trinity's eyes flew first to Neil Oates, then to Breck. "No! I mean, that—that isn't necessary."

Three responses fell with the speed of raindrops striking earth.

"I'm headed there anyway."

"He doesn't mind."

"You can't walk it alone."

There was a brief silence, the staccato kind that punctuates an outburst most effectively, before Breck said, "Ellie's right. You shouldn't walk it alone. Virginia City can be as dangerously spirited as a runaway colt."

Ah, but Mr. Brecker, Trinity thought, *who shall protect me from you? And for that matter, who shall protect you from me?* Because she didn't want to create a curious scene, she replied simply, "Then I remain most grateful for your generosity."

"Don't you dare!" Ellie said suddenly, drawing both Trinity's and Breck's attention. As she spoke, she swatted at her husband's hands, which were in the process of scooping her up and into his massive arms. "So help me, Neil Oates, if you embarrass me in front of these people, I'll...I'll... well, I'll just make you wish you hadn't. Besides, I'm perfectly capable of walking—" she stood to prove her point "—home, for that matter, and to the buggy most certainly."

"El, you're stubborn."

"I am not," she said, starting from the dining room, her bustle properly swaying.

"I'd like to know what in thunderation you call it if it ain't danged stubbornness!"

"Justified determination. That's what I'd call it."

"Thunderation on determination!"

"Oh, good night," Ellie called prettily over her shoulder to Trinity and Breck. To Trinity, she added, "I'll see you tomorrow at rehearsal."

"Maybe," Neil called back. "If Doc Dawson—"

"Doc Dawson?" Ellie said. "I am not seeing Doc Dawson."

"I think you might."

"I think I mightn't."

Trinity and Breck watched the couple walk from the room. A stab of something—envy?—jabbed at Breck's senses. There were moments, especially of late, when the night fell hard and full around him, that he wondered what it would be like to belong to another human being. To a woman. To a woman who'd care enough to laugh with him, fight with him, love with him. But he had never belonged to anyone, man or woman. He was a loner—today, tomorrow, to the end. Unconsciously, the way he'd done for a lifetime, he withdrew into himself, hiding behind eyes that were distant, shielding himself with a heart numb to all human needs save one: The need to survive.

For the second time that day, Trinity reflected on how lucky her friend had been to find a man like Neil Oates. What did love feel like? What did passion feel like? No man's kisses had ever made her burn; no man's arms had ever left her breathless; no man's body moving against hers had ever made her desperate to know what lay beyond her rigid control. For her, hate had been the driving force, bringing with it its own sinister sensuality. Hate had made her burn, hate had made her breathless, hate had made her desperate for its own vengeful release.

And so, in a gaudy Victorian dining room, swathed in the mandates of proper society, distant eyes met hate-rimmed eyes . . . and neither noticed the other's despair. Rejection and revenge had blurred their vision to all except the hurt within.

Virginia City, approximately seven miles long, was laid out lengthwise on the slopes of Mount Davidson, which rose to a height of nearly eight thousand feet. The railroad, coming in from the north, curled into the center of the city, although the

depot, its waiting room a furious red, as were many of the
public buildings, clung to the side of the mountain. The city, at
present spread out beneath the clear, starlit canopy of a night-
black sky, continued to the Divide, its highest point, then faded
down to Gold Hill, which was the south end of the rich Comstock Lode.

The city's eight main streets, striping the town in a north-
south pattern, were designated by letters of the alphabet. East-
west streets went by such imaginative names as Glory Climb
and Puff and Pant Grade. All were dirt, although the better
streets had board sidewalks, even though wood cost a silver
dollar an armful. Water, too, was costly, but almost every
house nevertheless had a small, well-kept front yard. The ultimate luxury was a crab apple tree, which, despite loving care,
was sure to be stunted in the rarefied air.

The homes were neat and trim, their fences fastidiously
whitewashed. Inside, a visitor would find a collection of hair
sofas and cane-bottomed chairs, rocking chairs with cushion
and shawl, and wallpaper so domineering it could rob your
breath more surely than the thin mountain air around you.

Trinity, huddling in her woolen cape against a chill as crisp
as a starched petticoat, was passing such a home—a two-story
structure with French windows and green blinds and a porch
with white pillars beneath a veranda—when she arrived at the
conclusion that Madison Brecker hadn't wanted to walk her
back to the hotel any more than she'd wanted him to. The silent minutes ticking by offered more than sufficient evidence to
support that conclusion. She doubted, however, that his reason was anything personal. He merely seemed the type who
preferred his own company. Which fit the image she'd had of
her mother's killer—a man who moved in shadows and whispers, a man who stood solitary and friendless.

"You said you, too, were headed to the hotel." Trinity made
herself speak, feeling it would appear unnatural to say nothing. She must act as if this man meant no more to her than any
other man conscripted into escorting her. She must not, now or
ever, do anything to give herself away.

At the shattering of the silence, Breck looked over at the
woman beside him. She had interrupted his usual mental exercise: Going over the columns of figures in the ledger book of
the Sierra Virginia, columns that were soon going to read in the

red if something didn't give concerning the robberies—and give damn quick.

"I rent a room there," he answered, but volunteered nothing more.

She tried again. "How long have you lived here? In Virginia City, I mean?"

"Several months."

"And before then?" She hadn't been able to resist.

He slanted her another look, dry and barren, giving no clue to his thoughts. "Anywhere, everywhere, nowhere."

His answer had the indisputable ring of finality to it, and Trinity abided by it, primarily because she could think of nothing else to ask. Except what she most wanted to, but didn't dare. At least not now. She'd ask him why he killed her mother when the time was right—and that right time would be right before she killed him.

The thought, or the wind, or a chilling combination of both, made her shiver. She noted that the streetlamps had been lighted and that the knee she'd slammed into the train's smokestack was beginning to hurt from all the walking.

"Are you cold?" Breck asked.

"No," she lied, unwilling to admit any weakness to him, however small it might be. She wondered, not for the first time, how he was keeping the autumn briskness at bay when he wore nothing but a buckskin jacket. The truth, of course, was that he wasn't keeping it at bay; he simply wasn't visibly reacting to it. His control annoyed her even as she admired it.

"It's just a little farther," he replied, as if he'd detected her lie.

In the silence that followed, Breck's boots thudded against the planks of the sidewalk of C Street, the city's principal thoroughfare, which was dotted every fourth door with a saloon. These drinking establishments, which no doubt offered other sundry services, ran the gamut of respectability, from the Hangdog Bar, where the whiskey guaranteed a shudder, to the Crystal Saloon, where gentlemen met for polite, polished conversation. As they passed the Last Drink Saloon, which boldly displayed the wanted posters of the train robbers, its louvered doors swung wide and two men, both pickled to the gills, were washed forward on a tide of loud music and louder chatter. Despite their inebriated state, they backtracked out of Breck's way. He didn't notice their reaction. Trinity did. It simply confirmed her image of a feared killer.

"This is the quickest way," Breck offered, apparently feeling he owed her an explanation for their colorful route.

"Does the wind always blow like this?" she asked, shoving the sight of the reward posters and the incident with the two drunks aside.

"No. Sometimes it's worse."

As though it had heard its name spoken, the wind whined and trailed its icy breath across the strong, shaven cheeks of Breck's face and across the ivory porcelain of Trinity's.

"It'll snow soon," he volunteered, taking Trinity so by surprise that she could find no sensible reply. Her mind filled with visions of snowflakes and snowbanks and snowmen, all of which would tamp down the dust that seemed to constantly wander from one corner of the city to the next.

Breck's mind, too, turned to thoughts of snow . . . and of a cabin tucked in the nearby hills. Winter was his favorite time to be there. Winter, with its pristine snow, its cleansing purity. Winter, when a hush descended upon the land and he could almost pretend that no one else existed. He'd long ago accepted the fact that he was a loner, in the beginning because life and circumstance and small-minded people had forced him into the role, now because he preferred it.

Silent minutes later, the Chastain Hotel, nestled behind a whitewashed fence, came into view. Trinity could have kissed the white three-story building.

"Thank you for walking me back," she said as Breck pushed open the gate and ushered her forward. Her sherry-colored dress rustled past his bronzed hand, its silken folds caressing the star-emblazoned scar.

"I was headed here anyway," he reminded her as they climbed the three steps to the hotel entrance. Trinity noted that he hadn't said it had been his pleasure; she also noted that her knee felt weaker still, and she forced herself not to favor it.

Warmth rushed toward them as they stepped inside, while a cozy light from the chandelier overhead rained down around them, illuminating the speckled marble floor and the wall hangings of scenes from the English countryside. Trinity's eyes took in one thing only: the wanted posters that had been added during her short absence. They were prominently displayed on the foyer table. Trinity's heart gave a tiny *pitter-pat*.

"We put out the posters, Mr. Brecker," an eager-eyed young man called from behind the receiving desk.

"Thanks, Gordy." Breck lowered his voice to ask Trinity, "Which floor is your room on?"

"You don't have—"

"Which floor?"

"Three."

He gestured toward the stairway, and Trinity had no choice but to proceed, needles of pain shooting through her knee. Because of the knee, because of the posters, because of how small the stairway suddenly seemed with this man looming beside her, Trinity felt the need to speak.

"Do, uh . . . do you think the posters will help?" she asked, picking that topic because she felt it the most natural—and because the self-preservationist in her really wanted to know.

"I'm hoping," was his sparse reply as his boots struck the oak stairs sharply.

"I hear the robbers might be part of the same gang."

Breck shrugged. "Maybe. Maybe not."

Trinity's eyes cut to his expressionless face. "What do you mean?" she asked, disciplining her voice to sound normal.

"Could be someone wants me to believe that. Could be there's only one man after all."

She waited. Impatiently. But it was clear that he was going to add nothing more. Damn! she thought, cursing his reticence, her fluttering heart, her aching knee.

"Well, I, uh . . . I hope you get them . . . or him," Trinity said after an endless silence.

When Breck spoke, his voice was totally without inflection, which made what he said seem all the more dramatic, all the more sinister. "Oh, I will, Miss Lee, even if I have to make a deal with the devil. And whoever's robbing my train may wish to hell that the devil had found him first."

The threat reverberated through the stillness, sleeting through Trinity's heart. At the same time, her bruised knee buckled from the strain of having climbed two flights of stairs. Her right hand shot out for the wooden balustrade; Breck's hand reached for her elbow.

The imprint of his fingers penetrated the voluminous yards of fabric—dress and wrap—with such force that she could easily believe she'd never been touched at all until just that moment. Lightning. His touch was like concentrated lightning, burning her, even as his eyes were burning into hers. But unlike fire, his eyes, cool, aloof, flamed with coldness, a frigid remoteness that cut her to the bone.

His hair, as pale as frost and scattered across his forehead by the wind, perpetuated the illusion of coldness. He was no dark-haired devil from the hideous, heated pits of hell; he was a fair-haired creature from a soulless world of ice, and in that moment she had no doubt as to what length he would go to to protect his railroad. Any other woman—any sane woman, she told herself—would turn and run, abandoning all fragile plans of revenge, but she wasn't any other woman, and she, too, knew about soulless worlds. Besides, though his touch frightened her, it also fascinated her, drawing her to its compelling power in a way she couldn't understand and could only forcibly resist. This dark attraction startled her, even as she accepted it as truth.

"Are you all right?" he drawled, his voice low and all too near.

She eased her elbow from his piercing grasp. "Y-yes. Yes, I'm fine."

She took the remaining stairs without mishap. On the third floor, she eased the key into the lock of the fourth room on the right, twisted her wrist, and opened the door. She turned.

"Thank you," she said.

Breck gave a nod, followed by a curt "Good night," then walked—swaggered—on down the hall.

Stepping into the room, she closed the door behind her and leaned back against it. Her breath was coming hard and fast, and she knew the irregularity had nothing to do with the mountain air. What it had to do with was the sure knowledge that a battle lay ahead, that her opponent was dedicated and ruthless, that he'd give no humane quarter...and that she, heaven help her, was looking forward to the fight.

Chapter Five

"No," Trinity murmured as the dream figure stepped toward her. The knife he held dripped teardrops of blood that glistened like rich rubies caught in a splash of moonlight. The same moonlight illuminated his eyes, making them translucent, eerie, the color—no, the absence of color—of melting blue ice. His hair was pale and tumbled, his stride certain and purposeful, as he advanced toward her. Trinity moaned, tossing her head back and forth against the already-crushed pillow.

"Come here, little girl," the specter called. *"Come here, come here, come here...."*

"No," she breathed, urging the wispy word through dry lips.

The figure drew closer; the little girl edged back; the woman in the bed writhed in rising fear. As he always did in the recurring dream, though it had not happened in real life, the man dropped the knife. It fell mutely to the floor, and the lack of sound was oddly frightening. Rivers of blood streamed over the man's hand like scarlet serpents, though the star remained clear, a pristine, untouched white. An evil white. Then, as always, the hand reached out for her.

"No!" Trinity cried, jerking to a sitting position. The ebony night, shrill with silence, crouched around her. Only her breath could be heard, filling the black void with butchered fragments of sound. Despite the room's prickly chill, perspiration dotted her forehead, and the thin fabric of her lawn gown clung to her sweat-clammy chest.

The dream was always the same, Trinity thought, spearing her trembling fingers through the tangle of her raven hair. No, actually, it had been different this time. Always before, the man in the dream had retained the youthful face she'd seen long ago, her imagination failing to add the passing years. Tonight, however, that face had aged. Now the face was that of a man in his mid-thirties, the face of Madison Brecker as he'd looked walking her back to the hotel a scant hour before.

Trinity flung back the covers and lowered her bare feet to the rug. The rug, the entire room, was frigid. She plucked up the woolen cape and slung it around her goose-pimpled shoulders, making her way in the dark to the farthest chair, which she dragged to the window. There she drew back the drapes, seated herself, and, snuggling her feet beneath the folds of the warming cloak, stared out at a sky so full of stars that it seemed close to bursting with twinkling lights.

Out of habit, she started to search the heavens for a shooting star.

How many times had she and her mother stared starward in just this way? Countless times, Trinity knew. It had been one of their favorite pastimes on those special occasions when they spent the entire night together, on nights her mother wasn't . . . working. Trinity always had trouble visualizing the specifics of her mother's job. Or, more to the point, she had trouble dealing with the specific visualizations that came to mind. She thrust those painful pictures away, remembering, instead, how she and her mother would climb into an open window on a warm summer night and travel to the starlit world beyond. For her mother, Trinity suspected, the voyage had been tantamount to fleeing, that the fragile, soft-spoken woman had chosen to live among the stars rather than in earth's harsh reality.

"Up there, where dreams sparkle," she could hear her mother say in a voice that put the sweetest of birdsong to shame, "there is no hurt or pain. Only joy."

Joy. It was such a simple word. The adult Trinity was sure Su-Ling Chang had known little joy in her life. Piecing together bits and scraps of what her mother had said, Trinity suspected that the woman had loved not wisely but too well; Trinity suspected, further, that the object of that reckless love was her father. Once, when Trinity had asked why she didn't have a father like other children, her mother had explained that she did—a kind, loving man, "a man in whose heart gentleness dwells." When Trinity had asked why he didn't live with them, her mother had answered that it was their destiny to live alone, his destiny to live with someone else. Trinity had commented innocently that destiny didn't sound very nice.

"Destiny is neither good nor bad, nice nor unnice," Su-Ling had answered. "Destiny simply is. See?" she'd said, pointing. "It's in the sky. Each person's destiny is scattered among the stars."

The youthful Trinity had rebelled against such a callous destiny. The mature Trinity still rebelled against it. She could not believe, *would not* believe, that one could not forge one's own fate. Yet, in moments like these, sitting alone in the dark of night, the nightmare clutching savagely at her senses, she was hard-pressed to explain, outside the boundaries of her mother's belief, the paths one was forced to walk. How else could she explain why her mother had seemed destined to sadness? And she herself to bitter revenge? How else could she explain why, though she'd searched a thousand ebony nights, she'd never seen a shooting star, which her mother had always said promised peace to the soul? Why had the only significant star in her life been on the back of a man's hand, bringing everything but peace?

Out of weariness, Trinity closed her eyes to ponder these questions. Outside, in the midnight-black sky, a shooting star blazed a brief, fiery path. In its wake, a dozen rooms away, came the sulfurous flare of a match. In the golden-orange light was outlined a man's hand, a hand that bore the imprint of a white star.

Breck brought the flame to the tip of the cheroot and inhaled. The smell of aged tobacco wafted through the still, dark room, while its smoky taste swirled upon his tongue. Though the smell and the taste were pleasant enough, more than once he had wondered why he smoked. It always left him feeling disappointed, as if he were somehow missing some of the intended pleasure. Come to think of it, Breck decided, blowing out the match and plunging the room back into darkness, the same could be said of his life. He was always left with a consummate sense of disappointment, as if he were missing some nameless something, as if life were a blankness, a void, that he could not see or hear or feel beyond.

Recoiling from the disturbing thought, he rose from the rumpled bed and reached for the denim Levi's crumpled on the floor. Teething the cigar, he tugged the pants up over his bare, hair-dusted legs and lean hips. Without bothering to fasten the jeans, he crossed the room. He ignored the chill air clutching at his chest and feet and puckering the copper-hued nipples nestled amid golden-brown hair.

At the window, Breck parted the drapes and stared up at the sky. Millions of glimmering stars stared back. Suddenly he was overwhelmed by a warm, familiar feeling. The feeling was named Su-Ling. How many times had the two of them gazed skyward, playing what she called her star game?

"The one to find the brightest star first shall possess all the wisdom on the earth," he could hear her saying, her delicate-featured face wreathed in the magical smile that had made her look even younger than he, though she had been ten years older.

"Wisdom? Who wants that?" he had teased her. "I'd rather have wealth."

"Wisdom *is* wealth, my fine, jaded, young friend."

"Yeah? How do you know?"

Her smile broadened, and her eyes fairly danced with glee. "Because I've just found the brightest star and possess all the wisdom in the world. See," she'd added, pointing upward excitedly, "there it is!"

Though a distance of eighteen years separated him from that night, Breck smiled, along with the Su-Ling of his memories. The smile sat awkwardly on his lips, as though it were a guest seldom invited and unsure of how to behave when it was. As slowly as the smile had come, it died, washed away by another poignant recollection.

"The first human being to count all the stars will gain eternal happiness," he could hear his friend saying.

"Where did you hear that?"

"I just know it."

"Because you possess all the wisdom in the world?"

She had smiled the smile of a child, the smile of a woman. "Yes."

"But counting all the stars is impossible, Su-Ling," he'd countered with manly logic.

Her smile had slowly disappeared, replaced by a sadness that weighted her small shoulders with stoic resignation. "I know," she had said. "The pursuit of happiness is all we have. Only up there," she said, once more gazing out the window, "is there happiness. Only up there is there peace and joy."

Happiness. Peace. Joy. Did they exist up there among those twinkling heights? Breck wondered, exhaling a stream of smoke that lazily curled into the inky darkness. He answered the question with a sardonic sneer. What the hell would he know about where to find them? The only things he knew anything about were isolation and loneliness. But then, if Su-Ling were alive, she'd point out that it was his destiny to be a loner. God only knew that was what he'd been all his life, almost from the moment of birth. Abandoned by his mother, ignored by his father, he'd been on his own for as long as he could remember.

To this day, he wondered what made a mother choose to leave her three-year-old son. His father had never talked about her or their life together. What little Breck did know about his mother—that she'd been Swedish, named Inga, and that she'd moved back to the East Coast—he'd learned from his father's drunken ramblings. He'd learned naught from the sober James Brecker, primarily because his father had seldom been sober. And those few times when he had, he'd been studying how not to be. Yet, drunk or sober, James Brecker had been consistent in one thing: He had never paid his young son a moment's attention. In fact, he had seldom been around to do so.

For days, even weeks, on end, James Brecker had left his son to fend for himself in their shack on the outskirts of St. Louis, Missouri, while he plied his trade as a teamster. Looking back, Breck guessed he would have starved if it hadn't been for the kindness of an old mountain man who'd taken to leaving buttermilk biscuits and an occasional slab of cooked meat on the doorstep. Eventually Breck had learned to cook and to hunt and even to steal what people weren't keeping a close eye on.

As hard as the solitude had been, however, he'd preferred it to his father's presence, for every Saturday night when James Brecker was home, he would drag his towheaded, snot-nosed son into town, and, despite the severity of the weather, plant him in front of the saloon and proceed to get drunk. He would then haul him over to the town brothel, where he'd again abandon him, oftentimes until the next morning.

In front of the saloon Breck had been introduced to the bowie knife by a half-breed Indian with steady hands and steadier eyes. In front of the brothel he'd learned to read and write from the ladies of the evening. In front of both he'd become known as "Brecker's brat," a phrase that had elicited pity, or, worse, disdain. "Come along, Alvin, Harold, Billy," the muffled voices would whisper, "you can't play with him. He's Brecker's brat."

Brecker's brat. Even now, the phrase angered him. In fact, it angered him more now than it had then. Then it had only hurt the tender heart of a young boy. That young boy had learned to hide the hurt deep within himself. He'd also learned to fight. And he'd honed his skill with the bowie knife.

At fourteen, his life had changed dramatically. When James Brecker had gotten himself killed over a poker game—one of the few times someone had cheated him instead of vice versa—Breck had felt an obligation to avenge his father, though he'd never clearly understood why, since his father had earned no such devotion. At any rate, within a week of his father's death, Breck, with an immature lack of discretion, had slit the throat of the man responsible. The killing, Breck knew, had given rise to his reputation, a reputation that had served to isolate him still further from the mainstream of Victorian society. Brecker's brat had become a lawless outcast.

Lying about his age, he, too, had worked as a teamster for a while, but soon the glitter of California's gold had beckoned him westward. It was there he'd received the scar on his hand. In an argument over a claim—he'd been in the right, but the other man, older and more experienced, had had the might—a fight had ensued, and Breck's own knife had been plunged through his hand, impaling it to the side of a wagon. Because of the mining camp's isolation, a doctor hadn't been available. The wound, instead of being sutured, had been cauterized. The tissue had healed in the vague shape of a star.

The incident had hardened Breck even more. Never again, he had resolved, would anyone take from him what was his. Later, when the same man had stolen a claim from another miner, a grizzled old codger Breck had taken a liking to, the troublemaker had mysteriously disappeared. Though none could prove it, everyone had thought Breck was responsible—and they had been right. His reputation had grown. As had his skill with the bowie knife. As had the coldness in his eyes. As had the emptiness in his heart.

Some women, he'd learned, found his dark reputation irresistible, but he had always been careful to keep relationships uninvolved, at least from his point of view, because his mother's abandonment had left him with a basic distrust of the female gender.

But then he'd met Su-Ling.

Su-Ling Chang.

As soft-spoken as a whispered rain, as gentle as a pastel dawn, as fragile as a beautiful wounded bird.

Incredibly, she had been a prostitute in a Sacramento brothel. Though he'd gone to visit her for the usual reason, he'd discovered that what he most wanted from her was simply to talk. Both of them, he eighteen, she twenty-eight, had been hurt, and each had found in the other a consoling friend. He'd shared things with her that he'd never shared with another human being. In return, she'd told him of her love for a married man. Though she had never revealed the man's identity, she had told Breck that the Caucasian man was the father of her child. Over a four-month period Breck had seen her regularly, though he'd never touched her in a carnal way. He had known, however, that there were those who did touch her in that way, men with varying degrees of lustful appetites. Some among them had cared little for her pain. Concerned for her safety, he had given her a knife to use as protection against any rough, unruly bordello patrons.

One hot, rowdy Saturday night, as he'd been nearing the brothel, he'd collided with a woman hastening from the alley behind the house. Fleetingly he had stared into pale gray, highly excited eyes. There'd been a streak of blood on the woman's fashionable dress, which she'd clumsily tried to hide. Minutes later, he'd discovered Su-Ling dead.

Dead.

Even now, Breck thought, a tide of emotions covering everything from disbelief to rage washing over him, he could see her sprawled on the hard floor, her life already having seeped out into a crimson puddle. Her body had still been warm, deceptively warm, and he had pulled the knife from her stomach, had shaken her, as if doing so would restore life to her. When it hadn't, he'd crushed her to him, trying to share his life with her. But he hadn't been able to work a miracle. The only miracle that night had been his clearheadedness. He'd seen his own predicament instantly. Because she'd been knifed, because he himself had bought the knife at a local store, because of his reputation, and particularly because he was now covered with her blood, he'd fled...but not before confronting the child who'd unexpectedly walked in on the scene. Those frightened brown eyes he'd never been able to forget. Any more than he had forgotten the guilty gray eyes of the woman fleeing down the alley.

From there, he'd drifted. Eventually, he'd ended up laying track for the railroad, the pet project of wild-minded investors who arrogantly suggested that the East Coast could be joined with the West despite unscalable mountains, uncrossable deserts, and unfriendly Indians. While thus employed, he'd met the railroad baron, Jedediah McCook, who had favored him with his friendship.

Increasingly weary of drifting, Breck longed to settle down, longed to have something solid in his life. He told himself he was getting old—at thirty-six he'd seen and done too much—but it would have been closer to the truth to say that he was just getting tired, tired of that empty feeling, tired of going through the motions and still coming up pleasureless, tired of having too many people still look at him as if he were lower than the sun at sunset.

Surprising the town of Virginia City—hell, maybe even surprising himself!—he'd bought the Sierra Virginia Railroad when Wilson Booth had been forced to sell it. And, damn it, he thought, viciously grinding out the cheroot that gave him so little pleasure, no one was going to take it from him! Least of all some two-bit bandit who tied people up with women's drawers! Marginally—he was more comfortable with such a decision in the margins rather than in the mainstream of his thoughts—he realized that the survival of the railroad had somehow come to mean his own survival. And for that reason, he vowed, crossing the room, shucking the Levi's, and crawling back into bed, he'd do whatever he had to to save it.

Whatever.

"Whatever happened to your knee?" Ellie asked the following evening.

Trinity glanced down at the navy-blue bruise showing through the slit of her yellow silk wrapper. The dress rehearsal had concluded minutes before, and she and Ellie, ensconced in the best dressing room at Piper's Opera House, were changing out of their stage clothes.

"Uh . . . on the trip down yesterday I, uh . . . I hit it boarding the train." She rushed to change the subject. "You're sure you're feeling all right? The rehearsal didn't tire you too badly?"

"I'm fine, I'm fine," Ellie answered, as if it were a question she'd heard a hundred times since the night before. "No nausea, just a little fatigue, and I promise," she added, sensing her friend's disapproval, "to tell Neil about the baby as soon as the play is over tomorrow night." When she saw the look on Trinity's face, Ellie repeated, "I promise. I swear it on the enormous size of my bosom." She giggled as she unabashedly stripped off the man's shirt and trousers that constituted her costume. "Do you think I'll fill out now that I'm pregnant? Oh, Lord, I'll starve my baby to death if I don't. 'Course, if I do fill out, it'll so take poor Neil by surprise that he'll most likely pull a Maude Terrill and faint dead away."

Trinity, unable to suppress a grin at her friend's accustomed ribaldry, stepped behind the dressing screen. Though Ellie's nakedness in no way embarrassed her—the two had shared too many dressing rooms—she couldn't share her friend's casualness about nudity. It had something to do, she knew, with having been raised in a brothel, with having seen far more than any little girl should have seen, with knowing that her own mother . . . As always, she let the thought drift away without completion.

"Who was the man who sat in on the rehearsal?" Trinity asked instead. The man, she did not add, who had been far more interested in the low décolletage of her stage dress than in the rehearsal. As a general rule, none of the troupe liked an audience at dress rehearsal. It was bad luck.

"Wilson Booth. He's a friend of Mr. Piper's."

"Ah," Trinity said. Being a friend of the theatre's owner brought certain privileges.

"He's also the former owner of the railroad."

Trinity peered over the dressing screen.

"He had to sell out—financial reasons. Neil said he couldn't meet the debt service required. That's fancy bank talk for 'went flat busted.'"

"And Madison Brecker bought the line?" It was the first time the name had crossed her lips all day, although she had heard it more than once. The air was saturated with muffled ruminations on the mine owners' discontent, all of which she had inhaled with secret satisfaction. Neil Oates, however, seemed disposed to give Madison Brecker the benefit of the doubt in terms of righting the wrongs being perpetrated against his railroad. Trinity sensed that Neil respected Madison Brecker, which was at odds with her preconceived notion about this man she knew to be a murderer. She prudently didn't dwell on the jarring inconsistency.

"Uh-huh," Ellie said, shimmying into a rose-pink dinner dress. "Rumor, however, says Wilson wants to buy back the railroad."

"But if he hasn't any money, how can he?"

"Rumor also says he now has the backing of a bank in San Francisco. Wilson even approached Breck with an offer."

"Oh?" Trinity asked casually, unhappy with the prospect of the Sierra Virginia changing ownership. The sport lay in Madison Brecker's financial destruction, not the railway's.

"Breck said no. Rather emphatically, I hear," Ellie said, reaching for her cloak. "Ready? I'm positively famished. Neil said he'd meet us out front."

"Yes, I'm ready," Trinity answered, smiling over Breck's refusal to sell the railroad. "And suddenly I'm very hungry myself."

The troupe dined together amid talk of scenery, costumes, and the following evening's presentation—the scenery in the second act was less than ideal; makeup would have to be applied conscientiously because the oil-lamp footlights would reveal far more than candles; had everyone heard that the show was already sold out? Shop talk soon dissolved into giggles and idle chatter as everyone was cocooned in a warm camaraderie, some in the warmer-yet effects of several glasses of wine. Though the hour was growing late—it was nearing nine-thirty—the dining establishment was still crowded. Trinity had just raised her wineglass to her lips when she saw Breck.

He sat alone at a table not far away. How could she not have noticed him before? He seemed to occupy the room so thoroughly that she could not imagine failing to see him enter the restaurant. Even as she watched, he, obviously finished with his solitary meal, stood, grabbed his buckskin jacket from the back of his chair, and slid his shoulders—his wide shoulders, Trinity couldn't help but note—into it. Then, as though he sensed her gaze, he looked up.

Their eyes met.

The chatter around Trinity receded, the laughter faded, the world shrank until it accommodated only two people. The lightning power was there again, she thought, feeling once more what she had felt the night before. As then, what she saw in his misty-blue eyes frightened her, even as it paradoxically appealed to her. She felt both repelled and compelled. She felt...touched. As surely as if he had reached out and brushed his fingers across her skin.

"Trinity?"

The voice shattered the fragile moment. She shifted her gaze to Neil, who was poised to pour more wine into her glass, which now hovered in midair.

"More wine?"

"No," she answered, already feeling drunk from those blue eyes. "No, thank you."

When she looked back, Breck was gone.

Thirty minutes later, Trinity, aching for both bed and solitude, stepped through the doors of the Chastain Hotel. Its lobby was empty except for the young night clerk and a man sitting alone in the plush waiting area. She smiled at the clerk and ignored the stranger as she headed for the stairs.

"Miss Lee?"

Trinity turned sharply. The stranger stood before her. He was a rather ordinary man, tall and thin, with a large, hawklike nose and a thick gray mustache. He held a black hat in his hands, the rim of which he toyed with in an awkward way. Her first assessment was that he was a shy admirer. Out of long habit, she smiled, even though she longed to be left alone.

"Yes?"

"Miss Lee, forgive me for intruding at such a late hour, but I was wondering if I might have a quick word with you."

He wasn't an admirer. He was too formal, too businesslike. And on second glance, there was nothing awkward or shy about him. If you peered beneath his plain surface, the man fairly reeked of confidence. He was also beginning to look familiar. Where had she seen him before?

"What about, Mr...?"

"Truxtun. Oliver Truxtun," he said, reaching inside his coat pocket and producing a shield, which he flashed at Trinity. "I'm employed by Pinkerton's, the detective agency."

The sight of the badge and the gun strapped to his waist, the latter revealed when he opened his jacket, brought a sudden dryness to her throat. So this was the Pinkerton agent Madison Brecker had hired. The man who'd unexpectedly thundered his presence upon the baggage car door the day before. The man she'd momentarily seen at the station when Breck had boarded the train, a curse on his stern lips.

"How—" she swallowed "—fascinating, Mr. Truxtun. And, of course, you're investigating the Sierra Virginia robberies." It wouldn't be prudent to play coy, she reasoned. This man would spot coyness a mile away—maybe two—with those sharp, intense, never-miss-a-thing eyes.

"Yes, ma'am."

"I'm afraid I don't see how I can help you. I didn't even know the train had been robbed until the conductor told me."

"You didn't see or hear anything?"

"I heard what I thought might be a shot, but I convinced myself it was merely my imagination. Later, Mr. Harlan, the conductor, told me I had been right, that a shot had been fired." She started to add that Dancey Harlan had said that Truxtun himself had fired the shot, but she couldn't remember if the conductor had mentioned that fact or if she had simply assumed the agent had shot the lock off the door.

"But you saw nothing?"

"No, I regret to say I didn't. I remained in my coach the entire journey."

"You saw no one get on, say in Reno, who would match the description of the robber?"

"No."

"Then you're aware of his description?"

Sharp. The man was sharp. Trinity allowed herself a hint of a smile. "One cannot have been in Virginia City for ten minutes without knowing it—mustache, glasses, scar."

Oliver Truxtun made no comment. Instead, in the span of a second, he produced a leather glove.

"Ah, the glove left behind," Trinity said. The trick to the deception was to play it as naturally as possible. At the slight arching of the Pinkerton agent's eyebrow, she explained, "It was mentioned last night at the Anthony party."

Still no comment from Oliver Truxtun, though he did pass the glove forward. Trinity had no choice but to take it. Simply touching it made her heart skip. She ignored the fluttering and turned the glove over in a studying way. "I'm sorry. I'm afraid it means nothing to me. It's really quite common, isn't it?" she said, handing it back.

"Quite," he agreed, fishing in the breast pocket of his jacket. He produced a card. "Should you remember anything, would you contact me?"

"Of course."

He nodded. "Sorry to have bothered you."

"No bother," Trinity said, relief slowly trickling down her spine, while his card burned her fingertips. Without another word, the man donned his hat and stepped away. Trinity started for the stairs once more.

"Oh, Miss Lee," he called out.

She turned.

"You've been aboard the train every time it's been robbed, haven't you?"

The question chopped Trinity's breath into halves. "Yes," she managed to say.

"How inconvenient for you," Oliver Truxtun said, the tone of his voice that of the true cavalier.

"On the contrary," Trinity said, "all the inconvenience belongs to that poor Mr. Brecker."

Careful. She'd have to be careful, Trinity thought. Oliver Truxtun was no fool. She was certain, at least reasonably so, that he suspected nothing, that all he was doing was throwing bait in a wide circle to see what he'd catch, but she'd have to be careful and make certain it wasn't her he caught.

Whether because of the encounter with the Pinkerton agent or because of the earlier encounter with Breck's disturbing blue eyes, Trinity slept poorly that night. She struggled so hard to keep the usual dream from recurring that she spent most of the long hours staring into the shadowy canopy of the bed. The shadowy canopy of the big, lonely bed. What did it feel like to share the night with a man? Was Ellie in Neil's arms this very moment? Were they making love? Or simply sleeping peacefully side by side? As she rolled onto her side, a weary sigh escaped her lips. Trinity had never longed so desperately for a strong pair of arms to console her. The longing was a jagged, almost unbearable pain in the region of her loveless heart.

Breck, on the other hand, slept well for a man under such extreme pressure. He even dreamed pleasantly. Of soft honey-brown eyes, eyes that held a siren's promise, eyes that stared into his with a mysterious intensity, eyes that, for a reason he couldn't explain, looked familiar. Come morning, however, the dream was only a filmy vagary he could neither recall nor forget, a vagary that tauntingly whispered the name of Trinity Lee. By that afternoon, however, the dream was pushed entirely aside by reality.

And the reality was that the train was a full hour late.

Chapter Six

"A God-almighty damned tree thrown across the track!" Dancey Harlan puffed, his face blooming with scarlet agitation as he whipped his cap from his head, passed his hand over his naked, scalped pate, and jerked the cap back into place.

Breck had jumped aboard the steaming locomotive even before it shuddered to a stop at the station. He had known something was wrong, very wrong, when the train hadn't shown up on schedule.

"If you ask me," a grimy Abe Dustin said, breaking his usual silence, "I think somebody felled it a-purpose."

"Well, of course somebody felled it a-purpose!" Dancey raved. "Some godless heathen axed it in two, dragged it across the track, and if it wasn't for Charlie's quick eye and fast hand, I can tell you now that we'd all be singing with the angels—or flapping out the flames singeing our backsides. If we'd a hit that tree, it a wrecked us for sure. It a stopped anything, including Judgment Day."

"A deplorable waste of timber," Charlie Knott, the man with the quick eye and fast hand, said as he brought the train to a halt with the appropriate application of whining brakes. In an area short of trees, timber was precious.

"Was anybody hurt?" Breck asked, so calmly that the quiet rage in his eyes seemed suspect.

"A lot of pantalooned bottoms in the air, a few scratches, and a chorus of praying to the Maker, that's all," Dancey answered.

"Where did it happen?" Breck asked again, with deceptive composure.

"Last curve before you hit the stretch into the city," Dancey replied.

Breck knew the curve well. In fact, he knew every inch of the rail line—every curve, every incline, every tunnel and trestle. The curve that Dancey spoke of wasn't a sharp one, and for that very reason it was an ideal place to block the rails. Though an experienced engineer most assuredly would slow for it, he'd still be traveling at a considerable speed—too fast to easily avoid ramming anything in his path.

"Thought for sure we was going to be robbed again," Dancey said, "but everything was as quiet as a harpless heaven."

"Are you certain it was deliberate?" Breck asked, wanting desperately to believe it hadn't been. God, didn't he have enough trouble without adding harassment to the list? "Maybe the tree was rotted, maybe lightning—"

"It was deliberate."

At the sound of the strong voice, which boomed upward from the station platform, Breck whirled. Before him stood a man in his early sixties, a man of average height but with a patrician carriage that was anything but average. The gentleman was neither thick nor thin, but somewhere in between, with a solid build suggesting good, crisp health. Few wrinkles creased his square face, and those that did only streaked it with character and wisdom. His eyes shone the weathered brown of a mature autumn and were filled with intelligence, insight, and a vigor many a younger man might have envied. Everything about him said imposing, powerful, wealthy—everything from the expensive English cut of his suit to his manicured nails to the immaculate trim of his white hair. Equally white, equally trimmed muttonchops sprigged his full cheeks, while a bushy white mustache sloped downward like the snowy eaves of a house. Only his chin, strong and tucked, remained clean-shaven.

Despite the troubling situation, a gleam of pleasure sprang into Breck's eyes. "Damn it, Jedediah, why didn't you let me know you were coming?" he asked, climbing down from the brass-bound locomotive and extending his hand.

Jedediah McCook grasped the hand of the man to whom he was both mentor and friend. "I didn't know myself until earlier today. I had business in Reno and decided at the last minute to catch Trinity Lee's performance tonight." The older man's face darkened as he returned to the previous subject. "You've got enemies, my friend."

Breck's laughter, bark-rough and totally mirthless, pierced the cold October afternoon. "Tell me something I don't know."

"You think the robberies and this incident are related?" Jedediah asked.

"What else can I believe? Even though there was no holdup this time, everything seems too coincidental to be anything else."

The white-haired man nodded in agreement.

"Hell, Jedediah," Breck said abruptly, hiking his hands to his lean hips, "what's a man supposed to do?"

"Have a drink, my friend," Jedediah McCook replied. "When the world seems to be falling apart, the only sane thing to do is have a drink."

"Amen," Dancy seconded.

Jedediah glanced up. "Gentlemen, would you care to join us?"

Abe Dustin and Charlie Knott declined.

"Dancey?" Breck asked, his eyes meeting those of the conductor. Though a friendship existed between Breck and Jedediah McCook, it was newer than the one Breck shared with Dancey Harlan and did not yet run as deep.

"Got some things to finish here," Dancey said. A warmth passed between the two men. "I'll join you later."

Breck acknowledged his friend's reply, adding, "If anyone needs medical attention, send them over to Doc Dawson's." It went without saying that the bill was to be sent to Breck. It also went without saying that it would be a bill he could ill afford.

Dancey nodded.

In short order, Breck was swigging down a bourbon—"hold the water"—at the Crystal Saloon. While the liquor didn't obliterate his problems or offer any solutions, it did provide momentary distraction, for as the raw bourbon slid down his throat, it was impossible to think of anything but the liquor's force and fire.

Across town, in a room in the Chastain Hotel, the mellow taste of heated apple cider and cinnamon caressed Trinity's taste buds. Her lines had been rehearsed, her costume readied, and she was now doing what she always did in the final hours preceding a performance. She was resting and collecting herself emotionally.

"Will that be all, ma'am?" the maid asked as she finished turning back the bed.

"Yes, thank you."

"Did you hear about the train, ma'am?"

Trinity glanced up sharply from the task of nestling the gilt-edged porcelain cup in the cradle of the gilt-edged saucer. "What about it?"

"Near-accident, ma'am. Someone felled a tree across the track. It's the work of those infidel robbers, everybody says. Robbing's one thing, but risking the passengers' lives is another. Nobody was hurt this time, but I can tell you . . ."

Near-accident. Tree felled across the track. The words fell with the same heavy *thud* Trinity imagined the tree falling with. For a moment she was disoriented as if the tree had landed on her. The disorientation was immediately followed, however, by the clearheaded realization that she didn't much like—make that didn't like at all!—having the irresponsible incident blamed on her. The maid was right. Robbery was one thing, potential injury to innocent strangers quite another. On the heels of that came the all-important question of who had done it. Who besides herself had a grievance against Madison Brecker?

" . . . people were jostled around like a whirlwind . . ."

And why did she suddenly feel guilty for not being able to warn the man of his enemy?

" . . . packages thrown hither and yon . . ."

Don't be ridiculous, Trinity told herself. What do you care what happens to Madison Brecker? What—

"Don't you just think it's awful, ma'am?"

Trinity glanced into the expectant eyes of the maid. "Ah, no . . . no, thank you. There's nothing else."

There was the briefest of hesitations before the maid answered, "Yes, ma'am." She then closed the door behind her, shutting out a look that judged Miss Lee beautiful but not overly bright.

Long after the maid had left, long after the warm cider was nothing more than a cool memory at the bottom of the cup, Trinity continued to wonder who.

Who, besides herself, wished Madison Brecker ill?

And why?

Why?

Why in hell had he let Jedediah talk him into going to the

play? Breck questioned later that night from the red-velvet box seat in the horseshoe-shaped balcony of Piper's Opera House. True, there was nothing he could do to solve his problems that night, but it seemed a sacrilege to be sitting here, twiddling his thumbs, when the Sierra Virginia was struggling for its very existence. He'd much rather be at the office. He'd much rather be poring over the books. He'd much rather—

"Wonderful turnout," Jedediah McCook bellowed, trying to be heard over the din, even though he sat at Breck's elbow.

The theatre's many sections, from the Pigpen at the back to the loges to the Diamond Horseshoe skirting the stage, were filled to capacity, and discreet conversation had risen to an out-and-out roar. The noise came equally from newly made millionaires and crudely garbed miners, one and all impatiently eyeing the curtain, a canvas depicting snow-capped Mount Davidson in all its glory. Above the mountain was a picture of the American flag, proudly bearing its thirty-seven stars. Wedged between flag and mountain ran the advertisement FRED'S LIVERY STABLE, HAY AND GRAINS.

"Ah, here we go," Jedediah announced as the oil lamps dwindled and the curtain began to rise.

Loud applause, whistles, and welcoming shouts erupted as Trinity stepped onto the stage. She acknowledged them with a regal demeanor, which consisted of a slight smile and a slighter bow, and then she began to do what critic after demanding critic said she did best in the world: She committed herself to the role she was playing.

The men in the audience simply committed themselves to watching her.

"I can't see," Maude Terrill complained, trying to peer over a coronet of zinnias encircling the head of the woman seated in front of her. A single zinnia perched tauntingly on the woman's crown.

"Mmm," Dub Terrill answered, already lost to the beauty of the woman on the stage.

"I said, I can't see."

"Mmm."

"Dub—"

"Shh!"

"Shh!"

"Madam, be quiet!"

"Well, I'm sure I'll faint dead away at this rudeness!"

Farther up in the loge, Oliver Truxtun watched the Eurasian beauty, thinking that she was, indeed, magnificent to look at. And she was intelligent. That he knew from speaking with her the evening before. A rare combination in a woman—beauty and intelligence.

In even less expensive seats sat Dick Kingsman and Hollis Reed, their mouths agape at the pulchritude confronting them, while, a few seats away, Dancey Harlan, Abe Dustin, and Charlie Knott were quietly experiencing various degrees of respectful appreciation. On the other hand, Wilson Booth, from his ostentatiously plush seat, wasn't even trying to hide his salivating.

Captive that he was, Breck, too, allowed his attention to be absorbed by the woman on the stage, though only in an abstract, detached way. It was the way he looked at all of life, and certainly the women in it. His eyes ambled across her face, which, despite what he presumed to be theatrical makeup, appeared a pure-honey color. The same shade deepened to the hue of aged whiskey in her almond-shaped Oriental eyes, eyes he couldn't see clearly at present but could clearly recall, eyes that still inexplicably—here he frowned—intrigued him. Following the blade of her nose, Breck's gaze sauntered to her lips—red and curved, lush and full. Just the way the low-cut bodice of her costume revealed lush feminine roundness. He stirred in his seat, thinking with masculine mechanicalness that he hadn't been with Millie Rhea in a while; too many other things, too many grim other things, had occupied his mind.

Because the feeling flirting with his male senses wasn't appropriate for his surroundings, his eyes roamed upward from Trinity's breasts to the raven hair knotted atop her head. It seemed so neat and precise and...*silken*. The word came from nowhere and, like the sound of silk, swished through his mind. The word was followed by a question. What would this woman's silken hair feel like disengaged from that neat precision and tangled about his hands? What would it feel like to have his fingers plunged to the hilt in it? What would—he stopped, genuinely surprised, uncomfortably aware that abstraction had fallen by the wayside, that detachment had been shot all to bloody hell.

As he was fretfully pondering the why of it, the how of it, applause burst out around him. Incredibly, the first act was over.

"Bravo!"

"Wonderful!"

"I couldn't see a thing," Maude Terrill reiterated peevishly as she peeked into the petals of the highest-perched zinnia. Dub replied with exuberant clapping. Beside him, a man whistled through his fingers. The shrillness made both Maude Terrill and Harriet Dawson, who was seated over and up a row, grimace.

"Thank goodness you listened to reason and forbade Victoria's coming," Harriet Dawson said, crisply adjusting her already crisply fitting gloves.

"I still think she might have enjoyed it," Doc Dawson replied, not bothering to mention that it hadn't been he who'd forbidden their daughter to come.

"Oh, I've no doubt she would have enjoyed it. One always enjoys what isn't proper."

Though he wondered what his wife could possibly know about what was improper—and, more specifically, the enjoyment of it—Doc Dawson said nothing. He simply joined in the applause.

"Will you just listen to this vulgar racket?" Harriet said. "And wasn't her costume scandalous?"

"Oh, I don't know about—"

"Well, of course you do. What else could you call it?"

The word *nice* begged to be spoken, but the good doctor prudently chained it to silence.

"I repeat," Harriet Dawson said, squaring her shoulders to the stiffness of a slab of lumber, "thank goodness Victoria isn't here."

Upstairs, even as her mamma was speaking, Victoria Dawson and her friend Molly Flannery were searching through the rows of seats for the numbers marked on their tickets. While Victoria hadn't planned on arriving at the play's start—she had to avoid her parents—she hadn't planned on being this late, either. She had thought the Flannerys, at whose house she'd asked to spend the night, would never go to bed. Now it was nine-thirty, and they'd missed half the play! Which she'd spent every dime of her quilting money buying two tickets for!

"Oh, Vicky, we're gonna get in trouble," Molly whined.

"We are not."

"We are, too. We can't even find our seats."

"Will you stop sniveling, Molly Shane Flannery?"

"I am not sniv— Oh, no, the lights are dimming."

"There!" Victoria whispered. "There's our seats."

The two girls slid into them just as the curtain rose on the second act. At the sight of Trinity Lee, Victoria sighed. A mere glimpse of her would be worth a month's punishment if, God forbid, she did get caught.

Below, as darkness descended upon the theater, one zinnia was plucked from the zenith of a coronet. So deftly was it done that not even a startled gasp was heard.

Breck had spent the intermission deliberately dismissing his earlier thoughts concerning Trinity's hair. He had no idea what the fantasy had meant. He knew only that it had left him vaguely unsettled, as if some part of his known world had shifted subtly. In true masculine fashion, he chose to deal with the discomfort by ignoring it. He encouraged his mind to return to the business of the Sierra Virginia Railroad. Once again, some twenty minutes later, he was startled when the curtain rang down the act and the finish of the play. Perfunctorily, he joined in the applause spreading through the theatre like a storm. Applause turned into a standing ovation as the cast members each took a bow. The last to do so was a male figure who, when he whipped the hat from his head, revealed masses of blond hair.

Ellie Oates! Breck thought. And he hadn't once suspected! Sweet Jesus, what was wrong with his perception tonight?

The applause rose to a deafening crescendo as Trinity took one last bow, and then the evening was over. The famed actress had charmed her way once more into the hearts of her fans.

"Wonderful!" Jedediah announced as the lights brightened. "Come, let's make our way to her dressing room."

"Thanks, but I should be getting back. I need—"

"Nonsense! I've already sent round a note. She's expecting us."

Breck knew she was more likely expecting only Jedediah, but when the older man ushered him forward, he sighed in defeat.

Upstairs, in the throes of rapture, Victoria Dawson sighed. "Did you see her hair? And her dress? Oh, Molly, isn't she the prettiest woman you've ever seen?"

"C'mon," her mousy friend said, trying to pull Victoria from her seat. "If Mamma or Papa checks on us, we're dead."

"They won't check. Oh, Molly, did you hear the way the men—"

A masculine voice interrupted her. "'Scuse us, miss."

Victoria glanced up. Two men were seeking passage into the aisle. The one nearest her was in his early twenties and had truly the finest gray eyes she had ever seen. He also had a cut on his lip.

Victoria smiled and stood. "Certainly," she murmured with appropriate demureness.

The two men passed by her and the agitated Molly. Once in the aisle, the man with the gray eyes stopped and looked back.

"Say, aren't you Doc Dawson's daughter?"

Startled, Victoria answered, "Yes."

The man grinned. "Your father tended to my lip. I was in the train robbery. Me and Hollis was," he said. He refrained from mentioning exactly how his lip had gotten cut.

"Of course," Victoria said with her prettiest smile as she at last recognized the man all spiffed up in his finery, "you're Dick Kingsman. I heard Papa talking about you." She didn't feel it necessary to mention that the town was giggling over how his lip had gotten cut. A robbery was a robbery and a cut was a cut, as far as she was concerned.

"Oh, this here is Hollis Reed."

"Mr. Reed," Victoria said, acknowledging him. Then she introduced her friend.

"We need to go," Molly whined.

"You two ladies aren't here alone, are you?" Dick Kingsman asked.

It was the first time a gentleman had referred to her as a grown-up lady, and the occasion filled Victoria with a faint warmth. "My mamma and papa are here," she answered, immediately feeling as daringly scandalous as Trinity Lee, "but the truth is, Mr. Kingsman, I'd just as soon they not know I'm here. Mamma has this ridiculous notion that viewing a play is improper."

Victoria's lips puckered into a smile. Dick grinned. Victoria felt they were sharing something wickedly personal.

"I do believe, Miss Dawson, that there's a back door to this theatre," Dick offered.

"What a lovely thing to suggest," Victoria said, falling into step beside the Sierra Virginia's baggageman. "Don't you think so, Molly?"

In answer, Molly whined.

Downstairs, at the door of the dressing room, Jedediah reached into his pocket, extracted a neatly folded bill from a gold money clip, and handed the currency to the young man holding a dozen crimson roses. The young man, whose presence at the appointed hour had been prearranged, smiled appreciatively at the large gratuity. Roses in hand, Jedediah knocked on the dressing room door with all the authority expected of the wealthy part-owner of the great Central Pacific Railroad.

Breck, standing a discreet distance away, viewed the scene with the flowers and wondered for the first time just what Jedediah's interest was in Trinity Lee. He had always assumed Jedediah to simply be a patron of the theater, but was his friend, even though married, interested in a liaison with the famed actress? Breck was surprised at how little he liked the idea. He told himself it was solely because he'd hate to see his friend make a fool of himself.

Trinity herself opened the door. Her face erupted in a bright smile at the sight of white-whiskered Jedediah McCook.

"Jedediah!" she cried, taking his hand in hers even as her eyes raced beyond the older man and lit on Breck. Her breath, as well as her voice, caught. She felt as if she'd just stepped into the cool pools of the eyes intently watching her. To keep from sinking beneath the surface of their blue depths, she drew her attention back to the man before her. "Jedediah, what a lovely surprise."

"My dear, the loveliness is all yours," Jedediah answered, handing her the bouquet of roses. "And you were superb tonight."

Fond. They were fond of each other, nothing more, Breck guessed, analyzing the genuine emotions playing back and forth. And there was undeniable pride emanating from Jedediah.

"Wasn't she superb, Breck?"

Ignoring the relief he felt at the discovery that the two were merely friends, Breck answered, "Yes."

How had he managed, Trinity thought, her eyes once more on Breck's, to make the one word sound so orchestrated, as if it contained each note known to the human voice, certainly each low, rough, masculine note? And why had it washed over her so warmly, as if it mattered what he thought of her performance?

"I'm sorry," Jedediah broke in. "Trinity, this is my friend—"

"Mr. Brecker and I have met," she answered.

"Breck. Everyone calls me Breck."

She toyed with saying the abridged name—it was probably expected of her—but it simply wouldn't form on her tongue. It sounded altogether too personal. Too intimate. Too forgiving. Instead, she said what had just occurred to her: "I didn't know you two were friends."

"Jedediah headed me in the right direction when I bought the Sierra Virginia," Breck said.

Trinity heard the possessive pride in Breck's voice when he spoke of the railroad, almost sensually stroking the words *Sierra Virginia*. For an instant she almost, *almost*, regretted that she was going to take his lover away. She pushed the thought aside and glanced down at the flowers, then up into Jedediah's glowing eyes. "Thank you for the roses."

"My pleasure, my dear, but they're nothing in comparison to what your performance deserved."

"You spoil me," she said with a smile that did strange things to Breck's senses—things like reminding him again that he'd been a long while without a woman, things like making him admit that smiles you paid for never quite seemed real, things like making him wonder again if her hair would feel like silk.

Jedediah laughed at her comment. "Hardly, though I do have a proposition that'll bring me closer to it. Get the cast, their friends, their families, and let's go for a drink. Champagne for everyone."

"What a charming idea," Trinity said.

At the same moment that Trinity was declaring Jedediah's suggestion charming, Victoria Dawson, all swoony-eyed, was declaring Trinity lovely. The search for the back door had brought her, Dick Kingsman, Hollis Reed, and the whining Molly to the wing of the theatre housing the dressing rooms. The sight of Trinity Lee, in the flesh and so close, pushed Victoria toward a case of the vapors.

"Just look at her. Oh, my word, isn't she pretty?"

Dick Kingsman, though hardly opposed to discussing Trinity's loveliness, regretted leaving behind a subject he felt even more warmly about. Victoria had so praised his bravery during the holdups that his chest was puffed out like that of a bantam rooster on parade.

"Y-yes," he said, reluctant to let the old topic die such an ignoble and incomplete death, "she is lovely."

"Is that Breck?" Victoria asked disbelievingly. "I mean, Mr. Brecker?"

"Yeah . . . sure is," both Dick and Hollis Reed chimed in.

"You don't suppose you could ask him . . ." Victoria began. She trailed off with a calculated "No, of course not."

"Ask him what?" Dick said, eager to recoup her praise.

"You work for him . . . I mean, is it possible . . . Could you ask if I—we—could meet . . . her?" She raised her eyes to Dick Kingsman, a sweep of blond lashes fanning up over blue eyes the color of supplication. "I don't know of anyone else brave enough to approach Mr. Brecker. . . ."

Mr. Kingsman's deflating chest swelled once more, making him courageous beyond his norm. "Well, shucks, it won't hurt to ask, will it?"

Breck saw his baggageman approaching and scarcely had time to wonder why before the man asked, shyly, nervously, "Could I speak with you, sir?"

Trinity, too, had seen Dick's approach, had recognized him immediately as the baggageman she'd held up three times, and had just as immediately stopped breathing. Had he recognized her? No, he couldn't have. But what, then, were he and Breck whispering about?

Breck turned back, his eyes finding hers without giving away what he was about to say. "It appears, Miss Lee, that there's a young lady who'd very much like to meet you. A Miss Victoria Dawson."

Relief tripped through Trinity. On the heels of it, she recognized the name. This was the daughter of the society snob. Trinity smiled, placed the roses, which she'd crushed to her bosom, in Jedediah's arms, and stepped forward. "Certainly," she said, feeling remarkably charitable now that she knew she hadn't been found out.

"Miss Lee," Breck said, "this is Dick Kingsman and Hollis Reed—they work for me—and this is Miss Dawson and Miss . . ."

There was a noticeable silence before Molly whined, "Flannery."

"Gentlemen ... ladies," Trinity acknowledged.

"Oh, Miss Lee," Victoria began, "you're ... I ... you're ... you're so beautiful."

As always, Trinity couldn't agree with the word *beautiful*. "Thank you, but the truth is, I've always longed for lovely blond hair like yours."

"Oh, no, ma'am, you mustn't wish that. I mean, yours is so—so perfect." Victoria Dawson swallowed, stammered, worried about the gloves she was wearing. "I'm—I'm going to be an actress."

"Good for you."

"Just like you."

"No, better," Trinity said, turning to Jedediah. "Would you hand me a couple of programs?" In seconds, she had scrawled her name and passed the programs forward.

Victoria thanked her, then giggled. "Imagine me talking to Trinity Lee. Why, Mamma would skin me alive if she knew I was talking to y—" The young woman suddenly realized what she was saying. "I mean, Mamma wouldn't want me talking to an actress ..." She wasn't making the situation any better. "Mamma thinks that actresses aren't ladies ... I mean, that plays aren't proper ... that they're vulgar...." Victoria let her words trail off, mortified into silence.

Breck saw the hurt that leaped into Trinity's eyes. He saw how it clouded the sherry-colored irises, leaving them dull and filled with a kittenish kind of vulnerability. Outcasts. They were both outcasts—he because he'd always been out of step, she because of a profession that kept her just beyond the gates of acceptable society. Anger, sharp and hot, coursed through him at the unfairness of fickle society. And while he was at it, he thought, he'd take the liberty of being angry for Trinity Lee, as well!

"I'm certain that nothing you could do would be improper, Miss Dawson," Trinity said softly.

Moments later, the young ladies departed through the theatre's back door. The choice of exits was an added, though unintentional, insult. As Trinity turned, her eyes met Breck's. He had seen her pain. Recognition was etched in his blue eyes—blue eyes that unswervingly, unnervingly, watched her. Strange, she thought, no one else had ever been able to see it. The realization that this man had brought a dichotomous reaction. On the one hand, it was comforting to touch, heart-to-heart, a kindred spirit; on the other hand, it was unsettling for that kindred spirit to be Madison Brecker. For the dangerous truth was, if he could see that, what else could he see? She shuttered her eyes, bringing thick lashes down to hide anything better left unseen.

Overbrightly, and with a smile that Breck thought looked as if it had been paid for, she said, "How about that champagne?"

The Crystal Saloon was loud with gaiety. Breck had tried too beg out of said gaiety, but Jedediah would have no part of it—of course he would join in the cast party! And so, detached as usual, Breck sat slumped in a chair, a glass of untouched champagne going flat before him. The crowd seemed to include half the town, with conversation covering a wide assortment of topics: The performance, backstage antics, the robberies, the tree dragged across the track, the troupe's next performance in San Francisco—all punctuated with giggles and laughs and sometimes ribald teasing. Breck complacently took it all in without adding anything. He was the only one who said nothing when one of Virginia City's elders invited Trinity to return the following month for the lavish Territorial Ball, sponsored by the town. Everyone else begged and cajoled her to accept the invitation—for heaven's sake, Nevada's governor himself would be present!

"When?" Trinity asked.

The date coincided with a scheduled shipment of mining payrolls.

Breck listened to her acceptance. Seconds later, their eyes met. He said nothing. She glanced away... and into the pawing look of Wilson Booth. Breck's glance slid to Wilson Booth, as well. The man looked the way he'd looked ever since joining the party uninvited—as if he'd like to see, to feel, Trinity buried deep in a mattress. Breck struggled to hang on to his complacency. It was a hard battle, given his feeling that if anyone buried anything, he'd like it to be his fist deep in Wilson's face.

He was just asking himself why he should care if Booth was drooling like a sex-crazed adolescent when a voice roused him from his troubling reverie. It was a drunken voice—one that belonged to Ben Buford, of the Buford Mine.

"You're sitting here whoopin' it up when you oughta be out there puttin' a stop to these here robberies," the man said, his hair tangled by liquor-trembling hands. "If you think I'm a-goin' to keep riskin' my mine's money, you've got another think a-comin'."

"You're drunk, Buford," Breck said quietly, calmly, never moving out of his slouched position by so much as the flexing of a single muscle. "Come talk to me when you're sober."

"I'm a-talkin' to you now. And I'm a-tellin' you that I don't need to rely on some two-bit railroad run by some trashy riffraff."

The room grew silent by degrees as people became aware of the confrontation. The last comment left only a smattering of dim peripheral conversation.

"But then, I guess we're a-gettin' what we deserve," Ben Buford said, drunkenly smearing his words together. "What can you 'spect from a man whose daddy was a cheatin' drunk and whose mamma was a whorin'—"

The sound of Breck's chair toppling thundered throughout the suddenly tomb-silent room. In the place of Ben Buford's words came a strangled gasp as Breck's strong fist clutched the man's throat. Ben Buford's face instantly pinkened, then turned red. His eyes, dark and wide, bugged, froglike, from his head. Breck, his eyes frozen to a frosty blue, took it all in in his typically detached way.

Second after tense second passed.

"My God, he's going to kill him," somebody said.

The man, now fighting for even a wisp of air, flailed his arms, striking Breck an occasional blow that seemed no more powerful than if it had been delivered by a babe.

Breck slid his fingers tighter, tighter, tighter...while his lips curled, curled, curled....

Ben Buford began to sag.

"Breck," Jedediah called softly.

Nothing. Except the gurgling sounds of the dangling man.

"Breck," Jedediah repeated more urgently.

Suddenly, Breck released his hold. Ben Buford sucked in a deep draft of life...seconds before he crumpled to his knees on the floor.

The crowd watched as Breck, without a word, without a backward glance, stalked from the saloon.

"Damnation!" someone said into the cloying silence.

The instant Trinity realized she had risen from her chair was the moment she felt the acute need to return to it. She also realized that her fingers were folded about her throat. It seemed the only way to hold back the scream. There was nothing, however, to hold back the fear spilling across her winter-cold body.

Chapter Seven

"Are you all right?"

The question mingled with the *clickety-clack* of the train as it chugged its winding way from Reno to San Francisco. Earlier, before dawn had crept over the sleeping horizon, Trinity and Jedediah McCook had boarded the Sierra Virginia, had ridden it to Reno, and there had switched the private car to the mighty Central Pacific. They now sat aboard the private car, surrounded by emerald-and-crimson luxury. Trinity quietly stared out the brocaded window at the passing landscape, which alternated between vast plateaus of sagebrush and austere desert mountains. Jedediah, more often than not, simply stared at Trinity.

At the sound of Jedediah's resonant voice, Trinity glanced over at him. He sat erect and perfectly groomed on the fringed, cushioned bench across from her. She smiled. "I'm fine."

Though she hoped they were convincing, Trinity recognized her smile and her answer for the lies they were. She wasn't fine. Nor had she been since last evening in the Crystal Saloon. While she hadn't seen Breck before leaving town, his image remained as sharp as if she'd seen him two dozen times. In fact, there seemed little she could do to dislodge him from her mind. No matter how hard she tried, she couldn't dismiss the sight of Breck's fingers squeezing until the knuckles were white, of Ben Buford's florid face, of Breck's empty, emotionless eyes as he'd calmly choked the life from another human being.

She had *felt* Breck's violence. It had stormed her senses with its bilious smell, its brittle sound, its bloody taste, which had seeped onto her tongue from her fear-bitten lip. At first she thought it was his violence, his ruthlessness, that frightened her, but she was slowly coming to realize that what frightened her most was the fact that he was nothing more than a reflection of herself. With her plans of murder, she was every bit as violent, every bit as ruthless, as he.

"You've been awfully quiet, my dear. Are you sure nothing's troubling you?"

"I'm fine. Truly. Just woolgathering." She smiled again, and this time it was a more genuine wreathing of her lips. "Do you never woolgather, Jedediah? Or do successful railroad magnates have time for nothing beyond counting their money?"

She expected him to join in her humor. Instead, taking her quite by surprise, he answered seriously. "As a matter of fact, I do woolgather. Mostly about the good old days when I was rich only in dreams." He sighed deeply. "I'll give you a piece of advice more valuable than anything I own. Be careful what you wish for. You might get it."

The man who now sat before her was so unlike the powerful, commanding Jedediah she'd come to know over the past year that she could find no ready response. None proved necessary, for Jedediah himself filled the silence.

As though he'd suddenly grown embarrassed by his emotional outpouring, he added with a smile, "Another piece of advice. Pay no heed to the ramblings and ravings of an old man."

"You're far from old."

"Ah, but I travel the road toward it more surely each day."

Telling herself she was changing the subject for Jedediah's sake and not because his advice, coupled with her own dark scheme of revenge, was troubling, Trinity said carefully, "I had no idea you knew Madison Brecker."

"I had no idea you did."

"Oh, I don't," she said hastily. "I mean, I just met him. My friend Ellie had spoken of him before. And of the robberies."

Jedediah nodded. "Bad, bad business, these robberies."

"Then, uh . . . then you've known him a long while?"

"A number of years. He helped to lay track for the Central Pacific. Worked his way up from nothing to track boss. You could count on him to get done what he said he would, when he said he would."

"Do you think he intended to kill that man last night?" She hadn't meant to ask the question, but the image was still hauntingly clear. With the slightest exertion of her imagination, she could feel her own throat being crushed by the pressure of Breck's long, strong fingers.

"No," Jedediah said simply, as if he knew his answer to be fact. "If he'd intended to kill him, he would have. Regardless of anything I could have done or said."

"What a savage mentality our Mr. Brecker has," Trinity said, not entirely convinced that Jedediah hadn't at least given Madison Brecker pause for thought. She was also unable to avoid a sliver of annoyance at what she sensed was Jedediah's respect for Brecker, despite everything the man appeared to be—despite everything the man obviously *was*. She conveniently overlooked the fact that her own plans proved that she was capable of being every bit as savage as he.

Jedediah shrugged. "Savage, perhaps, but honest. You always know where you stand with Breck."

Trinity laughed sardonically. "Yes, if you're alive, you know you're in his good graces."

"Last night frightened you, didn't it?" Jedediah asked, his voice quiet with understanding.

Yes, and for reasons you would never guess, she thought. "I'm not accustomed to seeing men murdered," she answered.

"The man wasn't murdered, my dear—that's a salient point to remember. And don't judge Breck too harshly. You can hardly force a man to create his own rules, then punish him for not abiding by yours." At her inquiring look, he explained, "The man last night—Ben Buford—was right. At least from what I hear he was. Breck's pa was no-account, his ma even less. And the kindhearted, churchgoing citizens of the world never forgave Breck for surviving on his own terms."

"You like him." It was a statement, not a question.

"Yes."

"Why?" She really wanted to know; she really *needed* to know.

"Because he knows what he wants... and he goes after it." A wistfulness returned to Jedediah's eyes. A melancholy wistfulness. "And he doesn't let anything—especially what people think—stand in his way."

Trinity gave her friend a measuring look, for a moment entertaining the notion that he was hiding something, some great sadness. But then, what would someone who had everything have to hide?

By tacit agreement, the subject of Madison Brecker was dropped and not mentioned again until the almost seventeen-hour journey had ended. The train had arrived at Vallejo, where the passengers, trading the smell of locomotive steam for the smell of the sea, had been transferred to a boat for the final leg to San Francisco.

Once at their destination, Jedediah said, "Breck is planning a trip to San Francisco in a couple of weeks—he wants to give final approval to a new engine he's ordered. He'll be staying the night with Ada and me. Why don't you plan to join us for dinner?" When Trinity hesitated, he grinned. "Maybe you can tame the savage beast."

In the span of her hesitation occurred a thousand thoughts, chief among them that she could reply with a simple "No, thank you" and still save her soul. Jedediah's warning to be careful what she wished for, for she might get it, also rang shrilly through her mind and conscience. Her answer, however, was foreordained. She'd lived with hate too long to abandon it now.

Smiling her famous smile, she replied, "I shall leave the savage beast for another to tame, but I should be most delighted to dine with you and your wife."

The days passed.

Trinity threw herself, body and soul, into a production of Shakespeare's *Macbeth*. In those restless moments when she couldn't help herself, she pondered the irony of performing a play devoted to the subject of murder. Normally, however, she worked herself to the point of fatigue and distraction, to the point where she could not think, where she could only feel a sense of relief that the day was over, where she could only hope and pray that she did not dream.

Breck, too, did his share of hoping and praying, and on the fifteenth of the month, when there was no attempted robbery, when the payrolls arrived as safe as a babe in a new mother's arms, he breathed a sigh of relief. His relief, however, was short-lived. A scant week later, a shot was fired at the engineer from the same spot where the tree had been felled across the track.

"I ain't hurt. It was a clear miss," Charlie Knott said, feeling the need to say something that would ease the tension

straining at the seams of Breck's small office. Breck had received the news as he always did—with his face wiped clean of
all expression, with his eyes coolly unreadable. His lack of reaction accounted in large measure for the teeming tension.
Everyone was awaiting the volcano's eruption.

"That's hardly the point, is it?" Breck said, his voice unnervingly without timbre.

Dancey Harlan, Abe Dustin, and Charlie Knott, the third
wishing someone *would* shoot him to get him out of this emotionally suffocating room, murmured varying shades of agreement. Oliver Truxtun, who'd once more been aboard the train,
said nothing. He simply stared at Breck with his dark, beady
bird's eyes.

"The point," Breck said, still calmly, "is that you *could* have
been hurt. Even killed. And everyone in the train might have
followed. Innocent people, I might add. People who entrusted
their safe passage to the Sierra Virginia. The next point," Breck
said, splaying his hands on the Spartan desktop and pushing
himself up, "is that maybe next time you will be hurt or killed."
He was now standing at his full, imposing six-foot-plus height,
and his eyes had begun to burn with flames that appeared to
lick at his composure. "And the last point, my friends, is that
we're going to have to do something to make goddamned sure
there is no next time!" By this time, his voice had set the timid
glass in the door to rattling.

Everyone spoke at once, except Abe Dustin, who sat quietly, now sweating from Breck's anger rather than from the
usual furnaceful of wood.

"You think today was the handiwork of the robbers?"
Charlie Knott asked.

"'Course it's the heathen robbers," Dancey answered.

"What do you suggest?" Oliver Truxtun asked, his impassive voice overriding the other comments.

Breck walked to the coat tree, jerked his buckskin jacket
from a limb, and threw his shoulders into it. His eyes met those
of the Pinkerton agent.

"With all due respect," Breck said, "your way doesn't seem
to be working. And I'm sick of being a sitting duck." With
that, he yanked open the door.

"Where you headed?" Dancey called.

"To get a drink," Breck said, "and to leak word to anyone
who'll listen that the payroll shipment at the first of the month

will be double in value." Breck's eyes darkened. "Certain facts, however, gentlemen, will remain confined to this room."

When Breck had finished disclosing his simple plan, Dancey said gleefully, "Sounds like what we have here is a trap."

"Might just work," Oliver Truxtun said.

"It better," Breck replied, his voice once again frighteningly even. "And when I finish with the sonofabitch responsible for all this, he'll be too dead to bury."

Minutes later, at the Last Drink Saloon, a bottle of that establishment's meanest red-eye whiskey at his elbow, Breck took the entirety of Virginia City into his strictest confidence. One listener told two, two told four, four told eight—discreetly, of course, and with the solemn pledge that it would go no further. That night, for the first time in a long while, Breck felt, if not good, at least less bad. It suited his style to be doing something for a change instead of sitting passively by and letting circumstances act on him.

In his hotel room late that night, he allowed himself to be downright optimistic as he gazed at columns of figures that had been severely depressing only the day before. There was hope yet, if only he could stop the robberies. If only he could pay back the bank loans he'd needed to make up the payroll losses. If only the engine he'd ordered—

A knock interrupted his thoughts.

"Hi," Millie Rhea said softly when the door opened. When Breck hesitated, she asked, "Can I come in?"

Breck stepped back, allowing the woman to enter. Silently he crossed the room and reseated himself in a chair, his legs sprawled open before him. His eyes roamed over the auburn hair scattered alluringly about Millie's young-old face, then lowered to the ornately adorned black satin dress she wore. He wished just once she'd wear something simple—a simple dress that would showcase the sweetness she had despite the fact that she knew too much about the wrong kind of men. He also wished he could be better company for her tonight, because, while his mood had improved, he still felt an overpowering need to be alone. He wished he'd been able to get away to the cabin for a day or two.

"I saw you over at the saloon," she said. "I kept thinking we'd get a chance to talk."

"Sorry."

"I, uh . . . I heard about Charlie Knott getting shot at."

"Yeah."

"And about the next shipment having so much money on board."

"Don't spread it around, huh?" he said, knowing she probably already had, hoping she already had. She promised him faithfully that she wouldn't. "Want a drink?" he asked, forcing himself to be civil. Millie deserved that much, at least.

"No," she said, crossing the room and lowering herself to the floor between his knees. "You want to go to bed?" she asked with her usual candor.

"Millie, I'm not in the mo—"

"I've missed you," she said, placing her spread hands on the inside of his thighs. She started them moving upward. By a slow, tantalizing route.

"Millie—"

"I know you've had a lot on your mind lately, but you need to relax. Let me help you relax." Her hand slid over the heat of him. He responded in a hard, thick way, though he made no sound and his eyes showed not a flicker of arousal. "I've missed our being together," she whispered, a little desperately as she unfastened his jeans and began to stroke him intimately. "See," she said triumphantly, "you want me."

He could have argued that he'd never wanted a woman, only periodically needed one. But he didn't, primarily because his body was painfully pointing out that this might be one of those need times. Still, however, he resisted. He didn't want to need a woman now; he wanted to be left alone.

"Millie—" he began, only to have her fingers close around him in an experienced way. He grimaced and thought, Ah, what the hell!

He took her quickly, acting as if by rote, and without leaving a shred of his emotional self behind. At climax he thought two things. One, he felt no pleasure, only the release of pressure. Two, tawny-brown eyes flashed through his mind.

"Here, buy yourself something pretty," Breck said minutes later, avoiding her eyes as he handed her the usual payment for services rendered and hustled her to the door.

"I, uh…I was hoping tonight could be just between friends." She knew he'd never love her—she wasn't sure he was capable of love—but she'd settle for their being lovers. Real lovers.

"Buy yourself a calico dress," he insisted, stuffing the bills into her hand, finally looking down into her face and confirming what he most feared.

Millie Rhea's eyes were blue.

Blue eyes.

She had failed miserably at remembering the precise color of Breck's eyes, Trinity realized as she scanned the elegant parlor of the McCook mansion. A little more than three weeks had passed since that balmy night on the bay when she'd promised to join Jedediah and his wife for dinner. Now, observing unnoticed the man she'd known would be there, she chastised herself for remembering Breck's eyes only as a pale blue. She had not remembered their captivating color, somewhere between the blue of flame and the blue of ice. Nor had she imagined, even in her wildest dreams, that they could smile as they now were, obviously at something Jedediah had said. Nor could she have imagined how their smiling could so transform the face of Madison Brecker, nor how that transformation could cause a tiny fluttering in a woman's heart.

"Ah, Trinity, there you are, my dear," Jedediah said, noticing her standing in the doorway and starting toward her with his usual bold, confident stride. "Are you soaked to the skin? I was hoping the storm would pass us, but it seems to have settled in."

Ignoring the fluttery butterfly feeling within and summoning up her comfortable companion, hate, Trinity stepped forward. The parlor, high ceilinged and splashed with rich Aubussons, displayed tasteful, cultured wealth. Everywhere was the echo of success—heavy imported brocades, silver shined to a mirror finish, rococo furniture vividly carved with roses and curlicues and enhanced by sumptuous upholstery in a demure blue. Overhead, a Viennese chandelier christened the room in soft, gentle light.

"Your driver wouldn't allow even a drop of rain to splatter me," she answered, indicating the scalloped flounces of her ivory pongee dress. "See, I'm dry as powder."

"I'd fire the man on the spot were you not," Jedediah teased, taking her hand in his and squeezing it affectionately. Turning, he began, "Trinity, you remember—"

"Mr. Brecker," she interrupted, her eyes meeting the blue, blue,   how-could-she-not-have-remembered-that-shade-of-blue eyes of the man standing casually before the fireplace. Orange and red flames flickered behind him, snatching the chill from the room and illuminating his tall physique, which consisted of wide shoulders fitted beneath a fawn-colored coat, and long, lean legs encased in coffee-brown pants that caressed his hips and thighs like a wanton lover. Again, unbidden, unwanted, came a delicate fluttering in her chest.

"I thought we had agreed upon 'Breck,' Miss Lee."

"Then I must insist you call me Trinity." Not only had it seemed the logical, expected thing to say, but she had simply, suddenly, wondered what her name would sound like on his lips, lips that could be as harsh as a punishing winter storm, but that she now knew could smile like the beginning of a merciful spring.

"Trinity it is, then," he said, his voice low and lazy, as though it had been dragged through a hot, Southern summer afternoon.

The word *dangerous* passed through Trinity's mind. Her name on his lips sounded decidedly dangerous.

As this thought was crossing her mind, Breck's eyes were taking in the dramatic contrast between the ivory of her dress and the ebony of her hair, which she wore in a low chignon skewered with lacquered ivory sticks. His eyes then raked over the low neck of her dress. From there, he noted her red lips, the rosy bloom of her Orientally round cheeks, the . . .

. . . the tawny brown of her eyes.

He had known the night Millie had lain beneath him that it was these eyes—Trinity Lee's eyes—that he had thought of, but he had tried to convince himself otherwise. These eyes, however, were even more alive than the memory that had taunted his senses. From nowhere came the heated stirring of his masculine blood. The intensity of the feeling startled him. Disturbed him. So much so that he hastened to tell himself the feeling meant nothing, that it was nothing more than a healthy man's reaction to a beautiful woman. It certainly had nothing to do with wanting any woman in particular, when needing women in general had served him well all his life.

To be on the safe side, however, he withdrew deep into himself, to a place where he alone was allowed admittance. At the same time, Trinity was taking similar precautions. She reminded herself, with brutal images of her mother and Ben Buford, just who this man was, *what* he was. So intent were both that neither heard Jedediah.

"Trinity? Breck?"

Both glanced up sharply into the waiting eyes of their host.

"Could I get you a drink?" Jedediah repeated.

"White wine, thank you."

"Whiskey. Neat."

When Jedediah handed them their drinks, Trinity moved to sit on the edge of a blue damask lady chair and sipped her wine. Never once did her eyes seek out Breck. Breck palmed his squat glass, stepped back to the fire, and, without looking at the woman in the room, brought the honey-colored liquor to his lips and drank deeply.

Jedediah poured himself a bourbon on the rocks, but, before enjoying the aged spirits, he pulled his watch from the pocket of his elaborately embroidered gray vest, checked the time, and peered beyond the room to the curving staircase in the foyer. The empty staircase.

"So you found the Baldwin to your liking?" Jedediah asked Breck, repocketing the watch and resuming what appeared to be their earlier conversation. A round of thunder rumbled, and rain thrashed the lofty windows as though angry at the dry warmth inside.

"There's little not to like," Breck answered. "It's powerful, it's a work of art, it's beautiful."

"And what about a delivery date?"

"That's the rub," Breck said, swirling the whiskey in his glass. "They're demanding their money up front." His lips curled into a sneer. "Not that I blame them, with my recent history."

"I've told you—" Jedediah began.

He was cut off with "I'll not take your money."

"A loan—"

"No." Emphatic. Nonnegotiable. Breck brought the glass once more to his lips. Over the glass's rim, his eyes met Trinity's.

She had told herself silence was her best recourse—Jedediah, to whom she'd confided that she thought Breck savage, would think it strange if she was nice to him, while Breck would think it odd if she was openly hostile—but she found herself, nonetheless, saying, "I take it a Baldwin is a locomotive."

"An expensive locomotive," Breck said. Their eyes held for a moment longer—swam, actually, one pair into the other—before he glanced away and back to his host.

Jedediah was again checking both watch and stairway. "What in the world could be keeping Ada? She vowed another fifteen minutes at most."

"I believe women consider it important to be fashionably late," Breck said, trying to put the older man at ease. He, too, however, had begun to wonder where his hostess was. He had arrived two hours before, had been shown to his room, and had joined Jedediah some few minutes before in the parlor. Throughout the afternoon he hadn't even glimpsed his friend's wife, whom he was eager to meet.

"Fashionable or no, one shouldn't be late with one's own guests," Jedediah retorted in a tone Trinity had never heard him use before. While it wasn't clear-cut irritation, it was a sharp deviation from his usual joviality. "Could I freshen anyone's drink?" he added, stepping to the bar to do precisely that to his own. Trinity noted that he poured himself a generous refill.

"No, thank you," both Trinity and Breck answered.

"So, Breck," Jedediah said, "there's been nothing beyond your engineer being shot at?"

Trinity looked up so quickly that her wine threatened to overflow its crystal confines. Her eyes dived into Breck's. "Shot at?"

"Yes," Breck drawled with a menacing lack of emotion, "my engineer—"

"I'm so sorry to be late," came a feminine voice as rich, as polished, as the room into which it poured.

Everyone turned toward the doorway.

Ada McCook was a woman of average height, but with a stance, a set to her shoulders, that suggested royalty. She exuded a gentility, a quiet, ennobling grace, that swept from the brown curls of her carefully tended coiffure to the beaded kid of her evening shoes. Her dress, a sweet, innocent shade of pink, flowed to the floor in three flounces, with an overskirt of point lace draped behind *en panier* with ribbons tied in a bow. Pearls and a pink coral medallion adorned a neck unwrinkled despite her age, which was probably a few years beyond her husband's. Her smile was full and friendly, while her eyes, the gray of a peaceful twilight, were warm and inviting. All in all, she looked the embodiment of womanliness and motherhood.

Trinity disliked her immediately.

She could not for the life of her, however, have explained why. It was simply an uneasy feeling that drizzled over her senses. She was certain—as certain as she was that a storm was raging outside—that Ada McCook had purposely been late so that she could stage a grand entrance. Trinity felt an instant disappointment, even sadness. She had desperately wanted to like her friend's wife.

"Ah, there you are," Jedediah said. "We had quite given up on you."

At the sound of Jedediah's voice, which held what Trinity thought was a subtle note of censure, she redirected her gaze toward him. It lingered there for only a second, however, before being drawn to Breck. Trinity frowned. He was staring so single-mindedly at Ada McCook that, rather than merely looking, he was absorbing her like a desert traveler thirsty for a visual drink. Even as she watched, though, the usual unreadable curtain fell across his eyes, leaving her to wonder if his peculiar reaction had simply been her imagination.

"I do so apologize," Ada said, gliding into the room. "Oh, Henri," she said over her shoulder, whipping the demitrain of her dress to the side, "let's detain dinner a half hour, shall we?"

"Yes, ma'am," the short, dark-haired servant said, his face impassive.

"Ada, I'd like you to meet—"

"Miss Lee, of course," Ada interrupted.

The older woman's perusal of her, Trinity thought, was odd at best. Had she not just seen it happen, she would have called it impossible. Ada McCook managed in one quick sweep to thoroughly take in every facet of her and then insultingly dismiss her. She wondered if Ada McCook was another whose nose was hooked too high to associate with actresses.

"And, of course, you're Madison Brecker," Ada said, turning her attention to Breck. "Jedediah has spoken of you often."

"Mrs. McCook," Breck acknowledged, his voice without inflection.

"I hope you've found your visit to San Francisco enjoyable and productive," the older woman added.

"Both," Breck answered.

Ada took the wine her husband handed her, shifted her eyes back to Trinity, and brought the glass to her pink lips. Trinity felt her spine stiffen, as if to ward off something she sensed was coming. She, too, sipped her drink. Finally Ada said, "And so, Miss Lee, you're the actress."

The comment was casual enough, yet Trinity felt the sting of condemnation as if it were the prick of a viper. "Yes," she answered, her voice soft but strong, "I'm the actress."

"Strange. You don't look at all as I'd expected."

"Don't I?"

"No, I thought you'd look more . . . Chinese."

Trinity's chin tilted ever so slightly upward, and she looked the woman squarely in the eyes. "I'm Eurasian."

"Yes, of course. A half-breed."

"Ada!" Jedediah thundered, his tone one of absolute mortification.

"Half-breed in the best sense, of course. Tell me, Miss Lee, is it your mother or your father that's Caucasian?"

"My mother was Chinese," Trinity answered, subtly but deliberately turning the question around.

"Ah, and beautiful she must have been. You're quite lovely, Miss Lee. As well as obviously being very talented. Jedediah—" she patted her husband's arm and smiled with the beauty of an angel "—has good taste in friends."

Ada McCook's last remark heralded a new attitude—at least, that was how Trinity viewed it. From that moment on she was friendliness incarnate, laughing at Trinity's comments, encouraging her to talk about her stage career, asking interesting questions about the theatre when the conversation lagged. She was polite, considerate, she even touched Trinity lightly when the occasion merited it. So friendly did she become that Trinity began to wonder if perhaps she had misjudged her. Had she simply taken exception to innocent remarks? Had her perception been askew at that instant when they'd met?

"Ah, here's Henri to announce dinner," Ada said when the servant reappeared. Rising from the ornately carved blue velvet sofa, she added, "Jedediah, if you'll escort Miss Lee, I'll impose upon Mr. Brecker." As she spoke, she stepped toward Breck, her hand already seeking the curve of his arm.

Slowly, silently, Breck set his glass on a table and crooked his elbow. As he felt her fingers curl around his arm, he stared down into the warm, friendly eyes of Ada McCook. They were eyes he would have sworn he'd seen before. But where? And why did it seem so goddamned important that he remember?

Chapter Eight

All through a dinner of expertly prepared food and expensive wine, neither of which had his full attention, Ada Mc-Cook's familiarity nagged at Breck. Surely he had been mistaken about having seen her before. She, no doubt, reminded him of someone else. But even as he thought it, he knew it wasn't true. He *had* seen this woman before. Her patrician features, her gray eyes—

"For heaven's sake, Henri!" Ada McCook cried suddenly.

Breck, along with Trinity and Jedediah, glanced up quickly. The servant, refilling the hostess's wineglass, had dribbled some of the burgundy onto the bodice of her elegant gown.

"Oh, madame, je regrette . . ." the servant said, starting to dab at the scarlet spots.

Ada pushed his hands away. "I'll do it myself," she said none too kindly, using her napkin to blot the moisture.

The servant was clearly mortified.

"It'll never come out," Ada griped. "The dress is ruined. Ruined!"

"It's all right, Henri," Jedediah soothed. "It was an accident." He smiled. "I'll buy Mrs. McCook another dress. You know how she loves to shop."

"Mais oui, monsieur," the man said, anxiously withdrawing to the sidelines.

Everyone, even Ada, whom good manners belatedly forced to civility, returned to normal. Everyone except Breck. The hand cupping his own wineglass, which at the moment was suspended in midair, curled so tightly around the glass that his knuckles grew white . . . as white as the star-shaped scar beneath them. He was staring at the red stain on the pink fabric.

A red stain that looked like...blood. His eyes raced to Ada's gray eyes. Gray eyes he'd once seen gleaming with emotion...filled with guilt? The woman in the alley behind the brothel eighteen years ago!

Surely he was mistaken, he thought. He *had* to be mistaken. God, tell him he was mistaken! For Jedediah's sake, tell him he was wrong! But even as he offered up the desperate prayer, he knew he wasn't. This was the woman he'd always believed had killed Su-Ling.

But Ada McCook?

What possible connection could she have had with Su-Ling Chang? How could a woman of Ada McCook's social standing know anything about women like Su-Ling, except in the abstract? What had happened to make their worlds collide? And how could emotions have run so mountain-high, so valley-deep, that murder had been the result?

Maybe, just maybe, he'd been wrong about Ada's being the murderer. Maybe she'd only found Su-Ling's body—as he had. After all, he hadn't seen her kill Su-Ling. Which was another thought—maybe she'd seen her murdered and fled for her own life. Maybe... Yeah, and maybe he was grasping for straws, like some poor drowning bastard going down for the third time. There was no way in hell he'd ever believe the woman to his left, sitting casually amid the best damask, silver, china, and crystal money could buy, hadn't murdered his gentle, soft-spoken friend.

But why? He hadn't the least clue.

Without drinking, Breck set the goblet of burgundy down and uncoiled his aching hand. He studied the other two people at the table. Jedediah, his white hair immaculately parted in the middle, his muttonchops fastidiously clipped, sat at the head of the table as proudly, as commandingly, as a Caesar reviewing his troops. Breck noted that his host was drinking generously tonight. To Jedediah's right, and across from Breck, sat Trinity, who was smiling at something Jedediah had just said. Strangely, when she smiled, she appeared more Chinese; lights jumped into her eyes, bringing attention to their almondlike shape.

Eurasian. Ada had been borderline rude, and downright inquisitive, about Trinity's parents. Why? Breck's eyes shifted back to his host, who was responding to something Trinity had asked. Did Jedediah know his wife was a murderer? And had he known Su-Ling? At that exact moment, Jedediah and Trinity laughed—both with lips that were full and nicely curved. With lips that were almost perfectly bow-shaped. With lips that were remarkably similar.

With a force powerful enough to stop his heartbeat, an idea occurred to Breck. It was so preposterous, however, so unbelievable, with repercussions so widespread and damning, that he refused to consider it. Seriously. Or otherwise. This time he had gone too far; this time he had to be wrong.

Didn't he?

Like hearing a horn in the far, foggy distance, Breck heard someone calling his name. The voice belonged to his hostess.

" . . . some more dessert?"

Breck glanced down at the remnants of a slice of apple pie, pie he had no memory of having eaten. "No. No, thank you. It, uh . . . it was good."

"I know what Breck wants," Jedediah announced, shoving his chair back from the table. "A good cognac and a good cigar. Both of which we'll find in the parlor."

As if on cue, the others rose, as well, Jedediah reaching for Trinity's chair, the servant, still a shade of white, for Ada's. Ada treated him to a stern, disapproving look. As they stood, a wave of thunder rumbled like an angry oracle.

"Tell me, Miss Lee," the older woman said as they stepped out into the cavernous hallway that echoed with the rain, "shall we abuse ourselves with the masculine talk in the parlor, or shall we create our own more pleasurable feminine gossip in the sitting room?"

"Of course you'll join us in the parlor," Jedediah answered before Trinity could manage a word. "Breck and I promise to keep the talk agreeable, don't we, Breck?"

Breck offered no reply to the rhetorical question. Instead, he thought Jedediah seemed inordinately eager to keep Trinity at his side. And away from his wife? Lord, Brecker, you're letting your imagination run wild!

"What I probably should be doing," Trinity said, "is getting back to the hotel. The weather doesn't seem to be improving."

"No, no, it's early yet," Ada protested. "I won't hear of your leaving so soon. In fact, I don't know why you don't plan to stay the night. We certainly have plenty of room for—"

"Oh, I couldn't," Trinity interrupted.

Some emotion Breck couldn't define—displeasure? uneasiness?—flashed across Jedediah's face. "I'm sure Trinity needs to get back tonight," the older man said.

"But the weather's so frightful," Ada argued, "and I was thinking as much of William and the horses." Catching her husband's expression, she said quickly as she ushered Trinity forward, "Ah, well, we'll discuss it later. Right now, Miss Lee and I want some sherry. You gentlemen can have your old cognac!"

The subject wasn't mentioned again until almost ten o'clock, when the elaborately uniformed buggy driver appeared at the parlor doorway. Breck, cradling his cognac snifter in the palm of his hand, was thinking that this expensive cigar wasn't bringing any more pleasure than the cheaper ones he was accustomed to. Jedediah was on his second cognac and considering a third, while Ada McCook was talking incessantly about how the whole of California was insisting her husband run for governor—which she wouldn't encourage him to do, but then again, wouldn't *dis*courage him from doing. It was her feeling—which she made as plain as the fact that she was already packing her bags for the governor's mansion—that one couldn't fight one's fate. Trinity was simply wondering how much longer she could fight the feeling of suffocation. She tried to tell herself it was the cigar smoke wafting through the room and not emotional tension giving rise to the feeling, but she wasn't sure she believed it. Jedediah was drinking too much, Ada was talking too much, and Breck—he was watching them all too closely for comfort.

"Begging your pardon, sir . . ." the driver began nervously. Everyone glanced toward the door.

"Begging your pardon, sir," the man repeated, choking his cap in a fierce grip, "but the weather...she's getting worse, sir, and well, sir, if your guest—" he looked at Trinity and nodded his egg-shaped head politely "—if she'd like to return to the hotel tonight, it might be wise to be getting started. Some of them streets are likely to be impassable soon, what with the flooding and all."

"That settles it." Ada jumped from her seat with unnatural zeal. "There's no need risking man and beast. William, find Pearline and tell her to ready the guest room next to Mr. Brecker's. And tell her—"

"Trinity?" Jedediah called softly. When she turned toward him, his eyes were warm—and there was something else, as well. Beneath the soft warmth lay the steely protectiveness of a he-tiger. "If you prefer to return to the hotel, William will take you."

"That I will, miss."

Ada remained perfectly quiet, though Breck noticed the pinched set of her jaw.

Trinity considered for a moment, then smiled. "How could I possibly refuse such a gracious offer on such an ungracious night?"

"Wonderful!" Ada said. "William, find Pearline."

"Yes, ma'am," the driver said, obviously relieved.

Breck saw the warmth in Jedediah's eyes deepen into glowing delight, yet the delight seemed tempered with unease. Maybe even fear? As if to drown the negative emotion, Jedediah poured himself another caramel-colored cognac.

"Another drink, Breck?" the older man said.

"No, thank you," he replied, his eyes gliding to Trinity. Her eyes met his, and in the span of a flash of lightning a new and different tension stalked the room. This one had to do with the fact that the two of them would be in bedrooms side by side.

Trinity lowered her eyes, aware that the fluttery feeling had returned. She willed it to stop. Now. Instead of investigating the source of the feeling, which she was instinctively sure she didn't want to know, she concentrated on the two dozen other feelings warring within her. The evening had been a strange one, filled to overflowing with undercurrents she couldn't interpret, undercurrents that had left her vaguely uneasy and highly confused. Why had Ada McCook insisted so stridently on her staying the night? Not that it wasn't the best thing under the circumstances, but she'd virtually been left with no choice unless she was prepared, as her hostess had so indelicately put it, to risk man and beast. Still, she had felt . . . she had felt manipulated. She didn't particularly like the feeling of being imprisoned. Any more than she liked the headache the evening had bestowed upon her.

When Pearline, her expression as servilely starched as her cambric apron, announced the guest room's readiness, Trinity jumped at the excuse to call a halt to the evening. "Would it be too impolite of me if I retired to my room? I seem to have a headache."

"Of course not, my dear," Jedediah answered, courteously coming to his feet as Trinity rose from the sofa.

Breck, too, stood—or, rather, lazily pulled his tall frame from the chair.

"Then I'll say good-night," Trinity said with a smile, her eyes meeting Jedediah's before grazing Breck's.

Typically, Breck said nothing, vocally or with his hooded eyes.

"I'll show you to your room, miss," the servant began, only to be cut off by Ada.

"Never mind, Pearline, I'll show her."

"Yes, ma'am," the servant answered with a little curtsy.

"Ada—" Jedediah called out, his brow furrowed in displeasure as his wife fell into step beside Trinity.

The older woman turned, her skirt rustling like a snake slithering through autumn leaves. "You gentlemen enjoy the evening. I think I'll join Miss Lee in retiring. I'd like to get out of this dress." She acknowledged her husband with just the slightest hint of defiance. "Jedediah. Mr. Brecker."

Breck nodded, while Jedediah downed the remainder of his cognac in one swallow.

"Could I get you something for your head?" Ada asked as the two women began their ascent of the grandly curved wooden staircase. "A lavender-scented cloth? Some laudanum?"

"No, thank you," Trinity replied. "Rest will be sufficient."

"It's probably this chill, wet weather. San Francisco's a lovely place, but terribly damp." Ada glanced at her guest. "You're not from San Francisco, are you?"

Trinity, her skirt and petticoats bunched in her hand, replied, "No." She knew more was expected of her, but she stubbornly held back.

Ada recognized the silence for the rebuff it was but, undaunted, forged ahead. "I believe Jedediah said your current play has ended?"

"Yes."

"Do you plan on taking a break before beginning another?"

"A short one."

"Tell me, Miss Lee, was your mother an actress, too?"

Trinity cut her clear amber eyes toward her hostess. "Why do you ask?" She had learned a long time ago, from myriad interrogations by the hungry animals of the press, that the best way to avoid a question was to pose another.

"I simply wondered if you'd inherited your talent."

"I suspect my talent, what there is of it, is the result of an overactive imagination." Again, she had cleverly avoided the answer Ada sought, and both women knew it. What Trinity didn't know was why Ada Mccook was so doggedly interested in her parents. Probably just the idle curiosity she'd confronted a thousand times as a well-known public figure. Still, as always, she found it irritating. In retaliation, she smiled and repeated what she always said to inquisitive journalists. "My parents were the lovely Chinese couple who raised me."

"What a thoroughly sweet—" the woman made the word sound sticky "—sentiment." Stopping at an ornately fashioned door and pushing it inward, Ada motioned for her houseguest to precede her.

A fire had been lit, leaving the chill to tremble in fear at its approaching demise, although it was putting up a valiant fight in the dim far corners. The room was small but artfully decorated, with the focal point an enormous bed crafted by the famed Prudent Mallard of New Orleans. Its silk-lined half canopy, the color of a sun-ripened apricot, nearly reached the lofty ceiling; from the canopy hung sheer netting, this, too, in a rich apricot hue. The carvings, flutes, and moldings of the rosewood bed were dramatically highlighted in a lighter lemonwood. To the bed's right rested a marble-topped dressing table, on which Trinity noticed a washbasin and pitcher, a cloth and a hand towel, and a silver-handled brush and comb.

"Should you need anything—"

"I shan't, I'm sure," Trinity said, politely but unmistakably dismissing her hostess.

"I, uh... I had Pearline lay out one of my wrappers," Ada said, indicating the silken robe draped across the back of a chair. She seemed reluctant to leave.

"You're too kind," Trinity said, edging toward the door in yet another subtle indication that she would prefer the woman take her leave.

The woman had little choice but to say, "Then I'll say goodnight."

"Good night."

After one final meeting of their eyes, strong will viewing strong will, Ada swept from the room, pulling the door shut behind her. In the hallway, however, she paused, her hand still on the doorknob, her face deep in concentration, before finally moving on to her room.

On the other side of the door, Trinity sighed and refused to think. She was tired, and her head was throbbing in a rhythm identical to that of the pounding rain. She would simply admit that the evening hadn't gone as she'd expected and leave it at that.

Ignoring her hostess's wrapper, she undressed down to her chemise, fashioned from more lace than silk and heavily embroidered in white across the fullness of her breasts, the dark tips of which peered innocently through. Her drawers, equally thin and lacy, hugged her long, slender legs, at the apex of which rode a shadowy triangle of darkness. Stepping before the mirror of the dressing table, she raised her arms and plucked the lacquered sticks from the bun of her hair. The thick, velvety mass tumbled about her shoulders, and, not bothering with the brush and comb, she shook her head, scattering the ebony tresses to a playful freedom. With that, she extinguished the lamp, drew back the covers, and slid into bed.

Fairies of firelight danced about the room, their wavery waltz tattooed on wall and ceiling. Outside, the rain pummeled the house, while inside, Trinity's head thudded. She tried not to think, but she couldn't help herself. Curiously, she felt as if she had bedded down in an enemy camp. Ada McCook had left her unsettled, while Madison Brecker, a murderer, would be right next door. Only Jedediah seemed a safe haven. Jedediah, with his warm, caring smile. It was a smile she could see even now in her mind's eye.

Slowly, inexplicably, the smile changed owners. It now belonged to the Breck she'd seen when she'd first walked into the parlor. Just as it had then, a strange feeling claimed her chest. Moaning, she turned onto her side and willed her mind to blankness. Still, her last thought before falling asleep was that Breck was next door. And what troubled her most in those hazy moments that lent themselves to truth was not the fact that he was a murderer, but simply that he was a man. A dangerously attractive man.

Jedediah was drunk—or as close as a stomachful of after-dinner cognac, before-dinner bourbon, and during-dinner wine could make him. After the women's departure, his mood transformed itself from ill-concealed displeasure at his wife's antics to one of celebration. The celebratory mood, however, soon drowned in the tides of the bottled spirits, leaving behind one of philosophical profundity.

"My advice to you, Breck, my boy, is to be careful what you wish for, 'cause you might get it. Speaking of wishing, I wish I had another drink. How 'bout you?" Jedediah wrestled himself out of the chair.

Out of deference to his friend's sensibilities, Breck forced himself not to offer his assistance. "No, thanks."

"Nonsense," Jedediah said, ignoring his guest's response and pouring two glasses, "we need something to cap off the evening."

Breck refrained from saying that the evening looked pretty well capped off to him already. Instead, he politely reached for the newly filled glass Jedediah pushed his way. A nearly full glass set at his elbow.

"What shall we drink to?" the older man asked.

"What would you like to drink to?"

Jedediah considered. "To good friends, to good cognac, to good and wise wishes, to—" his voice faltered "—to children." His drink-bleary eyes lowered to Breck. "How come you don't have any children?"

Breck's lips twisted with a hint of a smile. "I don't have a wife, Jedediah."

The older man made an impatient gesture with his hand. "A mere technicality you could change if you wanted."

Breck's smile slipped away, replaced by visions of a soft, warm, blanketed bundle clasped to the breast of a smiling, dewy-eyed mother. The same woman, smiling and dewy-eyed, would be his soft, warm lover. It was an image the reality of which he'd never known...and never would. And, somehow, the stark deprivation of that *never* hurt more deeply than he would have thought possible.

"To someone else's children," Breck said gruffly.

"To the children I never had," Jedediah said, suddenly alone in his own misty and faraway world. "To the daughter...I never had." His eyes glazed with more than drink; his voice shattered like a cry in the wind. "To my—" his glassy eyes sought the staircase beyond "—daughter."

Breck halted his glass midway to his lips, his eyes studying the man before him and the staircase in the distance. If Breck could follow his friend's gaze up that staircase, he knew with certainty where the gaze would stop. At the door to Trinity's room. Strangely, the confirming knowledge left Breck more relieved than surprised. Ever since dinner, ever since Jedediah and Trinity had smiled together, ever since recognizing Ada, he had fought admitting what he knew must be the truth. Battle it or no, it was the only logical thing that bound the pieces of the puzzle together.

"To your daughter," Breck said quietly, and drank.

The sound of Breck's voice beckoned Jedediah from past to parlor. The transition seemed to confuse him. Passing his hand across his face and easing back into the chair, he admitted, "I'm drunk."

Breck gave a slow grin. "Nonsense. You're just not entirely sober."

Jedediah started to smile, but the smile never materialized. "Did I say anything... anything I shouldn't have?"

"No. Nothing." Relief washed across the older man's face. Abruptly, Breck set down his snifter of cognac and stood. "I'm going to bed, my friend. Could I walk you up?"

"No, you go ahead. I'll just sit here for a while—keep the fire company."

"Good night, then."

Breck had crossed almost the entire length of the room when Jedediah called out, "Breck?"

The younger man turned.

"You're sure I didn't say—"

"I'm sure." The two men stared at each other, one seeking, the other giving, reassurance. "Good night," Breck repeated before walking from the room.

He *was* drunk, Jedediah thought, resting his white-haired head against the back of the chair and letting the warmth of the mature fire ooze over him. No matter what Breck said, he was drunk. But not drunk enough to blur the remembrance that his daughter was sleeping upstairs. Trinity. Under his roof. Where she should have been from the very beginning of her life. Where she would have been if...

He sighed, regret piercing his heart until he thought it would cease to beat. Where she would have been if he hadn't been such a sightless damned fool! If he hadn't wished for all the wrong things. He smiled, his lips curling out of self-contempt, not mirth. He knew what everyone would tell him, that he had everything a man could want—prestige, wealth, power. Hell, he was even going to be governor of the state of California if he wanted it! But all of this he would renounce—gladly and in a minute—if he could but go back in time and remake a decision.

Su-Ling.

Not a day, and certainly not a night, passed that he didn't think of the beautiful, porcelain-faced Chinese woman who had so unexpectedly come into his life. He had been thirty-two, the year 1844, and though he would soon invest in the railway adventure sweeping the nation and make a fortune from those shrewd investments, at the time he had been the owner of a modest dry goods store in San Francisco. Months before, he'd commissioned a friend of his, a sea captain who regularly sailed to the Orient, to bring back silks for him to sell. What he hadn't known until later was that the captain had decided to make this his last voyage and to settle in the beautiful city by the bay. This in mind, the man had brought a Chinese couple back with him to be his house servants, a man and wife whose new marriage had been arranged long before. It was a marriage, however, that the young bride had been fully committed to. While at sea, yellow fever had swept through the vessel, killing her husband and the captain. By the time the ship had docked, Su-Ling Chang, at the tender age of eighteen, was a homeless widow. And thus, Jedediah thought, he had found his lovely silks... and a lovelier-still Chinese woman.

He could still see her standing on the wharf—the liquor seemed to make the past clearer, nearer, somehow—her hair flying like a silken banner in the salty breeze, her eyes dark and wide and innocent. And so damned frightened. Yet she'd never once whined, never once lashed out at her cruel fate, never once asked for help. Maybe that was the reason it had been impossible not to offer her a job in his store. The proximity had resulted in something he never could have foreseen.

They had fallen in love. Not the foolish kind of love that glorifies stolen touches in the dark, not the kind that thrills to whispered, illicit words, but the deep and abiding kind that lives out the night and glows brighter than the morning sun, the kind that thrills to the shouted silence of two hearts beating as one.

They would have lived happily ever after, save for one compli-
cating factor: He was married.

They lived through eight months of heaven and hell before,
having searched his soul to the fullest, he ended the affair. He
had told himself that to continue it would be unfair to Su-Ling,
but he had known in his heart, then as now, that he wasn't
ready to risk the public censure that would surely come with
divorce or disclosure. He had been a man with ambition, a man
who wanted wealth and power, a man who didn't want his
name whispered maliciously by the people he was trying to im-
press. Though he hadn't asked her to, Jedediah had been relieved when Su-Ling quit her job. He had made arrangements
for her to work in a friend's hardware store. Instead, Su-Ling
had quietly left town. Jedediah had quietly gone crazy, because the moment she was gone, he had realized how tragi-
cally wrong his choice had been. He had searched for her, but
in vain.

Eight years later, while in Sacramento on a political mission, he and Ada had run into Su-Ling—had simply, fatefully,
passed her on the street. She'd had a child with her, whom she'd
introduced as her daughter. With her blend of Oriental and
Caucasian features, the child had been beautiful. She had also
been his. Of that, Jedediah was certain. As certain as he was
that she was the only child he would ever have, because the
years had proven his wife barren.

It had taken all the strength he'd possessed to walk away
from them that afternoon. He could still remember the uneven rhythm his heart had beaten as he and Ada made their way
back to the hotel. He had alternated between feeling the deepest remorse—Dear God, all the years he'd wasted!—and the
loftiest happiness—he had found her! Or he would find her the
moment discretion allowed him to search for her!

Two days later, he'd discovered she was a prostitute. He'd
been stunned, but that reaction had been nothing compared to
the discovery that she'd been murdered two days before—on
the very evening of the day he'd seen her. He had never in all
of his life felt such acute grief. Nothing had been able to pen-
etrate it . . . except a sudden fear.

Though rumor had it that a blond-haired man was wanted
for questioning, a dark thought had occurred to Jedediah. Was
it possible that his wife had had something to do with the murder? She had pleaded a headache the evening in question and

had begged out of a social engagement, although she'd insisted he go on without her. When he'd returned, however, Ada had not answered his knock on the door of her private bedroom. The next day, she had said she'd taken a sedative and fallen into a deep slumber, although she looked strained, peaked, not like a woman who'd had a refreshing night's sleep. Though he'd refused to believe the worst of Ada—dear God, she was his wife! And how could he be sure she'd even known about the affair?—he nevertheless made a telling decision, one based on an instinctive fear for the safety of his child. Ada must never know the child she'd so briefly met had been fathered by him, and if she did know, she must never be allowed near her. With that in mind, he'd arranged for Trinity to be raised by a Chinese couple, and all during her childhood he had discreetly provided money for that purpose. Only with the greatest restraint had he kept his distance from her. When her acting career had begun to blossom, he'd been personally delighted. People with his money were expected to patronize the arts, and that had given him a valid excuse to be seen with his daughter.

Jedediah frowned. Maybe he'd paid her too much attention. After tonight, he couldn't doubt that Ada was suspicious. He never should have invited Trinity to dinner, but it had seemed like a safe thing to do, something that wouldn't draw undue attention with Breck's presence. Breck. Had he, his tongue loosened from too much drink, revealed something to Breck? No. Breck had said he hadn't. But would he have told him if he had?

A weary sigh beat against Jedediah's lips. He was tired. So tired. Tired of worrying about Ada, tired of wondering if he'd revealed something to Breck, tired of having to cover up his feelings for his daughter. Trinity. Asleep upstairs. The pink lips beneath the brush of the snow-white mustache smiled slightly. Tonight his daughter slept in his house. He hugged that warm fact close as the liquor lulled him toward his own slumber. Above the crackle of the fire, beyond the thrash of the rain, mingled with the soughing of the wind off the Bay, Jedediah heard Su-Ling's soft voice calling his name.

"Jedediah . . . Jedediah . . . my darling Jedediah . . ."

A single tear rolled from beneath a closed eyelid, and his heart felt so full of love, so full of grief, so full of regret, that he thought it would surely burst.

"Su-Ling," he whispered, then said no more, for in that single name was contained every note of his heartbeat, every note of his soul's sad song.

Upstairs, in a bedroom she had long ago ceased to share with her husband, Ada McCook likewise sat pondering the past. In particular, one never-to-be-forgotten sliver of it. It had been a hot summer evening in Sacramento. She could still smell the Saturday night fever in the air, could still hear the boasts and ribald shouts coming from the bordello's patrons. She'd never been inside a bordello before, and its interior had surprised her—actually, it had been very homey-looking—just as her being able to slip in the back door unnoticed had surprised her. Even more surprising was how simple it had been to locate Su-Ling. Money bought everything . . . including fast answers to questions about where a Chinese woman named Su-Ling lived. A merchant whose shop was on the street where they'd met Su-Ling had given her the information she needed, including the fact that her room was at the far back of the ground floor of the brothel. She hadn't questioned how he'd known this last fact, though she had questioned him about the child, of which he'd known little. Not even her name.

Su-Ling.

She'd never intended to kill her, truly she hadn't, but she had never regretted doing so. Of course, she had known of her husband's affair—a woman knew these things. She'd known practically to a night the first time he'd taken his employee at the dry goods store to bed. She'd also known the moment she'd seen the child that she was Jedediah's. Fearing he would acknowledge the child as his and thereby jeopardize their social standing and his political career, both of which she'd worked long and hard to cultivate, she'd gone to see Su-Ling simply to talk with her, to try to persuade her to leave town with the child. She'd even offered her money. A lot of money. Every penny of which Su-Ling—stupid creature that she was!—had refused. She'd grown angry, Su-Ling afraid. When Su-Ling had produced a knife, a scuffle had resulted, and Su-Ling had been killed.

Even now, she sometimes dreamed about the small body sprawled across the floor, and about the way Su-Ling's blood had felt upon her hands. Moist. Warm. Sticky. Even now, she could hear the woman's gurgled whispering of Jedediah's name. Her husband's name on another woman's lips, on a dying woman's lips—a prostitute's lips—had instantly hardened her. Before that, deep in her heart, she had been hurt by Jedediah's betrayal. If she had been younger or prettier, would he have continued to love her? Would he have continued to care if she'd given him a child? After she'd heard his name on Su-Ling's lips, all feeling for him had died, as surely as Su-Ling had died. She was glad she'd destroyed the one thing that meant the most to him. She would have destroyed the child, too, but she'd disappeared—totally, completely—from the face of the earth.

When Jedediah, a scant year and a half before, had turned his attention to the stage, she hadn't thought much about it. When he'd increasingly singled out Trinity Lee as the object of his interest, she had started worrying. Did her husband have a penchant for Oriental women? Were they having an affair? Or did he simply remind him of a woman he'd once loved? Or— the thought clotted her blood, as it always did—was Trinity Lee his daughter? Jedediah's political future might tolerate an errant affair, but never would it tolerate a bastard daughter. Nor would she.

Unconsciously, as she had that night so long ago, Ada smeared her palms down the skirt of her gown, as if trying to remove the bloodstains. Power. Her secret—that it was she who had killed Su-Ling—gave her power, the way unshared secrets often did. It was just she and her power against the world. It was a power she would need to do what she must. It was a power that, unlike Jedediah, wouldn't betray her.

Breck removed the detachable collar and cuffs from the tucked, starched shirt and tossed them onto the dressing table. After a few more deft manipulations, he had stripped the shirt off and recklessly flung it to join his frock coat, which was draped haphazardly over the back of a chair.

Everything made sense, he thought, ambling toward the fire warming the room. At the hearth, he propped a boot on a bucket of extra wood and absently raked his fingers through the golden mass of hair on his chest. Damn it, everything made sense! He had known that Su-Ling loved an older, married man, an American, and that he was the father of her child, though Breck had never known the child's name. Su-Ling had never mentioned it; he'd assumed it was her way of sheltering the child. Jedediah had to be that man, and, somehow, his wife must have found out about Su-Ling and killed her. But did Jedediah know Ada had murdered Su-Ling? No, that Breck couldn't believe. Jedediah never would have stayed with her had he known.

The flames hissed and popped and seemed to ask the question that was most important of all. Did Ada know Trinity was Jedediah's child? She had certainly gone on a fishing expedition that evening. But had she caught what she'd wanted? And what would she, a woman capable of killing, do if she had? He suddenly didn't like the way Ada had pressed Trinity into staying the night. He didn't like it one bit. He—

A sound threaded its shallow way forward into his consciousness.

Breck cocked his head to hear above the noise of the fire. Silence. Followed by more silence. He had just convinced himself he'd been mistaken when he heard the sound again.

A whimper.

A cry.

A low, tortured moan.

All coming from the adjacent room.

Chapter Nine

The room was dark except for gentle splashes of firelight. Breck, his body poised in a wary stance, his muscles taut with tension, stood at the door, the irises of his eyes widening in quick adjustment. Shadowy shapes filled in the murky landscape and jumped out to capture his attention—the rearing up of a mammoth canopied bed, the hulking squat of a dressing table, the crouching of an occasional chair. Beyond that ... nothing. Absolutely nothing. No sinister scene. No menacing murder. No Ada standing over Trinity with a gleaming steel knife.

Breck was chiding himself for his fanciful imagination when the sound came again, a soft, hurting groan that seemed more animal than human. It reminded him of a coyote he'd once found caught in the intractable jaws of a trap. Then, as now, the pathetic cry had ripped at his heart. Focusing harder, he sought the figure in the bed, a silhouetted heap in the room's thick grayness. Just like the imprisoned coyote, Trinity fought her captor by thrashing and flailing, twisting and turning.

She was dreaming, Breck thought, and started toward her. He never once questioned why he was involving himself in something private, in something that breached his mind-your-own-business loner's philosophy. Instead, he gave instinct the lead, raked back the net curtain, and eased down on the side of the wide, quilted bed.

Her black hair spilled over the pillow like ink flowing across satin, except that her hair looked far more satiny than the finest of fabrics and left Breck wondering, as he had during her performance weeks before, what it would feel like to have his hands buried within the ebony tresses. Deep within. She whimpered, drawing his attention to her parted lips. Her lips grimaced as the dream phantoms pursued her.

"Trinity," he called softly, the name rumbling from his broad, bare chest.

The dream was always the same. Her mother lay on the floor in a pool of her own blood, blood that was scarlet and smelled sickly-sweet. The stranger, pale-haired and with eyes a cool, distant blue, stood watching the child consumed with fear.

"Come here, little girl," he whispered. *"Come here...come here...come here...."*

Trinity moaned as the man in the dream advanced toward her, his hand outstretched and covered with blood, all except for the starlike white scar, which remained sacredly, malevolently untouched.

"Trinity," he called again, and on some plane of consciousness she thought how very real the voice sounded. Was he calling her by name? He'd never called her by name before. "Trinity," came the sound once more, and this time she was reminded of the way Breck had spoken her name earlier in the parlor—that soft, low, drawled rendition that had caused warning bells to clang in her head, simply because her name on his lips had sounded as sensual as the rustle of silk over skin.

Danger.

The man in the dream was stalking her, reaching out, out, out.... As his fingers closed around her arms—God, they felt so real!—she cried out a muffled "No! No, please..."

The hands began to shake her.

She fought, trying to shove the manacles away.

"Trinity..."

"No!"

"...you're dreaming."

"No! Please..."

The hands, tight bands of steel, pulled her from the smothered warmth of the bed to a sitting position. She came instantly awake with a gasp. Before her loomed the shadow-shrouded face of Breck—dark, intent, as frightening as a night warrior.

Breck took in her tumbled hair, the glistening sheen of moisture on her brow, the whimpers, the cries, the reedy rush of air still pouring from her trembling lips. She looked consummately vulnerable.

"Shh," he whispered, enveloping her in his arms and pulling her to him. Again he acted on instinct, without self-examination.

As he fitted her to his chest, Trinity fought to sweep away the vestiges of the nightmare, but her sleep-muddled mind could manage only to think how strange it was that the man who had frightened her in the dream was the same man who was comforting her now, and how strange that something deep within her told her she was safe with him. Stranger yet was the fact that her arms, after a tentative brush with his bare back, encircled him and clung...clung as tightly as he was clinging to her.

Breck felt the softness of her shoulders beneath his palms, felt the fullness of her breasts against his chest through the embroidered chemise she wore, felt the rich, tangled cascade of her hair caress the backs of his hands. She smelled of field flowers and fresh rain and the cuddly warmth of a sleeping woman. Her breath was still coming in fear-riddled hitches. Mingled with the breaths were occasionally needy whimpers.

"Shh," he murmured, smoothing his hands across her back in a rhythm of solace he'd had no idea he knew. No one had ever offered him any solace, and in turn he'd never offered any to another. Until now.

Like a kitten being stroked, she turned her head, fitting her face into the curve of his neck. Her breath was hot and filled with soft little sounds that rained against his skin. Irresistible little sounds that tugged sweetly at his senses. Unknowingly, unthinkingly, he turned his face toward hers.

"Shh," he whispered, and their breath merged. "Shh," he repeated, angling his head downward.

In a response as old as time, as everlasting as man and woman, Trinity lifted her head, instinctively seeking, searching.

"Shh," he whispered, brushing the sound across her parted lips again and again until—God, was he really going to do this? Yes, he was!—his mouth lingered and melted into hers. As warm flesh met warm flesh, unspoken need, unknown need, met its counterpart.

This time the sounds singing from her lips were not born of fear but of something she could not name. The word *pleasure* might have occurred to her had she had enough experience with men to recognize its sweet symptoms, but men were something she kept politely, comfortably, at arm's length.

Breck sipped at the nameless song, pulling it into his mouth the way he'd wanted to devour her cries. In a way, his mouth was as virginal as hers. He'd had his share of women, but when you paid for the easing of an ache, the subtleties of kissing mattered little. There were better ways to get your money's worth. Faster ways. Ways that left you alone that much sooner. He now kissed Trinity as if he were starved for something he'd only that moment discovered.

Curving his palm along her cheek, he tilted her face to better align her lips with his. When his tongue penetrated her mouth, Trinity whimpered again, this time at the strange sensations spiraling through her. Breck, too, felt the licking of a fire deep in his hair-dusted belly. He groaned and slid his fingers into the satin of her hair, which felt softer, warmer, more beckoning, than any woman's body, however intimately joined with his, had ever felt.

Trinity's senses had so smoothly gone from sleep to sensuality that her brain buzzed with feeling rather than reason. She opened her mouth to this man, her enemy, as though he were a cherished lover. Her hands glided across his unclothed back, luxuriating in the heat of his body, the swell of muscle, the ridge of ribs, even as she basked in the feel of his chest hair abrading the delicate buds of her breasts. She wanted, needed, something she could not imagine, could not define.

On the other hand, Breck knew exactly what he needed—the word *want* never once crossed his mind, for it was not a word he used with women—and the raw power of that need so frightened him that he trembled. Wrenching his mouth from hers, he simply stared. At the woman staring back at him. A woman whose lips were parted and still moist from his marauding mouth. A woman whose eyes were wide. Wide and familiar. Familiar because they were the eyes of a child he'd seen eighteen years before. Did she remember that night? If she did, what exactly did she remember?

And, dear heaven, when had he ever needed anything as badly as he needed to bed her?

"Are—are you all right?" he asked, deliberately breaking all physical contact with her. The strap of her chemise had fallen off her shoulder, leaving the thin fabric snagged on the roundness of her breast in a way that was, depending on one's frame of mind, either a threat or a promise. To Breck, it was a definite threat.

Trinity nodded, though she wasn't remotely certain she was all right.

"You . . . you were dreaming," he said, in explanation of everything, in explanation of nothing. Still Trinity remained mute. The silence was broken only by two sets of ragged breathing. Suddenly, because he was unaccustomed to the intensity of the pain gripping his loins, because he *was* accustomed to needing only on his own terms, Breck swore, darkly, viciously, and hurled himself from the bed. Without another word, he crossed to the door and out of the room.

Trinity was left with an erratic heartbeat, dewy lips that felt bruised and mercilessly abandoned, and two questions she hadn't the least answer to.

What in God's name had just happened?

And why had she let it?

They were questions Trinity asked often in the days that followed. Always, her answer, though feeble, was that she'd been half-asleep. Which led to the natural conclusion that Breck had taken advantage of her, a circumstance that served her conscience well, since the best way to minimize her complicity was to maximize his. In unguarded moments, however, a sense of guilt would betray her, and she would be left with another stark, uncomfortable question. If she didn't believe herself somewhat responsible, at least responsible in the sense of having responded, why did she feel guilty? And what about the tingly feelings the memory of his kiss inspired?

All in all, she spent the days looking forward, for behind lay only confusion—not only Breck's kiss, but also Ada Mc-Cook's curious behavior, which had carried over into the morning after that strange night. All during breakfast, Trinity had had the feeling she was again being grilled, subtly and not so subtly, about her parents. It was Jedediah himself who'd called for the buggy to carry her back to her hotel. As she prepared to leave the mansion, her eye had caught the eye of the man coming down the stairway, and her heart had seemed to forget how to beat. Neither she nor Breck had spoken. They'd only looked at each other . . . and remembered.

Two days before she was scheduled to return to Virginia City for the Territorial Ball, and therefore two days before the next robbery she had planned, she received a letter from Ellie Oates. It was as chatty as the woman herself:

. . . the town is in a dither preparing for the ball. A parade is planned down C Street. The Miners Band, a motley collection of little-to-no talent, is actually rehearsing so that hopefully (our prayers rise high and many!) they'll all be playing the same tune . . . or thereabouts. The school-teacher, a Mr. Higginbottom from back East, who clearly feels that being in Virginia City is a form of God's punishment, has even dismissed the children for the day, with the stipulation, however, that they learn the first three paragraphs of the Nevada constitution in deference to the governor's appearance. Victoria Dawson was said to give it such a dramatic reading she's been selected to perform it before the governor himself. Mamma Dawson beamed with pride until someone suggested her daughter's future might lie with the stage. I for one hope she's the next greatest thing to Trinity Lee—wouldn't that serve Mamma her just deserts?

Speaking of the Dawsons, did I tell you I saw the good ol' doc? Or rather that I was forced to? I told Neil about the baby (Oh, Trinity, he actually cried! Imagine me being lucky enough to find such a man!) and he whisked me off to Doc Dawson, who told me I was pregnant—then charged for telling me what I told him first. (The practice of medicine obviously lies in the art of listening.) He then proceeded to sling the news to the four far corners of the town and did such a thorough job of it that—and I swear this to be true—Maude Terrill was waiting on my door-step to wish me congratulations when I returned from Doc D's office. Incidentally, she brought me the most god-awful persimmon jelly.

Oh, we've had another bit of excitement since you left. Someone fired at the engineer, old Charlie Knott. Didn't hit him, but scared another few scriptural remarks from Dancey Harlan. Breck thinks it was the work of the rob-bers. Or maybe the robber. He told Neil, confidentially, that maybe it's only one person dressing up like a gang. He also told Neil, again confidentially, that the next payroll shipment will be carrying almost twice as much money as before. Poor Breck. My heart aches for him.

Well, I must close, but I look forward to your arrival. Safe journey.

It was the penultimate paragraph that enticed Trinity's interest. Two snippets of the news she was already familiar with—that the engineer had been shot at and that Breck suspected a single person was behind the robberies. She hadn't had the chance to pursue either topic, and neither sat comfortably. Who else wanted to hurt Breck? And why? And how much more careful did she have to be, since he was suspicious of only one person's involvement in the robberies? These questions were nothing, however, compared to the excitement that bubbled in her veins as she read the last of her friend's letter.

Twice as much money on the shipment?

Twice as much money meant twice as much revenge. Which, in turn, meant twice as much satisfaction. Ellie's letter still clasped in her hand, Trinity renewed her commitment to destroy, financially and physically, Madison Brecker. She didn't ask herself why the renewal of her pledge was so fervently important. She was afraid that if she did, the answer would come back, *Because you feel guilty—guilty because you like the way your enemy's lips feel pressed to yours.*

"You best be boarding, Miss Lee," Dancey Harlan said at the Reno station, his voice a frosted mist in the stringent November air. "We'll be pulling out shortly."

Trinity brushed a tie of her brown velveteen bonnet back from her cheek, where the careless wind had blown it. Ahead to her right, the locomotive, as though it were a chained beast raring to break free, impatiently puffed a column of milky smoke into the cloudless blue sky.

"Thank you, Mr. Harlan," she said, falling into step beside the massively built conductor and taking one last quick but thorough look at the baggage car hitched to the front of Jedediah's coach.

Oliver Truxtun, looking like a hawk perched in a tree, had stationed himself before the door. His stance suggested that he'd be riding shotgun on the payrolls during the last leg—the Sierra Virginia leg—of the journey. Trinity had disembarked,

ostensibly to take a breath of fresh air while the private coach
was switched from the Central Pacific to the shorter line. In
truth, however, she'd gone on a scouting mission. She hoped
to catch a glimpse of the payrolls being loaded. Was there, indeed, the increased amount everyone was whispering about,
and what added precautions, if any, had been taken? Unfortunately, she'd uncovered little. She had just missed the payroll's boarding, and, though she'd strolled the platform
numerous times, she'd seen nothing that hinted at added precautions. Which concerned her a little. Wouldn't twice the
money demand twice the protection?

"Tell me, Mr. Harlan," she said, bringing her dark-fringed
eyes to his, "is the rumor true? I mean, the one about carrying
all that extra money?"

Dancey lowered his gravelly voice conspiratorially as he pre-
pared to repeat the lie he'd spoken so often he was half begin-
ning to think it truth. "Between you and me, ma'am, it is."
Trinity allowed her eyes to widen with just a hint of concern.
"There, there, it's nothing for you to worry yourself about.
You're as safe as if you were in the arms of an angel."

Trinity, too, halved her voice, as if the two were sharing the
utmost of secrets. "That is the Pinkerton agent at the door of
the baggage car, isn't it?"

"Yes, ma'am, and there he'll stay. Armed to the hilt."

"What a brave man he is. Why, I'd probably surround myself with a dozen other agents."

"No one's gonna get by Truxtun," Dancey said, not really
addressing the possibility of other agents. His response did,
however, make her wonder how she was going to get past the
armed guard if no one else could.

"Why, thank you," Trinity said, taking the hand the black-
clad conductor offered and stepping onto the porch of the private car.

"We'll stop in Carson City for fifteen minutes, then arrive
in Virginia City by midafternoon."

With any luck, minus the payrolls, she thought, her eyes
drawn to the thin stream of gray trailing from the smokestack
of the baggage car. Obviously, the potbellied stove had been
stoked to drive away the building chill. Potbellied stove. Suddenly, an idea stepped from the shadows. Would it work? Possibly. The chances were at least favorable enough that she

smiled and said, "It's frightfully cold, isn't it, Mr. Harlan? Do you think it's going to snow?"

"I reckon, like God's grace, it ain't too far away." He tipped the rim of his visored cap, turned, and walked back along the platform. She watched him for a moment, noting that a man was coaxing a large black-and-white dog up the steps of the far passenger car. She didn't think it unusual, probably because she was too busy wondering whether her plan would work. And whether God's grace extended to someone whose heart was as black with hate as hers.

As though the jerky, fitful motion of the train was her cue, Trinity, ensconced within the privacy of her car, began to unfasten the buttons of her dress. Before her, methodically laid out on the bed, were various articles of men's clothing. Beside them lay a gun, a bag holding a plethora of theatrical makeup, a man's wig, and a huge roll of cotton batting. As her breasts threatened to tumble from her chemise, she reached for the roll of fabric.

Breck, too, reached—for the rail of the moving baggage car. Running a couple of steps alongside the train, he hauled himself up. He'd waited until the last possible second to board, hoping to avoid attention. He didn't want anyone to know, save those in on the plan, that he was on board.

"You cut it close," Oliver Truxtun said, bracing himself against the rattling sway of the car.

"I intended to," Breck answered, immediately twisting the knob on the door of the baggage compartment. The *ker-chung, ker-chung* of wheels over track sailed into the slender interior. Dick Kingsman looked up sharply, his hand folding around the gun slung awkwardly from his hip. When he saw who it was, his hand relaxed, though nervous energy still filled his gray eyes. "Kingsman, you trade places with Truxtun."

"But I thought—" Truxtun began.

"You're more valuable inside," Breck said tersely, cutting him off. "Kingsman, you stand guard here. Put up enough resistance to make it look good, but let the sonofabitch in if he shows up. Think you can do that?"

"Yes, sir," Kingsman said around a smile that trembled more than it curved.

"Why not pull the guard from the door entirely?" Truxtun asked.

"Uh-uh. That'd look too suspicious. Someone hit three times, carrying a large sum the fourth time out, would have a guard posted. We don't want to spook our pigeon away."

"You're not only laying a trap, you're inviting him in," Truxtun said, his prematurely gray mustache twitching in what Breck surmised was probably as close to a grin as the man came. But then, Breck had never seen a hawk smile. "Ever consider working for Pinkerton?" the agent asked.

"I may have to if the bastard outsmarts us again," Breck replied without an ounce of amusement. Turning back to Dick Kingsman, he said, "Remember, let him in. And don't get yourself hurt."

"Yes, sir," the baggageman replied. With adrenaline-driven excitement, he added, "We'll get him this time, sir."

"Yeah," Breck said darkly, feeling the weight of the Remington .44 that hugged his lean hip. "This time."

Time.

Like a lazy, meandering snail, it passed. Carson City came and went, and everyone grew restless. Dancey Harlan went about the business of conducting with half an eye, while Charlie Knott and Abe Dustin, one as he drove the engine, the other as he fed its voracious appetite, kept their ears peeled for anything suspicious. Which was precisely what Sheriff Lou Luckett, in accordance with Breck's plan, was in search of—anything suspicious. Or anything his dog, a vicious, growling mongrel named Ugly, found suspicious. In a town that hired only the roughest and toughest outsiders as lawmen—they were the only ones who stood a chance of lasting a full day pitted against frontier violence—Lou Luckett enjoyed an impressive reputation. He kept the jails filled more regularly than any sheriff before him. Due to his singularly unattractive features, many said he "uglied" the culprits behind bars, and that the only way you could tell him from his dog was by the badge on his chest.

As Sheriff Luckett prowled, fingers of disappointment clutched Maude Terrill's heart. They were nearabouts to home, all the way to Virginia City, and no robbery yet...even though her hopes had doubled along with the reported shipment. So hopeful had she been that she'd packed a pair of her finest cotton drawers. Though heaven only knew she would faint dead away to have her vaporous sensibilities abused again by the knowledge that for the second time a strange man had touched her most intimate apparel—the delicate fabric, the lace, the naughty red ribbon she'd used instead of the more ladylike pink. Why, to touch her drawers was very much the same as touching her, for behind that thin fabric had lain her soft skin . . . and the lace . . . why, it had teased places that . . . well, places that a woman, a lady, hardly thought of, let alone spoke of . . . and the red ribbon . . . why, its color was as hot as she sometimes felt . . . inside . . . in unspeakable places . . . as hot as a windows-open-all-the-way summer night . . . as hot as fireworks exploding on the Fourth of July . . . as hot as . . .

"Will you quit fidgeting?" Dub Terrill said at her elbow.

Maude jumped guiltily and fumbled with the jar of persimmon jelly in her lap.

"And watch that lip-pouting jelly."

"You're a mean-spirited man, Dub Terrill," his wife sniffed righteously, though ever so breathlessly.

Dick Kingsman, too, was caught up in a daydream. He couldn't wait to tell Victoria Dawson—Vicky, she'd told him to call her—how Mr. Brecker had chosen him to ride guard. *Well, yes, it was a dangerous thing to do. Scared? Hell, no—I mean, heck, no, I wasn't scared. . . .*

Inside the stove-heated baggage car, Oliver Truxtun neither dreamed nor spoke. Indeed, he and Breck had spoken only sparingly throughout the whole journey. They had simply waited. Then waited some more. Ordinarily, the waiting didn't bother him. It was ninety percent of a detective's job. But today it was frazzling his nerves. He wanted these men, this man, simply because they, he, had proven to be such a worthy opponent. He hadn't been able to turn up anything that even resembled a clue, and that galled him. Professionally. Privately. And at every point in between.

Breck, his hip casually propped against a crate of fresh vegetables, his boot nonchalantly hooked over the edge of an adjacent box, felt the claws of tension raking along every vertebra of his spine. Damn it, he was tired of waiting for something to happen! Passing a hand over his fatigued eyes, he sighed. God, he *was* tired. Of everything. Of worrying. Of working long into the night simply because he was afraid that if he didn't, he'd think about things he didn't want to. Things like a woman whose soft sighs and softer lips had done things to him—powerful, confusing things. Things he'd done a good job of refusing to confront until . . . until he'd seen her walking along the platform in Reno. The need for her had come back, swift and consuming, and he'd been left feeling... Jesus, he didn't know how he had felt! He only knew he didn't want to think about it.

Not now.

Not ever.

He snatched a cheroot from the inside pocket of his jacket, lit up, and watched a stream of smoke coil from his pursed lips... lips that betrayed him by remembering a woman's kiss.

A car away, Trinity tested the black mustache bushing above her upper lip and, finding the glue set, reached for the black mask, which she tied around her eyes. Their sherry hue showed through the oval slits, though there was no hint whatsoever of the epicanthic fold. Good, she thought, forcing herself to calmly go over the revised plans. The Pinkerton agent standing watch at the door probably meant that Dick Kingsman was inside. Poor Dick Kingsman. She'd have to find a quiet way to make all this up to him. Grabbing the unloaded gun and a roll of cotton batting, she headed for the door before her nerve failed. She allowed herself one last thought of Madison Brecker—in the abstract, as the object of her hate. She deliberately kept at bay the concrete Madison Brecker, the one whose lips, one dark of night, she'd intimately tasted.

The biting cold instantly pricked her cheeks. Ignoring the discomfort, she heaved herself from the landing of the private car to that of the baggage car. From there, employing the steel grab irons, she shinnied up the side of the car and onto its top. Spread-eagled, she hugged the roof, feeling the jostling motion shimmer through her. She also felt the painful imprint of the gun tucked in the waistband of her pants biting into her stomach. The wind, flecked with soot and cinders, most of which came from the nearby smokestack, whipped at her senses, and she partially shuttered her eyelids before starting to crawl forward. Carefully, silently, she inched toward the smokestack, where she stuffed the cotton batting into the flue. She then edged toward the side of the car and proceeded to wait. And to pray. And to fight the uneasiness that had begun earlier, when she'd realized that the lone agent was the only protection the increased shipment had. She couldn't seem to shake the feeling.

Inside the car, Breck crushed out his cheroot after only a few puffs. Even so, the smell of smoke hung in the air. He noticed it only peripherally, intent as he was on nursing the impatience flooding his body. When? Damn it, when was the sonofabitch going to make a move? A crazy thought occurred to him. What if he didn't make a move? What if after all this planning . . . Damn, he had to get a breath of fresh air or explode into a million pieces!

"I'm going to check on Kingsman," he said, crossing the floor.

Truxtun nodded and skirted a cough. Then he gave in to it. He leaned his shoulder against the wall and waited. Seconds passed. He coughed again, this time inhaling a thick, viscous knot of smoke. He glanced toward the potbellied stove, which was suddenly spewing a blizzard of white. What the hell? A malfunctioning stove was just about the last complication they needed. Stifling an oath and a cough behind his hand, Truxtun stepped forward warily. Seeking ventilation, he reached to slide back the side door of the car, inched it open two feet, and received exactly that in the face for his effort. Two feet. Two booted feet. Stunned, the agent stumbled and fell to his back. He snatched at his gun, but even though Trinity had to yank hers from the waist of her pants—she'd had to use both hands to swing herself down from the top of the car—she outdrew him.

"I wouldn't if I were you," she told him, her voice deep and masculine. She pointed the gun directly between his dark eyes. She thought she saw a quick flash of admiration before it was covered by a black emotion that had everything to do with staring up the nose of another's gun from the embarrassing position of being flat on his back.

At the realization it was Truxton who lay before her, the uneasiness Trinity had been fighting doubled. Why hadn't he remained at the door? What was he doing inside the car? And where was Dick Kingsman? She looked around quickly, saw no one, and, despite the hammering of her heart, motioned for the agent to rise.

"The money," she said, automatically glancing toward the safe. "And let's take that gun out of the holster real slow and easy and toss it through the crack in the door."

Pushing himself upward from the cold wooden floor, Truxtun rose with a cocky, stare-her-right-in-the-eye confidence that Trinity found disconcerting. She swallowed, felt her palms grow wet within the leather gloves, and wished to God she were a thousand miles away. Something just didn't seem quite right.

"C'mon, move!" she bellowed, jerking the gun, which her other hand now helped support. The weapon had suddenly grown heavier. Or had her arm grown weaker? "The gun," Trinity reminded him.

Slowly, he drew it, hesitated as if he hated parting with a friend, then threw it outside.

"Now the money." Instead of stepping to the safe as she'd expected, Oliver Truxtun nodded toward something behind her.

"The money's there," he said, and Trinity thought she heard a smooth note of satisfaction in his voice. She dared a quick look over her shoulder. A plain wooden box, some four feet by five, sat in all its common, ordinary splendor. Trinity's uneasiness grew a size larger. The smoke was beginning to sting her eyes, too.

"Open it," she ordered, easing away and instinctively placing herself nearer the back door, through which she'd once exited before, preparing for a fast getaway.

"Certainly," Oliver Truxtun said willingly. Too willingly? Moving forward, the agent flipped open the lid of the box. It creaked, and the noise seemed strangely muffled in the veil of smoke filling the car. Trinity fought back a cough as she watched the man, without being told, untie one of the three bags in the chest. A jingling sound danced through the room. An unnerving jingling sound. Then, to her horror, she saw Oliver Truxtun reach inside the bag and draw out a handful of gold coins, which he let dribble—smugly—through his talon-like fingers. "If you can carry it," the hawk said with the greatest of pleasure, "you can have it."

A trap.

The silent words thundered throughout the car, borne along on every innocent *clickety-clack* of the rocking, pitching train. She'd been set up. Trinity fought back the scalding rush of panic that jumped into her throat.

Easy. Easy. Just take it easy, she told herself, stepping toward the back door. The gloating smile on Oliver Truxtun's face seemed like a hand pushing her backward.

"I feel it only fair to warn you," he said, "you can't get out that door. It's been bolted from the outside."

Trinity ignored the remark and tried the door. It was bolted. Tightly. Which was pretty much the way her breath felt in her chest. Tight. Too tight. So tight she couldn't breathe. She fought to keep a clear head. *Options. What were her options?* Exiting through the sliding door would require more agility than she had. The back door was out. That left only the front door. Where Dick Kingsman stood guard? Perhaps, but it was a risk she'd have to take. Quickly she crossed the room and, motioning for the agent to stay back, she eased open the door. The monotonous song of rail and wheel greeted her ears, while nothing—no one—greeted her eyes.

Thank God!

Her Colt revolver trained on the Pinkerton agent, she backed out of the baggage car. One step. Another. Then another. Freedom was only one more step away when she backed right into the hard steel nose of a gun. The pressure thrusting it forward was mean and uncompromising and unmistakably unforgiving.

"Welcome aboard the Sierra Virginia," she heard a dark, dangerous-sounding, and all-too-familiar voice growl.

Chapter Ten

Trinity's heart dropped to her feet, while fear rushed to her head.

Please, God, a tiny voice within her bargained, *if you'll just get me out of this, I vow never to rob another train.*

"Move," Breck snarled, the gun digging deep into Trinity's back, leaving her to conclude that God must be tied up somewhere else. Stumbling forward at the painful command, she grimaced—and wished she could slap away the smug smile tugging at Oliver Truxtun's lips. She also wondered what it felt like to get shot. Funny, why had she never considered that before? Would it burn? Would there be an overwhelming pain? Would she be able to stand it? Or— Or would he simply kill her dead out? For that matter, she was surprised he hadn't already. Clemency wasn't Madison Brecker's strong suit.

Dear heaven, what was he doing on the train?

Laying a trap for you, idiot.

"Just put the gun on the crate," he drawled, "and then turn around." When she hesitated, he snarled, "Now!" and buried the gun another inch between her shoulder blades.

Trinity was on the verge of complying—what choice did she have?—when abruptly, without warning, the train's brakes screeched and shrieked. The cars shuddered and trembled, metal moaned, and the train threatened to jackknife before it wrestled itself to an unsettled stop. In one of the passenger cars, on something between a curse and a prayer, Dancey Harlan was hurled into an unoccupied seat, while the passengers in both cars, some screaming at the top of their lungs, were thrown from theirs. Packages and parcels from the overhead racks tumbled into the aisles and onto a tangle of squirming arms and legs. At the bottom of the heap sprawled Lewis Rice Bradley, the distinguished governor of the state of Nevada. Nearby, Maude Terrill, catapulted from both seat and daydream, sat squarely on her backside, while her jar of persimmon jelly crashed at her feet. It landed in the path of Sheriff Luckett, who, along with his snarling, sure-footed dog, was one of the few people left standing.

"Boulder on the track!" came the word from the front of the train. From the back echoed Dick Kingsman's cry: "The train's been robbed!" Both fevered announcements caused a swell of excitement at the midpoint where they met.

Assuming the first pronouncement to be tied to the latter, Sheriff Luckett hastened, as much as was possible under the circumstances, toward the baggage car. En route he struck a patch of persimmon jelly with the heel of his boot and, nearly somersaulting in the air, fell into Maude Terrill's lap.

Maude Terrill screamed and threatened to faint dead away.

"Sorry, ma'am," the ugly sheriff apologized, trying to rise but doing nothing more than touching Maude Terrill in places she'd been touched only in daydreams.

Maude Terrill blanched. Sheriff Luckett blushed. And Dub Terrill tried to drag his wife's dress down over her exposed modesty.

"Sorry, sorry," the sheriff chanted as he shuffled to his feet. "C'mon, Ugly," he said, trying to pull the dog forward by the wrinkled nape of its furry neck. The dog, curious about the sticky pink substance, took a lick. Its mouth instantly puckered. So ugly was the dog naturally that the pucker smoothed out the unattractive features until, for once, they were pleasantly tolerable to look at. Whining pitifully, the animal repeatedly cuffed its paws up and down its snout as if hoping somehow to remove the acidic taste.

"Damn it, c'mon!" Lou Luckett barked, but the meanest dog in the Comstock Lode only puled and pawed.

Chaos reigned equally in the baggage car. In the moments of pandemonium when the train had jostled to a hollering halt, Oliver Truxtun, Breck, and Trinity had all been knocked off their feet. Trinity's hip slammed into the wooden floor, and pain, sharp and clear, shuddered through her lower body. The gun fell from her hand and skittered across the floor. It disappeared in the cloud of smoke that seemed to be crowding every corner and crevice of the car with its hazy, stinging presence.

She could hear Truxtun coughing, and her own throat tickled with the same need. Even as she automatically rolled from her hip onto her back, something told her this was the fateful intervention she'd prayed for...and that she'd better make the most of it, because she wouldn't get another.

That in mind, she half crawled, half scampered toward the door. Breck's hand, coming out of nowhere, ensnared her ankle and jerked. The air whooshed from her lungs as her chest struck the floor. Struggling, she kicked her leg free and took another couple of crawls forward. This time an arm, a band of mighty steel, encircled her waist and literally yanked her through the air and threw her flat on her back. What little breath she had left fled, leaving her dazed and gasping and certain she was going to die from the empty feeling in her chest. Or from the cold, murderous look she saw when her brown eyes met the blue of Breck's.

"No," she whispered, trying to shove him away, but she was no match for his strength, which suddenly seemed to fit all along the length of her as he fell atop her. She felt his hard, broad chest smothering her, felt his stomach aligned with hers, felt his masculinity, large and bold beneath the denim of his pants, crushing into the tender cradle of her feminine body. His hand reached up to yank the mask from her eyes. She thrashed her head from side to side—miraculously, the wig didn't budge from her head—as a new desperation seized her. He mustn't discover who she was! From somewhere deep within her, she found one last ounce of strength. Bringing her knee upward, she jammed it between his legs. At contact, the bulge of his masculinity shifted and rode unnaturally—and what had to be painfully—high.

Baring his teeth, Breck rolled from her, doubled over in a knot, and uttered an obscenity that Trinity had never heard spoken aloud before. Taking advantage of the distraction, she scrambled to her feet and, alternating between weaving and falling, hastened toward the door. From his bent position on the floor, Breck's fingers brushed against the cold steel of a gun. Grabbing it, he dragged himself to his knees and, ignoring the agony in his groin, aimed the weapon at the back of the fleeing man. It never once crossed his mind to maim; he intended to kill, which he knew he couldn't fail to do at such close range. The sweet taste of victory already on his tongue, he pulled the trigger.

Click.

Nothing. Nothing except the hollow sound of an unloaded gun discharging.

"Damn!" Breck bellowed, throwing down the pistol and frantically searching for his own in the soupy maze of the smoke-filled car. In the background he could hear the Pinkerton agent giving in to a spasmodic fit of coughing. His eyes and hands working in desperate harmony—he couldn't let the bastard get away!—Breck ferreted out and seized the Remington .44 from under the edge of a crate, whirled, aimed, and fired just as Trinity reached the door.

Suddenly it felt as if someone had driven a red-hot poker through her. Clutching her left side, she cried out and stumbled against the door, knocking the wig askew. For split seconds that seemed endless, astonishment and pain warred with the intuitive knowledge that she had to move. Fast! Now! To her right, through the chilled air gliding about her, she could hear the uproar from the passenger cars—any minute someone would burst through the door and discover her—while from her left came the sound of Breck's scrambling and Truxton's coughed "You hit him!" Acting on gut fear, running on pure adrenaline, she hurried from the still train and toward the private car. With each unsteady step, she prayed that no one could see her.

Once inside her coach, she leaned back against the door, her eyes closed, her breath coming rapidly, the burning in her side feeling now as if someone were holding an undying fire to her skin. A pulsation had begun. Not a pain, exactly, but an unnatural throbbing of her flesh.

"He can't have gotten far," she heard the Pinkerton agent say from what sounded like only feet away. "He took a slug in the side."

"Yeah, well," Breck said gruffly, breathlessly, as though he were perhaps still in pain from being kneed, "he's probably halfway back to hell by now. But check underneath the train anyway. And inside every car."

"Yes, sir," said someone Trinity thought must be an excited Dick Kingsman.

"Look for blood!" Breck shouted. Kingsman's reply was muffled.

"Think the boulder was accidental?" someone asked. "It could have rolled down—"

"As accidental as sin!" Dancey Harlan interjected.

"Not likely an accident," came another voice, behind which a dog growled.

"The boulder was to provide a getaway," Breck said, adding sarcastically, "which it did. Effectively." His booted feet crunched irritably into the earth, and when he spoke again, Trinity knew he was walking away from the private coach. "And see what the hell he used to clog the smokestack!"

Trinity heaved a deep sigh at the receding voices, but pain hitched the sigh in midbreath. Pushing away from the door, she forced herself into action. She had to get out of the disguise and back into her clothes. Somehow. Some way. Because someone might come to her door, and she had to be prepared to answer it. Tearing off the drooping wig, mustache, and mask, she started to slide the jacket from her shoulders. She gritted her teeth against the pain that jabbed at her and let the jacket fall to the floor. Even though she knew she had been shot, the blood smearing her knuckles startled her and made her stomach turn over. She looked down at the red stain blossoming on her shirt, and for a fractured second past and present blended, and she saw the image of her mother lying in a similar pool of crimson.

Trinity shook her head against the troubling memory and tugged the shirt from the waist of her pants. The motion caused a rush of blood, which she tried to stem with the hem of the shirt. With effort, with unsuccessfully muffled cries, she pulled the shirt over her head and quickly stripped away the cotton batting binding her breasts. They thrust forward, as though affronted by the callous treatment they'd received. The shirt in her hand, she stepped toward the mirror. Blotted the profuse blood. Stared. Turned. Stared again. The slug had entered her back and exited her abdomen right below the rib cage. As bad as the entry wound was, a hole the size of the end of her finger, the exit wound was worse; in leaving her body, the metal had ripped the flesh until it looked like a piece of freshly butchered meat.

Trinity fought back a wave of nausea, caused in part by the sight of the injury blaring from her stomach, in part by the knifelike pain now hacking through the burning ache. She stared as streams of red oozed down her side, across her belly, and into the waist of her pants.

Stark reality struck her: She'd been shot.
Dear God, what did she do now?

What she did was open the door minutes later when the brief but forceful knock came. She glanced up into Breck's almost translucent blue eyes. As always, they looked cold, aloof, making him appear unapproachable.

He had left her until last to check on simply because he'd wanted to check on her first. He excused his checking on her at all by telling himself maybe she'd seen something, heard something, that would give him some idea as to what had happened to the thief.

"Are you all right?" he asked instead, and wished he hadn't. He also wished the memory of her mouth hadn't intruded a thousand times in the days following that rainy night in San Francisco. Just as he wished it wasn't intruding now. He didn't want the memory of any woman cluttering up his life.

Trinity nodded. "Yes. I'm fine," she said, hoping her voice was even and her breathing didn't appear ragged. The searing, burning feeling had turned into out-and-out pain, the kind that started off like a dull roar and promised to convert into a sharp shout at any moment. She had stanched the blood as best she could with the cotton batting she'd removed from her breasts, but she feared it would seep through at some unguarded moment. "I'm fine," she repeated, as if she needed to hear it herself. "Just trying to stay out of everyone's way."

"He got away," Breck said, assuming that she, like everyone else aboard, knew there had been an attempted robbery. "You, uh . . . you didn't see, hear anything?"

"I heard a shot."

"Yeah, I hit him. I don't know how bad. I wish I'd killed the bastard." And he would have, he thought, if the man's gun hadn't been unloaded. Why would someone rob a train with an unloaded gun? Breck smiled maliciously. "Maybe I'll get lucky and he'll bleed to death."

Trinity's hand tightened on the edge of the door, a door she deliberately stood behind.

"Yes, well, I guess we could all use a little luck."

"Are you sure you're all right?" he asked again, noting her pallor for the first time.

She smiled and wondered if it looked as feeble as it felt. "I'm fine. I'm just not accustomed to this kind of excitement."

"We, uh . . . we should be on our way soon. If you need anything, let the conductor know."

"Thank you. I will."

He didn't leave. Why, neither knew. Both were aware, though, of another time, a time neither was comfortable remembering, much less mentioning. He had comforted her then. It was a comfort she desperately needed now. Even from the man who'd shot her. Particularly, though she knew not why, from the man who'd shot her. Because the pain was growing and growing. And because she was suddenly frightened. Frightened she might bleed to death.

"Mr. Brecker?" A voice from below carried upward. Breck turned toward Dick Kingsman, who bobbed his head politely at Trinity. "I'm sorry, sir, but Charlie wants to know if you're ready to get underway."

"Yeah," Breck answered roughly, as if angry with himself for standing there when he should be tending to business. He swung down to the ground. Glancing up at Trinity, he nodded in quick acknowledgment, then tromped off without a backward look.

Trinity watched him disappear, feeling curiously alone when he had. When she closed the door, it was just she and the pain, the fear. And the realization that the whole side of her dress was puddled in blood.

The train arrived to a festive, jubilant greeting from the Miners Band, but the disharmonious notes trailed away as news of the attempted robbery spread through the ranks of those congregated on the platform. As the governor disembarked, a horde swarmed him, wanting his comment concerning what he'd just been through.

"Villainous!" the former mule-trader, farmer, and cattle-raiser roared as he stroked the long, wavy gray beard hanging to the middle of his chest.

Trinity, smiling her way through the crowd that had gathered about her and giving an occasional shaky autograph, neither heard nor saw anything she could have recalled later. She simply felt—primarily pain, secondarily the sticky wetness concealed beneath her brown velveteen cloak. She'd started to change dresses but reasoned that she had nothing better than the batting, even though it was already soaked, to stanch the blood. Another dress would be ruined within minutes of her putting it on. No, she'd wait until she got to the hotel.

"Trinity!" Ellie called, waving her petite hand in the air.

Trinity plastered a smile, or a facsimile thereof, on her face. "Hi," she said, shielding herself as best she could from her friend's hug. Pain shafted through her nonetheless, and she trapped the cry behind gritted teeth.

"Can you believe it?" Ellie began. "The train robbed again! Or an attempted robbery, anyway. I mean, can you believe it? The nerve! The outrageous nerve! And the governor aboard. To say nothing of the Pinkerton agent and the sheriff. And Breck. Why, the man must be crazy!"

"Maybe he didn't know they were all aboard," Trinity said, offering nothing else. Which served the situation well, since Ellie seemed inclined to do all the talking, and since Trinity had discovered straightaway that she needed to conserve her energy. She'd never noticed before how far the hotel was from the station. But then, she'd never made the trip in gut-twisting pain. Increasingly, she grew clammy. Increasingly, she felt beads of perspiration, despite the cold winter air, pop out on her brow. Increasingly, she entertained the idea of fainting. If she could just make it to the hotel, she could rest. And maybe the bleeding would stop. Or at least ease up. She couldn't last if it didn't.

Finally the hotel came into view, and within agonized minutes the door stood open before her.

"I've already got your usual room," Ellie said as the two women stepped inside the Chastain. Then, bubbling with excitement, Ellie grabbed her friend and hugged her tightly. "I'm so glad you're here!" At Trinity's gasp, Ellie released her hold. "What is it?"

"Nothing," Trinity said, fighting to maintain her composure as pain scored each and every cell of her body. "I, uh . . . I think I bruised something when the train stopped unexpectedly. It threw me down."

"Let me get Doc Daw—"

"No! I mean, it's only a bruise."

"You look pale," Ellie said, touching Trinity's bleached cheeks with her fingertips.

"I'm all right. Just tired from the trip." She smiled wanly. "Too much excitement."

"What about tonight? Will you feel like—"

"I'll be fine after a rest. You don't mind if I rest this afternoon, do you?"

"Of course not. Listen, if you're not better by tonight, I'm going to get Doc Dawson. And I won't take no for an answer." The granite hardness of Ellie's green eyes stood behind every word she said.

"I'll be fine." At her friend's continued appraisal, she added, "Honest."

Five minutes later, when she and the maid were alone in the room, Trinity asked, "Will you do something for me?"

"Yes, ma'am, if I can."

Plowing through her purse, Trinity said, "Batting. I need some cotton batting. Lots of it." Without showing the least surprise at the request, the maid left to do the errand. Trinity eased to the edge of the bed, her cloak still about her, and carefully lay back. Despite her resolve not to cry, tears sprang to her eyes. She knew now what it felt like to get shot.

It hurt like hell.

That evening, Trinity wore an outrageously expensive scarlet gown created by the fashion designer Charles Frederick Worth, an Englishman working in Paris who had three queens among his clientele. Trinity, sharing the escort of Neil Oates, might well have been one of those queens when she entered the drawing room of the mansion where the Territorial Ball was being held. Whispered *ooh*s and *aah*s flitted about the room, and not a single man was oblivious to her arrival.

Not even Breck. Who cursed himself for noticing her. Just the way he'd cursed himself a hundred times for showing up at a party he had no desire to attend. He'd had little choice, however. As a serious businessman, it behooved him to associate with the governor whenever the opportunity presented itself. His attendance also served him socially. While on the one hand he didn't give a damn what Virginia City thought of him, on the other hand he was determined to make the townspeople accept him as their equal—a paradox he'd long ago given up trying to make sense of. He conveniently ignored the possibility that maybe he'd attended the ball simply because Trinity would be there.

In retaliation against this last thought, he turned away, walked to the bar, and ordered a bourbon and water. His hand in the pocket of his black pants, his buckskin jacket pulled back to reveal a tucked shirt and a string-thin tie, he surveyed the room. People milled about everywhere. Oliver Truxtun talked with Dancey Harlan and Charlie Knott, Dick Kingsman whispered to Victoria Dawson, whose mamma watched with an unswerving eye, and the governor, known as "Old Broadhorns" because he'd introduced longhorn cattle into Nevada, shook hands with a wide-smiling Wilson Booth. Beyond them were Maude and Dub Terrill, gossipy Doc Dawson, who was hurrying through a drink to go deliver an inconsiderate baby who wasn't due in the world for another two weeks, Neil and Ellie Oates, and . . .

She looked beautiful. Though he would have liked to, Breck couldn't ignore that. Her gown, as shiny and scarlet as a ruby, fit her in every way a gown should. No doubt expensive, he thought, but to show the magnitude of his spirit, it was worth every penny she'd paid. Every damned penny, he reiterated, bringing the glass to his lips. His eyes roamed upward, taking in the midnight-black hair piled atop her head, not severely, as he'd seen it in the past, but loosely, with wisps plunging about her face and down her neck in alluring disarray. From there, his gaze lowered to the cameo-ivory of her shoulders, shoulders scooped fashionably, provocatively, from her gown. His eyes followed the slit of a socially acceptable hint of cleavage. He remembered. Things he didn't want to remember. Things like the feel of her breasts cushioned against his chest. Things like the supplicant whimpers coming from her lips. Things like how soft—

Damn it, Brecker, give it a rest! he thought, deliberately looking away and swallowing a hefty belt of the expensive bourbon known for its velvet-clad kick. He forced his thoughts elsewhere. To the man who'd attempted to rob the Sierra Virginia. Curiously, the word *soft* occurred to him again. Why, he wasn't sure; it had seemingly come out of nowhere. The way the yellow-brown smears on the shirt he'd worn during the robbery had appeared out of nowhere. Possibly as a result of the tussle the two had engaged in, the ball-busting tussle that, in and of itself, was reason enough for him to kill the bastard! He had no idea what the smears were. Or, for that matter, why a man would rob a train with an unloaded gun. Breck frowned. Or why he kept getting the image of sherry-brown eyes peering from a black mask.

Breck raised the glass to his lips but stopped halfway. Over the rim, from all the way across the room, he saw a pair of pale brown eyes looking at him. As always, they were hauntingly familiar, but now he understood why. They were the eyes of Su-Ling's daughter. What he didn't understand was why it seemed impossible for him to break this visual contact, as if in doing so he would shatter something fragile and precious, some something his lonely life couldn't stand to be without. It was Trinity who glanced away, to receive the attentions of Governor Bradley, while Breck watched and downed the remainder of his drink. He wished to hell it was cheap whiskey, the kind that gave a stomp-you-in-the-gut-and-memory kick.

In the background, a band brought out from Sacramento began to play.

Trinity smiled at the governor—or tried to through the pain tearing at her side. Dear God, she hadn't known a body could hurt like this! Or that one could continue to function through the pain. So far she had managed, but her thinking was growing fuzzy. How much longer could she carry on this charade?

Governor Bradley was saying something—what, she couldn't exactly decide—but she smiled appropriately, nodded appropriately, and hoped she didn't faint inappropriately at his feet. And that the blood didn't seep through her dress. The wound—the wounds—had bled profusely but had slowed to a manageable ooze, probably because she'd lain still all afternoon after changing, with the greatest of difficulty, the batting bandage. *Had slowed* seemed to be the operative words. Once she'd dragged herself up and started to dress, the wounds had begun to bleed again, not as badly as before, but badly enough.

She was also getting stiff, so stiff she'd been able only to haphazardly arrange her hair. In addition, she was beginning to tremble, and her head was buzzing in earnest.

If she could just sit down, maybe she could hang on. Then, at an opportune moment, one that wasn't suspiciously early, she'd call a halt to the evening. Her goals beyond that were nebulous and moved along the vague path of getting through the remainder of the night, reboarding the train, and somehow seeking discreet help somewhere en route back to San Francisco.

If she could make it that long.

Which she could. Because she had to.

But only if she could sit down.

"...dance?"

The word snagged her attention with all its painful implications.

"Thank you, but..."

A small round of encouraging applause began and grew louder as eye after eye, from what was fast becoming a ring of spectators for this first dance of the evening, turned toward the governor and the famed actress. Only a few whispers breached the limits of good taste by mentioning that this was the same man who preached against allowing a flood of Chinese into Nevada. Instead, most eagerly watched Governor Bradley reach for Trinity Lee's hand.

Trinity hesitated but ultimately did the only thing she could under the circumstances: She took it. She bit back the sawtoothed pain that shot through her, recovered her breathing around a sharp and, she hoped, silent, intake of air, and smiled...shallowly. Then she followed as the older man led to the strains of the music.

It was the single most agonizing experience of her life.

The guiding pressure of his hand at her back was hell, since with each rhythmic stroke, he brushed the injury at her side. Trinity thought she wouldn't be able to withstand the pain. Her jaw hurt from gritting her teeth, and beads of perspiration, like diamonds on delicate pale porcelain, spread across her brow and upper lip. The perspiration felt cold and clammy. Nausea roared from the pit of her stomach.

"...party."

Trinity tried to focus her thoughts, her eyes. "I beg your pardon?" she said breathlessly.

"Nice party." The gray-bearded man smiled and leaned into her conspiratorially. The move ignited a hot pain that practically cut her in half. "Though I'll tell you a secret. I despise them. But it's all part of this thing called politics."

Trinity sucked air into her lungs. "Yes...I'm sure."

"Will you be in Virginia City long?"

"What? No. Tomorrow. I'm leaving tomorrow."

"So am I. I'm . . ." He chatted on, with Trinity hearing little and feeling far too much.

The music ended an eternity later, again to the accompaniment of applause. Her head spinning, Trinity mumbled her thanks to the governor and started for a chair. God, please let her get to a chair! The music began again, and gaily dressed couples pounced on the chance to claim the floor. She had taken only a few steps when Wilson Booth, black-haired and indisputably handsome, with a white smile that made all kinds of masculine promises, blocked her path.

Through the haze of her pain, Trinity saw that smile now flash its promises brightly.

"Miss Lee, I'll claim this dance, if I may."

"I . . . Please . . ."

The smile grew until it was blindingly brilliant . . . or maybe the brilliance was simply the lights beginning to do their own dance inside her head. "I'm afraid I can't let you say no," Wilson Booth said smoothly, as though he'd oiled the words to perfection. "In a roomful of men who want to dance with you, how can I be assured I'll get the chance again?"

"I . . ."

"Just one dance," he said, taking her into his arms with the vigor of a virile, single-minded man.

The lights in Trinity's head blinked, but, strangely, the pain didn't increase, even though his hand pressed, caressed, her side; the pain was already at the maximum level. He pulled her closer than convention allowed, and she could feel, vaguely, his breath on her neck. It felt hot. But then, maybe she just felt cold . . . cold . . . cold . . .

"You dance like an angel, Miss Lee," he whispered.

"Angel," she repeated, trying to hang on to any thread of reason.

"Like a tempting—" he whirled her in a finessing move meant to attract admiration, both Trinity's and the crowd's "—angel."

Trinity stumbled. Gasped. And felt Wilson Booth's hand slide over the naked skin of her shoulders in an attempt to right her.

"I'm sorry," she murmured, her breath gushing out.

"I'm sorry," Wilson said in tandem.

"I'm sorry," Breck echoed, his voice quiet but rock-hard. Wilson immediately shifted his startled attention to the man beside him. Breck was neither smiling nor frowning, but he commanded the moment by doing neither. "Miss Lee had promised me the first dance," he lied, visions of Trinity in Wilson Booth's overly eager arms still vivid. "The governor I was prepared to bow to, but I'm afraid now I must insist."

Age-old masculine tension crackled and popped. Would the man who held the woman in his arms relinquish her without a fight? Ultimately, though not before a muscle twitched in his jaw, Wilson Booth released her. Set on her own, Trinity fought for balance.

"Certainly," Wilson Booth said. "A prior claim is a prior claim." He managed to make the statement extend to the railroad he'd once owned, the railroad he'd like to own again. Suddenly, he smiled at Trinity, his lips overflowing with silent promises. "Miss Lee."

Trinity said nothing.

The lights in her head were growing dim, and the buzzing in her ears was growing louder. Pain seemed to be everywhere in the world.

"Trinity?" Breck asked, noticing the glaze of her eyes, the moisture dewing her face, the unnatural rose splotches in her otherwise deathly pale cheeks.

"I'm . . . fine," Trinity said, coherent enough to know that this man was the enemy. She had to be strong. She couldn't give in now. She . . . Reaching out, she placed her hand on his shoulder as though readying herself for a waltz. In truth, she needed an anchor. Which she created by digging her fingers into his jacket. "I'm fi—" she started to say, but suddenly the world went blank and black. The last thing she felt was her cheek crashing against the width of her enemy's strong shoulder.

With lightning speed, Breck threw an arm around her waist and hauled her limp body tightly against him. Balancing her weight, he shifted his arm to her back. Then he saw it.

The blood.

The blood smeared on the sleeve of his buckskin jacket.

Chapter Eleven

Suddenly it made sense.

Suddenly all the subtle clues added up: watching Ellie perform weeks before and realizing how easy it was to be deceived by a clever disguise; the dark smears on his shirt, which were most likely theatrical makeup; the robber mimicking Dancey; the train being robbed only when Trinity came to town; the familiar sherry-brown eyes that had been consistently shielded by glasses or a mask; the small stature, the small glove, the soft body struggling beneath his. The smokestack, for God's sake, had even been stuffed with some of the same batting she'd probably used to bind her breasts!

But why? Why had she done this to him?

The question twisted and turned in his gut as he scooped her unconscious form into his arms, carefully keeping the bloodstain hidden. Trinity's arm dangled lifelessly, while her breath, slow and reedy, trickled between her slack, pallid lips. She made no sound whatsoever.

In contrast, gasps and smothered cries drifted about the room as everyone's attention, like lined-up dominoes falling in rhythmic tandem, turned toward the couple. Breck plowed through the curious ranks, heading toward the staircase. From out of nowhere the party's hostess appeared to lead the way. Ellie, her face almost as white as Trinity's, raced forward and, with Neil at her side, fell into step beside Breck.

As Breck passed Dancey Harlan, who'd edged his way to the foot of the stairs, he ordered in a low voice, "Come with me." Without hesitation, Dancey joined the strange entourage. A quarter of the way up the stairs, Breck, as though compelled, angled his head, scanned the sea of intent faces, and zeroed in on Oliver Truxtun. The hawk's eyes were filled with quiet questions . . . none of which Breck answered with so much as a blink.

"Here," the hostess said, throwing wide the door of the first bedroom. Careful not to hurt the woman in his arms, Breck wedged through the door and, without invitation, headed for the expensively covered bed. When he gently laid Trinity on her side in the soft, ecru depths of the spread, her pallor was even more frighteningly evident.

"There's water there, and—" the hostess began, only to be cut off.

"All we need is some privacy," Breck said abruptly.

If the woman was offended by her guest's rudeness, she hid it well. "Certainly," she said, already backing from the room. "If you need anything, just ask." With a click, the door closed behind her. The delicate sound ended the silence the quartet had tacitly agreed upon.

"I knew she wasn't well when we picked her up this evening," Ellie began, taking her friend's inert hand in hers and chafing its deathlike coldness. "She wasn't well when she arrived in town. I tried to get her to see Doc Dawson, but she wouldn't. Said she'd just bruised herself in a fall when the train stopped for that boulder. You don't suppose she hurt herself bad? I mean, maybe broke a rib or something?"

"She's bleeding," Breck said curtly, reaching for the knife he always kept sheathed inside his boot.

"Bleeding?" Ellie asked, as if she'd just then become acquainted with the word. Neil laid his hand on his wife's shoulder, not only to comfort her, but also to draw her out of the way.

"Yeah, bleeding," Breck said, his voice as cold and thin as an early-winter layer of ice. As he spoke, he rolled Trinity slightly forward, nudging her cheek into the bed and bringing the splotch darkening the scarlet gown into view.

Ellie gasped at the saucer-size stain and unconsciously stepped into the shelter of her husband's massive arms.

With an expertise that was both captivating and unsettling, Breck poised the knife at the gown's sculpted neckline and sliced through the rich fabric in a way that would have brought tears to the eyes of the gown's renowned designer. A lacy ivory undergarment greeted him. Breck swore. As though he had every right to be intimately familiar with the woman lying unconscious before him, he gripped a fistful of the bloody fabric and, his knuckles grazing her naked flesh, tore it with his bare hands. The rending cry of cloth was loud in the still room. Beneath the silken garment, the once-white batting lay crimson against Trinity's bleached skin. Breck, his hands already smeared with her blood, severed the batting and peeled back the edges.

When she saw the raw, gaping exit wound that, without warning, stared outward, Ellie plastered her hand to her mouth. Her husband tightened his hold on her.

Dancey assessed the situation quickly and said, not without a trace of surprise, "She's been shot."

"Yeah," Breck said, his icy voice freezing thicker. "By me."

The room might have become a cloistered nunnery for the profound silence suddenly dwelling there.

Finally, Ellie said, "I...I don't underst—" Abruptly, her complexion blanched as realization slapped her full in the face. "Oh, my God," she whispered, "she's the one who... But how? Why?" She looked to Breck for answers.

He didn't have any. "I don't know," he said gruffly, "and if we don't stop this bleeding, we'll never find out." His implication was all too clear.

"I'll get Doc Dawson," Ellie said, breaking from her husband's arms.

"No!" both Breck and Neil shouted.

Confused, Ellie stopped, dragging her eyes from one man to the other.

"Unless you want every man, woman, child, and lamppost to know by morning," Breck explained, referring to the physician's loose tongue. "Which means that Truxtun would be circling overhead, just waiting to pick her bones clean."

"It doesn't matter, anyway," Dancey threw in pragmatically. "Doc's already left to deliver Mrs. Whitehead's baby."

"Good," Breck said. "We won't have to explain why we didn't send for him."

"What are we going to do, then?" Ellie said, suddenly strong and capable of handling whatever had to be done.

"We've got to stop the bleeding. Or at least slow it down," Breck said, glancing back at Trinity. Part of her stomach, all of her side, and a good portion of her back lay exposed. Breck couldn't help but notice the delicate curve where her back eased, with classic femininity, into the suggestive swell of her hips. He also couldn't help but notice that, while both wounds were bleeding, it was primarily the exit wound that was spurting small but continual rivers of red.

"She's bled too much already," Dancey said.

"Yeah," Breck muttered, the word burning around the edges with an anger he didn't know where to aim. At himself? After all, he *was* the one who'd shot her. At her? She was the one who'd forced him to. At Fate? She was the capricious bitch who moved mortals about on a whim. "We need something to stanch this," he said, mentally spitting out the anger before he choked on it. He scanned the room, considering tearing one of the drapes from the window.

"What about her petticoat?" Ellie asked.

"That'll do," Breck said, yanking back the hem of her skirt and plunging his knife to the hilt in a froth of cotton lawn. With jagged motions, he hacked off the ruffle of the undergarment.

Trinity moaned, as if consciousness hovered nearby, as if pain were once more seeping through the blessed darkness.

Breck glanced up at her and saw her eyelids twitch from the pain; he felt her pain so strongly within himself that he had to turn away from it emotionally. He continued to cut the petticoat.

"Lie still," Ellie said, moving to her friend's side and laying a hand on her shoulder. Despite Ellie's comforting touch, Trinity flinched when the petticoat made contact with her wounds.

Breck seemed to ignore her reaction, but his tone was once again harsh with feeling when he said to Neil, "Here, help me tie this around her to hold the bandage in place."

The two men, with Dancey's assistance, tied a strip of cloth around the petticoat dressing, then fitted her clothes back into place as far as was possible. Throughout her jostling, Trinity moaned but didn't come to. Her continued unconsciousness both pleased and troubled Breck.

"Get her cloak from downstairs," he told Ellie when they were finished. "And make her apologies. Tell everyone she fainted from fatigue and is going back to the hotel to rest." Breck glanced over at Neil. "Find a back way to get out of the house without being seen by the people at the party."

"Right," the miner said.

"And bring my horse around," Breck said to Dancey. The conductor was halfway out the door before the order was fully given.

"You're not going to take her back to the hotel, are you?" Ellie asked incredulously.

"No, I'm going to take her to my cabin in the hills. She'll be safe there."

For endless heartbeats, Breck and Ellie just stared. He knew the question she wanted to ask; it was the question he was asking himself. Why was he protecting the woman who had singlehandedly driven him to the brink of financial ruin? He told himself it was because she was Su-Ling's daughter. The answer was a good one, but somehow incomplete. There seemed to be more, some personal feeling he couldn't put a name to. Or, more to the point, some personal feeling he wasn't willing to put a name to.

It had begun to snow. Tiny grains drifted to earth like dainty crystalline flowers falling from an ice-sculpture paradise. Breck hunched deeper into his jacket and angled his head so that the wide brim of his hat deflected the wind's numbing breath. Pulling back the thick fox fur serving as a blanket, he peered down into the face of the woman cradled in his arms. She was silent, still, though occasionally her restless moans mingled with the *clomp-clomp* of the horses' hooves. He wouldn't even allow himself to imagine the pain she must be in or the blood she was still losing.

"How much farther?" Dancey called out from behind. Breck heard his friend's horse snort, as if the beast, too, were protesting the cold night journey. At the last minute, Breck decided that Dancey would accompany them, carrying what sparse medical supplies he could round up without attracting suspicion.

"Not far," Breck called back, the wind whipping his voice into frosty tendrils of sound.

"Why not just fire the Pinkerton agent?" Dancey said. It was his only comment so far regarding their unusual journey. Next to Trinity's condition it was the subject most singly occupying both men's thoughts.

An image of Truxtun watching him carry Trinity upstairs flashed through Breck's mind. "Because there's no way he'd walk away now."

The finality of Breck's tone, coupled with the truth of the words, discouraged further suggestions.

The cabin, nestled among the sloping foothills less than an hour's ride from town, had never seemed so far away, and Breck himself was beginning to wonder if it would ever come into view. He had never taken anyone to it before, not even Dancey. It had been the sanctuary to which he fled when his need to be alone prevailed, when his need to restore himself with silence outweighed all else. Now his need was to reach the isolated cabin with the woman in his arms still alive.

His horse, a stallion of the purest black, seemed to sense Breck's impatience and whinnied. The sound, or maybe the jarring motion of the animal as it struggled for a foothold on the narrow, rock-strewn path, jolted Trinity into groggy consciousness. She moaned.

"Easy," Breck said, tipping the fur back from her face. Even in the starless, ebony night, he was aware of her paleness. He *felt* it. Just as he felt her hand fluttering at his chest, clenching and unclenching, as though the pain denied it any peace.

"It . . . it hurts," she whimpered hoarsely.

Frustration shot through him, a frustration so deep, so wide, that he dared not entrust it to words. He simply pulled her tightly against him. And swore silently.

The cabin appeared just as Breck was despairing that it ever would. With thick stone walls and a sod roof, it huddled amid shadow-dusted piñon pines and night-tinged clumps of juniper. A wooden porch spanned the length of the one-room structure, beckoning the cold, weary travelers to shelter. To the right stood a small shed, with an adjoining corral of enduring cedar posts lashed together to make a stockade.

Breck stopped his horse as close to the porch as possible and forced himself to wait quietly for Dancey to slide from his saddle.

"Careful," Breck cautioned, lowering the woman into Dancey's arms.

Trinity, her face pinched, moaned as a sharp pain pierced her.

"There, there, miss," Dancey cooed. "We're here. No more bobbing around on those horses. And I'm a-thinkin' we'll be as warm as God's love in just a bit."

"Get her inside," Breck ordered, wanting to take her back into his arms but knowing the transfer would only hurt her more. Instead, he grabbed the reins of both horses and started off toward the shed. "There's wood already laid in the fireplace!" he shouted, his voice mingling with the wind's keening lament.

Relying on the provisions he always kept stocked, he needed only minutes to properly attend to the animals. The same state of readiness was maintained in the cabin—nonperishable staples stored in the cabinets awaiting his next unexpected visit. Hurrying back through the snow-speckled night, he stomped his feet on the porch and threw wide the door.

"How is she?" he asked, glancing toward the deathly still figure in the bed and shrugging out of his jacket, hat, and gloves. He was so cold that the fragile, hungry warmth coming from the hearth actually hurt, causing his skin to prickle in rebellion.

"She's bleeding bad," Dancey said as he lit the second of two globe-shaped oil lamps. One sat on the kitchen counter; the other he carried to the table by the bedside.

Breck had already seated himself on the side of the bed and was tossing back the fur. The sight of blood greeted him. The side of her gown was soaked, disturbingly so, and the petticoat bandage looked as though it had never once in its cotton life been white.

"Damn," Breck whispered, drawing his knife from his boot and slashing the thin strap they'd tied everything in place with. He pulled back the dress, removed the wet wad of petticoat, and examined the wounds by the light of the lantern. Both wounds, particularly the exit tear, ran red. "She's bleeding to death," Breck said, his voice devoid of feeling, as if he were totally unmoved by what he was seeing.

"Yeah," Dancey agreed solemnly. "We have no choice but to cauterize them if we want to save her." What he didn't say was that it might already be too late.

Breck had known what had to be done when he'd first seen the wounds back at the ball. He'd rejected the idea every second since. The thought of putting a searing-hot blade to her skin, her soft skin, was nauseatingly repugnant, but the unavoidable moment had come.

Damn it, why did you force me to shoot you?

"Here, help me with her clothes," Breck growled, starting to pull the dress from her shoulders. With complete disregard for her modesty—the issue had become a simple, uncomplicated matter of life and death—he bared her breasts, which only subliminally registered as full and firm and crowned in dark brown. Neither did he seem to notice the peachlike fuzz on her stomach, or the thicket of midnight black that grew between her delicately sculpted thighs.

As the two men tore her clothes away, Trinity groaned.

"There, there," Dancey whispered, throwing the fur back over her naked form.

The massively built conductor, who at some point had shed his hat from his scarred head, heaped the ruined clothes unceremoniously on the floor, while Breck, his jaw tense, his mind forced into detachment, stepped to the kitchen and, opening a drawer, searched through the knives. He selected the widest blade he could find. Then, squatting before the fire, he angled the knife until the blade rested in the red-and-blue flame. In the firelight he could see that his knuckles were painted with her blood. He made no attempt to wipe it away.

Neither man spoke as the blade heated. Finally—minutes, years, heavy heartbeats later—Breck pulled the blisteringly hot knife from the fire and pushed to his feet. His eyes met Dancey's. Breck's irises had faded to an icy, aloof, emotionally uninvolved blue.

"You want me to do it?" Dancey asked.

"No," Breck answered, feeling the inexplicable need to do it himself if it had to be done. "Just hold her still. I'll do the worst first, then cauterize the smaller wound with the other side of the blade."

Dancey nodded, yanked back the fur covering, and placed his big hands on Trinity's bare shoulders. She moaned. And laced with the sound was Breck's prayer that she remain unconscious just a little longer.

Indenting the feather ticking with his knee, then looking up at Dancey, he asked, "Ready?"

"Ready."

He didn't hesitate. He laid the hot steel across the bleeding, gaping wound just below her stomach. The sickening smell of burning flesh wafted throughout the room, piercing Breck's nostrils with a fetid fragrance he remembered only too well. The memory of the poker cauterizing his right hand had never died. It never would. He fought the memory of that pain, knowing that if he listened to it, gave in to it, he'd tear the burning blade from her body. And that he couldn't do. Because her only chance for survival lay in stopping the bleeding.

At contact, a searing pain clawed through Trinity, jerking back the foggy, blissful curtains of unconsciousness and thrusting her into a semiconscious world of raw feeling. Her body bucked in reaction, her slender hips heaving off the bed in search of surcease from the scorching swath of steel; simultaneously, a low, guttural moan spilled from her lips.

"Hold her still!" Breck hollered, pressing down on her hips with the palm of his free hand.

Dancey slid his knee across her thigh, pinning her to the bed, even as his hands tightened on her shoulders.

No! she pleaded silently, flailing ineffectively. *Let me up.... Please... please... please don't hurt me!*

Her moans turned into whimpers, then cries, one bubbling up on top of the other, until a gurgling scream tore through the quiet. The agonized sound slashed at Breck's heart.

"Roll her over," he growled.

"Maybe we should wait—"

"Roll her over!"

Pulling the knife from the heat-reddened skin, Breck impatiently tugged her onto her side and, turning the blade over, rammed it against the smaller entry wound. Again she cried out, but this time the pitiful sound was muffled by the pillow. Again she whimpered. Instead of trying to free herself, however, she began to twitch. Breck could see the muscles of her back, the femininely curved back that flared gently into the cheeks of her hips, convulse into one contraction after another, ripples that skittered across the ivory of her skin. And then the contractions stopped. Abruptly. As her body went limp from blessed unconsciousness.

Breck drew back the knife, pushed away from the bed, and crossed to the small area that served as a kitchen. He dropped the knife onto the cedar table, walked to the cabinet, pulled out a bottle of whiskey, and, holding it lovingly by its slender neck, downed a more-than-generous swallow. Followed by another. He turned and watched Dancey quickly bandage the wounds before carefully lifting Trinity in his arms, yanking back the covers, and gently laying her in the midst of the muslin sheets. He spread the top covers about her, ran his hand over his bald head, and looked up.

"I don't think the slug hit anything vital," Dancey said. "'Course, she's lost a damned sight of blood." When Breck didn't acknowledge his remark, he asked softly, "You all right?" He stared into a pair of eyes that looked as if they felt nothing, as if they'd never felt anything, as if they never would.

"Yeah," Breck answered, wondering why, if he was all right, his hand was trembling so.

"I guess there's nothing to do now but wait," the older man said tiredly, rounding the foot of the bed.

"Yeah, wait," Breck agreed tonelessly, bringing the bottle once more to his mouth...with a blood-smeared hand that still trembled, despite the fact that he was all right.

Wait.

There were a thousand ways to wait, Breck discovered, not one of which didn't challenge a man's sanity. He and Dancey waded through the long hours of the night, he sitting on the cold floor, his back braced against a wall that was colder still, Dancey sprawled uncomfortably in a straight chair. Neither man spoke. They simply waited for any sound from Trinity.

None came. Not even the rustle of sheets. Not even a moan of pain.

With the snowy sunrise, Dancey took his leave to go into town and manage the railroad in Breck's absence. The plan was for him to return the next day. Which left Breck to hold a lone vigil. Tending only to the direst of personal needs, he sat beside the bed from sunup to sundown, growing increasingly frustrated at the silence that had once served the cabin, and him, so well.

Shoving his fingers through his uncombed hair, he stood, paced, put another log on the fire, and paced again. If only she would moan, groan, shift—do anything to indicate she was alive. At that unnerving thought, he eased once more to the side of the bed and sought the pulse point at her throat. Her skin was neither warm nor cold, but he found a faint, steady throbbing that momentarily reassured him.

As soon as his hand came away, however, worry again sprang from the shadows of his mind. She had to live. He wasn't exactly certain why; he just knew she had to. He had to make her live. Yet how could he if Fate, scrawling its fickle message in the faraway stars, had decreed otherwise?

The sigh came seconds shy of midnight and instantly penetrated Breck's fitful doze. His chin rose from where it had been tucked on his chest, his weary, sleep-blurred eyes hurriedly taking in the woman only inches from him. He waited and watched...for any sound, any movement. The sound came again. A soft soughing. From beyond the windowpanes. Breck's heart, beating fast with hope, plummeted to his feet.

The wind.

Damn it, it was only the wind!

Biting back the bitter taste of disappointment, Breck hurled himself from the chair and walked to the curtainless window. Snow dusted the panes in triangular patches of fragile, lacy flakes that seemed to huddle together in search of warmth. Nearby, the wind moaned, a keening song whose mournful notes were born in the shadowy mountains rearing skyward in the distance, then trailed through the high trees and low scrub to become a soulful wail.

It sounded as if the wind hurt. Hurt. *He* hurt. Hurt from waiting, watching. Hurt from praying to a God who never seemed to know, or care, that he existed. Hurt from... He couldn't have put it into words, only into beats of his heart, but it had something to do with being forever alone—living alone, dying alone, forgotten as soon as the earth was indifferently shoveled over you. When had his beloved solitude turned into nothing more than barrenness? When had the fullness of silence become nothing more than the empty absence of sound? When had—

The wind howled again, rousing Breck from his unsettling reverie. He passed his hand over his face and exhaled a weary breath. When had he ever given in to such sappy thoughts? When had—

A sigh, more fragile than thinned hope, drifted over his shoulder. He whirled. And dared not believe that the sliver of sound had come from Trinity. He waited. Watched. Prayed to a God who didn't know or care that he existed. The sigh came again. Along with the gentle rustling of the covers as one arm moved restlessly. Breck hastened forward.

Trinity's eyes were open, though hazily unfocused, as if only experimenting with consciousness. As Breck's weight crushed the side of the bed, those dull, pain-streaked eyes slid to him. He couldn't tell whether they recognized him or not.

"Am I—" she swallowed and paused, as though trying to find the strength to go on "—going to die?"

"No!" he said, the harsh, grating word abrading his throat with its force. He searched for, found, and surrounded her hand with his. Hers felt chilled, limp...lifeless. "You're not going to die. I swear it. Do you hear me? You're not...going to die...." The words trailed off because she could no longer hear them. She had once more slipped back into unconsciousness.

Breck had no idea how long he sat holding her hand. At some frail hour between midnight and dawn, he lay down beside her, simply because he could no longer go without sleep, simply because every bone in his body, every lonely part of his heart, hurt.

By midmorning, Dancey had arrived with a vial of morphine.

"Good," Breck said, running his fingers over his chin. He hadn't shaved in over a day, and his face was stubbled with a dark-brown beard that made him look like a renegade on the run.

"Told the druggist we needed it and some bandages—" here he produced another offering "—around the railroad yard, 'cause there's always busted fingers and such."

Breck nodded. "What's happening in town?"

"Tongues are wagging." When Breck jerked his head away from the steaming mug of coffee he'd just poured, Dancey chuckled. "Though not about what you're thinking. Seems Mrs. Oates got carried away with the story of Miss Lee's fatigue. Seems yes, she did faint from fatigue, and yes, she is up here in your cabin, but no, she couldn't possibly say more because...well, what goes on between a man and woman is nobody's business but the man's and woman's."

Breck let the hot coffee burn away the memory of Trinity's kiss and concentrated on the practicality of Ellie's gossip. "Good thinking. That ought to buy Trinity some time. And keep Truxtun sidetracked."

Dancey's smile faded. "How is she?"

Breck told him about her foray into consciousness, adding with a worried frown, "She's growing restless." He'd awakened to movement, which had pleased him at first, but he'd soon realized it was fretful movement. He'd also thought she seemed warm. Too warm. Fever wasn't something he'd allow himself to think about. There was no way she could survive a fever in her depleted state.

A short while later, Dancey returned to town, and Breck, grateful Trinity had again ventured into consciousness, tried to get her to swallow the morphine.

"Come on, that's it," he urged, spooning the powder past her lips, lips that had once been so unexpectedly soft beneath his. Would they be that soft again, if they were kissed? And could he stand it if they were? Ignoring the truant thought, he gently laid her back on the pillow. And stared into her colorless face.

Despite the morphine, her restlessness grew, punctuated by moans, dollops of sound that knifed at his heart. The evening hour of eight o'clock had barely arrived when she began to twitch convulsively and speak deliriously.

"No...hurt...M-mamma..."

"Trinity?" he asked, quickly feeling her brow.

Burning! She was burning up! His heart turned over, then sank to the bottom of his stomach.

"No...make it go away...make the pain..."

Jesus, what was he going to do? The answer came with lightning swiftness. Get the fever down. He had to get the fever down! But how? He looked around the cabin, his eyes quickly taking in everything within...and without. He sprang from the bed, grabbed a wooden water bucket, and threw open the door. Snow, flaky and cold, fell from the heavens. Breck scooped up a bucketful and raced back inside. Snatching a rag, he yanked back the covers and, sitting on the side of the bed, began to bathe her.

"No!" she protested as he drew the freezing wetness along the curves of her shoulders, down the column of her neck, across the plumpness of her breasts. The nipples contracted into hard, pebbled knots, which the serious moment allowed Breck to notice only in the most clinical of terms.

"Be still!" he ordered, leveling a heavy arm across her trim waist and drawing the snow-filled cloth along her stomach and down her thighs, being careful not to disturb the bandages.

Trinity shivered from the cold even as her body burned with a raging fire. Breck, too, worked with a fever, a fever born of fear. Over and over he bathed her, over and over he fought her as she, growing more delirious, fought him.

"Don't!" he growled, ensnaring her thrashing arms with one hand, while with the other he bathed the satiny undersides of her arms, the velvety undercurves of her breasts.

But the more cold he applied, the hotter her skin seemed to become.

She was going to die!

That realization came to him, with the stealth and speed of a nightmare, after long, exhausting hours of rubbing her down only to have her fever spike higher and higher. He'd lost all track of time and knew only that daylight, mocking daylight, had come. And that it had stopped snowing. Good, some part of him said. It would make burying her easier. At that thought, something rebelled within him, and anger, pure and strong and vile, surged through him.

No, damn it, no! You will not die! I won't give you that out!

"C'mon, China, fight!" he whispered roughly as, denying his tiredness, he started bathing her again. "You will not die. Do you hear me? If you die, I hope you burn in the hottest hell. But you're not going to die . . . you're going to fight . . . even if it kills you doing it. Damn it, China, I won't let you die!"

Throughout the day, he tended her—fearfully, furiously, fervently. At some point, as the sun was setting, he dropped his head to the side of the bed. Just for a minute. He'd rest for just a minute. Then he'd . . . The thought was never finished. The bucket of snow melted. The fire died. The cabin reeked of silence. Dead silence.

Breck woke abruptly. His first thought was that the bucket of snow had spilled on the bed, for the covers were soggy. Then he saw that the bucket sat upright at his feet. Next his full attention was captured by the sweet sound of Trinity's even, restful breathing. He touched her. She was dripping wet. The fever had broken.

Breck forced himself to feel nothing. The elation threatening to swamp him made him feel uncomfortable. Even fearful. He was unaccustomed to feeling anything this deeply, and certainly not an emotion that centered around someone else. So he shunned it and instead, carefully, practically, bathed her once more, this time washing the sweat from her body before changing the wet linens and tucking her cozily inside dry ones. Not bothering with a jacket, he then walked outside.

The night was cold and clear, with stars glittering by the millions in a Nevada sky that seemed to have no beginning, no end. Standing on the porch, his shoulder braced against a column, he stared upward. Upward, where Su-Ling had believed destinies were unalterably written. Had Trinity's survival been scrawled among the glimmering patches of stellar light? Or had he simply willed it so strongly that he'd rewritten destiny?

He had no answer, only a warm feeling coursing through his veins, a warm feeling that, deny it, fear it, label it what he chose, felt a great deal like elation.

Chapter Twelve

The days following the shooting were a blur to Trinity, a montage of acute pain, searing heat that fried her skin from without, a scalding fever that blistered her from within. On the heels of the heat came cold, a cold unlike any she'd ever known, a cold that made her body shiver and shake in the cruelest of agonies. Then a deep, peaceful rest descended, broken only by broth forced past her lips, gentle hands, and a hard male body occasionally lying beside her. She came to look forward to the nearness of that body, for it supplied a quiet strength she desperately needed.

Exactly one week after she'd arrived at the cabin, Trinity opened her eyes. Really opened them. To see clearly. And to interpret what she saw.

The cabin was small and silent and smelled of cedar and...and something she couldn't identify, although her nose told her it was coming from her right. Slowly rolling her head to the side—instinct warned her to do everything cautiously—her eyes lit upon a blazing fire, over which hung a black kettle. Food. Probably soup or stew. The thought of food made her mouth water and her stomach growl, and she slid her hand downward...only to grimace with pain when her fingers stumbled over a bandage. Bandage? Why was she wearing a bandage? What had happened? What—

Suddenly, it all came rushing back—Breck shooting her, fainting in his arms, a night ride that seemed to last forever. But where had he brought her? And how badly was she hurt? Her gaze lowered to herself—to the shoulders and arms encased in a man's shirt, to her body, mounded beneath a thick, warm blanket, to the toes spiking the blanket upward, to...

. . . to the man sprawling quietly, negligently, at the foot of the bed. The man whose colorless eyes stared at her with an intensity that suggested that, besides himself, she might well be the only human being left on earth.

She looked at him with equal concentration, taking in everything, from his mussed blond hair, to his unshaven face, to his wrinkled jeans, smeared with what looked suspiciously like blood. Her blood?

At last, interrupting her silent question, he posed one of his own. It was a simple question, an all-important question. "Why?"

At the sight of Breck, at the sound of his voice, which was low-pitched but laced with more feeling than many a shout, Trinity's stomach tightened. It tightened even more at his query. She did not, however, pretend not to understand. On the contrary, she met his boldness with a boldness of her own.

"Because you—" her voice cracked from long days of disuse, and she had to shove the remainder of the whispered words forward "—killed my mother."

Breck had long ago ceased to be stunned by anything. Yet, emotionally jaded as he was, her accusation startled him. Not as much as a flicker of a reaction, however, claimed his face. Nor did he speak, though he mentally acknowledged that at last his earlier wondering about whether or not Trinity remembered him from her childhood had been satisfied.

His silence shredded Trinity's nerves, sparking an anger that demanded expression. "Aren't you going to deny it?" she rasped, wondering if she'd actually wanted him to defend himself and make her believe in his innocence. The realization that she might have only angered her more.

Still Breck said nothing. Instead, he pushed away from the bed, ambled toward the fire and the kettle, and, lifting the lid, lazily stirred the contents. A rich aroma wafted through the small, snowbound room.

"Well?" Impatience rippled through the word.

Breck glanced toward the woman on the bed. "No," he said, his tone frustratingly calm and even.

"No, you didn't kill her?"

"No, I won't deny it."

He'd hastily considered the situation from every angle. He'd thought of Su-Ling. He'd thought of Jedediah, a man who had finally found his lost daughter. He knew Su-Ling would approve of the latter. His silence was his gift to her. And his gift to Jedediah. At least until he could learn more about what had happened that tragic night. Besides, it was obvious that Trinity had long ago made up her mind about him. And that irked him. All his noble reasons be damned, her preconceived notion was the real reason he wouldn't deny her accusation. He was sick to death, fed up to the craw, with people telling him who he was and what he was without ever taking a good look at him. He was tired of bigoted assumptions. To hell with what everyone thought! But, why, then, did it hurt so much to see condemnation gleaming in Trinity's hate-filled eyes?

"Then you're saying you did kill her?" Her anger had made her stronger, and her shoulders inched up the wall behind the bed as she sought a sitting position. Grimacing, she had to settle for a point midway between sitting and lying.

Breck reached for a cup and ladled out some of the vegetable soup he'd made. "What I'm saying is that you can believe what you choose."

"I'd like to know the truth."

He turned, his empty eyes finding hers. "The truth? According to whom?"

For long moments they stared at each other. The fire hissed, the wind howled, snow fluttered against the window. "I'm going to kill you," she said calmly. "The first chance I have."

Breck, his eyes never wavering from hers, moved to sit on the side of the bed. He dipped into the cup and brought the spoon to her lips. "Then you'll need this to build up your strength."

"Are you awake?" Breck asked, edging to the side of the bed two hours later.

"Mmm."

"Is that a yes or no?"

"Mmm," Trinity mumbled again, hazily wondering how their earlier discussion, their earlier confrontation, and the consumption of a bowl of soup could have tired her out so. But it had, so much so that she'd instantly fallen asleep. Gloriously asleep. Until now, when two inconsiderate, marauding hands seemed intent on pulling down the covers and pulling up her shirt.

Pulling up her shirt? Trinity's sleep-riddled eyes flew open. "W-what are you doing?"

"I'm changing the bandages," Breck said, not even bothering to look up into her startled face, but rather hiking the tail of the garment upward until a whisper of the underside of one breast showed.

"I can do it," Trinity said, pushing his hands away and the shirt lower.

Breck's eyes locked with hers. His were a hard, flinty, nononsense blue. "Look, China, let's get something straight. I've seen every inch of you there is to see a dozen times over, and I'm not going to start kowtowing to your Victorian modesty at this late date. Now, move your hands—" he shoved them aside and her shirt back up, this time deliberately higher, until the clear swell of her breast, though not the nipple, was visible "—and let me change these bendages. You're damned lucky I gave you the shirt," he added, more roughly than the situation merited.

The truth was, he'd put the shirt on her more for himself than for her. Day in, day out, hour in, hour out, of seeing a body that had obviously been designed by a God at the height of his creative powers was enough to crumble any red-blooded man's restraint.

"You're too thoughtful," Trinity spewed through gritted teeth as the bandage on her abdomen fell away. While not exactly painful, it wasn't comfortable, either.

"Yeah. Aren't I, though?"

The cauterized wound had long since ceased to bleed, but the red-hot steel had left the skin red and blistered. Breck ran his fingertips over the water-filled bubble, then investigated the jagged edges of the gunshot wound the cauterization had seared irregularly together.

Trinity's breath caught slightly, though she admitted that, for a killer, Madison Brecker had a gentle touch.

"How bad is it?" she asked, nudging the shirt down over her breast and struggling to keep the blanket over her thighs.

"You'll live," he muttered.

"Your bedside manner leaves someth—" She gasped.

Breck, thinking he'd hurt her, jerked his head up. She was staring at the angry four-inch wound on her belly, and her stunned face had turned as white as the snow banked beyond the window. He longed to comfort her yet resisted the temptation—partly as a matter of principle, partly because he knew little about comforting people.

"You're lucky to be alive," he said harshly. "And if it's the scar you're worried about, let me assure you, people can live just fine with one." The scarred hand tending to her injury bore eloquent testimony to that fact.

Trinity took in the ragged seam where the uneven pieces of her flesh had been fused together under the strength of hot steel. She wasn't certain what she'd expected; she knew only that what she was seeing wasn't it. Her puckered skin looked as if it had been drawn together by whiskey-guided hands, and it was puffed into a blister surrounded by brilliant red patches. There was also a small, oval, purple bruise at her hipbone, which was peeking from beneath the blanket.

Trinity's eyes moved to the white scar that blemished the back of Breck's hand and, to a lesser extent, his palm, a scar that had been part of her life for as long as she could remember. She wondered if some poetic justice lay in the fact that now they were both scarred. But did the physical scars merely stand for deeper emotional wounds? And was there some significance in the fact that she was now more severely scarred than he? Had her hate turned her into a monster that even he was not? This last thought was too troubling to consider, so she let the question slip away as if it had never posed itself at all.

"It'll, uh . . . it'll look better as time passes," he said, damning himself for offering her solace when he'd just told himself he would offer none.

"I know," she said, her lips moving slowly, the words forming softly. "Really, I'm not . . . ungrateful. I'm really very thankful." She swallowed and, though the words were hard to say to the man she'd hated for so long, she found they were, nonetheless, genuine. "Th-thank you."

Thank you.

The words, spoken sweetly, hesitantly, by a woman whose lips had haunted his every waking hour, unlocked an internal door Breck hadn't known existed. From that cracked doorway wafted the realization that he had almost killed her. That he surely would have killed her, had her gun been loaded. That he surely would have killed her with his own, had he hit what he'd been aiming for. He had, of course, known this before, but he'd never faced it quite so squarely, so starkly. He supposed he'd simply been too busy trying to keep her from dying.

Dying. Dead. Without his efforts, she would be dead, not lying in his bed half-naked and wholly desirable. Some emo-

tion, an emotion he'd never before experienced, an emotion
that sailed far beyond temporal lust, cramped his heart, and he
suddenly felt as if it were he, not she, who'd had the near miss.
He didn't entirely understand the feeling, yet its power frightened him as he'd never been frightened before.

"Turn over," he growled, hiding behind a defensive
brusqueness.

"What?"

"Turn over!"

She rolled onto her side, her cheek buried in the downy pillow; she had no choice but to obey the insistent hand that
firmly, if gently, clasped her waist and pushed. His open hand
on her bare skin felt strange. No man had ever touched her so
intimately. The thought of what else he'd seen and touched—
by his own admission, he'd seen every inch of her—made her
skin burn with embarrassment...and with something more. It
was a tingly, white-hot kind of feeling, not unlike having been
caressed by the shocking fingers of lightning.

"Damn it, will you get that out of the way?" he barked,
thrusting the shirt and the blanket down until most of her back
and a goodly portion of her buttocks were exposed.

Trinity felt the cool cabin air lapping at her skin. She shivered, but it was only partially from the cold. Was he looking at
her? Of course he was looking at her. Did she think he'd close
his eyes? Her skin heated under his imagined gaze, and she
clutched the pillow to her, trying to hide within its folds. She
wanted to die of embarrassment, but even as she thought it, she
knew that before she died of embarrassment she wanted something from him....some masculine something that promised to
ease the unfamiliar ache he inspired. An ache she hadn't known
existed until, once upon a time, he'd kissed her.

Kiss.

What would it be like, she wondered in traitorous abandon,
if he lowered his mouth to the hollow of her back?

Breck looked at the creamy indentation in the small of her
back, the slender drape of her shoulders, the provocative curve
of her spine, the rounded swell of her hips, and cursed silently
but vilely. He swallowed and concentrated on the wound before him, which he deemed improved as he covered it with a
clean bandage. He ignored, or tried to, the velvet brush of her
skin against his knuckles, and the way that velvet skin begged
him to touch more and more and more....

"There," he announced huskily as he rolled her once more onto her back.

Their eyes met. Hers were the color of melted moonlight, with a hazy glow washing across them that reminded him of a beckoning nighttime fog. Her lips were parted, as though she were ready to say some delicate sweetness... or ready to receive an indelicate kiss. The top button of the shirt had worked itself loose, leaving a tantalizing view of her breast. Her incredibly dark-crested breast, his memory reminded him, as his eyes involuntarily roamed from the swell of her breast to her lips and back to her eyes.

Suddenly, he felt as if he were drowning.

Hurling himself from the bed, he grumbled, "I'm going to tend to the horse. And for God's sake, button up that shirt!" he added with a growl as he slammed the door behind him.

Both were too preoccupied to think it a strange remark coming from a man who wasn't going to kowtow to Victorian modesty.

In his absence, which turned out to be far longer than the time required to see to the needs of a single horse, Trinity found a chamber pot and, fighting the darkness of a faint, made necessary use of it. Breathing heavily and hard, she crawled back into bed, letting the swirling room settle about her once more. Physically depleted, she slept again, but not before realizing that the purple splotch on her hipbone was indeed a bruise—a thumbprint. Breck's thumbprint. And that it was accompanied by matching fingerprints that ate into her thigh, as if he'd had to hold her down by force. In those fuzzy moments between wakefulness and sleep, she fancifully interpreted the bruises as his brand. And proof positive that he had, just as he'd said, seen every inch of her. Even as groggy as she was, the thought was unnerving, disturbing, and enough to make her heart rate soar.

She slept for an hour, waking to the thwacking strains of an ax chopping into timber. Trinity frowned at the generous supply of wood already stacked by the hearth, then frowned again an hour later when Breck brought in a massive armload of firewood that raised the supply from generous to bountiful. She said nothing, however, and neither did Breck. They merely exchanged brief, let-me-tear-my-eyes-away-quickly glances.

Supper was another bowl of vegetable soup, served with hot-water corn bread that Breck fried in a black skillet over the fire. His crouched pose graphically supported Ellie's assertion that he wore incredibly tight pants, and Trinity, her throat dry, looked away, though her eyes insisted upon returning to play grazing games with his.

Neither spoke until it was time to eat, at which point Trinity swung her legs over the side of the bed and announced, "I can feed myself."

Breck looked her over consideringly before silently handing her the cup.

While the job proved more difficult than she'd anticipated, she was determined to see it through.

"It's good," she said. When he made no comment, simply glanced her way and gave what might or might not have been a nod, she said nothing else.

At meal's end, thoroughly exhausted, she lay back in bed and watched Breck's economical movements as he cleared away the dishes. She also watched him stoke the fire and found herself wondering, for what reason she knew not, if he was going to shave before the day was over. Which, technically, it already was, for night had crowded in, wrapping the cabin in its inky veil. Snow quietly peppered a winter song.

"You need some privacy?" he asked sometime later, startling her so badly that she actually jumped.

"What?"

"It's time to go to sleep. Do you need some time alone first?"

"Yes. Yes, thank you," she said, her mind quickly buzzing with the query of where he was going to sleep. It was out of the question for him to sleep with her now that she was conscious.

Oblivious to what was going on in her mind, Breck grabbed a fur-lined jacket from a nail beside the door, slung his broad shoulders into it, and disappeared through the doorway. A whirl of snow pirouetted, then danced inside.

As quickly as she could, Trinity tended to her personal needs, feeling less dizzy than before when she slipped back beneath the warm covers of the bed. As if sensing she'd finished, Breck entered the cabin, hung up his jacket, and dragged his fingers through his snow-dusted hair. Glancing briefly at her, he banked the fire and blew out one of the lamps. Only one remained, which, with the fire, cast a muted yellow-orange glow.

He reached for the buttons of his shirt and in seconds tugged it from his jeans and off his shoulders. Underneath he wore long-sleeved cotton underwear, which he whipped over his head, leaving his long hair attractively wild and his chest completely bare.

When she saw his rippling muscles, golden hair and copper-colored, coin-shaped nipples, Trinity's breath shallowed. She watched as he hiked his boot onto the seat of a straight chair, ran his hand inside the scuffed brown leather, and removed a knife, which he laid beside the lamp on the bedside table. As if challenging her to carry out her threat while he slept.

Their eyes engaged before he—indifferently, it seemed—turned away and said, just as insouciantly, "Ever hear that anyone considering revenge needs to dig two graves?"

"One will be sufficient."

"Then make sure it isn't your own."

"Thank you for your concern."

He cut his eyes back to her but said nothing as he unbuttoned the waist of his jeans. Color stole into Trinity's cheeks, and she quickly averted her eyes before rolling onto her side and away from him. She heard the sound of denim being peeled away, saw the room swallowed by shadows as the lamp was extinguished, felt the covers ripped back from her shoulders as his deep, impatient voice rumbled, "You want to move over?"

She jerked around, as fast as her injured body allowed, to face him. She pretended he wasn't standing beside the bed wearing only a defiant look and tight, tight, oh-my-God-tight long underwear that revealingly molded everything she'd once intimately kneed.

"What? Surely you're not—" Her throat was suddenly drier than the Nevada flatlands in summer's prime.

"You're welcome to the floor, China. Frankly, it's too hard and too cold for my taste."

"But—"

"C'mon, I'm freezing my ass off!" he ordered, burying his knee in the feather mattress and causing the bulge in the underwear to shift noticeably.

Anger, along with some emotion she refused to look at with the same conviction with which she refused to look at his jarred masculinity, purled through Trinity's veins. "You're certainly no gentleman, Mr. Brecker," she muttered, scooting to the far side of the bed.

"Nope. It's one of the few advantages of being a murderer. No one expects you to be a gentleman, as well."

"Damn you!" she muttered.

"Sweet dreams to you, too, China," he said with such infuriating calmness that she could cheerfully have slapped him silly.

She soon realized, however, that it was she, not he, who was damned. His back to her, his breathing unruffled, he seemed to fall asleep instantly. She, on the other hand, had never been more awake. Nor more aware...of everything. Clinging to the very edge of the bed, as if she'd been granted six inches and not an inch more, Trinity tried to rein in her runaway thoughts, thoughts encompassing everything from the sublime to the mundane. Shadowy, flickering figures cast by the fire bobbed and weaved with a strange life force. Life. Alive. She was glad to be alive. She had just realized that.

But there's a man lying beside me. Even from this far away, I can feel the heat of him.

Heat. Cold. It was cold outside. She could hear the silence of the snow as it blanketed the earth.

And the sound of Breck's breathing. He hadn't shaved. What would the stubble of his beard feel like if I touched it?

Touch. He had touched her. All of her. The thought made her feel...funny. As if her body were suddenly that of a stranger.

He's nothing more than a stranger, a stranger whose bare, golden-haired chest glistened in the firelight. And yet, he's more than a stranger; he's an enemy...an enemy whose chest is made of supple power and solid strength.

Strength. She had to build up her strength. She had to stand strong before him. She couldn't be weak. She couldn't be scarred.

Does he think my scars are ugly? Does he feel revulsion when he sees them?

Ugly. She must look ugly. Bringing her hand to her face, she traced her fingertips across cheeks worn free of makeup, lips dry and cracked from fever, hair tumbled until it was neither up nor down but sprigged and sprawled midway between. Searching for the remaining pins, Trinity pulled them from her hair and let it fall about her shoulders, finger-combing it as best she could.

"Be still!" Breck roared.

She jumped as though she'd been caught in the middle of some grave crime. "I am!" she thundered back, angry with him, angry with her thoughts, angry with feelings she neither wanted nor understood. In short, she was just plain angry.

"Like hell you are!"

As he spoke, he flopped onto his belly, propping himself up on his elbows as his eyes rooted through the darkness to find hers.

For shattered heartbeats, both ceased to breathe. Trinity was agonizingly aware of tousled blond hair and the provocative way the blanket fell away from his shoulders, creating a beckoning tunnel of shadow down his hair-matted chest. Breck was all too conscious of sin-black hair scattered alluringly about a naturally beautiful face.

"Go to sleep!" he growled, punching the pillow, collapsing into it, and once more rolling away from her. He damned the hard ache that had sprung to life below his waist.

"Go to Hades!" she retorted. She wanted to flee to her side, as well, but the injuries hurt too much for her to consider that position again. Instead, she stared at the ceiling. And thought... though she hated herself for it. A long while later, when the fire was but warm ashes, she sensed that Breck was still awake, too. Her anger now spent, the darkness making her bold, she asked the question she'd wanted to ask since regaining consciousness. "Why didn't you let me die?" she said softly.

"You were too much trouble to bury."

She ignored his flippant, grumbled answer and repeated, "Why?"

The silence that followed was the width and breadth of forever.

"I don't know, China," he said at last. "I don't know."

The bewilderment scoring his voice convinced her that he spoke the truth.

And thus the pattern of the days was set. By day Breck and Trinity, the latter still more dependent on her enemy than she would have liked, cohabited in a predominantly silent, more often than not strained, atmosphere, while at night they shared the same bed. Increasingly, sleeping together began to seem natural, and, awakening to the frigid mornings, she hastened less to disengage herself from the warmth of his body, a body she invariably found during the night.

Increasingly, too, for reasons Trinity never fully understood, Breck would unexpectedly storm from the cabin and fell another tree, or split to smithereens the chunks he'd already cut and split, all of which would eventually enter the cabin as firewood. Firewood that clearly wasn't needed. It was now stacked so high it would have taken a half decade of the most brutal winters to use, and the slightest whisper of sound threatened to send it tumbling. Breck had even begun to stack it outside on the porch. Yet he continued to cut more, or at least to split what he had, only grunting when she once asked him the why of it.

Nor did Trinity understand the insidious thing that had begun to happen to her. Their forced proximity had begun to wear away her resolve, and she had to keep reminding herself of her sworn mission to kill Breck. Whole days, days spent simply on the details of living, went by without it ever crossing her mind. Then she'd suddenly be jolted back to reality, which ushered in guilt and resulted in a reaffirmation of her cause.

On the eve of one such day, she watched Breck peeling potatoes with his bowie knife. Her eyes had followed him for a long while, taking in his every fluid yet ever economical movement. Something—the scar, the knife, her guilty conscience—reminded her that this man who was casually preparing her supper was the man who'd killed her mother. She felt the bilious taste of hate, which was instantly diluted when she remembered that this same man had saved her own life—had changed her bandages, had brought cool water to her hot lips, had cared when there had been no one else to care. This realization caused wildly contradictory emotions and in many ways tasted more vile than pure hate. To compensate for wavering, she staunchly rededicated herself to her purpose.

Glancing up, Breck saw that renewed avowal burning brightly in her amber irises. Finished with his task, he daringly plunged the knife into the cabinet top, then deliberately turned his back to her while adding the potatoes to the beef stew.

She made no move to carry out her threat. Later, on the way to bed, however, she picked up the knife from where he nightly placed it on the bedside table. She turned it over in her hands, then glanced up at him, blatantly conveying her silent warning that once she was stronger, she'd have her vengeance. Laying the knife back on the bedside table, she crawled into bed. Then, as happened each night once sleep had overpowered her, she melted against him, taking from him the strength she could never take from him while awake, the strength she would ultimately wield against him, the strength he willingly let her have.

A week's worth of days later, which placed the date squarely in the middle of November, a knock on the door shattered the silence before Trinity and Breck had had a chance to crawl out of bed—or maybe before they'd taken the chance offered. Trinity immediately pushed away the warmth of the hard chest cradling her.

"What—" she began, only to have the word drowned out by Breck's "Damn! We overslept. Yeah, just a minute!" he called toward the door as he dragged a pair of jeans over his underwear-clad hips. Not bothering with a shirt, he pushed his sleep-mussed hair from his eyes and opened the door to Dancey Harlan. The conductor showed up at regular intervals to bring supplies, but he had never come quite this early before . . . and never when it was so obvious that she and Breck had shared the bed, Trinity realized.

"Are we too early?" Dancey asked.

"No. We overslept," Breck answered, stepping back to let him enter the cabin.

Trinity, shoving her hair out of her eyes, was pondering the word *we* when Ellie's pert blond curls bobbed into the cabin.

"Ellie!" Trinity cried, delight streaming through her as sunlight began to stream through the windows. "I didn't know. I didn't—" Her words were lost in a huge hug.

"Oh, Trinity!" Ellie squealed, embracing her friend again, then holding her at arm's length. "Let me look at you."

Suddenly Trinity felt self-conscious. Her hair was in shambles; her body, clad in Breck's shirt, was still warm from his nearness. It was as obvious as snow in winter that Breck had lain beside her. His imprint was still in the mattress. He was still shirtless and shoeless. None of which seemed to perturb him in the least.

"You look wonderful," Ellie pronounced finally.

"I'm feeling better. Much better," Trinity said, hugging his shirt tightly to her as her eyes involuntarily sought him out. He was squatting before the hearth, giving birth to a new fire, which sent tender shoots of light outward. When he stood, pushing from the balls of his feet, his eyes found hers, but it was to Ellie that he spoke.

"Thanks for coming," he said, proving beyond a doubt that the moment had been planned.

"My pleasure."

"I heard about the baby. Congratulations."

Ellie smiled. "Thank you."

Breck's eyes raised once more to Trinity. "I've got to go into town to see about some business. Ellie's going to stay with you."

Trinity nodded, thinking he sounded very much like a husband explaining his actions to his wife. She immediately banished the ridiculous notion, along with the heavy feeling that came from nowhere at the thought of his leaving her.

"There're plenty of things to cook, and I've drawn plenty of water," Breck said, speaking again to Ellie. "We won't be long."

"We've certainly got plenty of firewood," Ellie said innocently.

"Yeah," Breck muttered, snatching his clothes and throwing them on. Without even looking in Trinity's direction, he stalked from the cabin, Dancey in tow.

The day passed pleasantly as the two women unpacked some of Trinity's things, which Ellie had brought from the hotel, and indulged in the idle, girlish talk of good friends. By some unspoken agreement, both avoided the topic of the train robberies. Ellie asked no questions; Trinity offered no answers. As morning faded into early afternoon and early afternoon into late afternoon, Trinity began to watch the clock. Why wasn't he back? He'd said he wouldn't be late. Surely nothing had happened to him. Surely— "What?"

"I said, I told everyone you and Breck were having an affair."

"You did what?"

"Don't get so excited," her friend said calmly. "I had to say something to account for him carrying you off." Ellie giggled. "And people love to believe in affairs."

Though Trinity could see the wisdom of her friend's act, the thought of an affair with Breck left her...more breathless than it should have.

"I don't suppose there's reason to hope?" Ellie said, the naughtiness in her eyes suggesting that she remembered how the couple had been found.

"Absolutely none! Breck is the last man I'd—" Trinity stopped at the sudden tears that had jumped to Ellie's green eyes. "Ellie?"

"You scared me so badly," the woman whispered. "I thought you were going to die."

The women tumbled into each other's arms.

"I have my reasons for doing what I did," Trinity said after her friend's tears had dried. "I mean, for robbing the train. Reasons that I can't tell you now. I will later. I promise." *After I kill Madison Brecker. You'd only try to stop me if you knew what I was planning,* she thought.

"Good reasons or no," Ellie said, "I only know that Breck worked like the devil to keep you alive."

"I know," Trinity answered, though she, like Breck himself, couldn't even have come close to explaining why.

The first Trinity knew that Breck and Dancey had returned was when Dancey's head popped around the cabin door. "You ready, Mrs. Oates? We're running a little late, and if we don't get started soon, it'll be night before we return, and that husband of yours will have my hide."

"I'm ready," Ellie answered, bundling up her things, hugging her friend goodbye, and promising to return soon. Trinity hardly heard the promise, however, over the thumping of her heart. Breck had come into view beyond the window, and she watched as he assisted Ellie onto a horse.

Dancey, bringing one last bag of supplies to the cabin, nodded his own goodbye to Trinity. "Good to see you looking so well, miss."

"Thank you," she said as he started to close the door. "Mr. Harlan?"

He turned.

"Have I, uh . . . have I thanked you properly for what you did? I mean, for helping Br—Mr. Brecker?"

"No thanks are necessary."

"Yes, they are. Thank you."

"Well, I reckon you're as welcome as a sinner to God's house." The big man, garbed in the folds of a fur coat and a cap, hesitated. Then, as if deciding to say something, he added, "About Breck, miss . . . Whatever differences you two have, remember, he isn't a bad 'un. He's hard—he's had to be—but he isn't bad. Not deep down. And I reckon you and I have something in common now. Breck saved us both. Me from a heathen Injun who decided to decorate his belt with my scalp. Breck carried me five miles to help. Five miles in cold weather . . . and I'm no little man. So you see, he may be rough, but he's got heart, miss."

Heart. That was what almost burst from her chest minutes later when Breck, their departing guests behind him, entered the cabin. Neither spoke. Neither could. Both simply stared as cold swept into the room, Trinity wondering how it was possible to miss one's enemy so much, Breck thinking that, for the first time in his life, he felt pleasure. Honest-to-God pleasure. And this elusive thing had finally been brought about by nothing more than the simple sight of this woman after what had seemed an unbearably long separation.

Silently he drew his eyes from hers, closed the door behind him and removed his coat; silently they ate the remains of the food Ellie had prepared for lunch. Still without a word, he started for the door. Night was falling fast, and evening chores awaited.

"What's this?" Trinity asked, seeing for the first time a small tissue-wrapped package on her side of the bed.

"Just something I thought you might like," he muttered uncomfortably, wishing now that he hadn't made Dancey and himself late by stopping at the drugstore.

As he spoke, she unfolded the tissue. An oval bar of ivory lavender-scented soap lay nestled within the paper. She glanced up, touched beyond words.

"It's nothing," he said gruffly when he saw the glaze of tears in her eyes.

Still Trinity said naught.

Ultimately, Breck had to get away from the suffocating emotions in the room, so he slammed out of the cabin. When he returned later, she'd had her hand bath and was already in bed. The lights were out save for one lamp, which he quickly snuffed. Removing his clothes, he crawled in beside her. Both hugged their respective sides of the bed, as if their salvation lay in keeping their distance.

That night, Breck made an interesting observation: Both heaven and hell smelled of lavender.

Chapter Thirteen

What do you mean you had nothing to do with that tree being felled across the track?"

Breck asked the question at midmorning the next day as he sat in a straight-backed chair before the fire, his hands wrapped around a steaming mug of coffee, a startled look wrapped around his unshaven face. With the first light of day, the smell of lavender so thick in his senses he'd thought he was going to die, he'd sprung from the bed and, without fixing breakfast, stormed out into the clear, cold Nevada morning to chop more unneeded wood. This he'd stacked alongside the rest on the cabin porch until the pile reached as high as the one inside the cabin, which was to say that both were as high as a new miner's dreams...and just as fragile. Exhausted, he'd come in, fried some eggs and a slab of fresh bacon, and had settled down to a second cup of coffee when Trinity made the unexpected announcement.

"Exactly what I said. I wasn't responsible for the tree. And I didn't shoot at the engineer, and I didn't roll the boulder across the track." When she saw Breck's look of astonishment, even disbelief, Trinity added, "Why would I lie? I've been honest about everything else."

Brutally honest, Breck thought, pushing to his feet as he tried to assimilate what he'd just heard. From the beginning, she'd shot straight from the hip about her plan to kill him. Strangely, grudgingly, he had to admire her straightforwardness, just as he had to respect her convictions—even if those convictions shortened his life. No, she wasn't lying. But if she hadn't been behind the harassment, then...

"Who?" he asked, verbalizing the thought on both of their minds.

On Trinity's was the additional question of why she was telling him this. Why didn't she simply let someone quietly assist her with his destruction?

"You don't have any idea who'd want to ruin you?" she asked, conveniently shoving the other bothersome question to the back of her mind.

Breck glanced over his shoulder from where he stood staring out the window. His eyes were edged with hardness and streaked with a sarcasm that streamed down to curl one corner of his mouth. "You mean besides you?"

Still in bed, cushioned against the pillows, Trinity didn't back down. "Besides me."

Breck snorted. "Well, now, China," he drawled, "I figure that could be everyone in Nevada and three-quarters of everyone outside it. I'm not exactly filthy rich with friends and well-wishers."

For a split second, Trinity thought she saw Breck's cold eyes thaw with vulnerability, but then they appeared to freeze over again, leaving her uncertain whether she'd seen anything beyond what—perhaps—she'd wanted to see.

"Surely you've some idea of who could be doing this. Someone who's made a threat. Someone—"

"Don't worry about it." He cut her off sharply and once more presented her with his back. "It's not your problem."

The tone of his voice was dismissive, the square of his shoulders an impenetrable, unbreachable fortress. Trinity suddenly had the strong, inexplicable urge to batter down his defenses, to see his eyes warm, to see his posture something besides unwelcoming. Suddenly she wanted to know why.

"Why do you shut people out?" she asked softly.

The silence stretched wide and deep, and Trinity was just reaching the conclusion that he wasn't going to answer the question when he slowly pivoted to face her. His eyes were emptier than she'd ever seen them, a hurting kind of empty that gnawed at one's soul.

"If you're smart, you learn to shut the door before someone shuts it on you." His look challenged her, with her murderous mission, to deny the wisdom of his remark. Minute dragged into minute, one silent note banding with another to form a heavy, soundless symphony. Finally, he swallowed the last of the coffee, slid the mug onto the mantel, and, grabbing his jacket from the hook by the door, strode out of the cabin.

Literally, and symbolically, he shut the door behind him.

It was late afternoon before he opened it again, this time to the succulent smell of food. His hand still on the doorknob, his gaze flew to Trinity, who stood testing a skilletful of corn cakes to see if they were done. She had traded his shirt for a jonquil-yellow silk wrapper, which had been among the things Ellie had brought. The silken garment clung as if well pleased to be reunited with its owner.

The bright, blaring rays of the sun had caressed Breck all afternoon, washing from his mind everything but the fact that someone besides Trinity was trying to destroy him. Though the fact was troubling, he had cherished the worrisomeness of it. At least for a while he had been able to think of something other than the haunting heat of a woman's body, the raven satin of her hair, the perfect porcelain of her skin, skin that smelled maddeningly of lavender. Now, all that he'd battled to forget came scurrying back—with a jonquil-yellow vengeance.

"What are you doing out of bed?" he asked harshly as he closed the door behind him.

"I was bored."

"You're supposed to be," he said, shrugging out of his jacket. "You're convalescing."

"I don't like convalescing."

"Then don't rob trains. And get back in bed."

"The trick is to stay away from ill-tempered train owners. And I'm fine."

"Get back—"

"What do you think's wrong?" Trinity asked him, swatting at a wisp of hair that had escaped the topknot she'd made. She longed to wash her hair, but, failing that, she'd done the next best thing. She'd pinned it up and out of her way.

Not a damned thing's wrong, Breck thought, looking at the gentle curve of her neck, the arch of her throat, the wayward tendrils of her hair, before suddenly realizing she'd meant the skillet of corn cakes. The skillet of flat corn cakes.

"No soda."

"Darn!" Trinity muttered. "I knew I forgot something." She gave a deep sigh that was part frustration and part sheer fatigue.

"Get...back...in...bed." When she still hesitated, Breck urged her forward. "Now!"

Where his palm touched the small of her back felt warm, as though his fingers were burning through the silk, but Trinity ignored the fervid feeling and edged back into bed. She tucked her feet beneath the covers.

"All I did was heat up yesterday's soup," she said, not wanting him to think any great meal awaited him. "And make some coffee. And the corn cakes. Look, I'm sorry about the soda."

"They're fine," he said, removing the remaining two pancakelike corn cakes from the long-handled skillet, "but you should have stayed in bed."

"When you didn't come back for dinner, I, uh...I thought you might be hungry...and I was bored, and..." She let her words trail off, wondering if she'd said too much. Could he discern from her words how she'd looked up each and every time she'd heard the slightest noise outside? Did the tone of her voice reveal the disappointment she'd felt? A disappointment that she couldn't in the least explain? Least of all to herself?

He glanced up—guiltily? "I, uh...I had some work to do in the shed."

Anything to keep me away from you, he might have said, but he didn't want to admit it, even to himself.

In minutes, he'd dished up a bowl of soup and handed it to her, along with a corn cake. After serving himself, as well, he drew a chair up to the cedar table and, facing her, started to eat. The soup was hot and tasty, the corn cake as dry and hard as a rainless prairie. Breck eased his teeth from the undented cake and sought another location in which to bury his incisors. He bit down, sawed back and forth, and finally tore off a chunk, which he folded into his mouth cautiously. Just as cautiously, he began to chew, with the result that the wad grew bigger...and bigger...and bigger. At long last he swallowed and was rewarded by having the pasty ball disappear down his throat. He prayed it wouldn't clog anything important. After ripping the remainder of the cake into pieces, he drowned them in the bowl of soup.

"You're cheating," Trinity said, an uneaten, undented cake in her hand, the traces of an elfin grin on her lips.

Breck jerked his head, like a little boy caught in a compromising act by his mother. Within seconds, the smile on Trinity's lips thretened to smear itself across his.

"Clever, China," he drawled. "When you said you were going to kill me, I thought you meant with a gun or a knife. I never suspected a loaded corn cake."

Smiles widened until bona fide grins wreathed both sets of lips. As it had once before, the beauty of his smile took Trinity totally by surprise and left her breathless. Breck, too, was having trouble getting a decent lungful of air.

Suddenly, slowly, as if they'd just realized what they were smiling about, both sobered. Trinity glanced down at her soup, Breck at his, and they finished the meal in their customary silence. After he cleared away the dishes, Breck shaved in a mirror angled on the mantel. Trinity deliberately refused to watch, though once she looked up to see his tongue spiked against his cheek. She remembered that tongue heatedly foraging in her mouth. The memory caused a curl of fire to shimmer through her. She quickly glanced away, but not before their eyes brushed in the mirror's silver surface. The curl grew hotter.

Later, when he crawled into bed beside her, she pretended to be asleep. Breck stretched out, trying to uncoil the bunched muscles in his neck and shoulders. He was bone-tired and needed to sleep. God, how he needed to sleep! He was tired of thinking. Tired of worrying. Tired of smelling lavender.

Jesus, why had he bought her that damned bar of soap?

Rolling onto his back, careful to keep a wall of distance between himself and the woman at his side, he draped an arm across his forehead and heaved a frustrated sigh. Forcibly, he willed his mind to another subject. Any subject. The shed. The horse. Going into town the day before. Dancey. Ellie. The unexpected pleasure of seeing Trinity after a day's absence.

Pleasure and lavender.

Breck gritted his eyes together, trying to destroy the sensory images. Unfortunately, all he managed to do was conjure up another—the mental portrait of a black-haired woman in a clinging jonquil-yellow robe.

Throwing back the covers, Breck slung his feet over the side of the bed. He grabbed his undershirt, which lay abandoned on the floor, and thrust his head into it, then ran his legs into jeans before wrestling on his boots. Crossing the room as quietly as he could, he snatched his fur-lined jacket from the hook, slid his arms into it, and opened the door.

Cold, grasping air hurried toward him as he stepped onto the porch. Leaning against a column, he turned up his collar and rammed his hands into his jacket pockets. He stared out into the night. Above twinkled a sky full of gray stars, while below, highlighted by silver moonglow, lay a coverlet of snow so pure, so white, that it demanded the world whisper in its majestic presence.

Where was a shooting star when you needed one? Breck thought. He could use a little peace of mind, a little peace of soul. Refusing to concentrate on what had driven him from bed—namely, the woman beside him in that bed—he focused on what had occupied a major portion of his thoughts throughout the day. Who was harassing his railroad? And why? There wasn't much he hadn't done in his life, though that truth paled in comparison with the rumors that tattled there was nothing he hadn't done. With that kind of reputation, one made one's share of enemies. One such enemy lay asleep inside the cabin, though, irony of ironies, he wasn't guilty of what she accused him of. Breck's usually sullen mouth quirked in a joyless smile. Hell, maybe that was sly Fate's way of paying him back for all he *was* guilty of.

And who was going to pay back Ada McCook?

He'd been so preoccupied the past few weeks that his grim discovery of who had killed Su-Ling had gotten pushed aside, trampled underfoot by higher priorities.

And what was he going to do with the woman inside the cabin? Assuming, of course, that the woman inside the cabin didn't do something with him first. He had no answers to any of these questions. He knew only one thing: He had to hang on to the railroad, because in hanging on to it, he hung on to himself. With the railroad, he proved his worth. Without the railroad, he had nothing, was nothing, because a loner, a misfit, the man he'd been forced to be all his life, cast no shadow.

Shadow.

Breck jerked around at the sudden shadow that fell from the silently opened doorway of the cabin. A shaft of moonlight drizzled about the feminine form, lending it a hazy, ethereal quality that mocked mere reality. She stood, her head high, her hair tousled, draped in the thick blanket she'd removed from the bed. She stood . . . beautiful. Utterly beautiful. And Breck thought that if she'd come to kill him, if his knife was hidden within the woolen folds, he would die with a sight before him that any man would deem worth dying for.

"I . . . I couldn't sleep," Trinity said, her voice gliding sweetly through the white winter hush. Wary, Breck said nothing. He simply watched. His muscles were tensed, though a casual observer would never have known it. "May I join you?" she asked, making no move to do so without his permission.

"It's cold out here." The breath frosting from his mouth testified to the truth of his words. He glanced away from her and back into the snowy, dark night.

Trinity interpreted the absence of a refusal as encouragement and stepped forward, angling around a mountain-high stack of wood to stand near an adjacent column. She, too, quietly peered at the moon-brushed landscape.

"You should be asleep," he said, his voice seeming to mingle with the prancing moonbeams.

"So should you."

Neither could argue the point.

"How far is it into town?" she asked.

Breck looked at her, and each of them knew what the other was thinking. It was a logical question, should she make the trip back to town alone. And each of them knew under what circumstances that would be.

"About an hour's ride—" he nodded to the east "—in that direction." Stillness, silence, the howl of a lone wolf. "Have you come to kill me?"

Trinity's eyes roved from the distant town to the man at her side. Breck's eyes dropped to the blanket hugged close about her. She could see that he was considering the possibility that she had a knife concealed within its folds.

"Maybe. Maybe not," she said casually. "Is now a good time?"

He shrugged. "As good as any."

"Where do you want to be buried?" she taunted.

"You have to kill me first, China. Which means you have to get a little lucky and I have to get a lot careless."

"Assuming I do get lucky and you do get careless, where do you want to be buried?"

"Assumptions granted, I guess anywhere out under the stars will do." He tilted his gaze upward, spanning the panorama of glittering, winking lights. Like a gentle thief, a memory stole through his thoughts, and he heard himself saying, ''Up there, where dreams sparkle, there is no hurt or pain. Only joy.''

Trinity's head turned sharply at the recitation of her mother's words, words she'd heard a thousand times, words she'd never expected to hear again.

Breck sensed her recognition, sensed, too, her confusion about why her mother would have shared such a personal sentiment with him.

''We were friends,'' he said, simply, sincerely.

His words only baffled her more. How could this man, the man who had killed her mother, have been her friend? It dawned on Trinity that she guessed she'd always thought Breck had been a client of her mother's.

No! The denial screamed through her head. The thought was far too unsettling, as was the thought of him with any woman. Except her? Shoving the harassing thoughts aside, she focused on the fact that Breck had known her mother.

''What was she like?'' she asked, her request filled with reverence. On some plane of reason, she realized what an odd inquiry it was to make of her mother's murderer. ''I, uh...I can't remember too well. I try to. Sometimes I remember some things—a smile, an expression, a touch—but mostly the memories are faded.''

All the years of wondering about his own mother made Breck sensitive to Trinity's plea. He heard the small boy in him uttering the same request, though the man in him would have shunned making it.

''She—'' He grappled for the right words. ''She was the gentlest person I've ever known.'' Poignant memories swamped him, memories that encouraged him to go on. ''She had a soft voice...sort of like wind playing through leaves...and a pretty smile...but a sad smile, too. And her eyes were sad...dark and sad. I think she'd been hurt . . . badly.''

''By my father?'' Trinity asked, refusing to try to reconcile the caring tone of Breck's voice with the act he'd committed.

Breck could see the interest in Trinity's eyes; it shone more brightly than the moon. ''Maybe. Probably.''

''Did she ever mention him?'' she asked eagerly. ''I mean, his name—''

''No,'' Breck interrupted, certain he had no right to divulge what he thought he knew to be true. The past, at least for now, was between a sad-eyed Su-Ling and maybe an even sadder-eyed Jedediah. Breck further excused his decision by telling himself he wasn't lying. Su-Ling hadn't mentioned the name of Trinity's father.

Disappointment marched through Trinity, but she hid it behind another question. "Was she pretty?"

Not as pretty as you, Breck thought. "Yes."

Trinity embraced this new information, letting it mingle with the faded bits and pieces she'd clung to so tenaciously over the years. Despite the chill of the night—a sudden wind breathed its frozen breath upon her—she felt warmed by Breck's remembrances of her mother. She gave a sad, wan smile. "As a little girl, I wanted to be like her...I wanted to wear my hair up with pretty pins in it...I wanted to wear perfume and smell like flowers...I wanted...I wanted to be a lady just like her."

The unhealthy smile died, lost in the bitter knowledge that society had labeled her mother everything but a lady. Just as she herself was viewed as a demirep, a woman of poor reputation. Appearances could be deceiving, however. Breck had betrayed her mother under the guise of friendship. Plus, she now knew that the older couple who had raised her never could have done it on their paltry earnings. She knew, too, that she'd spent a lifetime pretending not to care that her mother had been a prostitute.

"Your mother was a lady," Breck said, as if he had read her mind. Trinity raised her eyes to his. "A real lady."

The night deepened around them as each sought answers from the other to life questions neither could voice. They could only feel them...and be strangely comforted by each other's presence.

A brittle breeze exploded into action again, dragging Breck's blond hair onto his forehead. With his collar turned up, with the shadows settling in the creases around his expressionless eyes and mouth, with his hair ruffling to the rhythm of the wind, Trinity thought he looked wild, untamed. She realized, too, that she was afraid of him, but that that dark demon within him fascinated her as much as it frightened her. As it had from the moment she'd met him. Perhaps because she sensed a sibling demon within herself.

The breeze had also fluttered Trinity's hair to life, lifting streamers of silk from the topknot. The tail of the blanket flapped, as well, drawing Breck's attention to the swell of her hips, then to her shoulders, clad in jonquil-yellow silk, which had come into view because the blanket had slipped. Breck's eyes lowered to the point where her hands clasped the blanket to her breasts . . . the only spot where she could be concealing a knife.

The wind rose again. Breck stepped closer, shielding her from its cold fury with his tall body. And then he took one more step, leaving himself wholly, carelessly, vulnerable to attack.

Time stood still. His eyes met hers. Each pair of eyes lowered to a pair of lips. Lips each remembered, though both had tried to forget. Slowly withdrawing his hands from his pockets, he reached toward her.

Trinity's heart raced.

Breck leaned into her . . . and gently adjusted the blanket more securely about her shoulders. When he finished, he hesitated, his hands apparently reluctant to leave her body.

"You'd better go in," he whispered at last, his breath a hot vapor upon her wind-chilled cheek. Whom it would be better for—him or her—he didn't expand upon. He simply released her.

She stepped back. One long, slow look their only communication, she walked toward the door and, leaving Breck to watch her, disappeared inside the cabin. Her heart was still pounding as she spread the blanket back on the bed and crawled once more beneath the covers. Stretching the width of the bed, she laid the knife back on the bedside table.

It had been a mistake.

Breck knew it the moment the lamplight painted her nude silhouette against the sheet he'd strung across the room. Her request, made the following evening after supper, had seemed reasonable. A bath. She'd wanted to have a proper bath and wash her hair. Both he could understand, since he'd bathed several times to her none since they'd been in the cabin. The cold of the shed, where he'd washed, had seemed appropriate, considering the ever-increasing heat of his body. So tonight he'd agreed to her request. He'd even complied with her need for privacy. Which was where he'd made his real mistake. Her bathing stark naked before him couldn't be as provocative as the shapely shadows dancing on the muslin.

Damn her innocent, sensual movements!

Damn the smell of lavender!

Damn that fact that he needed a woman!

An image of buxom Millie Rhea started to form in his mind but wouldn't even complete itself. He didn't need Millie Rhea. He needed this woman. And what scared the living hell out of him was the fact that he could no longer distinguish between needing and wanting.

Snatching a log from the plenteous stack, he threw it on the already crackling fire. Every time he caught a glimpse of curved neck or stretched arm or rounded breast, he stuck another log on the fire, with the result that the disgruntled fire was about ready to spit them back. Reaching for the poker, he jabbed and probed and forced his mind elsewhere, though it was quickly yanked back by the sound of trickling water . . . and a little sigh of contentment that did big things to Breck.

He gritted his teeth and attacked the fire.

"Mmm," Trinity murmured, leaning her head back against the rim of the wooden tub and letting the warm water soak deep into her body. "It feels so good."

Breck grunted, thinking that the ache he was feeling was both good and bad and utterly unbearable. He was about ready to climb the walls. Which was the state he'd been in ever since he'd draped the blanket about her shoulders the night before.

"Thank you," she said. "For the bath."

"Yeah," he muttered.

Trinity didn't even notice his strained voice, so intent was she on enjoying the heaven she now had. Gradually, though, she became aware that the water was cooling, and she set about quickly washing her hair.

Breck could tell from her silhouette that her arms, unaccustomed to exercise, were growing tired. Probably, too, the wounds, which she now insisted on dressing herself, were still tender, restricting her movements. She could hardly lift the pitcher to rinse the soap from her hair. When she finally did, she almost dropped it.

"Are you all right?" he called. No answer. "China?"

"I'm fine," she said, her voice small and hollow. "I almost dropped the pitcher."

He longed to help her. God, how he longed to help her! "How much longer—"

"I'm finished," she said, and he saw her reach for a towel and turban her hair. She stood, water visibly sluicing from her slim body. Breck's mouth went dry. He told himself to look away, but he couldn't. Damn it, he couldn't! And so he watched as she stepped from the tub, then bent at the waist to pat her slender legs dry. His eyes were riveted to the shapely swell of her derriere.

Groaning, he jerked his gaze away and fed the satiated fire two more logs.

After rebandaging the wounds, she pulled back the corner of the sheet. Her eyes, looking tired from her efforts, grazed Breck's before she walked toward the fire, the folds of the yellow silk wrapper swishing with each barefoot step. With a grace that stole his breath, she knelt before the fire and released the turban, allowing her hair, dark and long and the subject of more than one of his dreams, to cascade about her in moist, bewitching disarray. She reached for a nearby brush and, grimacing at having to raise her arm so high, drew it through the rich, silky tresses.

Though he could see her pain increase with each brushstroke, Breck warned himself to stay away from her, not to go anywhere near her, certainly not to do anything as stupid as volunteering to...

"Here, give me that brush," he ordered, crouching beside her and seizing the brush before she could even consider relinquishing it.

Startled, she glanced up. "I can—"

"Be still!" he said, beginning to rake the brush through her hair with masculine awkwardness. A strangely endearing awkwardness.

Trinity allowed herself to be seduced by the soothing slide of the brush through the wetness of her hair. She allowed herself to be seduced by the warmth of the fire, the nearness of the man. Since the scene on the porch, when his breath had caressed her cheek, she'd told herself she hadn't killed Breck because she was still too weak to execute her plan, that she'd merely been walking through it to see how easy it would be to take him by surprise. But since that moment she'd felt a heightened awareness of him. She'd tried to deny it, tried to ignore it, but it lived and breathed as a dull ache within her. Now, tired of fighting it and herself, she simply wallowed in the moment, closing her eyes and, little by little, tilting her head back until her neck was fully exposed. She'd kill him—that she had vowed to do, that she would do—but for now she'd simply let him stroke her.

She looked like a sleek she-panther arched on a limb, soaking up the heat of a sultry sun, Breck thought, feeling the velvet strands of her hair wrap themselves around his hand as though eager for his touch. Soft and wet, her hair was an inebriant, and he was more than willing to drink of its heady black wine.

With each stroke, the tendrils of her drying hair, which fell to her waist, teased the front of his pants. Though feather-light, the tendrils seemed to fall against him with an unnatural weight that made him ache. God, he ached! God, he...

When had his hand grasped a fistful of her hair? When had she, her eyes still closed, rolled her head to the side? And which of them had uttered the strangled cry that sounded somewhere between savage and desperate?

Time stood perfectly still, though the room seemed to whirl with expectancy. Slowly, Trinity opened her eyes. Her hazy eyes. She and Breck stared as though they'd never seen each other before, as though they'd never seen anything *but* each other before. Memories, wild and sweet, drenched them, memories of a kiss that had burned its way into two empty souls. A primitive hunger gnawing at their senses, they dropped their eyes to each other's parted lips.

Don't! he told himself, his head already lowering. *Don't do this!*

"No," she whispered, but she didn't turn away as his body loomed closer and closer, shadowing her with its dark strength.

He kissed her.

His mouth, hard against hers, made their previous kiss seem tame and adolescent. Parting her lips, he thrust his tongue inside. When he met no resistance, but rather felt Trinity melt against him, he tried to appease his thirst, to satisfy his hunger, but each thrust of his tongue only demanded another and another and another. . . .

From within Trinity burst emotions foreign and new. This man, this stranger, this enemy, made her feel...different. He made her feel empty inside, as though some part of her were yawning wide open, yet he also made her feel full. Her breasts, beneath the silken fabric, felt heavy and tingly, while farther down, at a spot secretly hidden between her thighs, she felt a throbbing emptiness. Softly, wantonly, she whimpered.

Breck drew his mouth from hers and, angling her head back with the hand he had tangled in her hair, planted ragged kisses along the satin of her neck.

"Breck," she whispered, her voice reedy, thin, unfamiliar even to her.

"Say it again!" he rasped. "Say my name again!"

"Breck . . . Breck—" He kissed the valley of her throat and felt his name vibrate against his lips. "Breck . . . Br—"

His lips once more ground into hers, while his hands slid to bracket her face in a vise. Lost in emotion, Trinity placed an anchoring hand over his. It was then that she felt the scar. The painful reminder of her treason. Through the warm mist of feelings sinuously swirling through her woman's body, she latched on to a remnant of sanity and reeled it slowly toward her. This was the man who'd killed her mother, the man who didn't deny killing her mother, the man she'd sought for eighteen long years.

"No," she murmured, pushing her lover away. "No!"

Startled, Breck peered into her wide, defiant eyes. Her lips were still parted, still moist and red from his mouth's sweet plundering. Her hair was still damp from its washing, his name still lingered in the air, passion still swam in their bodies.

And yet . . .

Hate now stalked the room, burning the haze from her eyes, setting her oh-so-kissable mouth into a hard, thin line. In place of his name, hate substituted sullen silence. In all his life, silence had never sounded so loud. Nor had hate seemed such a hurting thing.

"Damn you," he grated, hating her as much as she hated him, simply because, for the first time, she'd made him care that he was hated. Without another word, he pushed to his feet and crossed the room. Grabbing his coat, he slammed out the door.

Within the cabin, the silence settled in, broken only once by a soft keening sound. It might have been the wind. It might have been the fire. But then, it might have been Trinity calling his name.

Chapter Fourteen

When Trinity heard footsteps on the porch the following morning, relief scored her bruised emotions. She hated herself for feeling relieved, but she couldn't pretend she wasn't. The night had been long, longer than she'd known a night could be. For the first time in the two weeks she'd been at the cabin, Breck hadn't slept beside her. In fact, he hadn't returned to the cabin at all.

Quickly busying herself at the hearth, where she unnecessarily shifted the coffeepot brewing a dark roast, she tried to present an image of disinterest. What would they say to each other? Would they merely pretend last night's kiss hadn't happened? Would they—

A firm knock sliced through Trinity's thoughts. She jerked her head toward the sound. Breck wouldn't have knocked. Given his personality, and given that the cabin was his, he would probably have entered with the same arrogance, maybe even the same anger, with which he'd exited.

Dancey.

It had to be Dancey Harlan, and, though she'd grown fond of the Bible-quoting, profanity-spouting conductor, she still felt the sharp sting of disappointment. She hid it, however, behind a manufactured smile as she crossed the room.

Before she could reach the door, the knock came again, this time clothed in the raiment of impatience.

Pulling open the door, she said, "You're up awfully—"

The words screeched to a halt as her eyes collided with those of the tall, thin, beady-eyed man before her. A man with a hawklike nose and a thick gray mustache. Wariness immediately crawled the length of Trinity's spine.

"Mr. Truxtun." She adjusted the jonquil-yellow wrapper about her, chilled more by the coldness in the man's eyes than by the cold of the morn.

"Miss Lee," the Pinkerton agent returned, not a muscle moving in his plain, unprepossessing face.

When he said nothing more, just continued to stare at her like a hunter who'd cornered his prey, she asked, "Could I, uh . . . could I help you?"

"Mr. Brecker," Oliver Truxtun answered. "I've come to see Mr. Brecker."

"You, uh . . . you might find him in the shed." She glanced toward the small building beyond and absently noted that Breck had turned the horse loose in the corral for its morning exercise. Breck himself, however, was nowhere in sight.

In wordless acknowledgment, the agent tapped the brim of the hat he hadn't removed from his head and turned, his measured pace taking him the width of the porch and down the steps. The snow had melted except for privileged patches in shaded areas, over which Truxtun's boot crunched loudly.

In the wake of his departure, Trinity allowed herself a silent sigh of relief.

"Oh, Miss Lee," Oliver Truxtun said, pivoting unexpectedly, "I trust you're feeling better."

Timing. Oliver Truxtun, Trinity thought, knew all about timing, the selection of precisely the right moment to carry an idea forward on the wings of drama. That was something an actress understood, and in that instant Trinity knew that, had Truxtun so chosen, he could have had at least one other career. She knew one other thing, as well. To show weakness before this man would be to know defeat.

She forced herself to smile sweetly. "Much better, thank you. Fainting before a roomful of guests, including the governor, is a most effective way to be convinced one needs a rest. The theatre demands long and late hours." Her smile brightened to a shade of wisdom. "Those candles simply will not burn from both ends . . . at least for long."

"No, I 'spect not," he agreed, adding so subtly that the remark fairly tiptoed, "no more than a gunshot wound can go unattended for long."

Trinity felt the blood drain from her body as surely as it had once before. Now, as then, she felt light-headed. Now, however, she didn't have Breck's arms to faint into. "I—I'm afraid I don't understand."

"Tell me something, Miss Lee," he said, negotiating the steps once more to stand on the porch. Trinity had the oddest feeling that he would have liked to travel on to the shed in search of Breck but that he simply couldn't stop himself from approaching her again. "Do you know a Beatrice Kroates?"

The name meant nothing to Trinity, and she said as much with what breath she could muster.

"Well, she's a maid over at the Chastain. A silly little creature, if truth be told, but nonetheless a woman with a good memory. 'Course, it wasn't likley she'd forget running a private errand for *the* Trinity Lee. Do you remember her now? I believe you sent her to purchase cotton batting. Lots of it, she said."

Trinity's mouth suddenly went drier than all the batting in the world combined, but she managed to say, "Of course, I remember her now. I, uh . . . I just didn't know her name."

"Then you did send her after batting?"

"Yes, but—"

"Why?"

"Why?"

"My question, Miss Lee."

Trinity's chin tilted up in defiance. "And one I don't have to answer." She was only vaguely aware that she'd stepped out onto the porch and that the cold was pebbling her skin with goose flesh. "However," she added, "I will in this case. Batting is used quite regularly for costuming. For taking away and adding inches. I was merely preparing for the play."

The hunter grinned, as if his sharp talons had connected with tender flesh. "Ah, but, Miss Lee, you weren't in town for a play. Simply for the ball."

The words suffocated her in their truth. Damn, she thought, her heart hammering in her ears, why had she backed herself into a corner?

Through the roar in her head came Breck's calm but unmistakably firm voice. "Get in the cabin, Trinity."

Both she and Oliver Truxtun whirled toward the vocal intrusion, but it was only to Trinity that Breck looked. Somehow, without even a single touch, he seemed to absorb her into him, to gather her in his arms as he had once before. Trinity felt his protection cloaking her, felt, too, a wild rush of relief...and some other emotion she couldn't put a name to, an emotion so warm it felt like buttery sunshine pouring down around her.

"Now," Breck said, his blue eyes brilliant with command. "Before you catch your death." When she still seemed frozen in place, he mounted the steps, walked past the Pinkerton agent, and, taking Trinity by the shoulders, turned her around and urged her forward. His eyes, cool and distant, then met those of the man before him. "We'll talk inside."

"I'd rather speak to you out here. Alone."

"We'll talk inside. The three of us."

The two men sized each other up. "As you wish," Truxtun was finally forced to say.

"Is that coffee?" Breck asked, closing the door behind them.

"Yes," Trinity squeezed through a throat that threatened to close.

"Good. Pour me some, will you?" He glanced up at their guest. "Coffee?" he asked, shrugging the jacket from his shoulders and tossing it carelessly across the bed.

"No," the detective answered, likewise refusing the chair offered him.

Casually, as though the morning were like any other, Breck lit a cheroot and took a lazy, deep draft before exhaling a stream of smoke, then straddled a ladder-back chair and folded his arms across the top slat.

"Thanks," he said when Trinity handed him a mug of coffee. She used both hands, since one helped to nullify the trembling of the other.

He took the mug, trapping her shaking fingers between his palms and the cup. When she glanced into his eyes, he gave her a quiet look of reassurance. Reluctantly, she pulled away and sought the warmth of the blazing hearth. She wondered how much Oliver Truxtun knew for a fact and how much was speculation. She also wondered how long she could keep her composure intact.

Composure. Breck was filled to overflowing with it, as usual, as he swallowed a long swig of the hot coffee. Even as Trinity admired his self-control, she resented it. She also thought it faintly unnerving, maybe even alarming, because there was no way of knowing how long it would last.

"Now," Breck said, his gaze shifting from the mug to Truxtun, "spit it out."

"All right," Truxtun responded from where he stood in the middle of the room. "I think Miss Lee's been robbing your train."

A deafening silence ensued, during which Trinity was certain everyone in the room could hear her erratically thumping heart. Intuitively, her eyes had gone to Breck.

His eyes displayed typical blankness, though even as she watched, a sudden twinkle skipped as fast as lightning through the light blue irises, while, in contrast, a slow grin lazed at his mouth. "You been robbing my train, China?"

Calling upon every acting skill she had, Trinity allowed a similar sparkle to glint in her eyes, while she pouted her lips prettily. "No. Though it sounds positively...exciting."

Breck's grin widened, as though he were deeply appreciating the woman before him—on every level there was to appreciate a woman. His eyes then wandered back to Truxtun. "You heard the lady."

"Surely you don't expect her—"

"What I expect," Breck boomed unexpectedly, shattering everyone's pretense of composure, "is a better return on the money I'm paying Pinkerton's!" He shot from the chair and slammed the mug onto the table, setting coffee sloshing, before stalking to the fire and flicking his newly lit cheroot into the flames. The face he turned back to the agent was wreathed in anger. A frightening anger. "What in hell do you mean riding in here making that kind of accusation simply because Trinity asked a maid to buy some batting?"

"Naturally, that isn't all I'm basing—"

"Then let's hear what you're basing the accusation on."

Outwardly, Truxtun looked unruffled, though when he spoke his speech was a note higher and a notch more hurried. "Miss Lee's been on board every time the train was robbed..."

"Coincidence. I could find a half-dozen other people who were, as well."

"...your Mr. Harlan has been buying bandages regularly, plus he bought a vial of morphine..."

"All standard procedure around a railroad."

"...batting was used to stuff the smokestack..."

"They'll sell batting to anyone with the money. And stuffing it in the smokestack isn't that novel an idea. I might have thought of it myself if I were looking to rob a train."

"...plus the batting probably served other—" Truxtun's eyes lowered to Trinity's breasts "—disguising purposes."

Breck tensed, as though he resented Truxtun's allowing himself even so small a degree of familiarity with the woman beside him. Truxtun sensed his advantage.

"We've known from the beginning," the agent continued, "that we were looking for someone small, someone who could wear this." He pulled a glove from his coat pocket and tossed it onto the chair he'd been offered. "We also suspected that a single robber was trying to make us believe a gang was involved. Miss Lee would have that costuming expertise. Just as it would have been necessary for Miss Lee to hide her... distinctive eyes behind either a mask or glasses. Actually, with a little imagination—" he dug into his pocket once more "— these two wanted posters look remarkably like her." He carelessly tossed them atop the glove.

Fear, as cold as a winter storm, shivered down Trinity's spine. She was vaguely aware Breck had stepped closer to her, and she greedily drank in the protective nourishment he was offering. She tried to stay calm, tried to key in on his stable voice.

"That glove would fit half the women in Virginia City," Breck countered smoothly. "Even some of the men. And surely you're not suggesting Miss Lee is the only one alive with any costuming skills. Furthermore, I believe it's common practice for most bandits to shield their eyes." Breck lowered his gaze to the posters. "As for those posters, it's purely a personal call who they look like."

"And how do you explain the unloaded gun?"

"I can't," he answered, "and neither can you."

The two men again engaged in a visual battle, a testing of wills. Breck broke the combative spell by running an arm around Trinity's waist and hauling her hip intimately against his. When he spoke, there was an insinuating man-to-man quality in his voice. "Believe me, Truxtun, if the lady had been shot, if she had a scar anywhere, I'd know it."

Trinity knew the implication was that he'd seen all of her, lover-to-lover, his lips, his hands, his body, carnally knowing hers. She knew, too, that her appearance and that of the room supported the insinuation that they were lovers with carnal knowledge of one another. Only she knew that her tangled hair, the mist in her eyes, the rumpled condition of the bed, spoke not of passion but of restless sleeplessness.

Telling herself it was a role she was playing, a role she must play, she eased her hip closer to Breck's. Though it was unnecessary to the performance, she relished the hard, unyielding planes of his body, luxuriated in the feel of his muscles, muscles that contracted subtly as her arm slid around his waist.

"So," Truxtun said knowingly, "this is how it's to be. You know, of course," he added, "that I don't need you to press charges. With this evidence, I can have her arrested myself."

Trinity tensed. Breck's arm tightened.

"Then do it," Breck dared. "But I warn you, the evidence won't look very convincing when it's learned you couldn't even persuade the man paying the bill. The man who wants the offender brought to justice more than anyone."

As Trinity watched Oliver Truxtun's eyes shade from brown to frustrated black, she wasn't at all certain the Pinkerton agent didn't want the perpetrator caught more than Breck ever had. It hadn't helped this professional investigator's pride—in fact, it had probably injured it considerably—that he'd once lain flat on his back, her gun pointed at his nose. No, he wanted his pound of flesh . . . her flesh.

Truxtun, refusing to give in so easily, made one last stab. "It's understandable how a . . . a dalliance of such brilliant proportions—" he glanced at Trinity, and she wondered vaguely if she was supposed to feel flattered by his comment "—could cloud one's vision. Others, however, will be seeing more clearly."

"What others will see, Truxtun, is that a dalliance is one thing, marriage another. Oh, I did tell you, didn't I, that Miss Lee and I are getting married?" Breck glanced down into the face of the woman in his arms. "You think we ought to invite him to the wedding?" he asked, his lips—lips that had so passionately kissed her the night before, lips that had so passionately cursed her—once more tilted with teasing.

At the word *marriage*, Trinity's entire body stiffened, but she quickly reminded herself that they were playing a game, presenting an illusion. In response, a smile, the sinner-saint smile that had left more than one man's heartbeat irregular, slunk across her lips. "I'll leave that up to you, darling."

At the unexpected endearment, a flicker of some emotion raced across the pale blue of Breck's eyes, but it disappeared as

rapidly as it had come, and he was once more confronting
Oliver Truxtun, his face a study in seriousness.

"How likely, how *believable*, is it that I'd marry a woman I
knew had stolen from me, practically ruined me?"

If it could be said that Truxtun had a predatory disposition,
it could also be said that he was clever enough to know when his
prey had escaped. He was also clever enough not to call this
man the fool he thought he was, for nobody, nobody, called
Madison Brecker a fool. Truxtun took a deep, resigned breath.

"Then I guess there's nothing left for me to do but congrat-
ulate you both," he said, his eyes clashing defiantly, resent-
fully, with Breck's before sliding to Trinity. He touched the
brim of his hat, which he had yet to remove, uttered a curt
"Miss Lee," and walked toward the door.

Relief swamped Trinity, leaving her legs almost unable to
support her when Breck withdrew his arm from her waist and
stepped to the window to watch Oliver Truxtun's departure. She
faced the fireplace, urgently held on to the mantel, closed her
eyes, and took a deep breath, but she could not will away one
fact. One panic-inducing fact.

"He knows I did it," she said, turning to address Breck's
broad back.

He said nothing. He merely continued to stare out the window.

"Oh, God, he knows I did it," she repeated, the full truth of
it hitting her. She raked her hand through her hair. "What am
I going to do?"

She knew it was illogical, but she seized the posters and threw
them into the fire. Flame bubbled around them, singeing, then
curling, the edges of the paper into brown wisps. She reached
for the glove.

"He won't do anything," Breck said, unexpectedly near her
elbow. "He can't. His hands are tied." Snatching the glove
from her before she could toss this remaining evidence into the
flames, he added, "If you think burning this will make the
slightest difference—"

"I know! I know! It just makes me feel better, all right?"

"No, it's not all right. It's stupid."

The two glared at each other, restored once more to the
woman who'd pushed him away the night before and the man
who'd damned her before fleeing the cabin. The woman,
though, longed desperately for the strong yet tender man who'd

stood so faithfully beside her minutes before. And the man longed to have the woman's sweeter-than-honey kisses off his mind for one restful moment. Both looked away, Trinity back to the fire, Breck to the jacket he'd flung across the foot of the bed. Jerking it up, he slung his arms into it, rammed the glove into his pocket, and started for the door.

"I'll have Dancey bring up a preacher," he hurled over his shoulder.

Trinity whirled. "You'll what?"

Breck pivoted as he adjusted his collar. "I'll have Dancey bring up a preacher. Unless you know a better way to get married."

"Married?"

"Yeah. You know—I do, till death do us part, and keep your ass out of jail."

"You—you're not serious," she gasped. She saw his eyes slit to thin strips of blue. "My God, you are serious." Her hand flew to her throat, as if she were choking on the idea.

Breck took two heavy footsteps back into the room. "Let's get something straight, China. The only thing between you and incarceration, maybe even hanging by that pretty neck, is marriage to me."

"That isn't true. Truxtun will forget about our marrying after a while," she said, though she was not at all certain that he would. The Pinkerton agent didn't strike her as one to forget or concede anything. "All we have to do is pretend to be . . . to be lovers for a while longer."

"Wrong," Breck drawled. "Even if Truxtun is willing to forget—which I doubt—I'm not."

"W-what does that mean?"

"It means, my little China star, that either you marry me, or I'll turn you over to Truxtun myself."

Trinity heard the words yet couldn't make sense of them. The cold, unyielding light in his eyes told her to try harder.

"And what's to keep me from turning you in as the murderer you are?" she retaliated.

"Nothing," he granted. "Though I wouldn't want to be in your shoes, trying to prove something that happened eighteen years ago. With no witnesses except a scared child. Besides, since I've so clearly got the goods on you, it might look as if you were simply trying to get even."

The wisdom of his reasoning wrapped its ugly tentacles about her. "Why are you doing this?" Her voice was a whisper of desperation.

He smiled. It was a mirthless twisting of his mouth that would have twisted the guts of anyone watching it. "So you can play the role of grieving widow when you kill me."

"Why?" she insisted, ignoring his flippancy.

The smile died, washed away in a tide of seriousness. "Let's just say that this way I can keep a better eye on you."

Minute sped into minute, yet time seemed to stand perfectly still. It was a time measured in fractured heartbeats and feelings neither of them could have explained—hostility, and some unfamiliar emotion inspired by the mention of marriage. Finally, Breck spun on his heels and threw wide the door.

"I won't marry you," she said, following him out onto the porch. The chill clutched at her, making her shiver in her yellow wrapper. "Whatever the price, I won't marry you."

"At the end of the week."

"I won't marry you!"

"Ask Ellie if you like."

"Are you listening to me, Madison Brecker?"

He stopped abruptly, his eyes finding hers. "Oh, and China, make no mistake about it—this'll be a marriage in every sense of the word."

Something as hot as the sunshine streaming down on the cold winter morning jumped between them. It sizzled, sparked, seared, leaving both of them puzzled by its scorching magnitude. And then Breck turned once more and strode toward the shed. He didn't look back.

"There won't be a marriage in any sense!" Trinity shouted after him. "I'll rot in jail first. I'll burn in hell first. I'll . . . Do you hear me, Madison Brecker? There won't be a marriage!"

"We are gathered here today, before God and man, to unite this man and this woman . . ."

The preacher's nasal recitation grated across Trinity's frayed nerves with the effect of chalk screeching across a blackboard. Would this farce never end? she thought. On the heels of that impatient sentiment she had to admit that, in reality, it had only just begun. Only seconds before, the minister had cleared his throat, drawing the errant attention of the other three people in the cabin—herself, Breck, and Dancey. The latter two had been huddled together for what Trinity suspected were business reasons. Her friend Ellie had not come; she had not been asked. Though the notion was crazy, Trinity thought she had glimpsed a flash of hurt in Breck's otherwise cool, emotionless eyes when he'd learned that she hadn't invited her friend. But why should he care? Moreover, how could she be expected to ask Ellie to witness this desecration of sacred vows?

There was still time, she told herself, still time to call a halt to this. Yet she knew she wouldn't. She'd known from the beginning that she wouldn't. Simply because she couldn't. She was caught, decisively and by the throat, in Madison Brecker's trap. She understood clearly why he was marrying her—hadn't he explicitly spelled it out? As her husband, he could keep a closer watch on her; as her husband, he'd be in a better position to effect her silence regarding his past. He might even be reaping his own revenge on her. Hadn't he once told her that those who plotted revenge should dig two graves? Maybe it had crossed his mind to eliminate, rather than placate, his adversary. Maybe the hunter had become the hunted, with the hunting grounds, ironically, the marriage bed.

Why she was marrying him was clearer still. For all her ranting, she hadn't wanted to go to jail. Which was precisely where Madison Brecker would have sent her had she refused his offer—his demand—of marriage. She had no doubt of that. Had she entertained any, the memory that he'd rescued the glove from destruction would have dispelled it. It was his ace in the hole, evidence, contrary to what he'd tried to make Truxtun believe, that she had robbed his train. How could she have been so stupid as to let him keep the glove?

Rather than answer the disagreeable and unfortunately belated question, she forced her attention back to the twangy-voiced preacher, who wore somber black from head to toe. At least he was dressed appropriately, she thought.

"Do you, Madison Brecker, take this woman to be your lawfully wedded wife, to live together in the state of holy matrimony..."

Unable to help herself, Trinity angled her gaze from the tattered Bible in the minister's hands to the man beside her. Breck was looking at her with those pale, unfathomable eyes of his. It was the first time they'd really looked at each other since Monday's confrontation. All week they'd avoided each other;

Breck had practically made the shed his home. He came into the cabin only for quick, silent, increasingly strained meals.

That afternoon, a cold, gray, overcast Friday, he'd come in, grabbed a change of clothes, then fled back to the shed. When the minister had shown up at three o'clock, Breck had appeared, garbed in a plain white shirt and sensually snug brown pants. Clean-shaven, his hair blown askew by a playful wind, he'd said nothing to Trinity. He hadn't even looked at her until this very moment. Was it possible that, even under the circumstances, she'd missed him?

"Yes," she heard him say in answer to the preacher's question. The one word vibrated through the small room, causing a warm frisson to scurry along her senses. Because of her alarmingly powerful response, she lowered her eyes from his.

"Do you, Trinity Lee, take this man to be your lawfully wedded husband..."

She concentrated on the skirt of her dress. Her feminine pride had forbidden her to ignore entirely the fact that this was her wedding day, no matter how much a mockery, so she had asked Dancey to bring the most modest of her dresses from the Chastain Hotel. The garment was simple, champagne colored, with a high, prim neck and ruffles around the hem. It was not what she'd envisioned as her wedding dress. That one was satin and lace and more beautiful than any wedding dress had ever been. Her long hair would have been fashionably styled to match the gown's elegance, not casually piled atop her head with little more to recommend it than the fact that it was clean. And she would have been smiling, a smile more radiant than the sun, a smile—

"Miss Lee?"

Trinity jerked her head. The preacher was looking at her as though he expected something of her.

"Do you take Mr. Brecker here for your husband?"

Trinity's heart began to pound. Now was the time to back out, she told herself, her eyes involuntarily going to Breck's. His were so cold, so empty...so silently threatening. He hadn't taken her hand at the ceremony's beginning, and now Trinity almost wished he had. She suddenly needed support, any support.

"Y-yes," she managed to get past trembling lips.

After Trinity's prolonged hesitation, the preacher beamed, obviously relieved that the wedding was going to proceed normally. "Well, then," he said, a smile on his thin lips, "the ring."

Ring?

There would be no ring, Trinity thought. A ring meant love. A ring meant a promise to cherish forever. A ring—

Breck drew a slender gold band from his pants pocket, and before a startled Trinity could do more than register the fact of its existence, he reached for her left hand and slid it onto her finger. The ring fit—perfectly.

Her eyes raced to his. Hers were filled with disbelief, his with both a dare and what she thought looked remarkably like a plea. He was daring her to refuse—that much was clear—but what was he pleading for? For her to like it, to want it, to wear it?

The preacher's fingers clasped their joined hands. Trinity could feel the warmth, the strength, of Breck's as it smothered hers.

"By the power vested in me, I now pronounce you man and wife. What God has joined together, let no man put asunder." The preacher released their hands. "You may kiss the bride," he said, the pride of having united yet another couple showing clearly in his eyes.

Her hand still in Breck's, her eyes still locked with his, Trinity felt her heart sprint. She steeled herself for his kiss. Would it be gentle? Proprietary? Or would it punish her for sins only the two of them knew about?

Second faded into second, and Breck made no move. A frangible tension invaded the room. Trinity could hear the shuffling of the preacher's feet, the nervous clearing of his throat. Abruptly, Breck released her hand and stepped back without kissing her.

"Well, now, I'd say there's plenty of time for that. Plenty of time, indeed," the preacher gushed overbrightly.

Breck busied himself with paying the minister for his time and trouble. Paying him generously, Trinity noted, still reeling from the fact that Breck hadn't kissed her. Her lips still tingled in anticipation, she felt a keen sense of humiliation, and she most definitely felt punished—and not one of those reactions made even the slightest sense.

"Mrs. Brecker," the preacher acknowledged politely on his way out the door. He was quickly followed by Breck, who spared his new bride not a backward glance.

"Congratulations," Dancey said, leaning down to peck her cheek. If he thought it strange that Breck had married the woman who'd robbed his train and nearly ruined his railroad, he had never let it show.

"Thank you," Trinity whispered.

At the door, the conductor, cap in hand, hesitated before saying, "He has heart, ma'am. It's just buried deep." He was gone before she could reply.

Trinity stepped to the window. Dancey, after a few words with Breck, mounted his horse, then led the way, the preacher following, down the narrow hill path. Breck, hunched in his jacket against the cold, gray encroaching evening, started off in the direction of the corral and the shed. Never once did he look back toward the cabin . . . or the woman framed in the window.

Trinity watched him disappear. Breck. Her husband. Suddenly, the magnitude of the moment tumbled down around her like boulders tearing down a mountainside in the throes of an avalanche.

What had she done?

What she had to, she quickly answered. Yet she could not keep at bay the dark feelings threatening to drown her.

She was wife to Madison Brecker. Wife to her mother's murderer. Wife to a man she feared. Worst of all, wife to a man who made her fear herself. For when he had placed the ring upon her finger, something deep inside her had longed for him to place it there out of love. And in that moment, revenge had not been a clear goal, but rather a hazy illusion seen through the eyes of the heart.

Squatting on his haunches, Breck stared down at the hungry flames of the small fire he'd built outside the shed, then at the glove in his hand. He knew what Trinity thought: That he was hanging on to the glove to blackmail her into doing his bidding. Maybe there was some truth in that. He'd certainly had no qualms about forcing her to marry him. What she didn't know was that he'd used the glove to get her ring size.

Ring.

She'd been surprised by the ring. But had she been pleased?

Irritated with himself for caring one way or the other, he added a few more twigs to the fire, encouraging it to blaze higher and higher.

Why?

Every trail, path, and road always came back to why. And the biggest why of all was, why had he forced her to marry him? He glibly told himself he had to protect her, that Truxtun wouldn't stop until he brought her to justice. He also told himself he'd married her to better know the moment she tried to kill him, which her pride would demand she try at least once. And then there was the matter of Su-Ling. Wasn't he marrying Trinity because he knew his friend would have wanted him to protect her daughter? Yes. Yes, to it all. But... But there was some other reason he was running long and hard from, some reason he refused to face.

Once more refusing to confront it, he dropped the glove into the fire and watched the flames consume it. Stupid. He'd told Trinity that burning the glove would be stupid. It *was* stupid. That he freely acknowledged. And yet he had this overwhelming urge to destroy the evidence, to protect her.

The fire rose in candent destruction, throwing off a gleaming, golden heat that bathed his spread legs.

Heat.

The heat of desire still burned deep within him. God, how he'd wanted to kiss her—his bride, his wife! But if he had, he wouldn't have been able to stop there, and he hadn't wanted to be personally responsible for the good minister's dying of embarrassment.

Breck watched the fire burn low before petering out entirely. Raking and dispersing the charred remains for safety's sake, he rose and peered around him. The hills, wearing white hats of snow, were silent. How many times had he come here for just this solitude? He answered the question with another question, another why.

Why had he forced her to marry him?

This time he heard the answer in the silent hills. He had forced her to marry him because it had suddenly seemed important to bind her to him in a way that bespoke permanence. A permanence he had never had in his life. But beyond that, and far more important, he had married her because for once in his life silence was not desirable. For once in his life, it seemed desperately important not to be alone.

Chapter Fifteen

Do you want another corn cake?" Trinity asked at supper.

It was the first time they'd eaten at the table since their stay at the cabin. Trinity assured herself that the gesture wasn't a concession to domesticity; preparing a meal and setting the table had simply evolved as an outlet for her anxiety in the hours following the tension-filled wedding. The same anxiety was making her unnaturally chatty.

"There's plenty if you do," she said, her eyes falling short of meeting Breck's. "I just kept adding a little here and a little there and, well, before I knew it, I had enough corn cakes for the whole of Virginia City." She smiled. Awkwardly. "At least I remembered the soda." She considered the puffy cakes stacked on the platter as if they were of monumental importance. She frowned suddenly. "Do you think it's too much soda? Maybe I put in too much soda. Maybe—"

"They're fine," Breck said, his deep, controlled, masculine voice—Trinity experienced a pang of resentment—surging through the room. As though to prove the point, he reached for the platter.

Needing any kind of activity, Trinity intercepted it and passed it to him. She forced her eyes to stay on his hand. His large, sun-bronzed, scarred hand.

Breck noted that Trinity's hand was trembling, as was her voice. He dragged another corn cake onto his plate, returned the platter, and wondered how long it would be until she launched into the next round of speech. He didn't have long to wait.

"We need some cornmeal. And this is the last of the bacon. Do you think there's any chance we could get some fresh eggs?

If we could get some eggs..." She let her words trail off, aware of the inanity of her chatter. God, what was wrong with her? she thought, dropping her forehead into her hand. The action forced her attention to the unfamiliar gold band on her finger. *That* was what was wrong, she thought with a rise of peevishness. That and the nerve-wracking waiting for heaven-knew-what. No, she knew what. All too clearly. At least as clearly as her inexperience allowed.

She felt as if she were standing on the crumbling edge of a very high precipice. Below was something dangerous, something to be avoided, and yet that something—fleeting thoughts of what it would be like to be Breck's lover—tantalized her, urging her to step closer and closer and closer....

"I'll get some eggs," Breck said, as if that were what was causing her distress. He noticed that she was still wearing the ring. His ring. That fact pleased him in a way he'd never been pleased before.

Trinity glanced up into his light, unreadable eyes, certain hers were all too legible. Suddenly, the precipice seemed perilously nearer. Suddenly, she couldn't run away fast enough.

Scraping back her chair, she started to clear the table.

"I'll get it," Breck said, standing.

"I can do it."

He reached for the platter just as she did. "I'll do it," he said, tugging.

"No, I'll do it," she argued, snatching.

The platter, wrenched between overly eager hands, fell to the floor with a *thunk*. Miraculously, it didn't break, though it scattered corn cakes everywhere.

"Damn it," Breck growled, "will you stop acting as if I'm going to throw you to the floor and take you right here?"

"I wish you would!" Trinity cried, her gossamer-thin composure ripped to shreds. "I wish you'd just get it over with!"

She knelt, frenziedly slapping crumbling corn cakes back onto the platter. Breck, too, squatted and snapped up the cornmeal disks.

"By *it*, I take it you mean the husbandly exercise of my conjugal rights?"

"I believe that was the threat," Trinity retorted, making an effort to keep her attention on the cakes and not his crotch.

"Ah, China," he said, his voice suddenly warmer than heated molasses, "that was no threat. That was a promise. And

I promise you one other thing," he added, his molasses-thick voice growing even hotter, even thicker. "When we make love, you're going to want it as much as I do."

"N-never," she said, clutching at the platter as though it were a lifeline.

"Never, my China star," he murmured, his finger tracing the underside of her jaw, "is a long, long, long—" he tilted her chin up until her eyes mated with his "—time."

The last word was nothing more than a whisper, a whisper that carried the promise of every intimacy known to man and woman. It also carried a threat. A threat to Trinity's defenses, for the whispered sensuality had sailed right into her heart, making it burst into a too-fast rhythm, a breath-stealing rhythm, a damn-her-to-hell traitor's rhythm.

Never.

All of never, from its infinite beginning to its limitless end, could not have been as long as that evening. Contrary to her assertion that she would prefer that he claim her and get it over with, she did everything she could to postpone going to bed. She dawdled in the bath he poured for her—this time he hadn't bothered to hang a sheet—then spent unnecessary time before the hearth combing out her hair, which she had swept up for the bath, but which had still managed to acquire moist tendrils. Her hair crackled in the dry heat of the cabin, flying waywardly in the wake of the brush. When she reached for a yellow ribbon to tie back the rebellious strands, Breck broke his long silence.

"No," he said, nonchalantly drying his bare chest with the same towel she'd used, "leave it alone."

Trinity hesitated, her eyes going first to the snug pants he'd obviously slipped over damp legs and hadn't properly fastened, then rising to his golden-matted chest, which still gleamed with crystalline drops of moisture. Her breath thinned, the way it had when she'd looked up to see him uninhibitedly bathing in the cool water she'd left. The water sluicing over his broad, bare shoulders, the power in his muscled arms as he'd soaped his chest, the strong, firm thighs she'd but glimpsed before averting her eyes, had left her feeling as if the frail mountain air had been stripped of even more substance.

Defying him, she ran the ribbon under her hair and arranged it in a bow atop her head.

"I'll only take it out," Breck said calmly.

"And I'll make you go to the trouble."

Coming to her feet, hugging the yellow silk wrapper about her, she stepped toward the bed with all the dignity of royalty going to the guillotine.

Annoyed with her martyrdom, Breck started to speak but checked himself. Instead, he banked the fire, smothered the lamplight, and yanked back the bedcovers.

Trinity flinched where she lay on her side of the bed. She listened to the nerve-splintering sound of his pants leaving his body. Seconds later, she felt his weight indent the mattress before he stretched out to his full length. Her heart stopped. Yet, curiously, she began to feel a heat building in deep and secret places.

Would he take her harshly? Would he hurt her? Would he be able to tell she was a virgin? Would a child grow from the seed he planted in her? A child. Their child would be beautiful, but it would be a child born of hate, of primal lust, of sacrilegious vows.

Cold bullets of sleet pelted the cabin, but the sound could not compete with her own jagged breathing. Breck's breathing, however, was even, smooth, controlled. Damn him to hell, did he never lose control?

Breck lay motionless, thinking of the lavender scent traipsing about his nose, thinking of the sight of Trinity's bare back as she'd bathed, thinking of her hair, wild and black as a fierce summer storm, raining about her shoulders as she'd brushed it by gilded firelight. God, he'd wanted to touch it. To touch her. To have her touching him...his lips, his chest, his stomach, the hard shaft of his—

"Come here, China." His voice was compelling, commanding, and, to ears more alert than Trinity's, just a tad out of control.

She rolled her head toward him. Through the shadowed stillness, through the expectant tread of time, their eyes merged.

"No," she said. "I won't come to you willingly."

Even in the firelit night, she could tell that his eyes darkened. "You want me to force you, don't you?"

"That's absurd. Why would I—"

"Because then you could salve your conscience. You want me as much as I want you, but if I force the issue, you can keep your hate, your precious revenge, intact."

"That's a lie!" she said, throwing back the covers, her intent to remove herself from him. Because when he was this near, she wasn't certain he wasn't right.

Like a sleek cougar long crouched on a limb, he sprang forward, driving her back into the mattress. His body pinned hers with its mighty, muscular weight. Capturing her wrists in his left hand, he jerked them above her head and anchored them firmly. Careful not to injure her wounds, which still wore small bandages, he slid his leg across her, hemming her beneath him.

"You want force, China?" he ground out, his face looming above her startled one. "Then it's force you'll get."

"You bastard!" she hissed, struggling against his hold, though her movements were less effective than a haggard parasol in a hailstorm. "I don't want you! I've never wanted you! I—"

The raw, impatient heat of his mouth silenced hers.

His kiss was the carnal embodiment of anger and punishment, though he could not decide where to aim his anger—at her or at himself. Her, certainly, for making him want her so desperately; himself, though, for being unable to resist her. And then there was the matter of punishment. Was the kiss her punishment or his? And then he could think of nothing, neither anger nor punishment, for the soft curves of her body writhing in rage beneath him, the taste of her struggling lips, seduced him, warmed him, inflamed his man's blood until his body vowed to have her, whatever it took.

Trinity felt the hostile slant of his mouth and tried to wrest her lips from his. She tried to turn her head, but his free hand gripped her cheek, forcing her lips to stay locked with his.

"No!" she spat, and he used the moment to plunge his tongue forward.

Like a velvet rapier, he speared the honeyed cavern, swirling, twirling, in a rhythm of stormy seduction. When her tongue tried to withdraw, his pursued, abrading, stroking, forcing hers to amorously entwine with his until, despite herself, a slow, disturbing heat suffused her body.

She heard herself whimper. And felt the tip of her tongue do the most outrageous thing: It curled around the tip of his.

The white-hot knife of desire cut sharply at Breck's senses, engorging his sex until it was hard, thick, and throbbing with an exquisite pain. He groaned and deepened his kiss.

She told herself not to kiss him back; she tried to fortify herself with images of her mother's lifeless body. Yet her mouth, as though it knew far better than she, opened to his like a flower opening to the sweetest of spring rains. Guided by forces he couldn't resist, Breck responded by gentling the kiss. Where he had once plundered, he now caressed. Where he had once brutally assaulted, he now brushed and teased and feathered, sinking his mouth so thoroughly into hers that neither was sure where one ended and the other began. The hand at her cheek departed, eased upward to untie the rebellious ribbon, and his fingers then tangled themselves in the wild mass of her raven hair.

His kiss, coupled with his hand buried deep within her hair, seemed somehow positively wanton to Trinity, and a tremor ran through her as though an arrow had been shot from her lips and traveled the length of her body, embedding itself in the valley between her thighs. She felt hot and heavy and in need of things she could not define.

No, she told herself, making herself lie still when she wanted to move, to search for, to find, something, anything, she thought desperately, that would ease this growing ache. And, dear sweet God, why must he kiss her so tenderly? A murderer wasn't supposed to kiss so tenderly. A killer wasn't supposed to know the ways of gentleness. An outcast—

She moaned as his lips broke from hers and began a steamy trail down her neck. At the vulnerable hollow of her throat, his tongue skipped inside before moving lower to the spot where the yellow robe formed a rumpled vee. Sliding his hand inside the fold, he parted the robe, sending the tie slithering away. His lips, impertinent with longing, moved to her breast at the same time his free hand palmed the plump flesh and urged it toward his seeking mouth.

Trinity gasped as his tongue flicked across the dusky peak, setting new and alien sensations exploding within her. No man had ever touched her so intimately. When his lips closed around the turgid bud, her breath beat against her throat in a ragged, tattered gasp. The feelings were so painfully sweet, so sweetly painful, that she felt obligated to offer some resistance, and so she tried to free her hands from the warm prison of his grip.

Breck merely tightened his hold...and sucked her nipple past his lips. Trinity writhed, but the action only thrust her more surely into the hot heaven of his mouth.

"No...no...no..." she chanted, uncertain whether she was pleading for him to stop or not to.

He'd shifted his legs, parting hers for his exploration.

"No!" she said, knowing what was coming. She fought to keep her legs together, but all she succeeded in doing was ramming her hip against the swollen shaft of his manhood.

"Yes!" he said, his voice harsh and grating, releasing her breast and showering her stomach with his warm breath and his moist kisses.

His hand played along her leg, slipping to the intimate inside of her thigh.

Sensations burst to erotic life at every spot he touched.

She closed her eyes and begged him, "No!"

He raised his head to watch her. Her face was contorted with blissful agony.

"You want me inside you, China," he growled, his teasing fingers caressing higher and higher.

She opened her eyes. "You're crude," she whispered with what breath she had.

His fingers glided tantalizingly through the nest of ink-black curls cradling her femininity. "Deep inside."

"You're vulgar," she moaned, involuntarily arching against the hand suddenly molding itself against her.

"And you're so wet," he murmured, slipping his fingers between the folds of her fevered petals, "that I could drown in you!"

As he spoke, his fingers slicked through her love-moisture, drawing the wetness against the small, nearly hidden nub of her desire.

Nothing in her life had prepared Trinity for the feeling that slashed through her. Nothing she had heard other women talk about in hushed and giggly tones, nothing she'd heard men more blatantly tout, had given her the slightest clue to the sensations that sang through her. She cried out, a harsh, loud, undisguised groan of pleasure.

Breck soaked it in and sent his finger on another stroking voyage, then another, until Trinity lay limp and whimpering beneath him, her eyes languidly beseeching him. It was then that he knew he could have her...without force. All he had to do was ease atop her and bury himself deep inside her. Nature would do the rest. For both of them.

Unfortunately, he realized one other thing, as well.

Just having her was no longer enough. He wanted her to come to him willingly. In all his life, no one had ever been *his*. No one had ever belonged to him, nor he to anyone. He'd been rejected by his mother, ignored by his father, shunned by society. On some deep, primitive emotional plane, he wanted to be wanted. By this woman. No one else mattered. Only this woman.

Slowly, he released her imprisoned hands; slowly, he edged his legs off hers and rolled away from her. Startled, Trinity sought his eyes.

"Come here, China," he commanded as he had once before. Unlike before, his eyes now glowed with a need he didn't fully understand, a need that raged throughout his body.

Trinity, too, was besieged by feelings—confusion that his hand had abandoned its magic, bewilderment at the thick, heavy, unsatisfied tremors still claiming her body, and...and one other feeling that washed across her like a scarlet tide. Shame. Shame at how easily she had been seduced. Shame at how completely she had forgotten that this was her mother's murderer. Shame at how easy it would be to obey him even now—to go to him, to make love to him, to lose herself in the wonder of his body.

And yet, was this not what he'd planned? Had he not meant from the start to bring her this far, then make her betray all her principles if she were to go further? His cruelty knifed at her heart. He would not even do her the courtesy of taking her by force.

Tears gathered in her eyes. "I hate you," she whispered.

Breck knew what she believed, what anyone would have believed under the circumstances. He could not tell her she was wrong, however, because doing so would reveal his vulnerability. And he must not appear vulnerable. Not in front of this woman who had a power over him that no one else had ever possessed.

"I know, China," he answered wearily as he rolled onto his back and stared into the shadowed night. His body ached, his heart ached, yet he could do nothing to ease either. "I know."

Trinity rolled onto her side and pulled her knees up until she formed a ball. Maybe this tight knot would ease the ache gnawing at her stomach. Nothing, she knew, would ease the shame.

They were both spoiling for a fight.

It was obvious within five minutes of waking the following morning that unfulfilled passion had channeled itself into anger. It continued to do so for the duration of one hellish week. By day they sniped and snapped at each other, by night they lay side by side, neither of them able to sleep for the ache that merely looking at each other could now induce.

Trinity no longer knew her body. It had ceased to belong to her. It was now the property of a woman who had shocking, wanton images constantly playing in her head. And feelings that tingled and burned and made her blush constantly shimmered through her. She preferred that more innocent time, when she hadn't known what to expect, she thought, although she still didn't know the whole of it. My God, how could anything be more powerful than what she had already experienced? And yet, she suspected there was more. Much more. A more she wanted, a more she hated herself for wanting, a more she hated Breck for ever having taught her to want.

Breck, on the other hand, knew his body all too well. He needed a woman. Which was an understatement comparable to saying that a little silver had been mined in Virginia City. What he didn't understand was what was going on in his head. Maybe even in his heart, though this latter he kept conveniently distanced. Trinity was tying his emotions into knots he couldn't unravel. Want and need had always been separate, and quite distinct, spheres of being. Now they had fused together until it was impossible to tell one from the other. And, damn it, everything about her pleasured him! Just seeing her pleasured him. Just hearing her voice pleasured him. Even arguing with her pleasured him, because it meant he was alive in a way he never had been before. And the more she pleasured him, the more he wanted her, which meant the more they argued, for anger was the only release they could agree on. So Breck spent his days in agony, chopping tree after unsuspecting tree.

"Why are you cutting all this wood?" Trinity snapped on Tuesday. "You've got enough to last four winters as it is."

"I like firewood," Breck retorted, unloading yet another armful in the cabin. Stacks, like little wooden soldiers, already lined the porch and the east side of the shed.

"Fine," she said, thinking that the wind had done a provocative job of rumpling his hair.

"Glad you approve," he shot back, wondering why in hell she didn't wear her hair up. For days—perversely, it seemed—she'd worn it down, so that it swayed invitingly with every movement of her body, so that it hurled a thousand memories at him.

"I don't care if you cut down every tree on the hillside. Which, I might add, you've almost done," she told him, exaggerating boldly. In reality, he'd probably chopped down no more than three or four trees, which the hillside, unlike the city, could spare. Mostly he'd split logs, then split them again, leaving them fit only for kindling.

"Then I'll start on the goddamned corral," he drawled before stalking out the door. In seconds, Trinity heard the fall of the ax, the splinter of wood.

Two days later, they were still waging their emotional war.

"I thought we had some eggs," Breck said, hoping to distract his passion with food.

"We, uh . . . we did," Trinity answered sheepishly.

When she offered no more, Breck asked, "Well?"

"I, uh . . . I kind of broke them."

"What do you mean, 'kind of'?"

"All right, I broke them!"

"All of them?"

"Yes!"

"How did you break a dozen eggs?"

"There were only ten," she pointed out.

"Oh, well, excuse me. That's different." He dragged his hands to his hips. His lean hips, Trinity reflected. His lean, muscular, hard . . .

She glanced up guiltily. "What?"

"How did you break ten eggs?"

Watching the muscles in your back and shoulders ripple as you chopped wood. "The basket . . . it fell out of my hands."

"Well, great!" he snorted, wishing she wouldn't wear that prim, high-necked, schoolmarmish dress she'd been married in. What he couldn't see, but could imagine, was far more potent than what was displayed.

"Why don't you just take me out and shoot me?" she offered with a sarcastic smile, erotic images of his mouth at her breast whirling through her mind.

Why don't I just throw you on the bed, haul that dress up, and make us both forget about eggs, he thought, but said, "Actually, I'd be content to wring your neck."

"Fine!"

"Good!"

"Great!"

"Fine!" he said, slamming the door behind him. Within minutes, the sound of splitting wood fractured the stillness.

The next day, which was the thirtieth of November, Ellie Oates and her husband paid an unexpected visit to the honeymoon couple. Though Breck continuously hounded Trinity to rest, she, bored to frustrating tears, had slipped from bed to wash out a few articles of clothing—both hers and his—only a few minutes before her friends arrived. Uncertain of Ellie's reaction to the marriage, and to not having been invited to the wedding, Trinity awaited her friend's initial comment with nothing less than trepidation.

After a fierce hug, Ellie burbled, "I'm not the least surprised. I saw it coming. Didn't I say I saw it coming?" she tossed over her shoulder to her husband. Without giving the brawny miner a chance to reply, she gushed on, "And married just like that, without friend or foe to attend, why I think it's—why, it's just plum romantic."

Romantic wasn't the word Trinity would have used; she would have used *blackmailed,* but she refrained from saying so. She also might have pointed out that Ellie couldn't have seen anything coming, though even as she thought this, she remembered a comforting kiss in the guest bedroom of Jedediah's mansion. Even then, she had responded to Breck. Trinity thwarted this line of thinking and concentrated on Ellie, who was busy informing Breck that she and he were now friends-in-law. She also insisted on kissing the groom, while Neil asserted his rights concerning the bride. Smiles were inevitable, even Breck's, which tripped Trinity's heart—especially when his eyes met hers and his smile actually lingered. The gay mood, however, was short-lived. For the life of her, Trinity couldn't figure out why Breck's attitude changed. She knew only that something happened when she served the coffee.

She tore into him the moment their guests left. "And just what is wrong with you? You were barely civil," she said, though she was fairly certain no one but her had noticed Breck's subtle change of mood.

"Considering my mood, *Mrs*. Brecker," he said, "you're lucky I was any degree of civil."

"And to what do we owe the pleasure of your surliness?"

By way of explanation, he grabbed her left hand—none too gently—and planted it before her eyes. "Where's your ring, dear wife?"

Ring? For a moment, Trinity honestly couldn't remember where it was. Then it all came swiftly back to her. Fearing the effects of the harsh lye soap, she had removed it to wash out the clothes. She started to tell him this when he spoke again, the dark expression on his face a formidable contrast to his light, unimpassioned eyes.

"What's wrong, China, you ashamed to be tied to me?"

The accusation, delivered in a tone suggesting hurt, left her speechless.

He sneered. "Well, like it or not, you are."

"Breck—"

"Put it on," he ordered quietly. "And don't take it off again."

His words were still ringing in Trinity's ears later that evening, when, heartily tired of the yellow silk wrapper, which now had the added disadvantage of reminding her of Breck's caress, she dressed in a white lawn gown. It was among the additional personal effects Ellie had collected for her from the Chastain Hotel. The sleeves of the gown billowed in a wild profusion of fabric, while an army of tiny pearl buttons stood virtuous watch down the gown's embroidered front. The material was satiny-soothing and deliciously soft, a marked counterpoint to the abrasive feelings scratching around inside her.

Ashamed.

He thought she was ashamed of him. Which raised a pointed question. Was she? The immediate answer was no. She told herself she probably should be ashamed of being the wife of a murderer, but the truth was, she thought of herself as the wife of Madison Brecker. And that carried no shame. Somehow the two—the murderer and the man—had become separate entities. Maybe, though, the truth was that she had no room for any shame but her own. How could she have responded so shamelessly to his touch? How could his kiss have so thoroughly seduced her into forgetting her mission? How could she forget her sweet mother and all the tea parties they'd never given, all the laughter they'd never shared, all the soft lullabies that had never been sung? How could she forget what it had been like to be eight years old and to be told your mother was never coming back?

Trinity flushed under a new assault of guilt. She would not forget. She could not. She owed it to her mother and to herself to end this charade, and her shame, right here and now. Why didn't she, this night, take the taunting knife that would soon lie on the bedside table and plunge it into his black, villainous...

...heart! The sight of her wearing a gown that concealed so much, yet left her body tantalizingly silhouetted against its sheerness, stopped Breck's heart in midbeat. He felt a wave of passion so strong that he almost staggered under its weight. He also felt a rush of pure fear. Fear. It was an emotion he hadn't felt often, but he felt it now. He was afraid of the power this woman had over him. He needed to have her need him, want him, because, sweet God in heaven, he needed and wanted her.

Their eyes met, both pairs inscrutable, both scrutinizing.

Slowly, he crossed the room, propped his boot on the edge of the chair, and removed the thin steel knife. He laid it on the bedside table near the lamp.

Trinity's eyes skipped to it, then back to his.

His eyes darkened, but only a fraction.

It was funny, she thought, how utterly calm she felt now that she'd made the decision. How unnaturally calm.

She watched as he lazily pulled off his shirt, then his undershirt. His chest was thickly swathed in golden hair, hair she'd wanted to touch the night he'd held her hands so securely above her head. Hair she'd wanted to touch many nights before that, hair she wanted to trail her fingers through this very moment. Prickles of longing danced through her.

"Which is it to be, China?" he drawled. "Passion or revenge?"

That he so clearly saw her dilemma angered her. That there was a dilemma at all shamed her. Both goaded her to action. Snatching up the knife, she curled her eager, angry fingers around it. Breck, faster than blond lightning, chained his hand about her wrist.

Brutal pain shot through her. "I'll see us in hell before it's passion," she grunted, her face contorted.

Breck effortlessly tightened his hold. "We're already in hell, China," he said as the knife tumbled to the floor.

With all the strength she had, she wrestled free of his grip, whirled, and raced for the door. She had but one goal: To get away from him. Maybe even to get away from herself. Heedless of her bare feet, heedless of the cold winter night, she stumbled forward.

Breck, with a frightening calm, bent and picked up the knife. With an expert's accurate aim, he sailed it through the tension-knotted air...and toward the woman whose hand had just closed around the doorknob.

Chapter Sixteen

The knife pierced the flowing left sleeve of the gown, impaling Trinity to the door like a delicate butterfly trapped by the pin of a zealous collector. She screamed and whipped her head back over her shoulders. Breck, naked from the waist up, was coming toward her in something more than a saunter and less than a rush. His usually emotionless eyes simmered with rage. Trinity's heart stampeded within her chest, and she scrambled to withdraw the knife. The hand that curved around its handle wasn't hers, however.

Breck yanked the knife from the wood and the billowy fabric, twirled Trinity around, and drove her flush against the door, imprisoning her there with his body. He gripped the knife in his left hand, holding it near her temple, where she could peripherally see its silver flash, while he slid his right hand around the exposed column of her neck. His fingers clutched her throat until both she and he could feel the tapping beat of her pulse. Everything about him spelled *man*; everything about him spelled *power*; everything about him spelled *fury*—a cold fury directed solely at her.

Trinity wondered if he was going to kill her. And if so, would he knife her as he had her mother, or would he slowly strangle the life from her the way he'd almost strangled the miner who'd disparaged his parents?

"Go ahead," Trinity whispered. "Kill me." A rage similar to his coursed through her. As well as some other emotion. Anger, helped along by the intimate nearness of Breck's body—his belly brushed hers, his thighs rubbed against hers, his manhood nestled at the apex of her legs—was metamorphosing into passion. And that made her defiant. She tilted her head in challenge.

Breck was sorely tempted to do something physical. Like take the knife and try to cut her out of his ... The word *heart* came to mind, but that suggested an emotional intimacy he couldn't face. At the very least, he'd like to throw her across his knee and paddle her senseless. Of course, there was one other physical option, which the lower part of his body seemed to think of before the rest of him.

Trinity felt him grow to life, felt the hard thickness of him swell against the softness of his woman's mound. Suddenly the fabric of her gown and the material of his pants felt tissue-thin, suddenly his chest seemed more vividly bare, suddenly...

On a groan torn from his throat, Breck's mouth swooped to hers. It slanted, drove, plundered, penetrated. The velvet rapier of his tongue met and tangled with hers, sending tremors of need spiraling deep within him.

Similar tremors destroyed Trinity's senses. It was as though she'd waited all her life, prayed all her life, for just this kiss. The moment his lips collided with hers, the moment his tongue demanded entry, she opened her mouth—gladly, willingly, damning all reservations.

Passion ruled.

"Breck..." she whispered, the word more feeling than sound.

He responded by taking her mouth again and again, from every hasty, fevered angle instinct dictated. He felt aflame, scorched to cinders by the heat of her arousal. That she was meeting him fully, without being forced, only sent the fire blazing higher within him.

The fingers at her throat eased aside, and his mouth, hungry for the taste of all of her, slid along the curved line of her jaw and started down her slender neck. He rained kisses, while his moist, tattered breath splattered against her skin. At the hollow of her throat, he called her name, a strained, uneven rendering of "China."

And then he was seeking access to the gown. His trembling fingers fought the tiny buttons but could force not one to abandon its prim watch. With a snarl of frustration, he took the knife and, in one swift movement, slashed the gown open. The soft lawn fell away, leaving her breasts, dark-tipped and full, exposed. He lowered his head, his mouth capturing the nearest peak.

Trinity moaned and swayed into him. In order to catch herself, though she cared not whether she fell to the very bottom of the sensual abyss yawning so sweetly before her, she splayed her hands against his chest. Luxuriantly soft, springy hair coiled around her fingers, and she sought out the copper-colored nipples hidden so provocatively from view.

She tried to tell herself that she shouldn't be doing this, that she shouldn't be letting him do this to her, but the sucking of his mouth, the laving of his tongue, clouded all thought, heightened all senses.

"I want you!" he growled, his mouth roughly seeking hers once more.

She heard herself sigh and knew that it was more than acquiescence; it was a plea.

Breck, too, heard her whimper, and, his mouth still on hers, he plunged the knife into the door again and scooped her up and into his arms. As he crossed the room, the toe of his boot clipped the edge of one of the many stacks of firewood piled high and wide. The log shifted, unbalanced another, and caused yet another to lose its barky footing. A hill of logs tumbled, taking with it the stack to its right, which, in turn, took the one beside it. Wood spilled across the cabin floor. Breck noticed only to the extent that he stepped over a log that rolled directly into his path.

Trinity noticed nothing except the surge of blood in her ears, felt nothing except Breck's hot lips and the steely strength of his body combined with the delicious power in the arms cradling her. And then the bed was beneath her, soft and inviting, while Breck loomed above her, hard and needing, sure and giving.

He deepened the kiss for one brief heartbeat before pulling away from her and rising. She reached out for him, as though his leaving her constituted the single greatest tragedy of her life.

"No," she whispered, clutching at his arm.

She wanted him. Not only was she coming to him, she was begging him to stay. Some emotion, headier than any he'd ever felt, consumed Breck totally. It was as if he were in a bright, glaring shaft of white light. The emotion cried out to be called *love*, but, loner that he was, loner that he'd always been, he did not know the texture, the weave, the nap of the word. Therefore, he could not recognize it to embrace it and would not have trusted the word had he recognized it.

"You have to let me get my pants off," he said, a tender smile on his lips. "Unless you know another way."

Trinity's face suffused with color, and she released his arm. He would know soon enough that she knew little about any way. She might have dwelled upon her naiveté, had not Breck at that moment shed his pants. His masculinity, strong and firm and growing in a bed of golden hair, jutted proudly against his stomach. All reason fled Trinity's mind, though she fought to hang on to the ragged threads of the one foundation upon which she'd built her entire adult life. She tried to hang on to her dreams of revenge.

When he eased back onto the side of the bed, her passion-glazed eyes found his. "This changes nothing," she whispered. "I still hate you."

"I know, China."

"I *will* kill you."

"You are," he muttered, placing his hands on her shoulders and lowering his head. "With desire."

Heaven could have been no sweeter than his mouth opening over hers, nor could hell have contained more fire than his kiss. Fever raged through both of them.

"Kiss me!" he said hoarsely, taking for himself what he was demanding.

As her mouth mated with his, her hands—tentative, though strangely brazen, too—spread across his chest, exploring contours and planes, comparing the texture of warm skin with soft hair.

"Touch me!" he whispered, taking her hand and guiding it to a flat, pebbled nipple. Her fingertips caressed; her fingernail raked.

Breck moaned. And, his hand on hers, he directed her lower, across his hair-dusted belly, across the indentation of his navel, to the shaft of his desire. As he closed her fingers around him, his breath gushed out, and he swore something dark that ironically sounded more sacred than any religious incantation could have.

Trinity had never touched a man this way, though in the thick of night she'd often wondered about such intimacy. Even imagined it. Yet she had not known to think in terms of such exquisite smoothness, such arousing fullness...nor had she known to think in terms of anything so large. She brushed her fingers along the rigid column, fascinated, enthralled, burning for the completion she intuitively knew it offered.

His patience at an end, Breck growled, ripped the remainder of the gown with his bare hands, and, brushing the fabric aside, levered himself atop her. Careful of her healing injuries, he fitted his knee between her legs. And then, because he could wait no longer, he took her, burying himself within the heated sheath of her damp body, feeling her swallow... swallow... swal—

Breck stopped cold at the unexpected wall of resistance. He whipped his head upward.

"No," she whispered, the word, drunk with passion, staggering from her lips. "Don't stop." As she spoke, her hands clutched greedily at his bare, sweat-dewed back.

Gently but surely, he thrust inside her, then stilled to let her tight virgin's body accommodate him. At his entry, her eyes had closed, while her mouth had opened to emit her sundered breath, which purled about her lips in little gasps. Little gasps Breck found irresistible. Tenderly lowering his mouth to hers, he worked his lips, his tongue, in a sensual accompaniment to the motion his hips slowly initiated.

Over and over, he pressed himself into her. Over and over, she rose to meet him. Never had she imagined anything this splendid, this wondrous, this... this perfect. Never had he, in any other coupling, felt this passion, this possessiveness, this... this unmitigated pleasure. And, at that moment, when both felt that nothing could be any more perfect, any more pleasurable, the end came, first for Trinity, in a blinding flash of light and sensation that made her cry out in the cabin's silence. Breck followed only strokes behind, his grunted breath emptying into the hollow of her throat as his body emptied itself into her. And even as their passion rode its highest peak, each knew, though neither could fully explain how or why, that far more than their bodies had just been joined.

She was crying.

Breck listened to the soft, bleated sobs and tried to make sense of them. It was difficult, however, because as an adult he'd never cried. It was something he'd promised the scared, lonely kid in him, the kid who'd cried himself to sleep night after night, that he'd never do again.

He tightened his hold on the woman in his arms and thought that probably the reason for her tears was twofold. The dramatic release she'd experienced, especially since it was such a new phenomenon for her, was no doubt partially responsible. God, she'd come apart in his arms! Every time he thought about her never having been with another man, he went a little bit wild with a feeling he couldn't identify, though it was closely akin to possessiveness. He supposed it had never occurred to him, one way or the other, but now the thought of her with another man, the thought of her coming apart in another man's arms, made him red with jealousy.

The confusion he felt at this realization reminded him of the second reason she was probably crying. She was confused. The reason he knew she was was simple: He was confused, too. About more than the jealousy. He was confused about what they'd just shared. They hadn't mated; they'd bonded. And, though the realization was traumatic enough for him, how much more traumatic must it be for her, since she so clearly hated him?

That thought cut at him like the sharpest of daggers, and for a moment, just a moment, he toyed with the idea of telling her the truth. He wasn't quite sure what stopped him. Thoughts of Su-Ling? Jedediah? Or was he simply afraid she wouldn't believe him, and that that lack of faith would crush him even more than her blind hatred?

Placing his finger beneath her chin, he tilted her face up. Without a word, he laid his lips against hers, slowly, tenderly, like the brush of a sweet spring breeze. He could taste the salty moistness of her tears, could taste, too, her womanliness, and the supplicating way her mouth received his. He thought he could live for the rest of his life on that taste alone.

Trinity's trembling lips gratefully accepted the kiss he offered. She wished she could stop crying. Wished, too, that she understood why she was crying. She didn't understand, however. She only knew that she was . . . and that it felt good. That she felt good. That Breck's lips felt good. And that what she and Breck had just shared had felt good . . . and that she felt more confused than she could ever remember feeling. Confused and good.

"Did I hurt you?" Breck asked, his hand stroking down her side and onto her stomach, where it brushed the bandage she still wore. That this might be why she was crying made him drag his lips from hers.

She looked up at him with tear-sheened eyes and sniffed. "No."

His hand slid lower, through the black tangle of curls. "Here?" he asked, his fingers touching her intimately.

She flinched. He stopped and frowned.

"I did, didn't I?"

"No," she quickly denied.

"Then—"

"It . . . it feels strange . . . funny."

It struck Breck that he really didn't know all that much about women. At least those you didn't pay to fake enjoyment. Some of what Trinity was feeling, however, he did recognize as the natural winding down of a woman's body after lovemaking.

"It'll stop feeling strange in a while," he said, unable to keep his mouth from hers. One other thing struck Breck. He was becoming addicted to kissing.

As his lips, now as gentle as they'd once been fierce, melded with hers, sensations flowed through her like warm, drizzly rain. Places that felt strange and funny began to tingle with new life.

"That's not helping to stop the strange feeling," she whispered as his tongue lazily flicked the corners of her mouth. She felt him smile. The feel of his smile was even more intoxicating than the rare sight of it. She felt herself smiling in response.

Breck pulled back until their eyes met. Slowly, their smiles died, replaced by deep, sober feelings neither of them could have explained. Nor could Trinity have explained why her left hand reached out and palmed her lover's—her enemy's—cheek.

Breck placed a hand atop hers. And felt the ring on her finger.

"You don't have to wear it," he said, his voice suddenly husky. An undeniable vulnerability had crept into his blue eyes, blue eyes that looked warm, not cold, blue eyes that were filled with emotion, not devoid of it.

Trinity saw that vulnerability, that warmth, that emotion, and couldn't help but respond truthfully. "I'd taken it off to do the wash. For no other reason."

Both realized that their discussion was an unusual, even a dangerous, one for a marriage based on blackmail. Just as their feelings were unusual, dangerous. And yet both seemed compelled to follow where those confusing, dangerous feelings led.

With a groan, Breck rolled her onto her back and, as though he had not kissed her for a lifetime, sealed her mouth with his. And then, over and over, until the black cloud of night gave way to the resurrection of dawn, they made love. With morning, however, came reality, and reality was a cabin floor impetuously, passionately, strewn with logs...and a knife, as hard, cold, and unrelenting as a vow of revenge, plunged into the door.

With morning, also, came an agitated Dancey Harlan.

The conductor, bundled warmly in a heavy coat and gloves, threw himself off his horse even before the animal had stopped.

"What's wrong?" Breck asked, his shoulders squared to take the brunt of what he sensed was coming.

Dancey whisked his hat from his head and stomped up onto the cabin porch. His breath, reflecting his excitement and the cold, issued forth in uneven puffs of white. "That sow-sucking bastard's at it again!" he exclaimed. Then he nodded toward Trinity, who stood in the doorway. "Morning, ma'am."

"Morning, Dancey."

"What sow-sucking bastard's done what?" Breck asked calmly. Too calmly.

"Some fearless heathen, the devil burn his soul, has tampered with the tracks. You know right there before the last trestle?" He didn't wait for a response. "Well, somebody pulled the spikes out of the track. Just ripped 'em right out like he had every right to do it! Charlie damn near didn't see it. The front end of the engine jumped the track anyway. Charlie says he's quitting quicker than a preacher at a rained-out revival if things don't stop."

Trinity had instinctively eased to her husband's side, as though sensing that was her place in time of trouble—his or hers. She watched now as Breck's eyes became cooler, more aloof, with each word Dancey spoke. She also felt a gurgling of her own anger. How dare anyone harass the Sierra Virginia!

"Was anyone hurt?" Breck asked tightly, thinking he was making a habit, a bad habit, out of asking his conductor that question. When Trinity had told him she wasn't responsible for the accidents, Breck had told his employees to continue keeping a watchful eye. His order had, regrettably, been justified.

"No," Dancey answered.

"What about the train?"

"I sent a crew out to pull it back on the track."

Breck turned to Trinity. "You think you can travel?"

"Yes," she replied without hesitation.

"Good," Breck said, his jaw tensed as he turned back toward Dancey. "It's about time I get back to town and find out just what in hell's going on." The words embraced a threat. "We'll be there by midafternoon. Get the train back on schedule if you can."

"Right," Dancey said, hurrying down the steps. He had just swung himself back into the saddle when he thought to add, "Oh, by the way, we received word that the new engine is being shipped. Should arrive in a day or two."

Breck frowned in complete surprise. "I thought they were demanding their money up front."

Dancey shrugged. "Looks like they changed their minds and are going to extend credit after all."

The name Jedediah popped into Breck's mind. More than likely, his influence was behind the change of heart. His friend knew he'd never accept his charity—giving him or loaning him the money was out of the question. Extension of credit was another thing, however. That Breck would consider taking from Jedediah, from his friend, from his . . . father-in-law.

"I guess we could use a little luck," Breck said.

"Amen," Dancey said, reigning the horse into a turn and starting back down the slender path.

Breck, impervious to the cold, looked over at his wife, who was hugging her bare arms tightly about her. "You're sure you can travel?"

She nodded.

"We have only the one horse, so try not to take much."

Again she nodded, but her mind was less on what she'd take than on how she'd have to travel back in Breck's arms. The thought was disturbing and guilt-provoking, for the simple reason that it was also undeniably appealing.

The chill, blustery wind blew them back into Virginia City exactly when Breck had predicted—midafternoon. Already the town was gearing up for a rowdy Saturday night. Rush-the-evening miners were already slapping backs and slurping beers, while a sad-hearted Millie Rhea—news of Breck's marriage had traveled like wildfire—rested in her room above the saloon, the better to cope with the evenings' aggregate of humping, slumping bodies.

With masculine authority, Breck bypassed Trinity's suite at the Chastain Hotel and ensconced them in his far more modest rented-by-the-month room. Trinity, more tired than she'd expected to be, put her few things on the desk and eased down on the edge of the bed. She brushed back a fallen wisp of her black hair.

"Tired?" Breck asked as he ripped open a telegram the desk clerk had handed him as they'd entered the lobby of the hotel.

"A little."

"Why don't you rest while I run by the office and then the station?"

"How long will you be gone?" It was a wifely kind of thing to ask, and she regretted the inquiry the moment she made it. And yet she really did want to know how long she'd be without him.

"A couple of hours," he said vaguely, reading the telegram before handing it to her. "Jedediah sends us his congratulations."

Trinity took the telegram and read it, never once wondering how her friend had learned of their marriage. She'd had too many experiences with bloodhound reporters who seemed capable of sniffing out things that smelled innocuous to others. She glanced up at Breck. It was obvious they were both considering the ethical implications of accepting genuine congratulations under the sham circumstances.

With a look that was part amusement, part sarcasm, maybe even part regret, Breck said, "Speaking of our unusual marriage, can I trust you not to go out, buy a gun, and be lying in wait for me when I return?"

"No," came Trinity's answer.

Breck walked the short distance separating them and tilted her chin up with the crook of his finger. He lowered his head and kissed her thoroughly, like the husband and lover he had become.

"And that, my dear wife," he said huskily when finally their lips parted, "is what I like best about you. I never know what to expect."

With that, and without a backward glance, he picked up his hat, crossed the room, and closed the door behind him.

Hundreds of miles away, a fashionably gloved hand knocked upon another door. The door's paint was peeling, not badly, but enough to suggest a landlord's indifferent neglect. The fashionably gloved hand, however, had picked a spot as acceptable as possible to its lofty standards, then tapped and rushed away. Its owner had immediately brushed at her knuckles.

"Yeah, just a minute," came from within.

Ada McCook waited with the impatience of a queen being forced to wait on a mere commoner. She told herself, however, that she could wait a few more seconds, since she'd already waited eighteen years. When the newspapers had pounced upon Trinity Lee's marriage, she had followed the news closely, not so much because she cared about the stupid wedding, but because one of the reporters had seemed so zealous on the subject of Trinity Lee. Five stories in as many days suggested a personal fascination on the part of the reporter, and, since much of the copy dwelled on Miss Lee's mysterious past, Ada had become convinced that the journalist might well play the part of her pawn. Her money and a few suggested avenues to pursue, coupled with the reporter's itchy nose, had turned up a name in Sacramento. The only thing that remained to be seen was whether the name proved useful.

The door opened unexpectedly.

"Yeah, honey, what can I do for you?" The voice was soft and sultry and belonged to a woman who'd put in a hard fifty-plus years. The robe she wore, a sleazy affair, looked as if it had been with her most of those fifty-plus years and had finally thrown up its satin hands and despaired of hanging graciously on an anatomy that had slipped and sagged and shifted with the sands of time. For all the woman's worn condition, however, there was a glitter in her eyes and a ready smile on her carmine lips.

"I'm looking for a Miss Ruby Landry," Ada said, forcing a civilized politeness.

—"Well, I reckon if you're looking for her, you've just found her." The woman smiled, producing a new set of wrinkles. "Actually, my name's Ruby Landry Wharton Davis Pip." The smile turned into a bawdy laugh. "The names hung around longer than the men."

Ada McCook smiled wanly. "Yes, well, I was wondering if perchance you were living here in Sacramento some eighteen years ago."

Ruby Landry laughed. "More like percertain, I'd say. Lord, yes, I was in Sacramento. Born and raised here and operated the best darned brothel in the whole city. And that wasn't just my opinion. Customers came from as far away as San Francisco. Everyone said my girls were ladies. Mind you, they knew when to be ladies and when not to be." She laughed again.

Ada McCook felt a wave of supreme disgust but covered it with "Did you have a woman by the name of Su-Ling Chang working for you?"

At the mention of the name, Ruby Landry's eyes softened with memories. "Su-Ling Chang. I haven't thought of her in years."

"Then she did work for you?"

"Lord, yes. She was one of my most popular girls. I knew she would be the moment I set eyes on her. She was so pretty, so different, with that alabaster skin and night-black hair."

"Did she, uh . . . did she have a child?"

"Well, I reckon she did. That was how I first met her. Found her living off of scraps in an alleyway behind a Chinese restaurant. She was about seven months pregnant, said she couldn't find a job 'cause nobody wanted a pregnant woman. Especially one who didn't have no husband. I brought her back to the brothel, fed her real good, cleaned her up, and told her I'd give her a job as one of my girls. 'Course, I made it clear she wouldn't start working until after the babe came."

"Naturally," Ada said, finding it hard to keep sarcasm from seeping into her tone. "About the child—"

"Born right there in the brothel. And from the moment we saw her, she was like our own. Lord, she had more aunts than she could shake a stick at."

"Then it was a girl?"

"'Course, by that time," Ruby went on, lost in her own world of memories, "everyone loved Su-Ling so, we'd have loved the babe simply because it was hers. Never saw a nicer person than Su-Ling Chang.''

''Yes, well—''

''But she was sad, too, if you know what I mean. Life hadn't been kind to her.'' Ruby suddenly turned pensive. ''I sometimes regretted bringing her into the profession. She was really too...tender for it. 'Course, that's what most of the men liked—that fragile quality.'' The woman smiled again. ''Ain't nothing that makes a man feel more like a man than a woman who needs protecting.''

''About the child...'' Ada repeated.

''Su-Ling used to say, though, that it didn't matter what she did to make a living. Used to say that she didn't live on earth, anyway, that she lived in the stars.'' Ruby sighed. ''Her death just about killed me and the girls.'' Ruby Landry looked up at her uninvited guest. ''You did know she was killed—''

''Yes,'' Ada said quickly.

''Everyone said it was that blond-haired man, but I never believed—''

''What happened to the child?''

''Well, now, that was a funny thing. A few days after Su-Ling's death, a Chinese couple showed up to claim her. Said they were relatives, but I could have sworn Su-Ling said she didn't have any relatives in America. Anyway, they took the child—and her scared stiff.''

Ada McCook could hear the blood surging through her temples. ''Do you remember the little girl's name?''

Ruby Landry smiled. ''I reckon I do. I named her. From right out of the Bible, I took it. We—my girls and I—had been studying the Father, the Son, and the Holy Ghost, and it just came to me to call that precious little baby girl Trinity. Trinity,'' she repeated musingly. ''Isn't that about the prettiest name you've ever heard?''

Ada McCook heard nothing except the blood surging against her eardrums.

''I think there's some famous actress with the name, but except for her, I never heard the name before or since. I—hey, lady, is that all?''

Ada McCook said nothing, but rather started back down the stairway.

Ruby Landry shrugged. ''Nice to meet you, too,'' she said, and closed the peeling door.

She had no choice, Ada thought, her feet sounding out *no choice...no choice...no choice* with each step down she took. Somewhere between the second and first floors, she saw the blood on her gloves—bright red against pale gray. She'd seen it there before—often of late. She hurriedly swiped her hands down her fur wrapper. Again. And again. Until her hands hurt. It was funny, but her hands had to hurt before the blood would go away.

Her breathing shallow, she forced herself to look at her gloves. She sighed with relief. The blood was gone. For now. She felt calm again. And in control. Her secret would make her strong. And she had to be strong. There were two things she had to do, and then she'd be safe—she and Jedediah, who would one day be governor of California. She had to make both of them safe. She had no choice.

Chapter Seventeen

You want to see the new engine?'' Breck asked four days later as he and Trinity were finishing supper at Molly Dodd's Eatery. It was the middle of the week and the beginning of December, the latter decreeing that they dine and turn in early, since nightfall came all too swiftly after sunset, bringing with it a chill that cut clean to the bone.

Trinity looked up from the last of her raisin rum pudding. The question surprised her. Since their return to Virginia City, he hadn't said or done anything that in any way shared the business aspects of his life with her. The only thing they'd shared was a bed... and breathless nights that they could neither resist nor quite accept. Now, however, she saw a boyish gleam of enthusiasm in his eyes, tempered by an adult's, a loner's, guardedness.

"Could I?"

If his question had surprised her, her answer startled her, for she realized she truly did want to see the acclaimed locomotive. Or was it simply that she wanted to be more than a fraction of Breck's life? She refused to answer the question. She also refused to confront the fact that she'd made no attempt to buy a gun. Nor had she availed herself of the knife he still kept by the bed. Tomorrow. She always told herself that she would tomorrow.

Breck scraped back his hair, his guardedness slipping away and giving full reign to enthusiasm. "We'll have to hurry. We've only got about an hour of light left."

Hastily he helped her from her chair and held her fur-trimmed velveteen cloak. As he handed her the matching fur muff, their hands brushed, and then their eyes. Both longed for it to be their lips, though, as always, Trinity experienced pangs of guilt. How could she so shamelessly give herself to this man?

"Ready?" he asked hoarsely.

"Yes," she answered, the word but a wisp of sound.

The cold air was a welcome balm to their impassioned bodies, and they let it bathe their hot senses. Trinity, lifting the hood of the cloak over her head, turned her face up, soaking in the stinging promise of snow. She let it momentarily drive away thoughts of the quiet man beside her. She tried to call forth a sense of peace, but, as always, perhaps as destiny had decreed, peace eluded her.

Breck, his breath freezing in the air, turned up the collar of his jacket and cocked the brim of his hat. He slowed his pace to match that of the silent woman beside him. A peace he'd never known descended on him. He turned it over in his mind, picking casually at it as one would a loose thread. He decided it was a peace based on belonging. Somehow he belonged to this patch of earth called Nevada, where mountains reared starkly in the distance, where eagles soared in summer-blue skies, where snow, like the fairy flowers of spring, blossomed on sagebrush. It was a land that taught the lesson of endurance. It was a lesson that epitomized his life. He had always endured. Alone. But now there was the woman beside him. Belonging frightened him—it threatened endurance—yet he could not deny that this woman's belonging to him was also part of the peace he felt.

"Is it much farther?"

Breck let the question chase away his troubling thoughts. "No. Just ahead."

They passed quickly through the snow, past the milliner's shop, where a fancy lace bonnet kept a nocturnal vigil, past the drugstore, which smelled of peppermint and camphor, past the general store, whose window displayed fabric and a set of yellow-flowered china dishes imported from England. There was also a doll that beckoned to every little girl. The doll had a pretty porcelain face. Because it was becoming harder and harder to reconcile what she needed to do—kill Breck—with what she wanted to do—lie forever in his arms—Trinity glanced away.

In the falling shadows of twilight, the railroad yard looked as though it had settled down for a slumbrous night. The yardmaster and the brakeman had called it a day, leaving behind a stillness that drifted about the scattered freight cars. Tin sheds flanked one side of the terminal track, while a larger wooden building swallowed the ribbons of track at the end of the yard. It was there that Breck, straddling rails and ties, guided Trinity. Sliding back the door, he ushered her into the deep cavern, then closed the door behind them. An eerie darkness swelled around them, and their intrusive footsteps beat loud and hollow in the silence. The smells of grease and stale engine smoke permeated the air.

Trinity felt Breck, who was little more than shadow himself, slip from her side, and moments passed before a lantern burst to life, shedding an amber glow into the dense blackness. An iron giant leaped into view.

"Well, what do you think?" Breck said, his pride as obvious as the locomotive itself.

Trinity considered the iron horse before her, and a strange excitement, based on appreciation of anything of such mammoth proportions, surged through her. "I . . ." She smiled. "I think it's big."

Breck grinned. "Yeah. She weighs thirty-four tons and could practically pull a mountain behind her."

"How do you know it's a she?" Trinity asked, the teasing, though atypical between the two of them, feeling somehow good and right.

Breck's uncharacteristic grin widened. "Anything this pretty has to be a woman." The smile softened as he gently ran his hand along a front bar. "She's an iron lady."

Trinity could feel his hand caressing her instead of the engine. Warm sensations hummed to life within her, and she tried not to think of what had happened every night since they'd arrived at the Chastain. Would he turn to her tonight, as well? Would she go to him willingly, as always? And would she later wonder how she could betray herself, her mother, her mission, so surely, so completely?

In an attempt to distract herself, Trinity, too, reached out and touched the black beast. It felt hard and cold to her bare hand. Hard and cold like its owner? Yes, but, like its owner, the hardness was also a strength, and the coldness could be thawed.

She watched as Breck dusted some minuscule something from the manufacturer's plate riding just below the headlight. Inscribed in a circle around the plate were the words BALDWIN

LOCOMOTIVE WORKS PHILADELPHIA. In the plate's center shone the huge number 11.

"It—she—*is* pretty," Trinity said.

"Yeah," Breck returned. When he spoke again, it was with a sobering sigh. "I only hope I can pay for her."

Guilt, that oh-so-close friend, once more visited Trinity. This time, however, it came from a different direction. "I, uh...the money, I—I mean, I still have it . . . all of it . . . in a bank in San Francisco."

Breck studied her long and hard before saying, "That'll at least pay back what I've borrowed for salaries. Unfortunately," he added, "it won't pay for the new engine. To come up with sixteen thousand five hundred dollars, I have to do a lot of business."

Trinity's brow wrinkled. "I don't understand. You were obviously planning on acquiring the new engine despite . . . despite the robberies. Obviously you thought the business could tolerate the cost."

"It was a calculated risk at best, but one I thought the odds favored, with everything going as it was. Expansion of the line into two engines seemed reasonable." He shrugged and gave her a half grin. "Okay. Maybe a little less than reasonable."

"You keep talking in the past tense."

Breck's gaze intensified, as if he were considering whether to speak honestly. "I've lost some business," he said finally. "Some of the mine owners have gone back to Wells Fargo for payroll shipments, although they're still forced to use the railroad for their ore. The payroll shipments were a steady, substantial source of income, however."

"You mean they've pulled out because . . . because of the robberies?"

There was a pause before Breck answered, "Yes."

"But surely since the robberies have stopped—"

"How do they know that?"

That fact hit Trinity squarely between the eyes. No, Breck could hardly reveal that the robber had been caught, imprisoned within the bonds of matrimony.

"But when they see the robberies have halted, surely they'll bring their business back."

"Possibly. But that realization may be a piece down the road." Breck's face hardened. "And all this damned harassment isn't helping things!" The words were hissed into the silence, and it took a moment for them to uncoil and slither away. When they finally did, Breck spoke again, his voice strong with conviction this time as he once more stroked the locomotive. "I'll find a way to keep her. Maybe I can make her pay for herself by doubling the runs." His fist clenched around the bar of the cowcatcher. "I'll be damned if I'll lose everything after working this hard!"

It struck Trinity that perhaps she'd accomplished part of what she'd set out to do: Ruin Madison Brecker financially. Funny, it didn't seem as satisfying as she'd thought it would. She spoke without thinking. "I have some money. I could help you."

Breck directed his eyes from the engine to the woman. Surprise, even disbelief, scored his face, but something flashed quickly in his unreadable eyes, hinting that her offer had deeply moved him. Maybe more than anything ever had.

"Now, why would you want to do that, China?" he asked, his voice warmer than the lantern's glow. "We're enemies. Remember?"

No, she hadn't remembered. For one unprotected moment, she hadn't remembered that they were enemies. How strange. And how very, very disturbing.

She was trying to sort through her confused thoughts when she sensed a sudden tension in him, which was followed by his low, abrupt "Shh!"

At his command, her own body drew to attention. They stood, their heads poised, listening for some sound in the silence. Nothing. Trinity heard nothing. Except an occasional settling creak of the wooden building and the ever-present whine of the wind. She was tempted to whisper "What did you hear?" when she heard a faint noise at the front of the building, then the scrambling sound of the door opening. In that same instant, Breck doused the light, plunging the cavern into total darkness. Apprehension raised the hair on the nape of Trinity's neck. Instinctively, she stepped back, going she knew not where.

Breck's hand shot out, unerringly finding her in the inky blackness, and pulled her tight against him. Trinity melted into the shelter of his arms.

She listened to the door closing, then to the hushed sound of footsteps shuffling across the floor planks. Suddenly, the footsteps halted. In the silence came a fumbling sound, followed by

the flick of a match, which was immediately touched to the
wick of a travel lantern. In the flare of the light, Breck eased
himself and Trinity farther into the shielding shadows and behind some stacked crates. A crowbar, obviously used for un-
packing, lay across one of the wooden boxes.

Peering around the edge of a crate, Trinity could tell that the
intruder was a man, but, because of the blend of dark and light,
she could distinguish little of the particulars of his face. She
could tell, however, that he was fair-sized and that he moved
with the agility of a man with well-honed muscles. Both his size
and his agility added to her apprehension.

What was he doing skulking around in the middle of the
night?

Even as Trinity posed the question, the intruder supplied an
answer. Setting the lantern on a box near the locomotive, he
pulled something long and narrow, and apparently heavy, from
inside his coat. A file? It looked like a file. But why would
someone break into the enginehouse carrying a lantern and a
file?

The man stepped toward the locomotive.

"Touch that engine and you're dead," Breck said, his voice
low, calm, lethal-sounding.

At the softly delivered threat, Trinity jumped. Her reaction
was nothing, however, compared to the man's. Like a top, he
spun on the balls of his feet. Lamplight streaked across his
startled face.

She'd seen him before, Trinity knew instantly, though for the
life of her she couldn't place him.

"Only cowards strike in the night," Breck said, stepping
around Trinity. "But then, we'd find a yellow stripe a mile wide
down your back, wouldn't we, Booth?"

Booth. Wilson Booth, Trinity realized. The man who'd
openly stared at her breasts during rehearsal. The man who'd
forced her into a dance. The man who'd formerly owned the
Sierra Virginia and who Ellie had said wanted to buy it back
again.

The man who was behind all the accidents?

"Well, well, if it isn't the owner of the Sierra Virginia,"
Booth drawled. His fear had vanished, replaced by a cockiness
made all the more arrogant by the fact that he dared to be cocky
under such damning circumstances. It was an attitude Trinity
assessed as dangerous. Very dangerous. Unconsciously, she

eased to Breck's side. "Ah, and your lovely new bride," Booth said, his smile revealing a full set of immaculate white teeth.

"Leave my wife out of this," Breck said with such lack of emotion that it sent shivers running down even Trinity's spine.

Booth's smile widened. "Whatever you say."

"What I say is that you're a bigger fool than I thought. Just how long did you think you could get away with sabotaging the line?"

Booth carelessly pitched the file to the floor, causing a *clunk* to echo throughout the massive room. "Actually," he said, "I was hoping the little accidents wouldn't be necessary much longer. I was hoping you'd come to your senses and sell."

"Not on your life," Breck said. "You were stupid to let the railroad go. I won't be that stupid."

A streak of ugliness flashed in the other man's eyes. "That's pretty highfalutin talk for a man who's about to drown in debt. By the way, I didn't have anything to do with the robberies."

"Only because you didn't think of it and wouldn't have had the guts to do it if you had. Your style is more crawling on your belly, rolling boulders onto the track, pulling up spikes, shooting at innocent people."

A smirk spread once more across Booth's lips. "C'mon, Brecker, you're gonna make the lady think badly of me." Booth's eyes shifted to Trinity, and for a moment she felt as if he could see straight through her clothing. His voice was smoky when he said, "We never did get to finish that dance, did we, Miss Lee?"

"Mrs. Brecker," Breck snarled, stepping forward protectively.

With the speed of lightning, Wilson Booth pulled a gun from inside his coat. Its silver steel winked in the lamplight, taunting, malicious. Breck halted in midstep, while Trinity sucked a gasp of air into her lungs.

"I wouldn't if I were you," Booth announced, his eyes fully on Breck.

"What are you going to do, kill us?" Breck asked quietly, edging back to Trinity's side. She clutched her muff in one hand, his coat sleeve with the other.

"I hadn't planned to. Really, I hadn't. But you've given me no choice, have you?"

Breck took another small step backward. Trinity followed. "Let her go."

"'Fraid I can't. She'll have to be found here with you. Too bad you two startled someone and got yourselves killed. People will probably wonder if those robberies and all those little mishaps had anything to do with your deaths. But I doubt they'll think twice when I offer to buy out the railroad. I might even be commended for doing it, since the railroad's future is so uncertain."

"The only place they'll commend you is in hell," Breck said, easing back another step.

Trinity felt the stack of crates behind her. And the point of something sharp sticking into her ribs.

Booth just laughed. "Maybe you're right, Brecker. Maybe—"

One moment the crowbar lay on the crate, the next it was sailing through the air. It struck an unsuspecting Wilson Booth in the chest, causing him to stagger backward. The gun fell to the floor...skidded...then made a pinging sound as it collided with the iron of the locomotive.

Simultaneously, Booth grunted, Trinity rushed her hands to her mouth, dropping the fur muff, and Breck raced forward. His fist caught Booth in the stomach before the man had a chance to right himself.

"You bastard!" Breck snarled, sending Booth to his knees. With one hand at the collar of Booth's coat, Breck dragged him to his feet and planted another fist in his stomach...then another...followed by another. Each blow was hard, heavy, ruthlessly uncompromising.

He's going to kill him. The thought traveled clearly and certainly through Trinity's mind and left her with a feeling of déjà vu. Once more, she was in the Crystal Saloon, watching Breck choking the life from Ben Buford. Just as it had then, the sight of Breck's cold, murderous fury chilled her.

Another grunt—Booth's—cut through Trinity's fear, and she watched as Breck struck the man again and again. She grimaced as each wallop of Breck's fist connected with its tender target.

Breck's ragged breathing cleaved the uneasy silence. Sweat popped on his forehead despite the cold, and a trickle of blood ran from the corner of his mouth, evidence that at least one of Booth's punches had landed. Breck, his hair tumbled, looked like a wild man intent upon savage revenge.

Revenge. He found the word so sweet, so damnably sweet, so sinisterly sweet, so—

Suddenly, he stopped, sending Booth to sprawl facedown on the floor. Breck stood over him, his nostrils flaring as he heaved in gulps of air. He wanted to kill him. That was certain. But he also knew he wouldn't. Why? Why wouldn't he? Maybe because he'd had his sickening fill of revenge. Maybe because killing had lost its punitive charm. Maybe because he wasn't the man he used to be.

"Get up," Breck said, the order filled with more air than speech. "Let's tell it to the sheriff." When Booth didn't move, Breck grabbed him by his collar. "Get up!"

Booth groaned.

"I'll send Dancey to walk you back to the hotel," Breck said over his shoulder.

Trinity nodded and watched as he disappeared, Booth in tow.

Breck had wanted to kill him, but he hadn't. Why? The question played over and over again in Trinity's mind, but no answer sprang to life. Other than one she didn't really want to consider: Maybe she had misjudged him. Maybe, just as society had mislabeled both her and her mother, appearances had once more been deceiving. Maybe Breck wasn't the cold-blooded murderer she'd believed him to be.

Maybe he hadn't killed her mother.

The realization of what she'd just conceded stunned her. No, he *had* killed her mother. She'd seen the blood on his hands with her very own eyes. That she could think for even a moment that he had not killed her mother filled Trinity with self-loathing, the likes of which she'd never known.

She stopped to pick up her fur muff but hesitated when she saw the gun, all gleaming and gray, peeking from beneath the locomotive. She stood, walked over to it, and bent and retrieved it. It felt cold in her hand, cold like the promise of revenge, cold like the porcelain face of a doll.

"I have some money. I could help you."

"Now, why would you want to do that, China? We're enemies. Remember?"

Trinity's hand tightened around Wilson Booth's gun.

With swift and sure knowledge, she knew that if she didn't complete her mission soon, she never would. Madison Brecker was making too many inroads into her life. Principally, he was making too many inroads into her heart.

* * *

Feeling a hundred years old, Breck entered the lobby of the Chastain Hotel. He told himself he should be relieved that the harassing incidents had finally been brought to an end, and, in truth, he was. But he was also tired, tired of the seemingly endless struggle that was his life. Furthermore, he hurt. His jaw hurt where Wilson Booth had clipped him, and his fist was pulverized from repeatedly pummeling Booth. Bringing his throbbing hand upward, he investigated the cut at the corner of his mouth. He grimaced. Lord, but he wanted a bath, a bed, and his . . . and his wife. The thought stole so naturally into his consciousness that he didn't even try to fight it.

Besides, he was tired of struggling.

Hastening up the stairway and down the hall to their room, he embraced thoughts of Trinity in his arms, her lips soft and pliant against his, her body writhing beneath his in the throes of passion.

Fitting the key into the lock, he turned the knob and opened the door. He stepped inside, then stopped abruptly. Trinity stood straight and tall in the center of the room. In the lamplight, her eyes glowed a rich brown, the color of shadow and honey, while her shoulders, alluringly scooped from the neckline of her dress, gleamed like sun-kissed alabaster. Her hands, a shade of pale ivory, looked incongruously feminine against the masculine gray steel of the gun she held. The gun aimed directly at him.

Surprise, followed by disappointment, streaked his weathered face. And then a sadness, complete and overwhelming, seeped through him.

Obviously, the struggle wasn't over.

Or maybe it was.

Slowly, as if nothing were amiss, he closed the door behind him and tossed his hat into a nearby chair. His jacket followed. He glanced back at Trinity, then over at his desk, which held a bottle of whiskey and a glass.

"May I?" he asked, asking permission to cross the room, though he didn't bother to await her response.

Trinity said nothing; she simply turned to accommodate his movement, keeping the gun trained on him.

At the desk, with steady fingers, Breck poured himself a shot of whiskey. Then he raised the bottle, asking silently if she, too, would like a drink.

"No, I guess not," he answered for her. "We wouldn't want to do anything to jeopardize your aim."

Tilting his head, he downed the entire contents of the glass in one blazing swallow, wondering if this would be his last taste of whiskey. He wondered, also, if the whiskey would ease the sadness he felt, or if it would take something more powerful, like death, to do that.

"So," he said, his eyes again finding hers as he blindly set the glass down, "it's come down to the moment of truth."

Trinity said nothing. She merely held the gun before her with both hands.

"It is the moment of truth, China. We end the game, one way or the other, right here."

Still she said nothing. When Breck took a step toward her, she—strangely, for the aggressor—took a step backward.

"Are you going to make it neat and fast, or does eighteen years worth of hate require it to be slow and painful?"

Trinity didn't answer; she just took another step backward as he took another casual step forward.

"The head, the heart, would be fast," he said calmly. "The gut slow and painful. I once saw a man take thirteen hours to die with a bullet in his gut. First he cried, then he prayed, then he couldn't do either, because the pain was turning him inside out."

"Don't," Trinity whispered, but not even she knew whether it applied to what he was saying or to the fact that he'd taken yet another step toward her. The latter forced her to take another step back.

"Which raises a point. Will you watch me die, or will you shoot and run? Oh, and you'll probably want to muffle the sound with something. Otherwise, you're sure to bring someone running, which would interfere with your watching me die—if that's your choice."

Relentlessly, he moved toward her. Just as relentlessly, she stepped back—until she felt the foot of the bed biting into the backs of her legs. Still he came toward her. One step. Another. Then another, until the hard planes of his stomach pushed against the barrel of the gun, daring her to carry out her plan.

Their eyes held. In both his and hers was raw, tender pain.

"I...I have to," she said, trying to justify what she was about to do—curiously, to both of them.

"Then do it," he said, adding in a voice that was merely a hoarse whisper, "If you can pull that trigger, I don't care to live."

And he didn't, Breck realized. On the one hand it frightened him, while on the other it liberated him, freed him from his loner's prison. In some deep, powerful way, this woman had changed his life. For the better. She had become sight to his blindness, sound to his silence, color to his emotionally drab existence. She had become...him. And he, her. A feeling strong enough to set him to trembling surged through him, though he could not, would not, give it a name. In the corridors of his heart, however, it whispered its name. And its name was *love*.

Trinity's mind was filled with equally chaotic thoughts. She'd vowed to kill this man, sworn on her mother's blood to kill him, but now that the moment had come... *Love. Hate.* The words swirled in her head, in her heart, until she could not separate them. Was it possible that the heart could not be made to hate what it was determined to love? Trinity's eyes glazed with a wash of tears until the man before her, the mission before her, was but a blur. Her hands began to shake.

Slowly, Breck took the gun from her and laid it on a nearby chair. Turning back to her, he saw the silent teardrops coursing down her cheeks, heard the uneven breath seeping from her lips. He pulled her into his arms, swaddling her with his body...and with feelings that threatened to burst his heart.

"I didn't kill your mother," he whispered in her ear. "I swear it. On everything holy."

Trinity tightened her arms about him and buried her face in his chest. She believed him. Dear God in heaven, she believed him.

Chapter Eighteen

Both damned thought and worshiped at the altar of feeling.

After taking the gun from her, after crushing her to him for what seemed an eternity, Breck carried her to the bed. His intention was to love her slow and long, but the moment he felt her beneath him, the urgent feelings that had just been played out between them demanded expression. He took her, she took him, quickly, mindlessly, with their bodies doing the talking. Afterward, as though in no way appeased, the need was still there, still demanding expression. Only this time, the need was willing to be patient. Relatively speaking.

Trinity, her black hair tossed about her bare shoulders, traced the curve of Breck's neck with delicate kisses, then planted the same sweetness along the contour of his shoulder. Tiny shudders erupted across his skin, and she could feel the tight control he had to exercise to lie perfectly still. Both could feel the second fire lapping at their senses; it was a fire that had built steadily with each kiss, each touch, each slow and measured caress. It was a fire that was singeing their already paper-thin patience.

"I've never kissed a man like this," she whispered, taking yet another taste of his skin, this a tiny nip of his biceps.

The love-bitten muscle flexed. "I've never been kissed like this," Breck said, his breath disintegrating into fractions of sound.

Her lips hesitated at the inside of his elbow. Her eyes went to his, questioning his comment. How could that be, with all the women who had surely been in his life?

How could he tell her about the paid-for, rote responses of prostitutes? How could he tell her that up until the last few weeks, their mechanical, sterile approach to lovemaking had been all he wanted? How could he tell her that knowing her had changed all that? He couldn't, so he simply repeated, "I've never been kissed like this."

As he spoke, he threaded his fingers through the softness of her hair, drawing it back from her face. Her beautiful face, he thought. He could see the tracks of her dried tears, could see their glitter in her passion-hazed eyes. Gently seizing her hair in his fist, he pulled her to him.

"Come here," he ordered, sultrily, sexily.

She went, allowing him to align her lips with is. He felt her lips take tentative command, and he gloried in her feminine authority. When her tongue teased the seam of his mouth, he groaned and admitted the probing tip, nuzzling it with his own tongue until he heard her moan. Sprawled across his chest as she was, he could feel her breasts nesting in the thickness of his hair. Her nipples had stiffened and now probed his skin. He could tell they ached, because she shifted restlessly against him. Ironically, the movement only made them harden more, which only made them ache more.

Which only made him ache more, as well . . . in a place that couldn't stand a whole lot more aching. In an attempt to still her, he ran his hands under her hair and down her back, sculpting her to him even as he quieted her. It didn't help; he couldn't stop himself from trailing his hands down her spine to the swells of her hips.

She responded innocently, instinctively, by arching into his thigh and drawing her knee upward. It brushed across the turgid shaft of his sex. At the same time, her aching breasts tunneled into his chest, their nipples wriggling against him.

A firestorm blasted through Breck, sending its hot rage to every quadrant of his fevered body. His heartbeat accelerated, slamming hard and furious against his eardrums. In that moment, he felt as if he'd never made love before, and he knew that if he didn't soon, there would be no hanging on to his sanity.

"Good Lord, China!" he gasped, taking control of the situation by rolling her onto her back.

"Breck..." she whispered, uncertain exactly why she was calling his name, uncertain exactly where she wanted him to touch her. All she knew was that the fire was building even brighter than before, and that it was threatening to consume all reason.

He seemed to know things she didn't, however, things like where she needed to be touched. He lowered his head, and his mouth closed around the swollen, hard bud of her breast. Warm tremors sluiced over her. She gasped at their savage intensity, then gasped again as his tongue flicked, then laved, the dark velvet crest. She could feel it tighten even more. It was a tightness she felt all the way down her body, a tightness that coiled between her legs, where a former tightness was only now easing away.

"Breck..." she whimpered.

"You're so hard," he said, drawing the pad of his thumb across the moist summit of her breast. "I'm so hard. Lord, how can I be so hard again, so soon?"

"Breck..."

"I want to come inside you again."

"Then...come," she pleaded, totally senseless, totally shameless, with this new and wanton desire. The feelings she'd experienced upon realizing she couldn't kill him were still very much alive, still shouting for expression.

"No...wait...gotta wait...this time..." His mouth found hers again.

The kiss was sweet and tender and...loving. Over and over, his mouth took hers; over and over, sensations purled through her body until she wasn't certain whether she stood at the gates of heaven or hell. His mouth left hers only to cherish the rest of her body. He kissed her shoulders, the hollow of her throat, her breasts, and the valley between. He kissed her stomach, her navel—his tongue flirted with its silken depths—then kissed the small bandage on her side so reverently that it erased forever her fears about the ugliness of the scars.

And then she felt his breath stirring the raven curls at the cleft between her legs. Sensations, tempestuously sweet, stormed through her, making her feel more alive than she could ever remember feeling. Need. Her whole body had become a throbbing need.

"Breck," she breathed, watching the blond-haired head sliding lower and lower and . . . She moaned when his lips, daring the most intimate of intimacies, brushed her; when his tongue dipped into her honeyed moistness, a moistness he'd helped create, she cried out. Clutched at his hair. And arched herself into the hot core of his mouth. He stroked her, teased her, guided her to within inches of a blinding bliss.

Finally, in desperation, she sobbed his name. "Breck!"

He crawled the length of her, nearly smothering her beneath him. Passion etched his wild features, but it was another emotion—one even more desperate than passion—that burned within his pale eyes.

"Tell me you believe I didn't kill your mother," he demanded. He trapped Trinity's face between his large, rough palms. "Tell me!"

His plea, his order, came from the deepest part of his soul.

"I believe you," she whispered.

Studying her, he gauged her reply, and when he was satisfied she had spoken the truth, he gave way to the passion ruling his loins. He crushed her mouth with his and buried himself deep inside her.

Trinity pulled him tightly against her, wanting the weight of him, the power of him, the hard strength of him. She splayed her hands across his perspiration-damp back, digging her fingertips into his bronzed muscles. She curled her legs lovingly about him.

He drove into her with a frenzied need.

She met him with the same frenzy.

For him, he needed to brand her as his—totally, completely, uncompromisingly. He needed to end the solitude of his life, the vast loneliness.

For her, she needed to give voice, physical voice, to the overwhelming feeling she'd experienced earlier, the feeling that had subtly, softly, replaced the hate of all the years. It was a hot feeling, a bright feeling, a feeling that exploded in her soul as Breck exploded in her body, taking her with him on the sensual, regal flight to heaven.

"China!" he growled, his breath warm and wild against her shoulder.

She held him, embraced him, eased his body with the feminine gentleness of her own. Each and all she did in the name of the hot feeling, the bright feeling, the feeling that had exploded in her soul. Each and all she did in the name of love.

Love.

Trinity contemplated the word much later that night as Breck lay asleep beside her. His hand rested possessively, peacefully, at her breast, with her hand lying atop his. The scar. She could feel the scar on the back of his hand. How odd, she mused, that the man she'd searched for for so long, the man with the scar in the shape of a star, was now her lover, was now the man she loved.

When had it happened?

And how?

She'd been so busy hating him, how could she possibly have found the time to fall in love with him? The answer, she knew, lay alongside the answers to such questions as: Why did the wind blow? Why did the rain fall? Why did fire burn?

But he had not spoken of love. Only of need. And that solely with his body. Yet clearly it was important to him that she believe in his innocence, which she did. But why? Did she really believe he hadn't killed her mother, or had her heart simply clouded her vision? No, she believed him, deeply, completely, and for a reason she never would have thought possible. If Breck said he hadn't killed her mother, then he hadn't. He was a man who'd done things; she didn't doubt for a moment that he'd killed his fair share of men, but *fair* was the operative word. Madison Brecker was a man of integrity, albeit an integrity that answered only to his own conscience.

But if he hadn't killed her mother, why had he insisted on marriage? A thought crossed her mind, one that knifed cruelly at her heart. Maybe Breck had been in love with her mother. Maybe he'd married her only because she reminded him of her mother. The possibility hurt, so painfully that Trinity could not catch her breath, so painfully that tears gathered anew in her eyes.

In the midst of the pain came the realization that she had to get away, away where she could think clearly, away where she could sort through her confused feelings, away where she could make sense out of having gone so quickly, so completely, from hating to loving.

Breck awoke with the first pink rays of dawn. He was instantly aware that his wife was not in his arms—a rare occurrence—and he reached out to rectify the breach of habit. When his hands embraced cool nothingness, he forced his eyes open groggily.

Empty.

Her side of the bed was empty.

Pushing himself up on an elbow, he glanced about the hotel room, from the chair to the desk to the washstand. Everything stood still and quiet, as if no human presence had disturbed it for hours. Trinity's clothes, which he'd stripped from her the night before and thrown to the floor along with his, were gone.

The birth pangs of panic began, but Breck deliberately ignored them. There were dozens of viable reasons for her not being in the room. Weren't there? He had just started to enumerate the more obvious ones when he saw the note lying on her pillow. The hand raking back his sleep-tousled hair halted in midsweep.

The panic began in earnest.

He stretched, picked up the square of paper, and noted idly that he'd never seen Trinity's—his wife's—handwriting before. It was strong and neat, with an occasional swirl and curve that pleased the eye. He further noted that the handwriting was a lot like the lady—except that the handwriting was here, while the lady was not.

Forcing himself, he read:

"Dear Breck, I'm returning to San Francisco. I need some time to think. Please understand."

An ache went through him, an ache made all the more insidious by its dull, merciless, agonizingly slow crawl into his vitals. Only one other time in his life could he remember a similar pain—when he'd been a little boy, a scared little boy, watching his father ride away without even a goodbye or a hint as to when he would return. Even as a child, he'd learned to hide the pain. He now hid it behind a curtain of anger, anger he distributed equally between himself and Trinity—Trinity for leaving, himself for giving a damn that she had.

She hadn't even signed it. No "Your loving wife." No "I'm sorry to put you through this." No "I'll be in touch." Nothing. A stone-cold nothing!

Crushing the note in his fist, he slung back the covers and, naked, crossed to the desk. The glass he'd drained the night before still sat where he'd left it, and he grabbed the bottle of whiskey by the throat and poured himself a generous serving. He downed it in a single gulp that burned his breath away. He poured another and allowed the flame to burn again.

Please understand.

Oh, he understood, all right. He sneered, dragging the back of his hand across his mouth. He understood completely. For all that he'd believed her at the time, she hadn't believed *him* when he told her he hadn't killed her mother. If she had, she couldn't have walked away from what they had together. God, what a fool he'd been to think she had believed him. What a fool he'd been to think she felt the same thing he did. What a fool he'd been to think he could hold her to him by force. What a goddamned fool!

He hurled the glass across the room, taking morbid delight in its shattering into countless pieces. When the tinkling abated, a silence heavier than any he'd ever known descended. In the silence, his soul whispered that he was once more alone... the way he'd always been... the way he always would be.

In the days, the weeks, that followed, only those who *had* to deal with Breck did. All others quickly turned aside when they saw him coming, his footsteps pounding angrily against pavement and path, while those forced to confront him did so with a nod, a mumbled greeting, and a speedy departure. No one wanted to get caught in his glacial stare; no one wanted to hear the heated wrath of his words. Charlie Knott threatened to quit a dozen times, while Dick Kingsman talked of nothing but Breck's bad mood when he and Victoria Dawson sneaked out under the moonlight. Even Dancey, friend though he was, admitted that working for Breck had become a lot like working for Satan, except that Satan was better-tempered.

Rumors were rampant that Trinity Lee—pardon, Trinity Brecker—had left her husband. No one, however, was suicidal enough to ask Breck to confirm them.

By the third week of December, the town was battening down for the Christmas holidays. The grain store on C Street boasted a live nativity scene, complete with a goat brought in in lieu of a camel. The ornery critter, determined to eat everything in sight, had broken into practically ever bag of grain in the store, and had topped one meal off with a wise man's sandal, followed by the baby Jesus's swaddling. People stopped by just to see what it would eat next.

Several doors down at the Last Drink Saloon, Millie Rhea and her sisters in sin were promising a little something extra for their customers' stockings, the implication being that they'd find that something extra in the sheer, lace-trimmed stockings they themselves wore. Harriet Dawson said their lack of piety was shocking, while Maude Terrill, secretly longing for a pair of sheer, lace-trimmed stockings, said she could faint dead away at their brazenness. Both their husbands, Dub and the good doctor, spent a lot of time at the grain store, principally because to get there one could innocently pass by the Last Drink.

The girls over at the Last Drink were the topic of conversation at the usual weekly business meeting Breck held in his office—a cheerless place that bore not a trace of the holiday season. Instead, it was decorated with human forms draped in chairs, sprawled on the floor, and reclining against the walls.

"Whoo-ee!" Hollis Reed cried from where he sat before the potbellied stove. "Have you seen the legs on that new girl?"

"Cindy Sue from St. Lou?" Dick Kingsman asked as if he knew her intimately. In truth, he hadn't been anywhere near her and wasn't about to go anywhere near her, 'cause Vicky Dawson would have his hide if he did.

"The same," Hollis confirmed. "She can tinsel my tree anytime she likes."

"And she can stuff my stocking," someone threw in. Someone else tossed out, "Hell, I'd rather stuff hers!"

Everyone except Breck burst out laughing.

"That's where you young bucks make your mistake," Charlie Knott said. He still wore the railroad man's badge of honor—a striped cap and a red bandanna. "What you need is a more seasoned woman, like Millie Rh—" He abruptly halted. Everyone knew that Breck and Millie Rhea, prior to his marriage, had been an item of sorts, and this reference to Breck's private life brought to mind the question the whole town was asking: What had happened to Madison Brecker's short-lived marriage? Charlie Knott, his gaze darting to Breck's cold eyes, then away, rephrased his comment. "What, uh . . . what you need is a more seasoned woman."

The talk and the laughter died, and the men stole glances at Breck, who leaned against his desk, looking more ornery than the nativity-eating goat. "If it wouldn't inconvenience anyone," he drawled sarcastically, "maybe we could discuss a little business."

Dick Kingsman fidgeted. Hollis Reed cleared his throat. Abe Dustin rubbed his shovel-callused hands together. Dancey Harlan said nothing; he simply looked concerned about his friend.

Breck shoved his hips from the edge of the desk and said into the awkward silence, "The week's been decent. The added run with the new engine's been well received, though the number of passengers was small. But that's to be expected in the beginning."

"You gonna hire another engineer?" Charlie asked.

"Not just yet. Can't afford one. You and I will have to split duty for a while." Since there was virtually no aspect of railroading Breck didn't know, he'd taken on the added responsibility of driving the new engine on its recently added weekly run to Reno. The extra job suited him fine, since it pushed him closer to working twenty-four out of every twenty-four hours.

Charlie nodded, as if to say he could be counted on.

"Heard Wilson Booth cut and run for California," Hollis Reed said.

"Yeah, me, too," someone added.

"He's lucky he could cut and run anywhere," Breck said, his expression hard as stone. What he didn't say was that before the sheriff had thrown Booth out of town, Breck had had a private chat with the man and had told him that he'd break his neck if he ever saw his face again. Booth had believed him. It was too bad, Breck mused, that he hadn't had the same persuasive powers with his own wife.

"I still think the sonofabitch was behind the robberies," someone said.

"Naw, the robber was smaller," Dick Kingsman said authoritatively.

"Much smaller," Hollis Reed added.

Dancey and Breck exchanged glances. Breck's was as cold as steel, as empty as old dreams.

"Gentlemen," Dancey said, "could we keep on track?"

Several of the men sniggered at the unintended pun.

Ten minutes later, the men eagerly filed out of the office, most headed for the Last Drink—or anywhere else where the atmosphere was less oppressive. Dancey was the last to leave.

Hesitating at the door, he braved the question he'd wanted to ask for weeks. "Have you heard from her?"

Breck never looked up from his ledger. "No," he answered flatly.

"Do you think in time—"

"No."

"Why don't you contact her—"

Breck jerked his head up, his eyes flaring with a mixture of fire and ice. "Just leave the subject be."

Dancey, despite all he knew about Trinity's involvement in the robberies, knew little else. Except that her relationship with Breck was as mercurial as quicksilver . . . and that it quite possibly ran deeper than either of them suspected.

"I'll be at the Last Drink if you want to join me," Dancey said, respecting his friend's privacy.

Breck instantly regretted the sharpness of his voice. "Checking out Cindy Sue from St. Lou?" he asked, forcing a smile as a peace offering.

"At my age, a good solid look is about all the damage I could do," Dancey said, returning the smile and slipping out the door.

Breck watched him leave before returning his attention to the ledger. But his attention wouldn't stay focused. Irritated, he slammed the book shut and scraped back his chair. Crossing the room, he stared out the glass of the front door. The night was black and cold, with flecks of snow beginning to flutter down.

Tired.

Lord, he was so tired, tired from head to toe, from soul to heart, and another restless night stretched out before him. As he'd done each night the last few weeks, he would stay in the office, dozing in a chair if he got lucky enough, exhausted enough, to fall asleep. What he'd try to do was not think of Trinity, which would prove impossible. Even though he hated himself for thinking of her. In fact, he hated—loathed—himself this very moment, for even as he stood watching the snow on this cold, dark night, his thoughts were all of her.

Where was she?

Who was she with?

Did she ever think of him?

Hundreds of miles away, Trinity stepped through the doors of the elegant Cosmopolitan Hotel in San Francisco. She looked around for the dinner companion she was scheduled to meet but saw no one familiar. Lifting her train of violet silk with a gloved hand, she swept across the expansive lobby and seated herself in the first chair she came to.

The wooden floors gleamed like ice under the glow of crystal chandeliers, while the scent of flowers freshened the air. In the middle of the lobby stood a tall spruce strung with chains of popcorn and cranberries. At the top stood a watchful angel; hundreds of glass ornaments hung from the evergreen boughs.

Christmas.

It was Christmas, Trinity thought with a startled laugh. She supposed she'd seen the signs before now, but now, for the first time, it really registered. The Christmas holidays, a time of joy and peace. *Joy and peace.* Those were words she had almost known the meaning of. Almost. Just as it was almost Christmas. Why hadn't she realized it was almost Christmas? Probably because she'd simply been too busy getting through the endless days, the restless nights, that had become her life.

She had returned to San Francisco, as she'd indicated in her note to Breck. Fortunately, a touring opportunity had immediately arisen. For the next two and half weeks, she had walked the stages of theatres the length of the West Coast. She had been pleased to have something to occupy her mind, though, even as she spouted her lines, her thoughts were always on . . .

Breck.

What was he doing?

What was he thinking?

Did he ever think of her?

She had tried to categorize her feelings more times than she'd tried to breathe. The truth was that she didn't know what she felt. Feeling her hatred turn to love had swept her into an emotional whirlwind. There seemed to be no foundation under her feet. No emotion, love or hate, seemed trustworthy any longer. No, that wasn't true. Her love for Breck was all too real, all too credible. Even though he was still a stranger in so many ways, she knew him thoroughly in all the ways that mattered. Except one. She did not know his heart. Did he care for her? Or did she simply remind him of someone else? On this subject, she was not ruled by vanity; she was ruled solely by her heart. She simply could not endure his being in love with another woman. Even if that woman was dead.

The thought that he might love her mother, even after all these years, left her cold and hurting, and she dredged her mind for something else to think about. What she settled on was not particularly placid, though it was distracting. She had returned to San Francisco from her tour less than a week before, and had found its citizens still talking about an incident that had occurred nearly ten days earlier. A reporter for a local newspaper, a hard-nosed, brazen investigator, had been mysteriously murdered. The same reporter who had hounded her about her parentage. His murder had left her oddly apprehensive.

"Trinity?"

She jumped, her eyes flying to her awaited dinner companion.

"I'm sorry, my dear," white-haired Jedediah McCook said, "I didn't mean to startle you."

She laughed nervously. "You didn't. I was just—" She came to her feet and took the two hands the older man offered. "How are you?" she asked, genuinely pleased to see her friend and somehow not surprised that he hadn't brought his wife along. When he'd issued the invitation to dinner, Trinity had sensed it would be just the two of them.

"I can't complain. How are you?"

Her smile faded a bit. "I'm fine," she lied.

Jedediah considered before saying forthrightly, "Let's get seated in the restaurant, order a drink, and then we'll discuss those circles beneath your eyes."

"What circles?" Trinity countered.

"The ones you're trying to hide," Jedediah said, his hand at her back urging her forward. Minutes later, he made good his gentle threat. "Now, tell me why you're not as happy as a new bride should be."

Having decided on a flippant denial, she said, "Jedediah McCook, you're incorrigible. You're also wrong. I'm hap—"

"Where's your husband?"

Trinity moistened her lip with the tip of her tongue. "He's, uh . . . he's back in Virginia City. He couldn't get away . . . with the railroad and all."

"I see," Jedediah replied, and Trinity feared that he did indeed see—far too much. "And so you, in the midst of your honeymoon, unexpectedly decided to tour."

"How do you know that it wasn't a prearranged commitment?"

"Was it?" he asked bluntly.

She toyed with the idea of lying, but she knew she could not, not to this man for whom she had such deep feelings. "No," she said, looking him straight in the eye. His silence encouraged her to add, "I had to get away for a while. I needed some time to think."

"Ah, time to think—the boon and the scourge of humanity."

Trinity glanced down, idly running her finger around the rim of her wineglass.

"And have you? Thought, that is?"

Trinity shrugged. "Yes . . . No . . . I don't know."

A silence followed, in which restaurant sounds intruded—low chatter, an occasional laugh, the sound of expensive tableware against fine china.

"You know," Jedediah said finally, "when word reached me of your marriage, I was surprised." He chuckled. "Actually, *surprised* may not be quite the word. I was stunned, but also very pleased. In fact, I can't think of anything that's pleased me so much in a long while."

Trinity raised her eyes, but said nothing.

"I know he's difficult," Jedediah continued. "Hell, *difficult* won't even begin to define him, but—"

"It's not that. I mean, you're right, he is difficult, but . . ." She let her words trail off.

"But what, then?"

She glanced down before once more letting her gaze meet her friend's. Her eyes misted, and she hated herself for the weakness. "I—I'm in love with him."

Quiet seconds strolled by before he said, "You'll excuse what may be an old man's faulty reasoning, but that doesn't sound like such a problem. I rather assumed that's what you would be feeling. It's certainly what you should be feeling."

"You don't understand. Our marriage . . . It's . . . it's unconventional at best." She longed to tell this man more, but could not. Some things were too personal to be shared with anyone. She heard herself, however, sharing one other thing. "He has not spoken of love."

"Ah," Jedediah responded knowingly. "And have you?"

"No, but—"

"Why not?"

Trinity sighed. "It's complicated."

"Love always is."

"He . . ." She hesitated, not certain she could give voice to her hurtful thoughts. "He may be in love with someone else. Someone from a long time ago. I may . . . I may only remind him of her."

"I can't imagine you reminding a man of anyone but you."

A smile slid across Trinity's lips. "You are a flatterer, Jedediah McCook."

Jedediah did not match his companion's smile. He simply reached for her hand, smothering it in the vastness of his. "You haven't asked my advice, child—" the word came naturally, and was received in the same manner "—but I shall give it anyway. Tell Breck you love him; ask him if he loves you." The hand enfolding hers tightened. "Never, *never*, turn loose of anyone you love—not without a fight." When he spoke again, his voice was strained. "I did once, and it was the biggest mistake I ever made."

Trinity had once wondered whether her friend harbored some deep hurt. Now he had laid his soul bare to her, eliminating all doubt. As strongly as she'd ever felt anything, she felt the need to comfort him, and so she laid her free hand atop his. They said nothing; they simply stared, each at the glaze in the other's eyes.

Finally, Jedediah sniffed, patted her hand, and said hoarsely, "Well, shall we eat dinner or cry in our soup?"

They ate. Later that night, Trinity, suffering as usual from sleeplessness, walked the floor. The next morning, before daybreak, she came to a decision. Penning a note to Jedediah, she asked if she could borrow his private coach again. Then she sent a telegram to her husband. It read:

ARRIVE VIRGINIA CITY ON NEXT TRAIN STOP I LOVE YOU STOP DO YOU LOVE ME

SIGNED MRS MADISON BRECKER

Chapter Nineteen

Jedediah was still in bed when Trinity's message arrived. At the servant's timid knock, he mumbled a sleepy "Come in" and proceeded to read the note presented to him. A smile in his heart, he checked his watch. Five-thirty. Since the train for Reno, and consequently the train for Virginia City, left at five minutes before nine, he hastily donned a silk dressing jacket and hurried down the stairs to his study. There, he dashed off a few lines, then proceeded to write a reply to Trinity. He had just completed it and was boldly inscribing his signature when a voice interrupted the silence.

"Is everything all right?" Ada McCook asked from the doorway.

Startled, doubly so because of the nature of his task, Jedediah jumped, knocking over the crystal inkwell and spilling a puddle of black across the lower half of the epistle to Trinity.

"Damn!" he muttered, righting the container and dabbing at the mess with his handkerchief.

Ada stepped into the room, drawing her wrapper around her. On her hair, slightly askew, perched a lawn nightcap with tucks and embroidery.

Jedediah glanced up. "It's all right, Ada. Nothing's wrong. Just business. Go on back to bed."

"But I heard—"

"It's just business," he repeated gruffly. When she didn't move, he gentled his voice. "Go on back to your room. I'm sorry you were disturbed."

Taking in the ink-stained paper, she turned and walked from the study.

Breathing a sigh of relief, Jedediah ripped the soiled note in quarters and discarded it in the wastebasket. He then duplicated it, this time without mishap. After placing the new version in an envelope, he rose, and, taking both it and his instructions to ready the coach, he went in search of William, his driver, and dispatched him to deliver the messages. Trinity's letter to him safe in his pocket, Jedediah mounted the stairs, intending to shave and face the new day. At the thought of Trinity's decision, a silent song once more sang in his heart.

While a silent song was singing in Jedediah's heart, curiosity was burning in Ada's. Stepping from the shadows of the adjacent room, she rushed into the recently vacated study and closed the door behind her. Relighting the lamp, she hurriedly searched the desktop. Nothing. She found no ruined stationery. Grabbing the wastebasket, she rifled its contents. Finally, she found what she sought and pieced the sections together.

Through the splotch of ink, which had obliterated Jedediah's signature but nothing else, she read:

My dear Trinity, your decision pleases me more than I can say. Of course you may borrow the private coach. And, yes, you're quite right. I would have your head were I to discover that you had returned to Virginia City without using it. I will immediately send 'round orders to ready it. The train, as per a new schedule, but which you may already know, leaves at 8:55 A.M. Safe trip, my child.

Always,

My child . . . my child . . . my child . . .
The phrase echoed in Ada's ears. It started softly, like a muted chorale in a vast cathedral, but soon rose in volume until it screamed pagan noises that hurled themselves from the study walls.

"Shh, shh!" Ada whispered, trying to quiet them before they beckoned the servants, before they told the world the one secret the world must never know.

As if the pagan noises understood and sympathized, they stilled, until the room was so quiet Ada could hear her heart beat. In the silence, her secret once more making her strong, she knew what she had to do. And she had to do it now, while she could still save Jedediah from his own folly.

"I'm sorry, ma'am, the train's already left."

"But it can't have," Ada cried, her breathing ragged. "It's not yet—"

She frantically raised her eyes to the wall behind the ticket stall. The large clock there read 9:05. Ada's spirits plummeted. She had rushed every second but simply had not moved fast enough. She had missed the boat from San Francisco to Vallejo but had had no problem finding a man to ferry her across—for a price, of course. In the end, she'd reasoned that the lone crossing might be for the best. She had avoided detection by Trinity, who was surely aboard the boat. But missing the train was not for the best. She couldn't very well carry out her mission if she couldn't get aboard the train.

"Is there another train—"

"No, ma'am, that's the only one bound for Virginia City."

Annoyed at being interrupted, Ada tilted her chin imperiously. "I quite understand that, young man, but is there another train leaving for anywhere else that connects with this one?"

"You mean at some point en route?"

"Naturally," Ada said, not bothering to hide her sarcasm.

The young man checked the schedule before him, then some maps hanging on the wall. In the silence, a locomotive whistled and belched a long, steady stream of smoke. The people hurriedly boarding the train gave the impression that it would be leaving soon.

"No, ma'am," the man said finally. "There's nothing till this afternoon."

"Where's this train going?" Ada asked, motioning with a gloved hand toward the one preparing to depart.

"Denver."

"It's not stopping anywhere along the way?" Ada asked, incredulous.

"No, ma'am, that's a through trip. Or near 'bouts a through trip. It only stops once in—" He checked the schedule. "Let me see, it stops in, uh . . . in Reno, ma'am," the man finished, awfully pleased with himself for having deciphered the information from the complicated-looking route schedules. He'd been employed by the Central Pacific for only two weeks, and he'd spent most of the time trying not to appear as ignorant as he felt.

"Reno?" Ada said, jumping on the word.

"Well, I'll be," the ticket attendant said in surprise. "The two do connect."

"When?" Ada asked, excitement flashing in her gray eyes. When the man hesitated, she pressed him. "When does the train arrive in Reno?"

The train preparing for departure whistled again.

"For God's sake," Ada barked, "will you look?"

"Uh, yes, ma'am," the man said, frantically beginning to search the schedule. "Uh, uh, here it is! The first train arrives at 8:01 tonight. And the one to Denver...uh, uh...it arrives in Reno at, uh...at, uh...at 7:53."

Eight minutes! Ada thought. Eight minutes between her being and not being first lady of the state of California.

"Give me a ticket," she ordered, scrambling through her purse.

"Yes, ma'am. Is that a one-way or round-trip?"

"Anything," she answered, casting a sharp look at the train on the nearest track. The conductor was pulling away the step. "Hurry!"

"Yes, ma'am, I am, but there's a certain procedure—"

"Give me a ticket!"

"But—"

"Now!"

Flustered, the young man ripped a ticket from the appropriate roll. "That'll be—"

Ada laid a bill on the counter and snatched up the ticket.

"Hey, ma'am!" the young man called after her. "You overpaid! Your change! Wait!"

But Ada didn't wait. She rushed from the building and boarded the train, without the benefit of a step, just as it began to roll.

"You know who that was, don't you?" an older man working at an adjacent window said. Without waiting for a response, he said, "Mrs. Jedediah McCook."

"The wife of *the* Jedediah McCook?" the other clerk asked, immediately recognizing the name of his ultimate employer.

"The same. I've seen her picture in the paper lots of times. Got her finger in every hoity-toity pie in town. She aims to be first lady of California, unless I'm missin' my guess."

"Well, I'll be skinned and hung out to dry. I wonder what she was in such an all-fired hurry about."

"Reckon that I don't know. No more than I know why she'd buy a ticket on a train her husband owns."

The young man said nothing. Instead, he glanced down at the overpayment in his hand and turned over an idea in his mind. Maybe, just maybe, Fate had handed him a way to compensate for all the beginner's mistakes he'd made. Maybe, just maybe, honesty could win out over incompetence. Maybe, just maybe, he could prove to Jedediah McCook what a fine, if still green, employee he was.

Reaching into the cash drawer, the young man made the correct change for the large bill and placed it in an envelope. He then laid it aside and said, "I'd like to go to lunch first today, if that'd be all right."

"Sure, son. You can go at eleven."

At eleven o'clock, Breck, as surly as ever, glanced up as the office door opened.

An instant apology tumbled from the intruder's lips. "I'm sorry, Mr. Brecker, but you, uh . . . you have a telegram, sir." The boy, no more than fifteen and fighting a bad case of pimples—to say nothing of the bad case of fear he was fighting at having to confront Madison Brecker—hugged the door with his back as if his life depended on being able to make a fast exit. Necessity forced him to edge forward. "Here, uh . . . here you are," he said, stepping only as close as he had to to drop the telegram on the desk. That accomplished, he snatched back his hand, whirled around, and started for the door.

"Wait!" Breck called out, recognizing the kid as a local orphan. His father had died in the mines two years before, his mother of fever last summer.

The young man spun around, his face pale.

Breck stood, ran his hand into his pocket, and pulled out some coins, which he handed to the boy.

The young man stepped forward, smiled shyly, and said, "Thanks." Noticing the generous amount, he added, "Hey, thanks!"

Breck nodded and picked up the telegram.

The boy, not wishing to push his luck with a man famed for his foul moods, hit the door and ran back to the telegraph office. The coins jingled all the way, causing the messenger to ponder just how bad this Madison Brecker really was. He decided maybe he wasn't bad at all.

Back in his office, Breck ripped open the telegram. It was probably a bill collector, trying a more direct, more threatening, approach. Maybe it had something to do with the new locomotive. Even though Jedediah had interceded on his behalf, the company had a right to know when to expect payment. Maybe—

ARRIVE VIRGINIA CITY ON NEXT TRAIN STOP I LOVE YOU
STOP DO YOU LOVE ME

                              SIGNED MRS MADISON BRECKER

Midway through the telegram, Breck's heart trebled its beat, though by the end of the message he would have sworn his heart had stopped altogether. He read the note again, this time forcing himself to go slowly to avoid what might have been a misinterpretation the first time. At the realization that wishful thinking had not penned the words, elation, warmer than the heat radiating from the wood-burning stove, bathed him; it was the same heated feeling he'd experienced weeks before, when he'd realized that Trinity was going to live. Now, as then, it was all-consuming, like being at the very heart of a fire.

I love you.

For a man who'd never before been the recipient of that sentiment—he'd heard it from neither parent nor lover—it burned its way into his frigid, solitary heart, thawing the chilled loneliness and heating it with promise. His eyes, always so empty, filled to the brim with emotions, tender emotions that budded and sprouted to new life, while the taut, world-weary lines of his face shallowed and softened.

Why had she left if she loved him? he worried. But did it really matter now?

No, Breck thought, caressing the telegram. No, it didn't really matter now. Nothing did, except—

His booted steps exploded against the wooden planking of the sidewalk, sending people scurrying out of his way. His hat pulled low, his jacket collar turned up, he noticed nothing, no one. He simply walked resolutely toward the telegraph office.

Do you love me?

Over and over the question repeated itself—with each footstep, with each swing of his arms, with each sway of his lean hips. It was one thing to be loved, quite another to love. The first was a pleasurable path, the second a treacherous one, one that could not be turned back from. Did he have courage enough to admit what he felt for Trinity? Did he have courage enough to give that feeling a name? Did he have courage enough to leave himself more vulnerable than he'd ever been before?

The telegraph clerk, green-visored and wearing an armband over his long-sleeved shirt, looked up as the door opened. So did the two men playing dominoes before the fire and the one who sat whittling on a nearby bench. The room grew silent and motionless, as if suddenly frozen in time. One by one, the men dropped their gazes.

Breck stepped inside. Crossing to the window, he said, "I want to send a telegram."

"Yes, sir, Mr. Brecker," the operator said, taking pen and pad in hand.

"To Mrs. Brecker, and I want it delivered when she boards the Sierra Virginia in Reno."

"Yes, sir. And what do you want me to send?"

Breck hesitated, waiting to hear what he was going to say, waiting to measure the courage in his heart. Finally, he said, clearly, distinctly, "I love you."

The pen halted; the man jerked his head up. In the silent background, a domino tumbled onto the board.

"Y-yes, sir," the operator said, quickly recovering. "Anything else?"

"No."

"A signature?"

"No." Breck pulled a bill from his pocket and laid it on the counter. "Just get it to her at Reno."

"Yes, sir."

Breck turned, briefly making contact with every curious eye in the room. His gaze, steady and lean, dared anyone to say anything. Finally, he tipped his hat in a curt parting and disappeared out the door.

"Well, I'll be a sonofagun," one of the men said.

Another drawled, "Who'd a reckoned the man was human?"

Human. That was exactly how Breck felt as he stepped out into the cold December day. Wonderfully human, frighteningly human, human enough to be in love.

At 11:17, the ticket clerk, perspiring under his high-collared shirt, was shown into the plush office of *the* Jedediah McCook. Staring into the strong, unwavering, and definitely inquisitive eyes of power, he was momentarily overwhelmed by a serious case of doubt.

"Yes?" Jedediah said when it became obvious the caller wasn't going to take the initiative.

The young man stepped forward. "I, uh ... I'm Garret Lathrop, sir. I work for you. Over in the ticket office." He gestured behind him, as if his grill-fronted cubicle were only feet away and not on the far side of the tracks. The faint squeal of an engine whistle gave evidence of the distance.

"Yes, Mr. Lathrop, what can I do for you?" Jedediah asked, so warmly that Garret almost could have believed the railroad baron recognized him.

"Well, sir, I, uh ... I think it's I who can do something for you." Encouraged by his civil reception, he advanced, simultaneously searching the inner pocket of his jacket with long, bony fingers. He pulled forth an envelope and laid it on the massive scrolled desk.

Jedediah's look was questioning.

"Your wife, sir," the clerk explained. "She overpaid for her ticket this morning."

Jedediah's look of inquiry turned to one of out-and-out perplexity. "I don't understand."

"Your wife. She overpaid. I tried to stop her, but she was in a hurry to board the train."

"Train? My wife caught a train this morning?"

"Yes, sir."

"Surely you're mistaken. My wife had no plans to travel. I left her in her room—"

"Oh, yes, sir," Garret Lathrop interrupted, his tone one of certainty. "I mean, she did catch the train. Sheldon Vance, my boss, he recognized her. Said he'd seen her picture in the paper before." Discretion forbade mentioning the boss's comment about her having her finger in every hoity-toity pie in town and her aspirations to be a governor's wife.

With each word, Jedediah's face had paled, until it was now the color of ash. "W-what train?"

"The one to Denver."

"Denver?" Jedediah asked, feeling the fear receding somewhat, though his curiosity was piqued.

"Yes, sir. She wanted to catch the train to Virginia City, but it had already left, so she caught the Denver-bound train 'cause it was going to rendezvous with the other one in Re—"

"Holy God!" Jedediah cried, jumping from his chair, rounding the desk, and racing from the room. The ticket clerk was left standing there with a dazed look on his face. "I want to send a telegram, Miss Evans," Jedediah said to his matronly secretary. "To Madison Brecker in Virginia City."

"Yes, sir," the secretary replied.

"I, uh... I'll just be going," Garret Lathrop said, edging slowly out of the room.

Jedediah picked up a pad and hastily scrawled a message.

"I'll just leave the money...."

"Send this immediately, Miss Evans. It's urgent."

"It was no problem. I mean, bringing the change over. I was glad to." Nothing followed. "It, uh...it was nice to meet you."

When the young man's remarks received no response whatsoever, he slipped from the room, disappointment dripping from his face. Damn! He could forget about his employer praising him for being honest. Maybe he could even forget his job. In fact, unless he was very much mistaken, he'd be lucky if he, like the famed bearer of bad news, didn't lose his head.

When the telegraph clerk in Virginia City saw the word *Urgent*, he immediately dispatched the message.

"Here, Billy," he said to the messenger, "take this to Madison Brecker's office. It's important." He had said Madison Brecker's office rather than Madison Brecker himself because it was common knowledge that Breck spent a major portion of his time there.

"Yes, sir," Billy said, visions of another meaty tip springing to mind. It was, therefore, a tremendous disappointment for the youthful Billy to discover that Madison Brecker's office was empty and locked. Darn! he thought as he slid the telegram beneath the door, he'd never be able to get those boots over at the general store at the rate he was going.

At the rate he was going, Breck thought, he was sure to be crazy by the time the train pulled in that evening at 11:33. Damn, the Central Pacific would have to be trying out a new schedule! Ordinarily, the trip from San Francisco to Virginia City would conclude in the afternoon, but every now and then the Central Pacific experimented with a new timetable. He checked the clock on the depot wall. Noon. God, he'd be crazy by 11:33 that evening!

He should go back to the office and try to stretch the money the length of the bills. Yeah, that was what he'd do, he thought, turning on his heel and heading for the station door. He stopped abruptly. No, he couldn't do that. He felt restless and higher than a kite in July. He simply could not face the discipline of the ledger that afternoon. So, what will you do, Brecker? Simple, came the answer. Hang around the railroad yard and go crazy.

One hour, two, three, then four, passed, followed mercilessly by another and another and yet another. At 7:48, Breck decided he'd drown the remainder of the time in a couple of shots of whiskey. The Sierra Virginia had long ago left to make the Reno connection. He'd toyed with riding in and meeting Trinity there, but even though she'd said she loved him, it was important that she come to him—all the way to him. And so he'd let the train depart without him.

"I'll be over at the Last Drink," he said to the yardmaster, who was getting ready to bed down the new engine for the night. The man grunted an appropriate response.

Minutes later, his hands buried deep in his jacket pockets, Breck was passing the telegraph office. His mind was on Trinity. Was she as eager as he? Would she still feel warm and clingy in his arms? Could he survive for another few hours? Out of the corner of his eye, he caught a glimpse of someone waving at him from beyond the glass.

Billy. Whose winter home had turned out to be the bench in the telegraph office.

"Evening, Mr. Brecker," he said, yanking open the door. His earlier trepidation had vanished, replaced by the hope of another generous gratuity. Nonetheless, he kept a safe distance between him and the man with the fickle disposition.

Breck nodded. "Evening, Billy."

"I slid it under your office door."

A frown settled on Breck's mouth.

"The telegram. I slid it under the door. Mr. Balcom said it was important, so I ran it straight over."

Breck's frown deepened. "I got another telegram?" The boy nodded. "What time?"

Shrugging, the waif said, "Noon or so, I reckon. I ran it straight over. 'Cause it was important, Mr. Balcom said."

"Thanks," Breck answered, starting off in the direction of his office. Disappointment scored the young boy's pimply face seconds before Breck pivoted, fished out a coin, and tossed it to him.

"Thanks, Mr. Brecker," Billy said, a picture of the handsomest boots he'd ever seen popping into his mind again.

Breck heard nothing of Billy's reply, saw none of the pleasure gleaming in his youthful eyes. Instead, his mind was on the telegram awaiting him in his office. Inexplicably, he felt a sense of dread, of foreboding. He realized the feeling was justified the moment he read Jedediah's cryptic message:

ADA TO BOARD SIERRA VIRGINIA IN RENO STOP KEEP HER AWAY FROM TRINITY STOP NO TIME NOW STOP WILL EXPLAIN LATER

SIGNED JEDEDIAH MCCOOK

Jedediah's desperation practically reeked from the paper. Breck could touch it, taste it, feel it deep in his gut. He didn't stop to analyze his own reaction. He simply knew, accepted the fact, that it matched Jedediah's. It was the same feeling he'd had when he'd rushed into Trinity's bedroom months before, half expecting to find Ada standing over her with a knife. Fighting a fear so cold that it threatened to leave him immobile, Breck jerked his head toward the clock.

A few minutes till eight.

Damn!

A telegram? Did he have time to send a telegram warning Trinity? Yes. No. Think! He shoved his fingers through his hair. Yes. He'd send a telegram, but, since the telegram in his hand was testimony to how delivery plans could go awry, he wouldn't rely upon its reaching her before the Sierra Virginia's departure. The only sure thing he could rely upon, he thought, dashing out of the office and leaving the door wide open, was himself.

He ran past startled passersby, past chatter and music, past the wind that seemed to stand still. He ran until his breath, which frosted the cold night, cut painfully into his lungs, and his boots pounded ruts into the hard earth. He spared not a single backward glance all the way to the telegraph office. From there, he ran like a crazed man toward the railroad yard.

The new engine, its tender in tow, rested like a giant sleeping panther guarding her babe in a jungle of iron railroad track. Breck boarded it in one mighty leap, breath heaving, orders flying.

"Release the track switch!"

"Mr. Brecker?" the yardmaster called.

"Release the switch!"

The man hurried to carry out the command, asking incredulously, "Are you taking her out, sir?"

"Yes. Ride tender and stoke her . . . fast."

"But, sir—"

"Now!"

"But, sir, she needs water. She's only half-full."

"I don't have time for water."

"But—"

"For God's sake, let's go!"

The engine snorted, then burst into life. Slowly, she began to move, in tentative steps that grew steady and sure, then surer still, until she was curving out of the yard and onto the track proper.

"Feed her wood!" Breck cried, frantically pushing and pulling all the necessary instruments. Smoke gusted into the air, while the whistle churned through the silence.

Ker-chung . . . ker-chung . . . ker-chung . . .

Speed mounted until the engine was knifing through the night, leaving the city and its petty problems behind. Then, and only then, did Breck allow himself a prayer. Please, God, he prayed, let the telegram reach her in time, let him reach her in time. Please, please, don't let him end up alone again!

"We're gonna burn her up!" the yardmaster called out, his comment in reference to the new engine that was the pride of its manufacturer, the pride and salvation of its owner.

Its owner's only reply was to open the throttle to full.

Chapter Twenty

Snowflakes the size of a child's delight had begun to fall by the time the train reached Reno. Adjusting the fur-lined hood of her cloak about her face, Trinity stepped from the private coach and onto the busy platform. The train had arrived in Reno on time, give or take a few minutes, and the Sierra Virginia was scheduled to leave in fifteen minutes. Other train schedules had not been so fastidiously met. Station gossip said the Denver-bound train, due to have arrived already, was still trudging through some of the worst snow that northerly route had seen all season. Trinity sympathized with the people who wouldn't reach their destinations on time.

She smiled faintly. Right now, she even sympathized with those who had arrived on time. Never had the trip seemed to take so long. Never had she been so eager to arrive in Virginia City. Her smile died. What if Breck didn't love her? What if he'd wanted her only because she was the daughter of Su-Ling? What if—

Stop it! Stop torturing yourself. You'll know the truth soon enough.

Occasionally giving a friendly nod to a stranger, she strode along the platform, stretching her legs after the long hours of confinement and trying to force her mind away from the singular subject of Breck. Her mind, however, refused to be controlled. She had half expected an answering telegram, or perhaps a handwritten message delivered by Dancey Harlan, who would, of course, have spent the earlier part of the day alongside Breck in Virginia City, but Dancey had had only a warm personal greeting for her. No message from Breck, no comment about Breck, except that he was expecting her. In the end, Dancey's eyes had apologized for his friend's reticence, for his private loner's ways.

Loner. Breck had always been a loner. And probably always would be. Maybe he chose that path because he could choose no other. Even if he wanted to, could he make room for her beside him? But what if he didn't even love her? What if he wanted her only because she was Su-Ling's daughter? What if—

Stop it!

The cold was threatening to pinken her nose, and Trinity returned to the private coach, now securely coupled to the Sierra Virginia. No sooner had she draped her cloak across the bed than a tap sounded on the door. Chafing her hands to rid them of their chill, she crossed the carpeted coach and pulled open the door. Dancey Harlan stood before her.

"We'll be leaving pretty soon, ma'am. Is there anything I can get you?"

Trinity smiled at the man who'd helped to save her life, at the man who'd tactfully fettered his curiosity as to why she'd been robbing the train, at the man who was becoming her friend. "No, thank you, Dancey."

"You're sure I can't get you some coffee or tea? It's a bit nippy out. Something hot might just hit the spot."

At the mention of something to drink, Trinity's stomach rumbled hungrily. The excitement of seeing Breck again, whether he loved her or not, had kept her thoughts from food and drink. "Now that you mention it, tea does sound tempting."

"Tea it is," Dancey said, moving away swiftly to accomplish the task in the little time he had before the train pulled from the station.

Trinity remained in the doorway a moment, watching him disappear. The platform suddenly seemed filled with a multitude of people, and she idly wondered if the Denver-bound train had at last arrived. Then, because the cold wind was biting angrily at her, she closed the door and began anew what she'd spent most of the day doing: Pacing. And thinking that the trip had never taken so long before.

She had just settled down, or at least had ceased her pacing, when a knock came again.

"That was certainly quick—"

Trinity stared, not into the face of Dancey Harlan, but rather into that of a woman she'd seen only once before. Now, as then, the woman appeared regal and genteel, her smile friendly and her gray eyes inviting. Her eyes shone with an animated energy that didn't seem quite natural. Trinity reasoned that its source was probably haste; though the woman appeared composed, she'd obviously been running. Her chest, hidden beneath a fur coat, heaved deeply in and out, and a thin film of moisture beaded her upper lip.

"Mrs. McCook," Trinity said, her voice revealing her surprise and—though she could no more explain it now than on their first meeting—her dislike of Jedediah's wife.

"Miss Lee," Ada said, her tone that of a civility that had been cultivated rather than bred.

"Mrs. Brecker," Trinity corrected.

The woman's features hardened, and the look in her slate-colored eyes grew just a little more . . . unnatural. But then she smiled. It was such a pleasant, *natural* smile that Trinity wondered, as she had weeks before, if she hadn't imagined the hard look and the strange eyes.

"Mrs. Brecker, of course," Ada conceded, instantly launching into another subject with a theatrical grandiosity that would have put many an actress to shame. "I've had the most tiring adventure. The train was late, and I was so afraid I wasn't going to make my connection." When Trinity didn't ask the expected question, Ada volunteered, "I'm on my way to Carson City, but I missed the train this morning. They booked me on the Denver-bound train—told me I could connect here in Reno." She laughed, setting the tie of her black velvet bonnet to quivering. "What they didn't tell me was that the train was going to be late. My dear," she hastened to add, "you wouldn't believe the snow farther north."

"Yes, I hear it's bad."

"Well, anyway," Ada said, her hand moving to her chest in a peaceful, settling gesture, "I made it. Jedediah told me you, too, were traveling this route and suggested that I look you up, that perhaps we could keep each other company."

Trinity doubted that he had proposed any such thing, but under the circumstances—she was, after all, occupying the family coach—she could hardly refuse Ada an invitation to join her. "What a lovely idea," she lied, stepping aside.

"Thank you," Ada said, sweeping in like a queen about to mount her throne. She instantly sighed. "Ah, this is ever so much nicer than those common, cramped quarters, although the red and green do clash, don't you think? I tried to get Jedediah to decorate in a blue or a mauve, but..." She let her words trail off as she slid her expensive coat from her shoulders and draped it familiarly across the bed. Her purse, black velvet and hanging from a chain, she kept with her.

"Jedediah's been very kind to lend me the coach," Trinity answered, ignoring the negative comments about her friend's taste.

"Yes, well, he can be counted on to be kind to his—" her eyes darkened "—to his friends."

A strange feeling, not fear, but rather wariness, crept down Trinity's spine. She was relieved when a knock suddenly sounded. "Excuse me," she said, crossing the coach to open the door.

"Here's that tea, as hot as a sinner's thoughts. Is there—" Dancey stopped when his gaze fell upon the other woman.

"Dancey, this is Ada McCook," Trinity explained, reaching for the tray he carried, which held a teapot and a cup and saucer. "She'll be riding with me as far as Carson City."

Dancey nodded. "Should I bring another cup, then?"

"Would you care to join me in a cup of tea?" Trinity asked, bound by the laws of civility.

"Yes, please," Ada replied with a huge smile. "I was just going to suggest it."

Trinity thought the prospect of tea seemed to please her unwanted guest inordinately; she also thought what would most please *her* would be a fast trip to Carson City.

When Dancey returned minutes later with an additional cup and saucer, he bore something else, as well, an unexpected something else, a something else that made Trinity's heart scamper.

"A telegram was just delivered for you," Dancey said, his eyes silently telling her he had no idea whether it was from Breck.

"Thank you," Trinity answered, reaching for the telegram with a hand that had begun to tremble. She fought back hope, because she could not live through the disappointment of a telegram from someone else...or of a telegram that said something other than what she wished.

"We'll be leaving shortly," Dancey said softly, then closed the door behind him.

Trinity absently set the cup and saucer on the tray, which sat on the table beside the bench seats.

"Shall I pour?" Ada asked eagerly—too eagerly.

Trinity, preoccupied, scarcely noticed. "Pardon?"

"Shall I pour?"

"Yes. Yes, please. Would you excuse me a moment?"

"Certainly," Ada replied, but her answer fell on deaf ears, for Trinity, in search of privacy, had already eased toward a far window, where she stood with her back to the other woman.

Her heart pounding, Trinity slipped the telegram from its envelope. She unfolded it, took a deep breath, and did what she had told herself she wouldn't do: She hoped. Then she read:

I LOVE YOU.

She reread the telegram. Again and again, as if she could not get her fill.

The words, like a gentle spring breeze, whispered through her, making tears spring to her eyes. He loved her. Breck loved her! That simple, beautiful fact was the only reality in her life, the only reality she needed in her life. She clutched the telegram to her, as if wringing the love from it. In her heart was an emotion so warm it threatened to scald her. Closing her eyes, she let the emotion consume her.

Across the room, hatred, chased by adrenaline, coursed through Ada's heart like heated venom. Working quickly and stealthily, she reached into her purse, removed a vial, and, glancing over at Trinity, tapped several drops of laudanum into a cup of tea. The drug, like a silken web, swirled on the amber surface before disappearing. Recapping the vial, Ada shoved it back into her purse.

She was taking a deep, quelling breath when she noticed the blood on her hands. Her heart skipped a beat. No, not now! she thought. The blood was appearing with more frequency, and always unexpectedly; it was also taking more and more pain to make it disappear. That afternoon, while on the Denver-bound train, the blood had sprung from nowhere, and she'd had to hold her hand over a lamp to burn it away. Blood. Now, as then, it was spreading all over her hands, threatening to drip into the tea. No! No! It mustn't drip into the tea! Trinity mustn't see it! Jedediah's daughter mustn't...mustn't... mustn't...

Ada curled her hands around the belly of the teapot. It was hot, unbearably hot, but she forced her hands to stay in place. One second. Two. Three. She was rewarded by seeing the blood begin to recede. Her heart slowly eased back into a normal rhythm. Seconds later, a composed Ada handed a cup of tea to Trinity.

As Trinity reached for the cup, a telegraph operator received and transcribed a curious message. The message was from a Madison Brecker and told one Trinity Lee to stay away from Ada McCook. The instructions indicated that the telegram was to be delivered immediately. The telegrapher glanced up at the clock. As he did so, he heard the Sierra Virginia's whistle herald its departure. Too late now, he thought. He'd have to forward the message. Which probably wouldn't make no never-mind, anyway. The note's urgency was suspect. Everyone always thought his telegram should be delivered immediately.

As Trinity reached for the cup, Breck reached for the throttle. He knew it was fully open, but he hoped against hope that he could coax something more from the engine.

"Damn!" he muttered as the locomotive rocked at its highest speed. Two curves back, Breck had almost lost control. Anyone else would have sought to slow his pace; he had only regretted he couldn't increase it.

Ada to board Sierra Virginia in Reno...Keep her away from Trinity.

The telegram burned in his mind. Like the wood burning in the tender. Like the love burning in his heart. Like the fear burning in his gut. What if she didn't get the telegram? What if he didn't make it in time? What if he lost the woman he loved before he'd ever really found her?

"She's dry!" the yardmaster called. "We're gonna have to stop in Carson city for water!"

"No!"

"She'll never make it without water!"

"Yes, she will!" Breck volleyed back. "She has to!"

But she didn't. A mile and three-quarters beyond Carson City, the locomotive chugged to a stop that was more than a stop. It was an irreparable death. Valves hissed, metal whined, instruments popped and cried.

"I told you she'd burn out," the yardmaster said, but Breck wasn't listening to the man's righteous lamentations. Instead, he was considering the farmhouse that lay in the distance. Without a word, he jumped from the engine and started running.

"Hey!" the yardmaster called after him.

Breck didn't respond. He just kept running. In less than ten minutes, his breathing hard and deep, he arrived at the farmhouse and offered every penny in his pocket—fifty-four dollars and ninety-nine cents—for the loan of the farmer's fastest horse. The startled farmer lent the horse, simply because he was afraid Breck would take it out-and-out if he refused.

Whipping the reins back and forth, Breck rode into the fury of the cold, snow-flecked wind. A thousand things crossed his mind: the warmth of Trinity's arms, the excitement in Ada's gray eyes eighteen years before, the lifelessness of Su-Ling, the sadness of Jedediah. And Fate. He thought of Fate, and how it had obviously decreed that he shouldn't be a businessman, for when the engine had died, so had his dreams. He'd never be able to recoup financially. All that was left now was to determine if Fate had decreed that he live his life alone, for if Ada did mean harm to Trinity, and if he didn't arrive in time, he would forever be alone. A loner, alone and lonely.

* * *

"Of course, Jedediah would make a splendid governor...."

Trinity heard the words, but couldn't hold on to them long enough to determine their meaning. It had grown so hot in the coach. So oppressively hot. She clawed at the high collar of her dress.

"Are you all right, my dear?" she heard Ada ask through a fog.

Trinity tried to focus her eyes on the woman. "Yes...just hot...and w-woozy." Every word she spoke seemed whispered through numbed lips.

"It is warm in here. Would you like to step outside for a breath of fresh air?"

Through the haze in her brain, Trinity could see the woman already rising. "No, I'm...I'm fine," she said, intuitively sensing that she didn't want to go anywhere with Ada Mc-Cook. The woman remained standing for what seemed like forever before she reseated herself. Trinity thought she looked displeased. She also looked increasingly blurred.

"Whatever you say. There's still time."

There's still time. What did that mean? Trinity thought fleetingly, but only fleetingly, for the heat, the dizziness, didn't allow her to cling to any thought for long. Reaching for her teacup, she sipped again. Bitter. The tea tasted bitter. It had obviously been brewed too strongly, but she had drunk it—almost all—because her empty stomach had demanded it.

"...Jedediah can sometimes be so naive. Why, he'd ruin his chance of being governor if I let him. But I won't let him. You do understand that I can't let him ruin his chance...."

Trinity didn't understand anything except the swaying of the train through the dark night, the keening of the snow-teased wind as it whipped by the coach window, the feeling of nausea that was sneaking ever so stealthily up on her. Maybe another sip of tea. Maybe— The cup, which she'd tried to lift to her lifeless lips, toppled over in the saucer, spilling the remainder of the tea in her lap.

Ada reached for the saucer, insisting, "You need some air."

Trinity felt Ada's arm encircle her waist, then felt herself being hauled to her feet. The world spun, blackened, then set-

tled back to a gray, confusing swirl . . . like Ada's eyes, which
were gray and strange and . . .

"I . . . I . . . What's wrong with me?" Trinity asked, passing
her tongue across her lips.

Ada said nothing; she simply drew—dragged—Trinity toward the door. Trinity had no choice but to hold on to
her . . . and to go where she was led. She could feel Ada's purse
pressed uncomfortably between them.

With the opening of the door, the loud rattle of the train assaulted Trinity's ears, while the frigid wind blasted her full in
the face. The cold cleared her head slightly; in that short span
of time, she realized that something was very wrong. She
shouldn't be feeling this way. Where was Breck? He'd know
what to do. He'd take care of her. Another wave of dizziness
claimed her, and the semilucid thoughts spun away like a
whirlwind that had only briefly touched ground. She almost
stumbled.

"Here," Ada said, supporting Trinity's slumped body with
hers, "hang on to the rail."

As ordered, Trinity reached for the railing at the back of the
car, curling her fingers around the cold iron. Cold. It was so
cold. Snow in the air. Snow beginning to whiten the ground.
The ground. God, it was speeding by so quickly. So quickly!
And Ada was urging her down, down, down the railing toward the head of the stairs. There, the railing played out, and
she could see the ground speeding by right below her.

Careful. She'd have to be careful. A person could fall. . . .

Trinity felt something—a hand?—press into the small of her
back.

Breck pressed his legs against the horse's belly, urging the
beast onward. He'd seen the smoke rising in the navy-colored
sky, had heard the piercing wail of the whistle; both had
taunted him with the train's nearness for the last five minutes.
One more curve, and he should see her. Time seemed endless,
the curve seemed endless, the nightmare seemed endless. Suddenly, like a shimmering mirage in the snowy distance, the
Sierra Virginia appeared, chugging dutifully down the track.

Trinity.

He'd reached her at last.

God, don't let it be too late!

"What the—" Charlie Knott said from his position at the helm of the iron maiden.

"Who in blazes?" the quiet Abe Dustin asked, his face, despite the cold, streaked with sweat and dirt from stoking the fire.

"Well, I'll be Sam Hill! It's Breck!" Charlie cried, watching his employer dash by the engine, swallowed up in the *clop, clop* of horse's hooves.

At a point midway down the train, Breck heard a sound that was half scream, half wail.

Stumbling from the insistent weight at her back, Trinity lurched forward, clutching anew at the rail, then crashed to the deck floor. The vibration of the car rolled her over on her back and slung her forward until her head was dangling off the train and over the steps. The fast-moving ground loomed only inches away, while the *clickety-clack* of the wheels on the track shot through her with deafening power. Above her, she could see Ada McCook. Even through her clouded vision, even in the dim wedge of light splashing from the open doorway, she could tell that the woman's mouth was grim, her eyes wild.

"Turn loose!" Ada hissed, trying to pry Trinity's fingers from the railing.

Trinity whimpered, her free hand flailing, her feet attempting to kick, both to no avail against Ada McCook's suddenly incredible strength.

Why?

Why was she doing this?

"Don't," Trinity pleaded above the roar of the wind and the train.

"I have to!" Ada shouted. "He'll tell the world you're his child!" With a fierceness that made Trinity cry out, she wrested Trinity's fingers from the iron rail. Trinity clutched at the front of Ada's dress, the ribbons of her bonnet—anything! "He'll ruin everything. I can't—"

Trinity's hands connected with a terrible nothingness, and she screamed. She was going to fall. She could do nothing else. She—

Abruptly, the brakes screeched, sending smoke spiraling from the wheels. The train pitched, then eased toward a slow, deliberate stop. The action jostled Trinity and Ada. Trinity grabbed at the hem of Ada's dark dress and fought to gain her balance.

Ada panicked. The train was stopping! Her chance was slipping away! A chance that would never come again! She had wanted Trinity's death to look like an accident—she had planned for it to—but her options had just been whittled away.

Kill her...kill her...kill her.... a voice as black as the night demanded.

Scrabbling in her purse, Ada pulled forth a small object...with a hand that was beginning to bleed again. The scarlet stain spurted over her fingers, her knuckles, with the rhythmic speed of her heartbeat.

Kill her...kill her...kill her....

In the sudden quiet, horse's hooves could be heard pounding the earth. They seemed to be coming from behind Ada, just as the sound of voices suddenly seemed to be everywhere in the air.

"What's wrong?"

"The train's stopped."

"Who's that man on the horse?"

Trinity saw the lamplight glance off something in Ada's hand. Metal. A gun? Yes, a gun, some rational part of her mind conceded. That same logical section of her brain told her that she was going to die.

She whispered but one word. With it, she was prepared to enter into eternity: "Breck."

Ada aimed, crooked her finger around the trigger of the pearl-handled revolver, and—suddenly, her eyes widened. Her shoulders slumped. Her lips emitted a grunt. And then, like a dancer who'd lost her balance, she tumbled forward, catapulting from the now-motionless train. She landed facedown on the ground, a knife sticking from her regal back.

A figure, riding a tired horse, then leaping onto the far side of the train, suddenly loomed before Trinity, its complexion etched in shadow, the dark lines of its face cut with concern.

"Breck?" she whispered, thinking that he, too, must be part of this foggy dream.

"Are you all right?" the dream figure asked hoarsely, kneeling and taking in Trinity's drugged state.

She tried to respond that she was, but could not. Hot tears stung her cheeks as she reached blindly, wildly, for the man before her. Her fingers knotted into the front of his coat, anchoring her to reality.

"She...she tried...to kill me."

"It's all right. It's over," Breck murmured, crushing her within the strength of his arms.

"Why would she..."

"Shh."

"She...she..." The laudanum claimed Trinity with its medicinal darkness, and she slumped against Breck. His own knees, after the endless burst of adrenaline, gave way, and he leaned on his haunches. Careful of the woman he held, he eased his back against the outside wall of the coach. Opening his jacket, he tucked Trinity inside, her body flush with his. Around them, the cold night sighed.

"What in the name of righteousness...?" Dancey began from below, on the ground. He held a lantern high. In its eerie light was outlined the fallen figure of a woman. From the knife wound in her back oozed a trail of blood; it pooled in the lacy white snow beginning to collect on the ground.

"What—who—my God!" came from the gathering throng of voices at Dancey's side.

Slowly, the conductor raised the lantern to the couple sitting at the back of the coach. All eyes followed.

What those eyes saw was talked about the length and breadth of Virginia City in the days and weeks that followed. Everyone agreed that Madison Brecker was holding his wife. Some even swore they could hear his softly chanted "I love you." What they couldn't agree upon was what was glistening from the cheeks of his hard-lined face. Some said it was but a trick of the light, while others insisted, both sober and over too many drinks, that Madison Brecker, the emotionless loner, was crying.

A month later, as January made preparations to shiver into February, Trinity and Breck once more stood at the back of Jedediah's private coach. The rhythmic motion of the train rumbled through them, while the cold, star-studded night swam about them. Moonlight shone down on the rails, giving them the appearance of silver threads magically sewn into the barren landscape.

"We're almost home," Breck said, his deep voice penetrating her back, which was flush against his chest. Home was Virginia City, with Ellie and Neil waiting for them at the station; home was a house Ellie had found for them, a house with a white porch, a gold doorplate engraved with the name BRECKER, a crab-apple tree they would coax and praise; home was a place to settle down for the future, a place for Trinity to return to from the few and select tours she would be making. Home was also the place to which Oliver Truxtun would be invited for dinner in the near future—and for enough of an explanation to salve his wounded ego. Breck respected the man's investigative talents, and, on his recommendation, Jedediah was hiring him to track down those responsible for some recent Central Pacific thefts. Breck had teasingly asked Trinity if she was up to her old tricks again.

"Good," she said now, easing back into the warmth of her husband's arms and wondering how she ever could have feared this man, for beneath his gruff, rough exterior was a core of gentleness. She often suspected it was a gentleness even he had not known he possessed—if he even knew it now.

They had spent the last few weeks in San Francisco with Jedediah. Ada's death had greatly upset him, on more planes of feeling than he could express. Trinity knew Ada and Jedediah had long ago drifted apart, perhaps even before her mother had come into the picture. That emotional distance did not mean, however, that Jedediah had wished Ada ill, that he had wished her dead. Even when Breck had disclosed that he believed Ada had killed Su-Ling, Jedediah had not been able to find it in his heart to hate her. Rather, he had felt a deep sadness and a deeper guilt, as though he himself had brought on the tragedy by pushing Ada to such lengths by so obviously loving another. Breck had told him that no one could assume such responsibility for another's actions. Trinity, uncertain how she felt about Ada's involvement in her mother's death, although she was certain her feelings weren't as charitable as Jedediah's, had simply held his hand—even when the police had arrived and informed him that Ada might have been behind the death of a San Francisco newspaper reporter. Of all that had happened, though, Trinity suspected that what had whitened Jedediah's already-white hair even more, what had put a stoop in his proud shoulders, was how close Ada had come to killing her, his daughter.

Daughter.

Father.

Trinity never ceased to be surprised by the revelation. Nor did she ever cease to be warmed by it. Had she been given a choice of fathers, she would have chosen Jedediah. That Fate had chosen him for her almost made her believe in Fate.

Fate.

It had almost betrayed her in this very spot weeks before. She had been certain, as she'd gazed into Ada's tormented eyes, that it would be her destiny to die by Ada's hand, but Fate had decreed otherwise. There were times when she lay in Breck's arms, her body flaming with need, her heart swollen with love, when she could almost believe him when he told her that he would have defied Fate, rewritten it, to keep her at his side. There were times when she lay in Breck's arms, his kisses hot upon her skin, his body quivering in the aftermath of lovemaking, when she believed that was precisely what he'd done...because she'd come so close, so very close, to dying.

"Stop," Breck whispered, tightening his arms about her. "Stop thinking about it. It's over."

"Is it?"

"If you'll let it be." He lowered his head and, nudging aside the hood of her cloak, kissed the side of her neck. "Turn loose of it, China."

She pivoted in his arms, her eyes finding his in the night. "Can you? Can you ever forget what I've done to you? Can you forget how I wrongly believed you guilty of my mother's death, how I hated you, how I practically destroyed you financially, how I almost kil—" She could not even force herself to say it.

Even in the dark, she could see the power in his eyes, eyes that were still pale but no longer cold. "You believed what was logical to believe, considering what you saw. Especially since you saw it through a child's eyes. And you did not destroy me financially." His lips curled into a grin. "Granted, you came close. If my father-in-law wasn't such a wealthy man, I'd be up a creek without a paddle. Make that up a creek without even a boat."

Trinity smiled, with her lips and her heart. That Breck had accepted Jedediah's loan, in the amount necessary to keep the Sierra Virginia solvent, had pleased her beyond words. There had once been a Madison Brecker, a lone man who lived life only in the singular, who would not have accepted help. Anyone's. Trinity knew it still was not easy for him, and that fact made his doing so all the more endearing.

"You shall pay royally for the loan. I think he expects you to provide him with a lapful of grandchildren."

A grin as lazy as a summer day strolled across Breck's lips. "I hope he's merciless." His smile suddenly disappeared. "I don't know anything about being a father. I never really had one."

Trinity's smile faded. He'd told her little of his past—a loner always kept a piece of his life to himself—but he'd shared enough for her to know that his childhood had been loveless and grim. "And you'll be a better father for it." She reached up to touch his cheek with her gloved fingertips, once again feeling drugged, but this time with love. "How could I ever have wanted to kill you?"

"When the time came, you couldn't."

"No."

"Because you loved me." Each time he spoke of her love, he did so with a hint of a question, as though he could not quite believe his good fortune.

"Yes," she whispered, "because I loved you, do love you, will always love you." Her fingers trailed across his lips, worshiping the lower lip's fullness, the upper's stern line, which gentled at her touch.

Suddenly, he moaned and, nudging her fingers aside, claimed her mouth with his. The kiss was fiercely sweet, his tongue thoroughly sweeping as he held her face between the callused palms of his hands. The hood fell from her hair, leaving it to shine like polished ebony in the moonlight.

"I love you," he whispered, his every move one of possession. "God, I love you!"

In a frenzy, he took her mouth again, this time leaving it only to deliver bite-size kisses to her neck and throat.

"Breck?"

"Hmm?"

"Did you... Did you love my mother?" It was the one thing she had not yet had the courage to ask him.

He halted, his eyes finding hers. He saw his own vulnerability reflected back at him, just the way he found his own worth reflected in her eyes. For a long while, he'd tried to prove his worth to the world, only to discover that it was to himself that he'd been trying to prove it. But he no longer was. He saw it every time he looked into his wife's eyes.

"No," he whispered. "We were friends, but even as a friend I didn't love her. I couldn't love. I didn't know how." His voice thickened. "You taught me to love, China. Only you."

When he pulled her into his arms, she went willingly, wantingly, satisfied that she'd found her mate. High overhead, a shooting star blazed through the heavens. Trinity saw it. Smiling, she closed her eyes and felt a sweet peace, her mother's promised peace, descend upon her.

* * * * *